Toil And Trouble

Book 2 of the Jolie Wilkins series

HP MALLORY

TOIL AND TROUBLE

by
H.P. Mallory

TOIL AND TROUBLE

Also by HP Mallory:

THE JOLIE WILKINS SERIES:

Fire Burn and Cauldron Bubble
Toil and Trouble
Be Witched (Novella)
Witchful Thinking
The Witch Is Back
Something Witchy This Way Comes

THE DULCIE O'NEIL SERIES:

To Kill A Warlock
A Tale Of Two Goblins
Great Hexpectations
Wuthering Frights

For Finn, I love you.

Acknowledgements:

To my mother, thank you for everything.

To my wonderful critique partner, Lori Brighton, thank you for all your help!

To my husband for being so supportive of my writing and of me.

To Mercedes Berg, one of the winners of my "become a character in my book" contest! Thank you for your help with the Wiccan rituals and for helping me shape your character. I hope you enjoy the part you played in this book!

To Christine Trum, my other winner! Thank you for all your help with German translations and German traditions. I hope you enjoy your character!

To my beta readers, Belinda Boring (reviewer for www.thebookishsnob.blogspot.com), Mary Genther (reviewer for www.sparklingreviews.com) and Evelyn Amaro (reviewer for www.paromantasy.com), thank you for all your guidance and help with this book. I'm thrilled to have you all so involved in my writing.

To my son, Finn, who never stops making me laugh. I love being your mom.

ONE

It was all I could do to open my eyes and take in my surroundings. I turned my neck and squinted against the bright light infiltrating the window in a garish display of brilliantly colored poppies. Blinking a few times, I tried to make sense of the scenery before me but my memory still wasn't with the program. I attempted to sit up but found I couldn't move. It didn't feel as though I were strapped down—it was more like my body decided to go on strike.

"She's awake!"

It was Christa's voice. Relief washed through me. Whatever bad situation I was in had just gotten more bearable.

"Chris?" I started, attempting to shield my eyes against the glare but I couldn't lift my arm.

Something is very wrong, I thought, a lump forming in my throat.

"I … I'm paralyzed," I stuttered. At least my voice still worked.

I blinked against an onslaught of tears and forced myself to focus on the bails of straw forming the ceiling of my abode. Where the hell was I? It was like I was playing hostage to Bilbo Baggins.

"Jolie, don't try to move," said a man and his voice was decidedly unhobbit like. It took me a second to realize it was Rand.

Rand … my warlock boss whom I was massively and totally in love with.

It was Rand who first enlightened me to my powers as a witch and although my life had since taken several twists and turns (some good and some really, really bad), I wouldn't have changed it for the world.

Rand leaned down into my line of sight, his pitch black t-shirt contrasting against his tan complexion. I wanted to smile but I wasn't sure if I could. None of that mattered anyway; what did matter was Rand's stunning face smiling down at me—the aquiline features of a Roman nose, chiseled cheek bones, deep dimples, and a strong and well-sculpted chin. Eyes the color of molten chocolate and hair a matching shade. Although his hair was mussed and dark circles decorated his eyes, he was male beauty personified.

I felt the heat of his fingers against my face and an electric current passed through me at his touch. It was the same feeling I always got whenever Rand touched me—I never had figured out what it was; maybe his energy. I closed my eyes against the feel of him, afraid I might start crying.

"Jolie, you're going to be alright," Christa said and grabbed my hand with an encouraging squeeze.

At least I could still feel my hands even if they weren't working. I glanced up at Christa and immediately noticed her swollen eyes—she'd been crying. I could only assume it was concerning my predicament.

"What happened to me? Why can't I move?" I whispered as panic began to stir in my stomach, sounding like a grumbling ogre in a cave.

"You defeated Dougal, Odran's fairy," Christa said in a tight voice. She quickly looked away and began dabbing her eyes. I closed my eyes again, trying to remember what had happened, what it meant that I'd defeated Dougal. Attempting to remember was like wading through tar—completely exhausting and, more so, useless.

"And because of it, you've lost a lot of power, Jolie," Rand added. "You absorbed Dougal's negativity thereby neutralizing most of your strength and now you need to heal."

And that was when the memories came pouring back as if someone had dumped a pitcher of realization juice over my head.

It was a freaking miracle to surpass all miracles that I was still alive.

Dougal just happened to be the strongest of the fae king Odran's, fairies. And I, like a dumbass, had challenged him to a duel whereby I had to defend myself against his fairy magic. Doesn't sound like a major deal? Yeah, that's what I'd thought too, but that was before I was stuck in bed, as immobile as an engorged tick.

So somehow I'd managed to prevail over Dougal's magical ambush and now my victory would force Odran and his fairy league to uphold their end of the agreement by allying with us in an impending war. Ah, yes, now the pieces of the puzzle were falling nicely into place. If only I wasn't paralyzed, I might have considered it a good day.

"What do you mean, I absorbed Dougal's negativity?" I asked.

Rand heaved a sigh and sat down on my narrow cot-like bed. His weight caused mine to shift, the straw of the bed poking me like the bite of a thousand ants.

"While you were defending yourself, using your own magic, you expended your life force. In the process, you absorbed some of the hostile negativity Dougal used to attack you."

"Oh my God!" Christa yelled and collapsed on top of me in a new deluge of tears. "Your life force!"

Rand chuckled, shaking his head. "Christa, Jolie just needs to sleep it off for a few days. It's similar to a bad hangover."

Christa sat up and wiped her tears away, looking a little bit embarrassed. If she was embarrassed, I was relieved. A hangover I could handle, paralysis was something entirely different …

"And speaking of a hangover," Rand started, leaning over me with a mysterious smile. He grabbed hold of my shoulders and lifted me up, pushing me back into the soft down of my pillows. Now I was propped in a sitting position—well, more like a slumped-over position, but at least my line of sight was more interesting. Rand reached to the wood table behind him and presented me with what appeared to be a tankard of something that smelled like … ale.

"Beer?" I asked.

Rand shook his head. "It's a fairy potion meant to aid in your healing. One of the elders gave it to me this morning."

"Can't you just heal me, Rand?" I blurted, remembering the many instances he'd used magic to heal my upset stomachs, headaches, cramps, the list went on.

Rand shook his head. "Unfortunately not. My magic is useless here."

By "here" he was referring to a fairy village in BFE, otherwise known as Glenmore Forest, Scotland.

Christa eyed the tankard of fairy juice suspiciously, her eyebrow arched in exaggeration like a cartoon character. And in her fairy provided blue gingham dress combined with the yellow ribbons in her dark hair, she looked like Pollyanna with dark hair.

"Are you sure that stuff isn't the tainted mead Odran was trying to make her drink the other night?" she asked.

The tainted mead in question had been exactly that—mead tainted with a love charm to get me to acquiesce to the king's sexual advances. And the stuff had almost worked—I'd narrowly escaped with my virtue intact. One thing I'd learned about the otherworldly is they're a randy bunch …

"Yes, I tried it myself," Rand answered and turned his smiling eyes on me. "We almost lost you once, I wasn't about to take my chances again."

His words, though meant to be comforting, had the exact opposite effect.

I had almost died.

It felt as if the weight of a semi had suddenly descended on me as I considered how fortunate I was to have survived at all.

"Jolie," Rand said, grabbing my attention. He gently tipped my chin up so it would be easier to swallow and held the tankard to my lips. I gulped a large mouthful before the taste of something akin to vinegar hit my tongue and I started to gag.

"Ugh," I protested as Rand dabbed the nasty stuff from my lips.

"You've got perhaps five more sips."

He repositioned the foul stuff on my lips and I had a vision of the black tar like substance bubbling into my mouth, reluctantly making its slimy way down my throat like a slug.

"I think she's gonna ralph," Christa observed.

I came damn close.

"She should get some rest," Rand said, facing Christa.

Christa nodded and dropped her eyes, fiddling with a piece of straw which had escaped the bedding or the ceiling. She glanced up again and offered Rand an apologetic smile.

"Rand, would you mind if Jules and I had some girl talk?"

"Of course. Take all the time you need." He stood up. "I'll just be outside."

Christa nodded and we watched his heavy stride as he neared the door. I wasn't sure if Christa noticed how his black kilt revealed the tiniest hint of his taut backside but I sure as hell did. He opened the wooden door which looked like it would be better suited to a makeshift fort and threw us both a grin. As soon as the sound of the door closing reverberated through the small cottage, Christa faced me.

"Jolie, I thought you were going to die," she said and started crying again, tears blurring her green eyes until they resembled glittering emeralds.

"Did I come close?" I asked, my stomach dropping at the idea.

She nodded. "You were in a coma for three days."

A coma! A new bout of anxiety visited me, turning my stomach sour. "Sounds like I've been through hell and back," I said and offered a weak smile.

"And I was so worried about Rand, Jules."

I wore my surprise. "Why? Did Dougal or Odran hurt him?"

Christa shook her head. "No, no. Rand is fine. I mean, no one hurt him. He just … seemed to fall apart where you were concerned." She sighed, long and deep. "He sat by your bedside day and night, Jolie. He didn't even sleep."

Warlocks don't actually require much sleep so that wasn't as big a surprise as it otherwise could have been. But still, the idea of Rand assuming the role of ever vigilant caregiver was something worth considering.

"I didn't know what would happen to him if you … well, you know … died," Christa nearly choked on the word and glanced away.

"He seems okay now." It was all I could think to say. I still hadn't moved past the fact that I'd been in a coma and nearly merged into the express lane of death.

"Yeah, he's okay," Christa said with a smile and then dropped her gaze to her fidgeting hands. "I just … I just wanted to tell you that I couldn't imagine what my life would be like without you."

I smiled and attempted to squeeze her hand but the attempt was useless. "Thank you, Chris."

She nodded and stood up, smoothing down the skirts of her blue dress. I couldn't see the outfit the fairies had magicked for me, but given the circumstance, fairy scrubs were probably in order.

"Guess I better go let Rand back in," she said, clearing her eyes as she started for the door. She opened it and Rand poked his head in, the sunshine outside acting as a halo around his head until he looked like an angel. All that was missing was a choir and organ belting out the notes to *Gloria in Excelsis Deo*.

"How is she?" he whispered.

"Seems to be better," Christa answered. "You probably want some time with her?"

"I can hear you," I said. "My ears are still working just fine."

Rand didn't say anything more but by the fact that I heard the door shut and Rand was the only one to approach my bed, I figured Christa had left.

"I don't remember feeling like this after dueling with Dougal," I said, starting to get annoyed.

Rand nodded and took a seat on my bed. "Your adrenaline was piqued. I knew it would be a matter of time before his fairy magic drained you."

"So is this paralysis thing just temporary, I hope?"

"Yes, but you have to rest, Jolie, that's the only way you're going to heal."

Did I mention Rand is English and therefore has that wonderful and melodious British accent? Granted, Rand is insanely hot but I think the accent makes him even hotter. But as it was, I had bigger things to think about than Rand's hotness. There was that whole subject of the fairies and our new alliance. Another thing I'd learned about otherworldly creatures was that they had a way of appealing to their own self interests. And to say Odran hadn't wanted to join our war was an understatement.

"Is Odran still on our side?"

"Yes, the fairies are perhaps the most honorable of creatures. Odran will not go back on his word."

Odran and honor didn't seem likely bedfellows.

"Are you sure?" I asked.

Rand ran a hand through his longish hair. "While you were sleeping, we discussed plans to go forward."

I just nodded, allowing all of it to sink in. And what a lot of it there was.

Bella's plans to become queen of all otherworldly creatures and Rand, believing in the ideals of democracy and probably more so in the lunacy of Bella, stood against her. Not surprisingly, Bella had declared war against us.

So far, she had recruited half the vampire population, the majority of the witches, and virtually all the demons as well as endless packs of werewolves. Until the fairies agreed to join us, we were exponentially outnumbered. Now we could wage war on a more even battleground.

"When can we go home?" I asked.

"It'll be a few days, Jolie," he answered. "You're in no shape to travel. You need to rest and let yourself heal." He stood up. "And having said that, I should leave you to get some sleep."

But I didn't want him to go. Now that we were alone, there was so much more to say, although I didn't know where to start. We'd been through so much together already—confessing our feelings for one another but never acting on them. Rand had told me a long time ago that love between a witch and a warlock wasn't the same as what humans consider love—it was all encompassing, a "union of souls" he'd called it. Well, after what had happened with Dougal, when certain death had seemed imminent, now seemed as good a time to talk as any.

"Rand, I'm not tired. There's so much to talk about, so much that's happened," I started, hell bent on making him stay.

He started to shake his head. "Jolie, you need to rest."

"I can't think about sleeping right now; I'm not tired and I've got way too much on my mind."

"That's a side effect of the potion," he said with a grin. "Just close your eyes and you'll be asleep before you know it." He looked as if he was about to stand up and I was suddenly seized with the need to keep him with me.

"Rand, I never slept with Trent."

The words tumbled off my tongue. It was weird because the thought of Trent, my ex-boyfriend (and werewolf), hadn't even entered my mind until I'd blurted it out. Rand paused and there didn't seem to be any emotion registered on his face. He picked at the seam of my coverlet before glancing down at me again.

"That doesn't matter. Your recovery is what matters."

But it did matter. It suddenly mattered more than anything. I wanted, no needed him to understand that Trent had never meant anything to me. He was merely a pothole along the Interstate Rand.

"I wanted you to know because I'm sure that's what you thought happened that night and I bet it really did look that way with him half naked in my house or had I been half naked? I can't remember now."

It was like I was waging a war with my mouth and it was winning. Words just came flying out and there wasn't anything I could do to stop them.

"He was half naked, if I remember correctly," Rand said, a smile toying with his lips.

"Is that what you thought?" I insisted. "I mean, that we, er Trent and I, had done it? Did you think we had? Cause it looked that way, didn't it?"

Rand chuckled. "It had appeared that way, yes."

"Were you bothered by it? I mean, did it bother you to think we'd been together?" It bothered me that I'd never cleared up this tidbit with him.

Rand dropped his eyes again and seemed like he was attempting to memorize the pattern of the hardwood floors.

"It caused me sleepless nights, yes."

Because I was possessed by the verbiage demon, I didn't even have a chance to ponder the fact that Rand was admitting things I'd never thought he would. Course, I'd never thought I'd actually have the guts to ask all these questions. Maybe the fairy potion wasn't such a bad thing ...

"Why didn't you ever ask me if I loved him or if I was happy with him, at least? You could have asked me if we'd had sex, Rand." I paused for a breath. "I would have told you eventually."

"Because it wasn't my bus …"

"You could've asked, you know? I really wanted to tell you at the time but it just didn't seem right. I mean, it had been super obvious that you were spying on me since you'd walked like two miles to my house in the rain and who does that?"

"Jolie …"

"And I knew Trent was just loving the fact that you thought we'd done … it. He had sooo many issues with you. God, he was such a jerk. What in the heck did I ever see in him?"

Rand appeared to be controlling a smile. He leaned into the pillow next to me, his kilt riding up and revealing the muscular swell of his thigh. I committed the image to memory for use the next time I needed a little one on one time with my hand.

"I don't know what you saw in him."

And neither did I. It was a good thing I was paralyzed or I would have jumped on Rand and sexually assaulted him right then and there. I suddenly started feeling a fuzzy warmth penetrating through my body like I'd just had something hot to drink on a really cold day. Maybe it was the potion but I suddenly felt sluggish and my eyelids felt even heavier.

"Yeah … jerk … right?" I managed.

Rand nodded and traced my hairline. "Granted, he was a jerk. Still is."

I couldn't help my yawn and I couldn't even cover my mouth.

"You're tired, Jolie," Rand said, running his fingers through my hair.

And just like that, the feeling of heaviness was gone, replaced with what felt like adrenaline bubbling through me. I had to restrain myself from spewing out another litany of meaningless drivel.

"Are you glad I told you about Trent and me?" I couldn't keep the words in—they'd mutinied and won.

Rand was quiet for exactly four seconds. "Yes."

"I'm glad I told you then."

"You know I have deeply rooted feelings for you, Jolie."

Well, I'd always known we had something between us. How deeply rooted his feelings were for me, I'd never been sure. Mine, on the other hand, were as deeply rooted as a super old tree.

"I … never really knew for sure," I said.

Suddenly, the bubble of anxious verbiage seemed to deflate in me and I expelled it with a sigh. I was exhausted again.

"How could you not know?" he insisted.

I tried to comprehend what he was saying but it was getting harder to keep my eyes open.

"Jolie, are you listening?" Rand asked with the hint of a smile.

I really was trying to listen but finding it near impossible. I felt my eyes close for a few seconds before I forced them open again. I'd wanted to have this conversation with Rand for a while and now that the opportunity was here, coupled with my liquid courage, I was suddenly a narcoleptic.

"Um, what? Yeah, yeah I'm listening."

But I wasn't listening, I was falling asleep.

"We can talk soon, Jolie," Rand whispered and ran his fingers down my cheek.

"No, Rand …" Yawn. "We should … talk now." Yawn.

He chuckled and pushed up from the bed. "Jolie, you need to heal." He grabbed hold of my hand and his warm electricity coursed through me.

"Don't go," I whispered.

"I thought I nearly lost you to Dougal," he said gently. "It would have killed me, Jolie. I'm not going anywhere."

I remembered the feel of his warm and lush lips on mine before the craptastic fairy potion took me to the Land of Nod.

~

I woke up with a start and this time my visitor wasn't exactly someone I was thrilled to see.

Odran.

Anxiety beat a path down my spine at the sight of the king of the fae. Hopefully he wasn't here to demand a rematch.

"I'm still not feeling good. Can't this wait until some other time?" I pleaded while attempting to wiggle my toe. No feeling … nothing. Maybe I needed more of that God-awful fairy potion because I didn't feel a damned bit better.

Odran shook his mane of hair and like a great lion, lumbered over to my bed and sat down, uninvited. Tendrils of his incredibly long and beautiful golden hair splayed over his naked shoulders like a cresting wave. Like Rand, Odran too wore a kilt but his was purple and blue, colors of fae royalty. But unlike Rand, I couldn't say I was much interested in what Odran wore beneath his kilt. Gorgeous though the king of the fairies was, fending off his sexual advances was in a word … exhausting. And I so didn't have the time or the interest for it now. Well, I guess I had the time …

"Nay, lass, I doona want to trouble ye with talk ah war."

The spectrum of Odran's conversation vacillated between war talk and sex talk and I could definitely say I preferred the previous. I frowned but didn't say anything. I'm sure he wanted to trouble me with talk of less noble subjects such as the carnal interests of the *Little King*.

"I doona want," he started and then stopped, fisting his hands in a great show of frustration.

"Out with it," I prompted impatiently.

He faced me in surprise, like most people wouldn't dare talk to him like that. Well, screw it, he wasn't my king. I didn't vote for him, as Monty Python would say.

"I hope ta change yer mind regardin' this war, lass."

I started to shake my head but he interrupted me.

"Nay, please listen."

I attempted to cross my arms against my chest in the universal sign of "I'm not amused" but forgot my arms weren't working. "Go on," I muttered, although I regretted the words as soon as they escaped. Odran should not be encouraged.

"Ye have ah gift, lass. Ah gift that all the creatures ah the Oonderworld would fight ta 'ave. Yer gift is too precious ta risk in ah war."

My gift was my ability to bring the dead back to life. How I gained this ability, I have no clue. It just sort of happened one day, and ever since then my life had changed dramatically. I'd been the victim of kidnapping and attempted homicide. Great gift, huh?

"I want ye ta reconsider ma offer."

His offer was to abandon my life with Rand and Christa and join the fairies whereby they could exploit my mad skills and let the rest of the otherworldly creatures destroy themselves.

"I won't reconsider, Odran," I said and then eyed him. "I hope you aren't breaking your word?"

Suddenly, the king's somewhat docile manner was thrown out with the kitchen trash. He stood up so fast he nearly fell over and proceeded to bash his fist into the wall, the plaster powdering the ground below him.

"I am king o' the fae!" he roared. "I doona break mah word!"

"Hot damn, Odran," I started, only slightly freaked out. His bark was worse than his bite. "Calm down. I believe you, jeez."

The blood in his face seemed to fade a bit but he didn't make any motion to sit down. Instead, he started pacing the room, arms crossed against his impressive expanse of chest. He was the epitome of some mythological being. But his wealth of muscles, immense height, and unappeasable sexual drive were lost on me.

"Ye 'ave ah way boot ye, lass. Ye are difficult."

Wasn't that the pot calling the kettle black? "You aren't much fun yourself."

"I will not offer again, lass."

What was he offering again? Ah, yes, the chance to live with him in fairyland with unlimited access to my bed until he tired of me. And then I'd keep the homefires burning while he proceeded to fornicate with the willing female population.

"I think I'll pass." I paused. "But thanks for the offer."

I was spared Odran's response when the door thrust open, and Rand, who could also be compared to a mythological being in his own right, appeared.

"What the bloody hell was that noise?" His gaze settled on Odran as he took the few steps separating him from the king. "And what the hell are you doing in here?"

Odran frowned, his hands on his hips. "The lass shows no respect."

A crimson wash stole over Rand's cheeks and his jaw was tight. "What did you do to her?" he demanded as his eyes found the remnants of plaster on the floor. "Are you alright, Jolie?"

I nodded. "I'm fine. Odran had a little temper tantrum but he's calmed down now."

"Temper tantrum?" Rand repeated. "I don't appreciate you scaring Jolie, Odran, especially when she's trying to recover!"

"He didn't scare me," I mumbled, though neither paid me any attention.

Odran dropped his hands from his hips and his face flushed like he was going to explode again. Before this became warlock vs. fairy, I thought I should intervene. "We were just discussing our plans to move forward," I said and gave Odran an encouraging glance. "Weren't we, Odran?"

His eyes narrowed but he succumbed by nodding. "Aye."

Rand wasn't fooled but chose not to comment, instead saying, "Jolie is tired."

Odran didn't say a word and without even a glance in my direction, lumbered out. Rand watched him and didn't turn to face me until Odran disappeared.

"What did you do to make him so upset?"

"He tried to persuade me to leave you and Christa."

Rand shook his head. "Well, I suppose that's preferable to what I assumed he was doing here."

"And what would that be?" I asked even though I knew the answer.

"Chatting you up again."

"And if I'd been into it, you certainly have a way of ruining any chance I get of hooking up with anyone," I said with a smile.

Rand looked entirely uncomfortable and started to say something but then stopped.

"I'm kidding, Rand."

He nodded and took a few steps closer to the door before turning to face me. "Yes, well, good. That's good."

He took another two steps and turned around again, running his hands down the front of his shirt nervously. “Well, rest and I’ll come and check on you in a bit.”

Then he turned and walked out.

TWO

One week later and I was nearly back to myself. Granted, I was still incredibly tired but at least I could stand and move my arms and legs. It might not sound like much, but after being bedridden for five days, it was an improvement I'd gladly take. Better still, I was back home in Alnwick, England, which was a creature comfort in and of itself. But though my surroundings might have been comfortable, my life was anything but.

Preparations for the war were in full effect. Odran and his ambassador fairy, Nigel, had already visited Rand's home twice in the course of the week since we'd been home. And the king of the fae wasn't our only visitor. We also played host to Sinjin, a vampire who was growing dearer to my heart. Sinjin had helped me escape from Bella, the would-be queen of the Underworld, after she kidnapped me. And since that great feat, I had to admit his approval ratings had soared, at least in my books.

The same couldn't be said for Rand.

"The Charter of the Witches dictates we announce when and where we will meet Bella's army," Rand insisted for the third time in twenty minutes.

We were in Rand's drawing room, centered around his grand fireplace (and by grand, I mean six feet tall and completely built of river rock). "We" comprised Odran, Nigel, Christa, Rand, and Sinjin. A roaring fire crackled and hissed from the hearth, sending macabre shadows around the room. Christa and I were seated comfortably in front of the fire, while the males paced around the room like anxious new fathers.

"Randall," Sinjin started, exhaling deeply as he came closer. The highlight of the fire heightened the harsh planes of his face and made his ice blue eyes appear to glow. He looked every inch the quintessential villain in his black slacks and black button down shirt. No one would ever use the word "casual" to describe Sinjin.

"Rand," the warlock corrected him, for the umpteenth time.

"Indeed," Sinjin smiled, his English accent thick. "Bella will not fight according to your doctrine, so why should we?"

Rand's mouth was tight. "Because we are honorable."

"Your honor will get us killed."

I grabbed hold of the top of my leather wing-backed chair, attempting to pull myself to more of a seated position. While I might have felt better than I had after defending myself against Dougal, I still felt like I'd taken one too many valium. Rand turned toward me and when it appeared Odran would assist me, Rand threw him a glare. He then bent down and hoisted me into his arms, moving me into an upright position.

"Are you okay?" he asked, his soft brown eyes enthralling.

I could only nod as I watched him reach for a small wooden stool in the corner of the room. He lifted it and walked back toward me, raising my legs as he positioned the stool underneath them.

"Better?" he asked.

"Yes, thanks," I replied meekly as I watched the warmth in his eyes dissolve once they re-encountered Sinjin.

"Stoop to Bella's level? Is that what you would have us do, Sinjin?" he insisted.

Sinjin shrugged and approached Rand and me, pausing just above me as he leaned against the side of my chair. He smelled of some foreign scent—clean and captivating.

"I do not care for it any more than you do but it is realistic."

"What time is it?" Christa asked and yawned, stretching all the while. When no one responded she shrugged and began searching for split ends.

"Do we even know where Bella and her army are?" I asked in a quiet voice.

Sinjin squatted down until his face was inches from mine. He didn't say anything but he didn't need to; his grin spoke volumes.

I just shook my head in resignation.

"What does he mean?" Odran insisted. Rand also turned to face me curiously.

"It means he's tasted her blood and now he can track her."

"Ugh," Christa said as she found a split end and tried to pluck it. I wasn't sure if the "ugh" referred to her hair or the fact that Sinjin and Bella had done the dirty deed. I was pretty grossed out by the latter.

"Bella is no fool. She would know Sinjin could track her," Rand said, ever the perceptive warlock.

"Aye, boot she wouldna know when we would coome for 'er," Odran added.

Nigel said nothing but just stood behind Odran. He was as silent and unmoving as a guard outside Buckingham Palace.

"Why don't we just assassinate her?" I asked and justified it with, "then we wouldn't have to worry about any of this."

Sinjin chuckled while Rand shook his head. "That is not our way. We would be excommunicated from our society," Rand said and threw me a disgruntled expression.

"Jeez Louise," Christa said, apparently losing interest in her hair. "Witches have so many rules."

I had to agree with that. Bella had already demonstrated that she was less than willing to comply with the very rules Rand relied on, so what did that mean for us?

"You are so concerned with propriety," Sinjin said, obviously unimpressed.

"If we killed her, Ryder would just take her place," I said. Ryder was a vampire and one of Bella's stooges. If I detested Bella, I hated Ryder even more. He'd been the one to kidnap me, all the while pretending to be on our side. And that hadn't been his last or least offense. He'd also nearly drained me to death. Only Sinjin had defended me against Ryder. Like I said, I was quickly becoming a fan of Sinjin.

"As far as I'm concerned, we fight with honor or we do not fight at all," Rand said.

Odran, Sinjin, and I all turned to observe Rand. Christa was too busy with her hair to realize the weight of his statement.

"What does that mean?" I asked.

"Yes, Randall, what does that mean?" Sinjin queried, his fingers plying the top of my chair. I could feel his cold breath as it assaulted my neck and a wash of excitement coursed through me, much though I tried to suppress it.

"It means I will not fight unless we do so morally and honorably. I will not stoop to her level."

"And if she attacks us?" Sinjin countered.

"We will be ready for it," Rand answered.

Odran rubbed his chin, as if in deep contemplation. Nigel could only stand there, like Odran's shadow.

"How do we prepare for it?" Sinjin demanded, his fingers now digging into the leather chair.

Rand sighed. "Everyone will camp here, at Pelham Manor. We will notify Bella of when and where we will meet her army. In the meantime, this will be our base. We will train together and live together."

"And die together," Sinjin finished with a scowl.

Odran started forward, lumbering as if his body wasn't accustomed to its great height and build. "If he will 'ave it nay oother way …" he started.

"I will not," Rand answered. He certainly was stubborn. I could only pray his sense of stubbornness would serve us and not be our death sentence.

"Very well," Odran nodded.

I glanced at Sinjin who smiled at me. "The leader has spoken," he said but I wasn't sure if he was referring to Odran or Rand.

"So we all live together here?" I asked, sounding stupid since I didn't quite grasp how this would work. "Where?"

Pelham Manor definitely had the acreage but it wasn't the ideal place for a bivouac, as far as I could fathom. I mean, there were no large open fields to house hundreds of soldiers. Instead, it was mostly packed with tall pines, a stream, and Rand's rose garden which was the only open flat land.

"We'll have to clear some trees to set up tents," Rand announced.

"I willna sleep in ah tent," Odran contended. "Officers shouldna be relegated to the ootside."

Since when was the fae king appointed an officer?

"If you are to sleep in your home," Sinjin addressed Rand while he glanced at me, "then so shall we. Odran is correct. Let the minion sleep in tents."

I smiled at his reference to the rest of our army as the "minion" but Rand's expression wiped the smile right off my lips. He was livid and his aura radiated with violet intensity.

I probably should have mentioned I can see auras. Even though I never thought much of this ability, having been able to see them since I was young, according to Rand, it was one of the first signs he'd had that I was a witch. I'm also psychic but apparently that wasn't as impressive as the whole aura seeing bit.

"And do not forget vampires cannot survive in the sun, as you know, Randall. We need a place to shelter us from the daylight."

"Then you can bloody well dig yourself a grave and sleep in it," Rand answered, the words "for all I care" hanging in silence.

Sinjin laughed derisively. "Excuse me, your honor, but I refuse to sleep in the dirt."

Rand began to protest but soon realized it was fruitless as his angry words expired from his lips. I caught Sinjin watching me with a rakish glint in his eye and returned my attention to Rand who was glaring at Odran, who was staring at Christa with undisguised interest.

"Jolie and Christa are under my protection," Rand snarled between clenched teeth.

At the mention of my name, Odran refocused his attention on me (mainly my legs) and smiled.

"Of course they are," Sinjin agreed. "No need to be a todger, Randall."

"If either of you lays one finger on either of them, I will kill you," Rand continued, dividing his icy glare between Odran and Sinjin. "No questions asked."

Sinjin's gaze didn't depart from mine. "What if they ... wish to be touched?"

"Hey, I have a boyfriend," Christa replied but was interrupted by Rand, who suddenly lunged and threw Sinjin into the wall. The entire house shook as Rand wrapped his hands around Sinjin's throat and suspended him mercilessly, their noses only inches apart.

"I do not want to catch you even glancing at them," Rand said in an arctic tone.

Sinjin's fangs exposed themselves but I could see him holding back, trying not to react. I mentally applauded him when his fangs retracted and his snarl turned into a smile.

"Of course, Randall, of course."

Rand released him and walked back to me. "Jolie needs to rest now. We can discuss all the details tomorrow."

"When do ye want yer recruits here?" Odran inquired.

"Immediately," Rand answered as he stood in front of the fire, finally quiet for a few seconds. "Odran, I will leave it to you to summon the fairies. By the time they arrive, I will have made arrangements for them. Sinjin, you take care of the vampires. I will handle all the werewolves and the witches."

I wanted to suggest I'd provide the pumpkins, carving knives, and Butterfingers but didn't want to be considered a smart ass.

And furthermore, it suddenly occurred to me that my sleeping arrangements hadn't exactly been detailed. Even though I did live on Rand's property, it wasn't inside the main house. Instead, my residence had once been the butler's quarters, almost two miles from Pelham Manor. I sensed maybe Rand intended for me to move back to the main house, but it was something I wasn't exactly thrilled over. I mean, it sounded good and all but the reason I lived on my own was due to the maddening relationship between Rand and me. And I couldn't imagine that relationship was now any less complicated.

"What about me?" I asked as Rand frowned. "Can I continue living in my house?"

He scratched his chin. "No."

"I don't want …"

"It's too far from me. I can't protect you if you aren't nearby. And with all the soldiers camped here, it won't be safe."

"Won't be safe?" I echoed.

"Jolie, while they might be on our side, they are still creatures of the Underworld and … male." He sighed. "I don't want to take any chances when your safety is concerned."

"And who will protect her against your advances, Randall?" Sinjin hissed.

"I'm not interested in starting a row, Sinjin," Rand warned.

"Perhaps you should apply your rules to yourself?" Sinjin persisted.

"Jolie, you and I can discuss this later," Rand growled before turning back to Odran and Sinjin. "As for our meeting, it is finished."

Sinjin said nothing as he moved toward the door. He grabbed the doorknob and turning it, seemed to remember something and whispered to me.

"Goodnight, Jolie, I bid you sweet dreams." The smirk on his lips told me exactly what type of dreams he had in mind.

~

Rand packed me into the passenger seat of his black Range Rover. It was late and I was exhausted, the thought of my welcoming bed the only thing bringing me consolation. Rand started the engine and cranked the heat up, pulled out of his driveway and headed for the dirt road that would lead to my house.

"Working so closely with Sinjin and Odran is hard for you, isn't it?" I asked.

Rand's eyes didn't leave the road. "Yes. If I had it my way, I wouldn't interact with any of them, save you and Christa."

He was quite the antisocial warlock.

"When do I need to move into the main house?"

"Once all the recruits arrive," he answered and glanced over at me. "I don't trust them, Jolie, and I want to make sure you're safe."

He smiled as he squeezed my knee playfully. A familiar warmth penetrated me and I clutched his hand.

"Every time you touch me, it still feels like a lightning bolt running through my body."

He smiled. "Well, it *is* energy."

"Do you feel it when I touch you?"

"No, you aren't yet a powerful enough witch. But in time, your powers will be strong enough for me to feel it."

I nodded, silently wondering when that day would come. I relaxed into the luxury of Rand's heated seats and had to fight the wave of exhaustion that threatened to submerge me.

"I hope I wasn't out of line warning Sinjin to keep away from you?" Rand asked, attempting to sound casual.

"What's that supposed to mean?"

Rand was quiet for a few seconds. "He acts as if there's something between you both."

I shrugged. "He's a vampire … they flirt."

Rand nodded and seemed satisfied enough to stop pursuing the subject. A few seconds later, we pulled in front of my house and he turned the car off.

"I thought you were just dropping me off?" I asked, somewhat surprised by the fact that he hadn't left the car running.

He opened his car door and walked around to open mine. He reached around my body and pulled me into his arms, lifting me up and kicking the door closed behind him. When we reached the porch, I fished inside my pocket and found my key. I only opened the door a sliver, trying to make sure my cat, Plum, wasn't about to sneak through. The coast was clear.

"I want to make sure everything is in order before I leave you for the night," Rand said.

As soon as we stepped inside, the lights came on, courtesy of Rand's magic. He carried me through the small living room and into my sparse bedroom, reclining me on my bed with the greatest delicacy. That was when I realized he'd have to undress me as I couldn't do it myself. Even though Christa was currently living with me to assist me with my daily needs, at the moment she was with John but due back any minute.

"You'll have to help me with my clothes," I whispered in a small voice. Ordinarily I could've just used magic to put on my jammies. But due to the latest course of events, I didn't have any magic left. That's why I felt so damned useless—my magic was in the process of healing.

Rand seemed taken aback, and I had to wonder why he wasn't thrilled with the idea of seeing me in the buff. Not like I was thrilled with seeing myself in the buff either … He didn't say anything, though, and quite matter-of-factly began the task of removing my shoes. He dropped them unceremoniously to the floor next to my bed and peeled off my socks. I could only hope my socks weren't sweaty. Talk about a turn off … Is there anything worse than foot sweat? Course, I hadn't done any walking so I was probably okay there.

"What do you sleep in?"

"My jammies are in the bottom drawer, far right," I said in a voice made weak by the toad currently living in my throat.

He opened the drawer, pulling out a Victoria's Secret pink cotton nightshirt. "This?" he asked.

"Yes, thanks."

He approached me again and appeared to be avoiding eye contact.

"You don't have to do this if you're uncomfortable, Rand," I said. "Christa should be here soon."

"I gave Christa the night off," he started. "And I'm not uncomfortable so there's no reason for you to be in jeans all night," he added, as if reassuring himself.

I had to wonder why he would've given Christa the night off but was spared the thought when he leaned over me and grabbed hold of the waistline of my jeans, his fingers brushing against my stomach. I fought to keep my eyes open as I relished the heat from his fingers while they undid my button and unzipped the jeans, sliding them down my body. He carelessly tossed them atop my socks and shoes.

"It might be easier to get my shirt off if you sit me up," I whispered.

He nodded and gripping my elbows, pulled me toward him. I tried to raise my arms so he could more easily slide the turtleneck over my head but my arms refused to budge. Instead, he gently pulled each of my sleeves and while running his hand underneath the material, pulled my arms into the square of the shirt. Then he carefully slid the shirt over my head and dropped it on top of the jeans.

Then he looked at me, somewhat bewildered. "Do you wear your sleepshirt over what you've got on now?" he asked, alluding to my bra and panties.

"No." I slowly responded.

He kneeled down in front of me, running his hands over the cotton of my nightshirt. A loose tendril of hair crested my shoulder and he gingerly positioned it behind my ear. His touch sent a ripple of shivers over my body.

"Rand," I started but couldn't finish. He leaned into me and I felt his hot breath against my neck. His hands cupped my face as he delicately brought his lips to mine. He kissed me softly at first, working his fingers through my hair. I moaned and his probing tongue plunged through my lips, eagerly seeking mine.

Suddenly, he withdrew and he was panting. "It nearly destroyed me when you were here with Trent," he said, drawing his fingers down my cheek. "I had ... nightmares ... about him making love to you."

I smiled. "And to think all you had to do was ask me."

"You must realize my self-esteem had already taken too much of a beating."

His finger continued down the line of my neck and further down until he outlined my bra strap. He traced it to the mound of my breasts and down to the hollow of my cleavage, his eyes fastened on mine the entire time.

"Move back to the main house, Jolie; I want you near me."

"You know where that led us before," I protested weakly.

"I know there are issues between us but I don't want you so far from me." He reached around with his other hand and unhooked my bra, dropping it carelessly to the ground.

His eyes were riveted to my breasts and I felt my nipples harden under his scrutiny. He drew one finger around my torrid nipple, teasing the knob with his thumb and forefinger. I closed my eyes and sighed at the ecstasy erupting from deep within me.

"We always seem to end up in the same situation," I said as I remembered Rand's inability to commit to me wholeheartedly.

"It's something that haunts me constantly," he sighed.

Any relationship between us could never be casual—it would have to be a permanent bonding of our souls. Hundreds of times more permanent than a human marriage. And that wasn't me just being dramatic—that's the way it was between witches—all or nothing.

"Rand," I interjected, quickly snapping my attention from the lazy circles he was drawing around my breasts.

"Hmm?" he responded, continuing to loop his fingers around my nipples, intermittently giving them a gentle squeeze to enhance their rigidity.

"Why did you tell me that love between witches was all consuming and that a witch can die if their lover dies?"

He stopped outlining my breasts and looked at me intently, his eyes not really seeing me but seeing through me as if into another time.

"I've seen witches die from losing lovers," he said in a voice fraught with pain.

It was a reaction you would expect from someone who knew this information from personal experience and even though Rand had told me he'd never dated a witch for this exact reason, I couldn't help but wonder if he hadn't been exactly truthful.

"Is this coming from your own personal experiences?" I asked, almost regretting the question as soon as it fell off my lips. Did I really want to know Rand's past where relationships were concerned?

He was quiet while his fingers traced the elastic line of my panties. He ran a finger across my stomach, from one side to the other.

"Yes," he said simply.

He lifted me up then and placed my butt atop the pillows at the head of the bed, arranging me sideways across the bed while he pulled himself next to me, lying on his side. He resumed painting the outline of my underwear, his eyes studying me as if he were an artist.

"Can you talk about it?" I cautiously inquired, just as Plum jumped up on the bed. Rand picked her up, gave her a kiss on the head and promptly deposited her outside the door, closing it after her.

He faced me again with a slight smile and lay back down next to me. "Yes, I think we should."

I felt his finger follow my panty line down my groin, to the inside of my thigh, and shuddered as it disappeared into the hollow between my legs. I dropped my head back into the pillows, relishing the feel of his finger as it traced up and over the other side of my panty line, up my inner thigh and over my stomach.

"Tease," I whispered.

He chuckled and turned my face toward him, outlining my cheekbones. "I was deeply in love once," he said and his eyes suddenly became sad and faraway.

The idea that Rand had been in love with someone hit me like a freight train. But the thought that he still hadn't gotten over her was something even harder to accept.

"I was so bonded with her that when she was killed, it nearly killed me. I was sick for months and probably would've died if not for Mathilda."

Mathilda was a fairy. She was also my teacher for many of the lessons I'd learned about magic. What I hadn't counted on was that she would be the reason Rand had survived the death of his … wife, for lack of a better word.

"Mathilda nursed me back to health," Rand continued. "She fed me and cared for me as if I were an infant. At the time, I suppose I was."

"You must have found the strength within yourself to have been able to survive such a loss, though?" I asked.

He cocked his head, as if he were pondering it for the first time. "I believe my survival was every bit due to Mathilda's strength, not my own. She was able to make me forget, able to take away the pain little by little. She erased it from my mind."

"What do you mean?"

"Just that, she erased my lover little by little until I couldn't remember her face or her name. I don't remember any of the details about her. All I feel now is an emptiness, a void. And I know that emptiness is due to the fact that I lost her."

"Do you remember how you lost her?"

He shook his head. "All of it's gone as if it had never been."

I couldn't imagine what it would feel like to live with such a blank space within you, knowing someone you loved had been prematurely taken from you. It was almost as if Rand wasn't complete.

"I wish you had told me this sooner," I whispered.

He turned and faced me with a sad smile. "It's difficult to think about."

"You would rather live with a void than live with the memories?"

"Yes," he said emphatically. "If I remembered the particulars, I don't think I'd be alive, or if I were, I don't think I'd be sane. That's what I meant when I said love is all encompassing. It's not something to be taken lightly."

And for the first time ever, I felt as if I was beginning to understand Rand, to understand his constant vacillations between wanting me and not. It didn't make our situation any easier; if anything it added another layer to the strata of difficulty that was knowing and loving him.

"Hold me, Rand," I whispered, wanting and needing to touch him.

He pulled me into him and squeezed me while resting his chin in the valley of my shoulder. "Once this war is behind us, Jolie ..." he started.

"Shhh," I interrupted. "Let's not think about it now. You're right, there's too much at stake with Bella and Ryder."

"Yes, that's so."

"Will you stay with me tonight?" I asked.

"I wasn't planning to leave," he answered and rolled me over so I could face him.

"You're breaking my rule," I said with a smile.

"And what rule is that?"

"You're not in your jammies."

He chuckled. "I don't sleep in jammies, as you call them."

"What do you sleep in?"

He smiled. "Nothing."

"Then I suggest you get ready for bed."

He pulled his sweater over his head, revealing the familiar broad expanse of his tan muscular chest. His pecs and taut stomach were just as glorious as they always had been. He stood and unbuckled his pants, allowing them to drop to the floor. But he didn't remove his boxers.

"I thought you said you slept naked?"

"One of us needs to be in control," he answered.

"Hmm, and what makes you think I'm not?"

He didn't answer but wrapped his hands around my ankles. Without any warning, he pulled me down the length of the bed until he was perched between my legs. Then he lifted me up and leaned against me.

"What are you doing?" I asked in a breathy voice.

"You'll find out."

And before I could formulate another thought, he slid my panties off.

"Rand!"

He pushed my legs apart and with a lascivious smile, forced his head between them. And that's when I felt his tongue prying me apart, eagerly lapping up my wetness. As his tongue darted in and out of me, I tried to arch up against him but my body felt limp, still too weak to respond.

My mouth still worked and I moaned and cried out unabashedly. At the moment of my climax, he replaced his tongue with a finger.

"Look at me," he said.

When I did, he was flushed, his eyes wild with desire.

"Rand," I breathed.

"I've wanted to taste you since the moment we met."

"Me too," I said like a moron.

"Tell me how you want me to touch you," Rand insisted as he outlined my entrance, a smile playing with the corner of his lips. "Like this or perhaps my finger inside you?"

He knew exactly how much this was torturing me. I didn't answer and he pulled away.

"Answer, Jolie."

"Oh my God," I groaned. "If you don't keep touching me, I'm going to murder you."

He chuckled and pushed his fingers inside me as I screamed out. "One or two fingers, Jolie?"

"Two, two please!"

And he plunged them back in me as I groaned. "I want you inside me, Rand."

"No, Jolie, not yet," and his mouth was back on me, sucking as his fingers dove in and out. I started moaning again, my lungs panting.

"I want you to come for me, Jolie," he whispered.

Bliss exploded within me as I opened my eyes to find his fixated on me, heavy with desire. He smiled, his dimples barely cresting, as his gaze traveled from my eyes, down to my breasts and further still, until he watched his fingers thrusting in and out of me. I clenched my eyes closed again, gripped the coverlet and allowed his fingers to take me to my own nirvana.

"Wow," I said with a smile as I returned to earth.

Rand chuckled but continued pushing his fingers all the way inside me, only to pull them all the way out again.

"God, I love watching your body react to me," he said in a raspy voice.

"Mmm, I loved feeling my body react to you."

His eyes clouded over with hunger and he dropped his head between my thighs again, pushing his tongue into me with renewed fervor. I arched up against him, grabbing his head as if to push his tongue further into me. Another rain of bliss showered down on me and I screamed out my pleasure.

"I could get addicted to your taste," he whispered.

"What about you?" I asked, motioning to the raging torpedo that was visibly straining against his boxers.

"Tonight is about you."

He got up and walked to his side of the bed, spooning himself beside me. He reached down and pulled the coverlet up and over us both, pulling me back into his erection. His hands cupped my breasts and he kissed my cheek.

"I shouldn't have done that," he whispered. "Now it's going to take you longer to heal. That must have drained all the energy you've been working on rebuilding."

"I don't care."

And that was the God honest truth.

"You know what I just realized?" I asked and turned around.

"What's that?"

"You didn't have to undress me in the first place. You could have just used your magic."

Rand chuckled. "I'm glad you failed to remind me."

THREE

Rand had been right—our carnal activities had zapped any improvement to my health I'd gained over the last week. But I couldn't say I regretted it. In fact, it turned out to be one of the best evenings we'd ever spent together. And believe me, I'd replayed the night's events at least one hundred times over.

Granted it was a major bummer he'd been in love with someone else but it helped me understand his attitude toward serious relationships, especially where bonding was concerned. This was a much better reason for us to be cautious rather than the fact that he was my boss (which he'd been throwing at me since I'd first met him).

It had been four days since our steamy tryst and we couldn't get any private time. Rand had been overly preoccupied with the various creatures being recruited into our army. Odran's forces had already arrived at Pelham Manor and quickly began felling trees and constructing rudimentary forts to serve as their shelters for the next few months. Almost immediately after the fairies, the vampires and their humans (think walking blood banks) arrived, followed by the werewolves.

What I found interesting, comical almost, was that each faction insisted on separating itself from the others. The fairies' camp was closest to the stream, allowing the pixies to find refuge in the water lilies. The pixies, who were about as tall as my thumb, scouted the banks of the stream, reporting to the fairies when any other creatures came too close. The werewolves chose a locale bordering the woods. The vampires busied themselves digging their pits and burying their caskets in the middle of the field while their humans set up tents along the perimeter of the caskets. There was no intermingling; they kept to their own in a great show of pride.

Although I found the hordes of vampires, fairies, and werewolves impressive, the same couldn't be said for Rand's coven of witches which numbered … twelve. In his defense, this coven had only recently become his. Rand was infamous for not allying himself with anyone. While witch covens were only able to stay in power by taking on outside jobs (exorcisms, tarot readings, palmistry, etc.), Rand, the recluse, opted to work singly and picked his own jobs. But after the estrangement between Rand and Bella was known, some of the witches migrated to Rand's territory and in the end he had no choice but to become their leader.

The twelve witches laid claim to a small piece of land ignored by the other creatures who outnumbered them twenty to one. The coven was comprised of eight warlocks and four witches from different nations; but the majority were Americans. Their skills were as varied as their backgrounds; some were newbies and others were pretty advanced.

As far as our war effort was concerned, Rand was determined to protect Pelham Manor, so the fairies had woven magical nets from tree to tree at the edges of his property; one misstep and you'd be as fried as a catfish in Louisiana. And if that weren't enough to keep our enemies out, Rand had insisted each of the creatures take turns scouting the property to ensure nothing got through the fairy nets.

In recent days, I had occupied most of my time by trying to relocate from the butler's quarters into Pelham Manor. Because I was still so weak, I wasn't much help—just telling the two witches Rand had assigned me where to put what.

It wasn't entirely thrilling to be living in Pelham Manor again. I mean, on the one hand, it was wonderful to be nearer Rand (my bedroom was coincidentally adjacent to his) but I cherished my privacy. Besides that, lurking in the back of my mind was the fact that the last time I'd lived inside the walls of Pelham Manor, my relationship with Rand had steadily and inexorably fallen apart.

I was also bummed by the fact that I had to leave the bungalow I called home and further bummed that Odran snatched the tenancy along with two of his fairy paramours (aka fairamours). Rand had jumped at the opportunity to relet it to Odran, knowing it would mean one less male in the house. But he still had Trent and Sinjin under his roof.

What bothered me more than the idea of Odran sleeping in my bed was the fact that I was now living in such close proximity to my ex, Trent. Despite our brief interlude, now I couldn't stand him. His reputation as a player hadn't stopped me from dating him even though I'd known this from the get go. Instead, I basically faceplanted for his charismatic charm. Our relationship had lasted all of a month when he dumped me, explaining he was just too dangerous to date. Stupid me.

The living situation was made slightly more bearable by Rand's insistence that Sinjin, Trent, and Odran only interact with us when absolutely necessary; that is, when discussing all things pertinent to the war. Otherwise we merely lived under the same roof while conducting very separate lives.

While our lives might have been separate, we were united by the impending war. The topic of war preoccupied every discussion in the house. It made me nervous to think about it and I couldn't help but think about it constantly, especially when war was the single topic on everyone's tongue. Truth be known, I was sick to death of it.

The war was to be held in exactly three months, on March 15th, otherwise known as the Ides of March. And the location? The battlefield of Culloden, in Scotland, the scene of the legendary Jacobite defeat by the British throne. Irony certainly wasn't lost on the creatures of the Underworld.

Rand, with the help of Odran, Sinjin, and Trent, had drafted what can only be referred to as an invitation to battle. The language seemed to have been borrowed from some ancient text and sounded as rudimentary as the act of delivering a war summons itself. Did one employ FedEx for such a purpose? I never found out.

Regardless, the war summons had been delivered and Rand expected Bella's response in exactly two weeks' time. Delaying any longer would just be downright rude.

It was almost funny to watch Rand, Trent, and Odran when the mail arrived everyday—you'd have thought they were waiting on Publisher's Clearing House. And as far as the postman was concerned, Rand had to resort to putting a spell on the poor guy so he wasn't aware of what was happening. Then Odran took a sample of his blood with one of my brooches and Rand used the blood in an incantation which gained the postman entrance through our barricade. We could only hope the postman wasn't one of Bella's employees.

"Push against him harder, Trent!" Rand yelled as Trent, in were form, battled Sinjin in the moonlight.

It was another night of training for the battle. I sat next to Christa, both of us bundled in a chenille blanket as we swung back and forth on a wooden swing which was attached to the bough of an ancient pine tree. The tree stood at the crest of a small hill which gave us a bird's eye view as our legions battled one another, bursts of light and clashing of steel weapons interrupting the otherwise still night.

It was like something out of a sci-fi movie—fairies weaving their magic while the vampires used their incredible speed to thwart their opponents and the werewolves were equally intimidating with their gnashing teeth and heart-stopping cries. It was nearly impossible to see the witches in the warring throng of otherworldly creatures.

And over all this, Rand played overlord. He looked like a coach as he weaved in and out of the faux battle, calling orders and offering encouragement. He disappeared into the moving sea of soldiers and I returned my attention to the scene directly before me—Trent getting his ass kicked by Sinjin.

It was a spectacle I couldn't say I didn't enjoy.

"This is not a challenge," Sinjin said.

Trent was on the ground, Sinjin's fangs poised above Trent's carotid. Even though Trent was in wolf form, which made him incredibly strong in his own right, he couldn't seem to break free of Sinjin's iron grip. Trent howled and Sinjin pulled away from him, his fangs retracting as he spotted me and stood up. He took two steps from the defeated werewolf and bowed theatrically.

"Did you enjoy the show, ladies?" he asked.

"It's getting a little old," Christa answered. "I mean, it was cool the first time but now it's like … a rerun."

"I apologize if you find us less than entertaining," he said with a smile. Never one to be offended, he seemed more amused than anything else.

"Apology accepted," Christa answered as she scouted the warring soldiers for a sign of John, her favorite werewolf.

Speaking of werewolves, as I looked past Sinjin to Trent, Trent got back up on all fours and panted breathlessly before transforming into his human shape, as naked as the day he was born. He stood up and smiled broadly at me.

"Ugh," I muttered and lowered my eyes.

"Cover it up!" Christa yelled.

Trent's hands were on either side of his hips and his limp thingy just flopped to the side like even it was unimpressed.

"Just wanted Jolie to see what she's missing."

He sort of gyrated his hips until he was hula-hooping sausage style.

"Oh my God," Christa said with disgust in her eyes. "That," and she pointed to his unit, "is so NOT impressive."

"Touche," Sinjin hissed in a serpentine sort of way. Then he turned to face his idiotic opponent. "Perhaps you should dress before you embarrass yourself further?"

Trent didn't say anything, just regressed into his wolf shape and trotted away.

Christa turned to me. "You good?"

I nodded. Trent would never get under my skin again. "I'm good."

I glanced up and found Sinjin leaning against the pine tree, watching us with unveiled interest. "Tonight Varick arrives," he said, grabbing my attention.

Varick was Sinjin's boss and a master vampire of the first order, being over one thousand years old. We'd been awaiting his appearance for some time now. I never knew why it was that Varick was arriving so late and just figured it was due to the nature of vampires—they conducted themselves according to their own schedules and a vampire was never on time.

"When?" I asked.

Sinjin shook his head. "He is close."

"How do you know?" Christa asked.

"I can feel him in my veins."

Christa frowned. "Are you guys like … you know?" she asked and wobbled her hand from side to side.

"I do not follow," Sinjin said.

I sighed. "She's asking if you and Varick have ever been together in … that way."

Jeez, I sounded as ridiculous as she did. Even though we both sounded moronic, it was a good question and one I'd wondered—not about Sinjin's sexuality necessarily but about vampires in general. It seemed that being alive, or in their cases, undead for century after century might cause one to consider alternatives to man-woman relations. I mean, there has to be a point at which you've been there, done that, right?

Sinjin chuckled and interrupted my inner monologue.

"I am afraid not, poppet. I prefer women, as you well know."

Well, that answered my question. And yes, I well knew which woman he was referring to. If I had a dollar for every lascivious glance or flirtatious smile Sinjin gave me, I'd be a wealthy woman. I really didn't mind—I mean, there was that whole achingly frustrating situation with Rand. If anything, Sinjin was a relief from the drama of agonizing over the what ifs with Rand.

Of course any flirtations with Sinjin weren't serious …

"Whoa, am I tired."

I turned to the sound of John, now in his human shape, as he threw a t-shirt over his muscular torso (he'd already covered his privates) and approached Christa. She dropped her side of the blanket and jumped off our swing, sending me into a tailspin before Sinjin reached over and steadied me.

"How did you do, babe?" Christa asked as she wrapped her arms around his neck and snuggled into his chest. He kissed the top of her head and I glanced away, not wanting to act the voyeur to their personal affection. And I immediately put the kibosh on the inkling of envy that started twining around my heart.

"Those vamps and fairies sure are somethin' to reckon with," John said.

Sinjin motioned to the empty spot next to me. "May I sit with you?"

"Sure."

In a blink he was next to me, his long legs swinging us forward and back. His uniquely masculine yet soapy clean scent danced around me as if flirting with the air.

"How are you feeling?" he asked.

"I'm better—I mean I can move my arms and legs but still can't walk."

Sinjin was about to comment when Rand's highly perturbed appearance interrupted him. "This is not social hour," he said, his eyes narrowing on Sinjin. "In case you haven't noticed, your men are still in battle. Shouldn't you play the part of leader and join them?"

Sinjin never appeared to be anything other than amused when it came to Rand. I had to give him props for that.

"I believe your recruits are in need of a reprieve," Sinjin said and exhaled as he leaned into the swing, throwing his arm around me. "And your ward is in need of company."

"Jolie doesn't need nor want your company," Rand spat back and leaned down, scooping his arms underneath me as he hoisted me up. "She needs sleep."

I yawned at the mention of sleep, realizing just how exhausted I was. Sinjin stood up instantly and wrapped his cold fingers around my arm.

"I do hope you sleep well, love."

I smiled and allowed Rand to carry me back into the house. It had to be late, so bedtime brooked no argument with me. Once in my room, Rand turned on my bedside table lamp and laid me down, reaching for the horrible fairy remedy sitting in the tankard on the table. The stuff could be compared to turpentine—having an endless shelf life, no need for refrigeration and probably tasting just as bad.

"Are you tired?" Rand asked with a small smile, the warm yellow of the lamplight illuminating his dimples until he looked like every woman's dream come to life.

"Exhausted."

He handed me the tankard and I grasped it with both hands, finding infinite enjoyment in the fact that I was now strong enough to hold it myself. I counted silently to five, closed my eyes and opened my mouth as I chugged the hideous stuff. My gag reflex kicked into gear and I had to keep my head back, lest any of it come back up.

Once I was in the clear, I handed the tankard back to Rand who placed it on the table and we both watched it refill itself with my next dose—something I wouldn't have to take until the morning, thank God.

Rand glanced at me and with a quick nod, the blanket fell off my shoulders, landing in a puddle of fabric around my feet. My jeans and sweatshirt dissolved, and in their place, my brown and pink striped PJs appeared. I couldn't hide the sense of disappointment that coursed through me as I remembered what had transpired the last time I'd needed help getting undressed. But Rand was extraordinarily busy and I needed my healing sleep, so ...

"Are you comfortable?" Rand asked and I could tell his mind was on other things besides me; the war, for example.

I nodded and pushed myself down into my pillows. "Rand, how much longer until I can start sparring with everyone else?" I asked and picked at a loose thread in the coverlet. "I'm feeling stronger everyday so hopefully it won't be much longer?"

Rand's brows furrowed. "I imagined this would come up."

I frowned but didn't say anything, just watched Rand go to my bedroom window, no doubt playing the role of sentry keeping track of his legion. The moonlight heightened the hard planes of his face and the cleft in his chin. It highlighted the breadth of his shoulders and how they narrowed into an athletic waist and narrow hips. He appeared so strong, so confident and capable.

"I don't want you to fight in the war, Jolie."

"What?" I asked and tried to sit up, which aggravated me when I failed. He faced me and I could see his jaw stuck in that stubborn clench that usually meant he wasn't going to bend.

"It's too dangerous."

I gulped down my anger. "I'm a good witch, Rand, I can help you."

"I know you're a good witch but your power isn't completely mature yet. You are young."

I was getting pissed off which meant my tendency to stutter was about to set in. It was bad enough I couldn't move but no one was going to tell me what I could and couldn't do. "Last time I checked, no one else could bring back the dead. Young or not, I'm powerful and you need me."

He shook his head and wrapped his hands around the bedposts. "No, Jolie, you aren't going."

Angry tears burned my eyes. This wasn't fair. I had promised myself I would see Ryder die, that I would kill him myself. When Ryder had kidnapped me months before and chained me to a bed where he'd nearly drained me and came even closer to raping me, the only thought to get me through the whole ordeal was my revenge. And now Rand was going to take that from me?

"So I'm supposed to stay here, knowing you or Sinjin could be killed any moment?" I had to marvel at the fact that it seemed my stuttering was on vacation. Hopefully a permanent one.

His eyes narrowed at the mention of Sinjin and he folded his arms against his chest. "You should have more faith in us. We are not easily defeated."

"But you are also not without your weaknesses!"

Rand's eyes dropped. "Be that as it may, it does not change the fact that you aren't going."

I suddenly remembered that prior to Ryder kidnapping me, he'd been training me in the art of self-defense, for what I thought had been training for this war. "Then why was Ryder training me, if not to fight in the war?"

Rand's eyes narrowed at the mention of Ryder. "That was for self-defense when I thought Bella might come after you."

"That's bullshit!" I railed, attempting to sit up again which proved useless and I just plopped back down. A hint of numbness climbed up my legs, starting at my toes. A few seconds later, it worked its way up to my waist and inched further upward into my arms and hands.

Rand shook his head and brought his hand to his forehead, looking as if he was exhausted and couldn't be bothered talking to me anymore.

"Jolie, I won't be able to focus on fighting if I know you're out there somewhere, possibly dying. I won't have a level head. You need to stay here if I'm going to be able to focus entirely on fighting Bella."

The weight of the fairy potion I'd drunk was now making itself known in the numbness which had overtaken my body. The heat of exhaustion was gently defeating me. My eyes started feeling heavier and I knew it was just a matter of time before I'd be asleep.

Rand grasped my hand and smiled gently. "Please just heal, Jolie. That's all you need to focus on."

He leaned down and kissed my forehead before opening the door and closing it behind him.

~

I opened my eyes and blinked a few times against the darkness of the room. Reaching over, I grabbed the corner of the curtain and pulled on it. A sliver of moonlight pierced the window and spotlighted the room in a Dali-esque array of shadows and exaggerated angles. Was I dreaming? Everything felt odd, muted, my mind buzzing. Maybe it was the after-effects of the fairy potion …

I turned toward the window, listening for the sounds of battling soldiers. Yep, they were still at it. Did they ever take a rest?

The eerie green glow of the alarm clock stated it was 3:32 a.m. God, I knew the creatures of the Underworld rarely slept but this was getting ridiculous. For the last four days, they'd battled all night. Some had slept during the day, but only the vampires and that was out of necessity more than anything else.

Suddenly, a shiver raised the fine hairs on my neck. Illogical fear began bubbling in my stomach and I pushed my palms into my down comforter and attempted to sit up. My muscles strained, but nothing happened. I collapsed into the mattress, holding my breath as my heart hammered madly. Something was wrong. Something was off. I just didn't know what …

I turned back toward the window and out of the corner of my eye I caught the image of two glowing eyes. Before I could scream, a brown wolf leapt through the door and landed on me. As he stared down at me, his eyes reflected the moonlight. His snarling snout revealed a great show of teeth as a line of drool escaped from his mouth and fell onto the coverlet.

I tried to scream but the sound stifled in my throat and refused to come out. The wolf growled and moved inch by inch up my bed. I wanted to grab one side of the bed to haul myself over the edge, thinking the floor might offer better traction. But moving still wasn't an option—my traitorous body failed. The wolf growled again and lowered himself to his haunches, approaching even slower, like he was taunting me, daring me to defend myself.

Rand!

I thought his name, hoping he wasn't so far away that our mental telepathy connection wouldn't work.

I brought my attention back to the wolf and in a split second, he leapt. His furry body was heavy against mine as his open snout buttressed my pillow. My first instinct was to reach for my alarm clock. I grasped it and bashed it into his eye.

He howled in pain and ripped the clock from my hand with his teeth, crunching and mashing it into a plastic mess before spitting it at me. He fastened his murderous gaze back on me and that was when I realized I was done. I was as ineffectual as a pancake and this wolf was going to kill me, no questions asked.

But I wouldn't go down without a fight.

Rand! I need you now!

I re-thought the words over and over again before attempting to tear at the wolf's throat but my fingers just freed up some of his fur. My defensive measures were so useless, I might as well have been grooming the damn thing. The wolf's eyes settled on my carotid and my heart thundered in my chest.

I pushed him away and screamed as his teeth sank into the flesh just above my collarbone. He ripped the skin away from me as I cried out against the agony. I forced my eyes open to find blood staining his muzzle and dripping down his chest, matting his fur. Closing my eyes against the incredible burning pain, I winced at the thought of being eaten alive.

The sound of the door crashing against the wall forced my eyes open. A black blur flew from the door and catapulted itself into the wolf, pushing it off me and sending it careening into the wall. The wolf howled against whatever had attacked it. I tried to get a clearer look at what in the hell was going on, but like before, I was unable move. I could only rely on my hearing. The struggling pair made intermittent gasps and groans then I couldn't hear anything besides an incredible roaring, as if I'd been sucked under a wave.

Heat radiated from the wound on my collarbone. It morphed into an all out burning until I felt like a volcano was erupting from inside it. I screamed, clenching my eyes tight, hoping the pain would abate but it continued to grow.

Suddenly, I felt cold fingers probing the wound and thought the pain would kill me then and there. I pried my eyes open to find Sinjin before me, spattered with blood. He'd killed the wolf—that much was obvious.

"Sinjin, it bit me!"

"Jolie." It was all Sinjin could utter before Rand bowled him over.

"Get the fuck away from her!" Rand screamed as Sinjin sidestepped him as fast as lightning.

"She has been bitten by a wolf!" Sinjin roared. "She will turn!"

"What?!" I demanded, realizing the weight of Sinjin's statement—I was about to get hairy. A scream sounded from the depths of my body as I attempted to face the facts.

When Rand came into sight, his concerned expression didn't fill me with much hope.

"Christ," he whispered as he inspected my wound. He touched it and all the burning within me seemed concentrated directly beneath his fingertips.

"Rand, it hurts!" I pleaded as the fire rained within me. Whatever was happening was happening fast. Rand's eyes were wide as he placed his hand on my forehead as if checking my temperature. Then he turned to Sinjin.

"She's turning," he said, his voice belying the fact that he was nervous.

"Stop it from happening!" I squealed before another spasm of pain racked my insides and I bit down hard, tasting the blood of my own lip.

"I can suck out the toxins," Sinjin said in a calm voice, his eyes glowing eerily in the moonlight as he took a step closer to my bed.

"No," Rand said, shaking his head. "I can heal her myself."

"You do not have time," Sinjin said as he glanced at me. "She is turning too rapidly."

At the hideous prospect of becoming a wolf, I gripped Rand's hand. If Sinjin could stop it, I needed his help. "Please, Rand."

Rand gulped hard and told Sinjin. "Do it quickly."

Sinjin's smile was wickedly purposeful. "You must charm her so she will not feel it."

Although vampires can bewitch their prey, rendering the victim an unwitting accomplice in the theft of their blood, vampires can't bewitch witches. That is, of course, unless Rand used his magic to make me susceptible to Sinjin's power.

Rand gritted his teeth, the emotions of whether or not to allow Sinjin to seduce me playing across his face. "No, I can't allow her to succumb to you," Rand said, tightlipped. "My magic will …"

"Very well but this will be incredibly painful," Sinjin interrupted with a shrug and sat down beside me, leaning over as he inspected the wolf's bite. As he looked at me, his fangs lengthened. I closed my eyes as another eruption of molten pain flowed through me.

"Please, Rand, please do what he's asking!"

Rand paused a moment more before kneeling down, placing my head between his large hands, riveting my attention. "Look at me, Jolie, and don't break eye contact."

I nodded and although another spasm seized me, I forced my eyes open. Rand didn't say anything as he gazed at me, almost like he was seeing through me. I could only gasp at the incredible pain that was now spreading into my stomach, feeling like my body was eating itself.

Seconds later, Rand released my head and stood up. "It's done," he said in a small voice.

Sinjin nodded and grasped my hand. "Look at me, poppet. This will not cause you pain, do you understand?"

I nodded dumbly and lost myself in the crystal blue of Sinjin's eyes. His pupils dilated until the black swallowed the ice blue only to immediately return to normal. Like a light switch turning off, the pain that had been coursing through me suddenly vanished.

And all there was was Sinjin.

Sinjin smiled as his fangs sparkled in the moonlight. He grasped my neck with incredibly cold fingers and maneuvered my head to an angle that pleased him. He leaned over me and I could feel his fangs sink into my already torn flesh. There was only a moment of slight pain—like the pinch of a vaccination but it was over almost immediately.

Sinjin squeezed my shoulders as his fangs sank deeper and I could feel the warm viscous blood seeping down my neck. His hands palpated my arms, plying my flesh as he continued drinking me. A moan escaped his lips and all I could think about was how good he felt, how his drinking me was the most erotic feeling I'd ever experienced.

I groaned when he withdrew from my neck and wrapped my arms around him, hugging him tightly, needing to be as close to him as possible.

"Jolie," Rand said but I wouldn't look at him.

I ran my fingers through Sinjin's thick, black hair and pushed his head back onto my neck. He pulled up from me and his eyes were bright with an unnatural light. He licked his lips which were covered in my blood and sunk his fangs into me again. I screamed with surprised pleasure, feeling the throes of an orgasm.

"Stop, goddamit!" Rand yelled. "What the bloody hell are you doing to her?!"

Sinjin didn't respond but merely withdrew his fangs again. Blood dripped from his mouth onto my face and he licked it off. "Do you want her to turn?!" he asked breathlessly.

Rand made no motion to back away. "No."

"Then let me finish."

Sinjin turned back to me and his eyes dilated again, weaving bliss in my stomach. I tilted my neck to the side and closed my eyes. "Please, Sinjin, please," I begged, needing to feel him, wanting to feel him.

He threw himself on me and bit me with renewed zest, sucking my blood feverishly. I was suddenly able to move my legs and I wrapped them around him, my body writhing with pleasure beneath his. He groaned slightly as I screamed out another orgasm.

"I want you, Sinjin, please," I moaned.

Rand smashed his fist into the wall. "Enough," he yelled.

Sinjin pulled away from me and his body heaved as he licked the blood off his lips and closed his eyes, panting ecstatically. When he opened his eyes, he glanced at my neck and examined the wound. His fangs retracted and I protested at the thought of him leaving me. I grasped his head, trying to bring his face back down.

He chuckled. "No, pet, you must keep the rest."

"Get away from her," Rand said in an exhausted voice, pushing Sinjin off me.

"I want more," I whimpered.

"No, Jolie, you're going to be alright now," Rand crooned in my ear. "These feelings are just temporary."

I heard Sinjin's chuckle from the door. "Randall, do not outstay your welcome. It is clear whom she prefers."

"I don't have the patience to deal with you now, Sinjin," Rand hissed.

I wasn't sure if it was sexual frustration or the werewolf in me but the heat suddenly began spiraling inside me again and I writhed against it. Rand grabbed hold of my flailing arms.

"Did you get all the toxins out of her?" Rand demanded.

"Yes," Sinjin responded. "She will heal."

I opened my eyes and grabbed hold of Rand, trying to pull him toward me. "I need you, Rand, right now!"

He held me and turned to face Sinjin. "When will this wear off?"

Sinjin smiled. "Another ten minutes or so. I had to charm her twice to ensure she would not feel pain."

Rand grumbled something unintelligible but I didn't care. I needed male attention and I needed it now. "Rand, please."

Sinjin's chortle was deep. "Apparently I awakened some dormant feelings in her. If you are not up to the challenge, I can satiate her."

Sinjin took a step toward us and Rand stood up, facing him. "I've had enough of you and your ulterior motives."

"Ulterior motives?" Sinjin questioned, feigning innocence.

Rand inhaled deeply. "Don't think I'm unaware of your interest in Jolie and it extends past mere physical attraction. I'm not a fool, Sinjin."

Sinjin shrugged. "I never accused you of being anything other than a gentleman."

"Just be aware that I'm onto you," Rand said in a constricted voice. "Now leave us and send someone for him," he said and motioned to the lifeless corpse in the corner of the room.

Sinjin bowed in his uniquely charming way and left the room. I exhaled the intense heat torturing my stomach until there wasn't anything left at all but a feeling of complete exhaustion. I closed my eyes wearily before remembering Rand was still in the room.

"I think I might be back to normal," I said, the sting of embarrassment over what had just transpired now making itself known in the heat of my cheeks.

Rand smiled. "You feel okay?"

"Physically, I feel better than okay, actually," I admitted shyly. As for emotionally, I was trying to beat down the memories of the orgasms I'd had in front of both Sinjin and Rand. Oh, God …

The memory of wrapping my legs around Sinjin invaded my mind and I clenched my eyes shut, hoping it would fade away. But what stuck out was not the fact that I'd wanted to jump his bones, but the fact that I'd been able to move my legs. I looked down at myself and attempted to lift my leg and … it worked.

"I can move again," I announced.

Rand nodded and didn't seem overly excited by the admission. "It's Sinjin's saliva. It must not only have healed the wolf's bite but the rest of you as well."

"It's that strong?" I asked, wondering why I hadn't just swallowed a tankard full of that instead of the fairy potion. Okay, gross, I know, but desperate times call for desperate measures.

"Yes."

I suddenly remembered the wolf and glanced toward the dead human heaped in the corner. "Do you know who he is?"

Rand shook his head. "No, but I do know he's one of Bella's."

"He was?" I almost choked. "But how did he get through the fairy nets and all your soldiers?"

"Inside job," Rand said with a sigh. "This is her way of saying she's agreed to our war."

FOUR

So while it wasn't exactly a great situation—having the werewolf attack me and all, I actually felt better than I had for the past week, courtesy of Sinjin's … spit. Even though the attack was only a few hours old, I had now regained full use of my entire body. Although, I wasn't one hundred percent back to normal because I still felt incredibly tired. It had taken a lot of magic to heal the bite the wolf had taken out of my shoulder and whenever I use magic, it exhausts me.

Exhausted or not, I was still livid over Rand insisting I wasn't allowed to fight in the war, especially when I was the reason for the whole stupid thing. And it wasn't like he didn't want me to fight because I was female. At least a third of his recruits were women! But I still had a few tricks up my sleeve where the war was concerned and what Rand didn't know, wouldn't hurt him.

But planning my strategy would have to wait. What currently occupied my mind was the fact that I'd nearly been turned into a wolf. And even though I'd dated a were and hadn't held his canine antics against him, that didn't mean I was ready to join him. What terrified me even more than the prospect of becoming furry was the realization that the war was no longer far off or abstract—it was now a definite.

Word of the attack had quickly spread throughout the legion, invigorating everyone with a renewed determination to prevail. Since the werewolf that attacked me had been one of ours, Rand had ordered every soldier to take a blood oath that involved an incantation whereby if anyone attempted to deceive us again, their blood would boil and they'd be cooked from the inside out.

Swearing in all the creatures had taken the entire day and was well into the night. Some of us were spared the duty because the fairies and Rand's coven had taken over the responsibility.

"Our legion will meet at the Clava Cairns," Rand announced to the group gathered around his dining table. The group consisted of Odran, Nigel, Sinjin, John, Trent, and Mathis, Rand's second witch in command. Christa was usually present during all of our meetings but tonight she was dozing on the couch.

Mathis wasn't bad looking but he wasn't really my type. There was just something about him that droned … bland. He was from Michigan and had mousey brown hair and dark brown eyes with an overall nondescript appearance. But in the sphere of witchcraft, he was pretty darn talented; otherwise, Rand wouldn't have selected him as second in command.

"What's the Clava Cairns?" I asked and leaned into the dark brown leather chair, admiring both Sinjin's and Rand's faces in the yellowish glow of the chandelier lights. Rand's dining room was like something out of a castle. The walls were stone but covered with floor-length tapestries he'd collected from around the world. The mahogany table was large enough to easily accommodate our group and the orange glow of a fire burning in the hearth gave the feel of a true English manor home. It was just missing an Irish wolfhound or failing that, Lizzie Bennett.

"Clava Cairns is an ancient Scootish burial ground, lass," Odran said.

"They are a series of stone circles," Rand added. "We will assemble at the Cairn surrounded by the eleven standing stones. Once there, we'll march to Culloden to meet Bella's forces."

Clava Cairns was just down the road from Culloden Battlefield. Why Rand didn't just meet Bella and her army at the battlefield was beyond me. But I wasn't well versed in the art of war or in waging it, apparently.

"And when are you going to send the declaration?" Trent asked, an angry red cold sore bubbling his upper lip. I tried not to focus on it, not wanting to be rude but it was next to impossible. It was the biggest cold sore I'd ever seen. In fact, it looked as if his lip was in the process of spawning another human.

"I await Bella's declaration and will respond accordingly," Rand answered.

"What's the declaration?" I asked.

"It's a letter regarding our proposal of terms should we defeat her," Rand said. "It's a way of informing Bella what's in store for her if she loses."

"Poppet, it is another attempt to allow Bella to politely step down from waging war against us," Sinjin finished.

I smiled at him, feeling a warmth toward him I never had before. I was sure it had everything to do with the fact that he'd basically saved my life. But what I couldn't decide was whether it was a feeling naturally born out of gratitude or a left over reaction to Sinjin's saliva.

"Then she will send a declaration letter to us also?" I asked.

"Yes," Rand answered.

"Do you think Bella will fight according to the rules?" I continued.

Mathis nodded. "The wolf attack was a sign of her agreement to our invitation since it came within the allotted time period."

"Yeah, never mind the fact that she almost killed me!" I countered.

Rand was about to respond but was interrupted by the entrance of someone I didn't recognize. He stood in the doorway and hesitated momentarily before striding in. A breeze suddenly blazed through the otherwise still room and the feeling of energy poured over my skin. I could only imagine it was in response to the stranger. He must have been powerful. He was nearly as tall as Odran and thin with a definite elegance about him. His hair was as orange as a sunset and his flawless skin whiter than seemed possible—almost translucent in its paleness. He wasn't necessarily attractive or unattractive. Like the ancient fairies, his sense of presence was such that it didn't occur to me to categorize him. He had no aura which could only mean one thing … vampire.

"Varick," Rand nodded.

Sinjin had already stood and solemnly bowed to his boss. He offered a seat to Varick who dismissed it with a wave of his hand. Sinjin remained standing. Subservient was not a role I'd ever seen Sinjin play and it didn't suit him.

"Rand, it has been far too long," Varick said in a voice the dialect of which didn't pay homage to any country. He made no motion to approach Rand which seemed to suit the warlock just fine.

"Thank you for joining us," Rand said stiffly.

"Yes, I apologize for my tardiness. I had to meet with two of my … informants regarding Bella."

And here I thought he was just fashionably late.

"And I've brought one of the informants back with me," Varick added.

"Pardon?" Rand surged to his feet, his anger palpable. The entire room was as eerily quiet as a murder scene.

Sinjin's eyes glowed red. "Who?"

"Grimsley," Varick said with a smile and turned back to the doorway.

I had already met the warlock Grimsley Jones at a recruiting party Rand had thrown to gain support for our side. At the time Grimsley had allied himself with Ryder and Ryder's ingénue, the half witch-half vampire, Gwynn. The fact that Grimsley turned out to be an informant was a surprise to all, as we'd assumed he was allied with the opposition.

"Grimsley?" Rand repeated. "Where the bloody hell is he?"

Varick merely chuckled and lifted his skeletal hand, beckoning toward the door with two pointed fingers. Grimsley appeared in the doorway and took a few steps forward, smiling insipidly. His attention then returned to Rand and he bowed his head, probably realizing he had to give us a damned good reason as to why he was standing in Rand's entryway.

Disgust crawled over me. I didn't trust him one bit.

"When I learned of Bella's intent to sick the wolf on your witch, I came as quickly as I could to alert you," Grimsley said and then inhaled deeply. "I hope I am not too late."

Not too late? He was way too late. If not for Sinjin, I'd be outside howling at the moon by now.

"You came very close to being too late," Sinjin snapped.

Grimsley glanced at me and smiled apologetically. "Jolie, are you alright?"

"Yeah, no thanks to you," I said, returning my attention to Varick who was busy inspecting his fingernails in a great show of indifference.

"Again, I apologize for not being more prompt," Grimsley said and offered Rand his weathered, old hand. "Rand, it is good to see you again."

Rand accepted his hand and bared a hesitant smile. Was he really falling for this crap?

"I'm pleased to have you on our side, Grimsley." Hmm, guess so.

"I wanted to alert you that I was on your side earlier, but couldn't risk it. I had to maintain the illusion that I was with Bella."

"But your coven …" Mathis started.

"My coven remains within Bella's ranks," Grimsley replied. "They have orders to stay there until the battle begins, then they will turn on her."

Jolie. It was Rand's voice in my head. *I don't trust him. Can you do a Liar's Circle?*

Thank God I wasn't the only dubious one. The Liar's Circle was a spell Rand had taught me—a quick charm that allowed the charmer to test whether or not someone had honest intentions. Sort of like a lie detector test.

Yes.

I watched as Rand continued to chat with Grimsley, eager to keep the old man's attention away from the fact that we were charming him.

I glanced down at my shoes and pretending to retie my shoelaces, closed my eyes, imagining a circle of bright white light surrounding Grimsley. I repeated the words in my head several times: *Grimsley Jones, are you sincere?* Then I awaited the answer. A bluish light began to usurp the white glow of my circle and that could only mean one thing.

He's telling the truth.

So I'd have to eat humble pie. I double knotted my shoelaces and sat up in time to see Rand smiling at me before he returned his attention to Grimsley.

"How many witches are still with Bella?" Rand asked.

"Thirty," Grimsley responded.

Rand nodded. "I am very pleased to hear that. We need all the help we can get."

"Boot ye 'ave anoother informant still within Bella's ranks?" Odran asked Varick. "Oother than the witches?"

Varick didn't even bother looking up from his nails. "Yes."

"This is good news," Rand said with a grin.

"We witches are few and far between so we must stick together," Grimsley said.

Nothing was closer to the truth. While there was a plethora of werewolves and vampires, the procreation of both not necessitating pregnancy, the same couldn't be said for witches. Our breed was slowly dying because females had a difficult time carrying to term. It was a subject I tried never to dwell on—I really had hoped for the large family with a white picket fence.

"Bella and her army are preparing in Arizona, as you know," Varick continued. "She received your war summons and should have already sent her response?"

"You could say that," I grumbled.

Grimsley nodded. "That would be the werewolf visit, I suppose?"

"Yes," Rand said as I frowned.

Sinjin looped a tendril of my hair between his thumb and forefinger, massaging the tress as if it were silk. "Without the wolf, we never would have had our moment," he whispered.

Varick suddenly brought his attention to Sinjin and his lips twitched slightly. "Is there something I should know regarding you both?"

If Rand had laser vision, he could have burned a hole through Sinjin's hand—the one now casually resting on the small of my back.

"There is nothing between them," Rand said furtively.

Varick nodded but his attention remained focused on Sinjin—it was almost as if the situation amused him, that of a warlock who couldn't possibly get any more uptight and a vampire that seemed to thrive on his ability to make the warlock uptight. I couldn't say it didn't amuse me too.

"Her army outnumbers ours," Varick continued, glancing back at his dagger shaped fingernails.

"I predicted it would," Rand said.

"But I believe we can still be victorious," Varick continued before addressing Odran. "Without the fairies, we would not stand a chance."

"Aye," Odran nodded.

"But they have demons," Trent remarked.

Varick studied Trent with narrowed eyes for a second or two and then exhaled deeply, as if he smelled something offensive and wanted only to extricate the foul air. He ignored Trent and returned to Rand. "Yes, she does have the support of the demons, but they are not as powerful as the fairies."

"They are noot," Odran agreed. "We can destroy any demon."

Rand nodded but said nothing to Odran, and turned his attention back to Grimsley. "What are your plans, Grimsley?" he asked, offering Grimsley a seat. The old man lowered himself so awkwardly, I worried he'd collapse before touching down. Witches could postpone their aging—slowing it to a mere crawl. So for Grimsley to appear as old as he did, he had to have been around for centuries.

As soon as Grimsley took his seat, Trent, Odran, and Varick also sat down. Rand and Sinjin remained standing. I occupied the only armchair in the corner of the room, offering the best vantage point.

"I must return to Bella to avoid suspicion," Grimsley said. "But I plan to return in just a few days."

"Isn't it a little too late for that?" Trent asked. "Doesn't she already suspect you're in cahoots with us?"

Grimsley shook his head and sighed, glancing down at the table. He took a deep breath and studied the men around him. "No, Bella believes I am en route, with more werewolves."

"And when you show up empty handed?" John asked.

"I had hoped not to show up empty handed," Grimsley countered.

"I would be happy to lend you some of my wolves," Trent said. "I would go myself, but I narrowly escaped Bella's clutches a few months ago so she'd probably sense something was up."

Grimsley nodded. "Very well. Thank you for your generous offer."

"How many do you need?" Trent continued.

"Twenty would suffice," Grimsley answered. I had to subdue my worry about offering up our men to Grimsley. My distrust was silly. The Liar's Circle was never wrong.

Trent asked Rand, "Can you cast some sort of truth spell on him? I want to make sure he isn't playing us."

Rand nodded. "He raises a good point, Grimsley. I hope you understand?"

"Yes, of course. I think it perfectly acceptable and will succumb to whatever spells or incantations you need to convince yourselves I am on your side."

Unbeknownst to him, he already had.

~

Later that night, I had insomnia. It seemed my schedule was adapting to that of everyone else—sleep by day and battle by night. I tossed from side to side and saw the green light of the alarm clock glaring at me. Not exactly comforting.

I sat up and rubbed my eyes, wishing I could vacate thoughts of the impending war and what it would mean to my future, to all of our futures. I gasped as the shape of a man met my eyes. He was dimly glowing like a weak light bulb and I could see right through him. It took me a second or two to recognize the resident ghost of Pelham Manor. He was a ghost I knew well and an old friend—the original master of Pelham Manor, William Pelham.

Pelham! I could only communicate with him through thoughts. *You scared the crap out of me!*

He grinned boyishly. I'd missed his ethereally handsome face. Pelham had died of cholera at age thirty-one but in his ghostly shape, he'd retained his vibrant light brown hair and rich brown eyes.

I am pleased to see you are unscathed.

It took me a minute to realize he was referring to the wolf-mauling. *You were there?*

Yes, I am the one who alerted the vampire. I knew there was nothing I could do to save you. I was looking for Rand but came across the vampire first.

Thank you, I thought and offered him a warm smile. *How have you been?*

Quite lonely, actually.

I didn't know what to say to that so I changed the subject. *I suppose you already know we're going to war with Bella?*

Yes, of course. I am nothing if not an eavesdropper, as you well know.

Yeah, poor ghost; not like he had much going on just being stuck in the house with only the home's inhabitants for company.

I snuggled down into my duvet and was silently thankful for the company. *So you already know that Rand won't let me fight?*

Yes, I think it for the best. You are not a soldier.

I shook my head, trying to suppress the disappointment coursing through me. *Ugh, I don't need to hear it from you too. There are plenty of other females fighting and I've got just as much ability as any of them, if not more.*

Pelham crossed his long ghostly legs at the ankles and leaned against one of the canopy banisters, actually sinking into the dark cherry wood.

Yes, but those females are werewolves and vampires. They are not like you.

I nearly choked on my irritation. *I'm a good witch.*

No one is arguing that. You are just too important, Jolie. Your gift needs to be protected.

I shook my head. *My gift is nothing without Rand. I need him to help me bring the dead back to life. If my gift is so important, he shouldn't be allowed to fight either.*

He is the leader, so he must. Besides, when the war is over, you will be extremely busy with resuscitating the dead.

I faced him with a question in my eyes. *What do you mean?*

You had not heard?

No.

Rand is requiring all creatures to supply him with a personal item, such as a piece of clothing. That way, if your side is victorious, you and he can begin bringing back the dead.

I'd learned it was much easier to reanimate the dead as long as I held something that had belonged to them in life. Hence, Rand's clothing drive. And it didn't surprise me that Rand hadn't already filled me in. He'd been so busy lately, I was lucky to get a quick hello. And while I was happy to help out, it wasn't enough. I wanted, no needed, to fight.

How do you know this? I asked.

He and the vampire discussed it in the rose garden last eve.

A knock sounded on the door, startling both of us.

"Jolie?"

It was Rand. I smiled at Pelham. *Speak of the devil.*

"Come in," I said.

He opened the door and seemed surprised to see Pelham. "I apologize if I'm interrupting?"

"No, you aren't interrupting," I replied, eager for any of Rand's time.

Rand nodded and glanced at Pelham. "Pel, a little privacy, if you don't mind?"

Pelham grumbled and disappeared into my coverlet while Rand glanced at me, a new concern in his eyes. "I knew you weren't asleep," he started, his brown sweater almost the exact shade of his hair.

Rand could send what he referred to as "feelers" to decipher when my brain was active or inactive, as indicated by sleep.

"I think my biorhythms are changing in accordance with everybody else's."

"Perhaps they are," he said and paused, as if something were troubling him. "I … I wanted to find out how you were holding up."

"I'm okay." I gave him a weak smile. "I mean, I have a mini meltdown every time I think about this war but other than that, I'm as good as can be expected."

Rand ran his hands through his hair. "I know I haven't been around much lately but that doesn't mean I haven't been thinking about you." He took a seat next to me on the bed and I had to keep myself from inhaling his masculine scent. "In fact, I think about you constantly."

At his words, a warmth started inside me and spread throughout my body. "I understand, Rand, you don't have to apologize. You've got a lot on your plate right now."

He sighed deeply. "I didn't know what happened when I saw Sinjin in here covered in blood." He paused, as if reliving the horror. "I thought HE attacked you."

"If not for Sinjin, I'd be a wolf by now."

Rand nodded. "As much as I hate to admit it, I owe him."

I shook my head. "You don't owe him anything. Sinjin doesn't do anything unless he wants to, for his own reasons.

Rand laughed but the laugh died on his lips moments later. "You know him well?" he asked, his entire body tuned to my response. I wasn't sure why Rand seemed to think there was something between Sinjin and me.

"I don't know how well I know him; but he's pretty easy to figure out."

He stood up and neared the window before facing me again. The moonlight seemed to exaggerate his already substantial height. I couldn't help but admire the strength of his figure, the breadth of his shoulders and the way his hair curled, just kissing his neck.

"I'm trying to figure out what he wants from you."

I shrugged. "Who says he wants anything from me, other than physical gratification?"

Rand's hands fisted at the mention of physical gratification and he was quiet for a few seconds. "I can't stop thinking about him glamouring you." He paused. "It was difficult to watch."

My heart fluttered as I realized how much Rand was opening up to me recently, freeing his feelings whereas he never had before. I stood up and approached him, throwing my arms around him. He pulled me into him and rested his chin on my head. I inhaled his scent deeply; I couldn't help it.

"Well, whatever I did or said, you know I wasn't in my right mind?" I questioned.

He nodded. "Yes, of course, I just hope it didn't bother you?"

I shook my head. "No, I'm okay with it. I mean, it's a little embarrassing, but I was under Sinjin's power … I wasn't really myself." I paused a moment and pulled away from him, trying to get a read on him. "Rand, none of this is your fault and you did what you thought best."

"I should've done a better job protecting you."

I clasped his hand, smiling at him. "Nobody knew that wolf was Bella's. What's done is done. There's no use saying what you coulda, shoulda, and woulda done."

He nodded and glanced down at me, a smile toying with his sumptuous lips. "I hated seeing Sinjin all over you."

"A little jealous, were you?" I asked with a laugh, relishing the heat emanating from his body.

"Yes," he said, lifting my chin to kiss my mouth. It started out as a quick kiss but when I wrapped my arms around his neck, he squeezed me tighter and slipped his tongue into my mouth. All too soon he pulled back. I resisted the urge to pout.

"I'm like a jealous school boy where you're concerned," he finished and pulled away from me.

"I can't say I dislike your jealousy."

He shook his head and sighed, as if overcome by the drama that was our lives most recently. He pulled away from me and took a few steps toward the door. "I wish I could stay with you but I need to get back to the training camp, Jolie," he said and smiled forlornly. "You know I'd much rather be with you."

"I know."

He grabbed hold of the doorknob and turned back around. "Don't forget I'm always here if you need me."

I smiled. "Thanks, Rand."

FIVE

I decided to give Rand a chance to change his mind about allowing me to go to war. I figured if I could prove myself on the battlefield, training with his legion, it might be enough to persuade him. My plan was a good one for two reasons—first, it could possibly persuade Rand to let me go, and second, it was just good practice. Regardless of Rand's orders, I'd already made up my mind to fight. But I didn't want to show up unprepared so I needed to get as much training as I could. Especially since I'd lost so much time during my recuperation.

On this particular evening, the sun had hurried its descent in the sky and it was just a matter of minutes before the vampires climbed out of their graves like something from a horror movie.

I pulled on some navy stretch pants, a sports bra to support the twins, and a sweatshirt, admiring myself in the mirror. Could it be possible that Sinjin's saliva had made me thinner? Nah. Combing my elbow-length blond hair into a ponytail, I put on my sneakers and went in search of Rand.

He wasn't hard to find.

Jogging to the training ground, I caught the image of Rand holding his own against Odran. The two were maybe six feet apart and Rand's white t-shirt was stained with dirt and sweat, but I was more concerned with the ample swell of his biceps as he exploited his powers against Odran. While Rand's t-shirt might have looked like it barely survived the Clash of the Titans, at least he was wearing one. The only thing separating Odran's nudity from the night air was a plaid kilt.

A bluish light glimmered from Rand's hands until it appeared he was holding a blue fire ball which he hurled into Odran's stomach. It sizzled a few times and then disappeared, leaving Odran intact, none the weaker.

Odran yelled something in Gaelic, or what I imagined Gaelic might sound like, and charged Rand, all the while glowing a bright yellow. He looked like an enraged *Lemonhead.* When he collided with Rand, the yellow glow amplified tenfold and Rand appeared to be straining as he hit the ground. The earth suddenly rippled in what felt like a mini earthquake. I stabled myself and found Odran was still on top of him.

Rand's eyes were shut in pain, and he pushed Odran's bare chest away, his hands glowing purple. A jolt bolted through Odran and in a matter of seconds he was sailing through the air, landing unceremoniously in the dirt. This time I didn't feel an earthquake. But I quickly discovered the answer to a question everyone asks …

Scots don't wear a damned thing underneath their kilts.

After reluctantly viewing that display, I jogged another twenty feet and thrust myself between the two plundering Titans, offering Rand a hand up. He was sitting on the ground, panting breathlessly, while not far off, Odran did the same. Rand looked up at me and smiled that boyish grin and my heart forgot to beat for a second or two.

His hair was mussed, going in all directions and dirt smeared half his face and covered his t-shirt. Beads of perspiration studded his brow like diamonds. He was nothing less than breathtaking.

"Jolie," he said, accepting my hand.

"You're a sight for sore eyes."

He grabbed a towel lying on the ground and blotted his forehead. "And here I was thinking how good it was to see you."

He casually laid his arm around me and kissed the top of my head as we started toward Odran, who was now nearly upon us.

"Good job," Rand said.

"Aye, ye too," Odran responded and threw me a cock-eyed expression.

"Hi, Odran," I offered.

"Lass," he answered and slightly inclined his head. "What are ye doin' oot here?"

I released myself from Rand's arm and faced him soberly. "I was hoping I could spar with you." His expression spilled curiosity and I continued. "I thought it would be good to take advantage of all this Underworld power and work on my magic, too."

Rand nodded. "That sounds like a good idea."

Great, he acquiesced, thank God.

He looked toward the warring throng of soldiers, scanning the horizon until he spotted John in the throes of a passionate kiss with Christa.

"John!" he yelled, catching the attention not only of John, who blushed instantly, but also of Christa, Trent, and Sinjin.

"Yessir?" John obediently responded and began walking our way. John would have made a perfect quarterback—he just had that jock sort of look.

"Are you interested in training with Jolie?" Rand asked.

John frowned. "But I thought you said she wasn't fighting Bella's …"

"She's not," Rand interrupted, glancing at me as if to reiterate the point while I offered my best expression of innocence. "It'll be good practice for you to defend yourself against her powers."

John obeyed and I grinned as he approached me. Rand observed on the sidelines next to Odran, Christa, and Sinjin.

"I could not miss this," Sinjin offered when Rand looked at him askance.

"John, go easy on her!" Christa yelled and then added, "I've got a twenty on Jules."

"Hey!" John admonished with a chuckle and Christa beamed right back at him.

"Give me all you've got. I can defend myself," I said, tired of witnessing their cow-eyed flirtations.

"You got it, girl." He ripped his shirt off and tossed it aside, then slowly walked around me as if measuring my worth.

"Mind if I cut in?"

I glanced behind me and found Trent facing us both expectantly.

"Trent, mind your own bloody business," Rand called, moving a few steps nearer us.

"It's okay," I yelled back, thinking there was nothing I'd rather do than spar with Trent and get a little payback from the asshole. "I'd be happy to fight him."

"Okay," Rand said, backing off as John returned to Christa in the sidelines. They were about ten feet from us.

I faced Trent and anxiety raged through me. Not so much because I was afraid of him but more so because I didn't want to be so close to him. "Don't hold back," I said.

Trent shook his head. "Never do."

And without further warning, he lunged at me, catching me off guard but I quickly reacted by envisioning myself a few feet behind where I currently stood and watched Trent do a faceplant at my feet. I couldn't help but laugh and imagined a fire ball of energy in my hands. It was just for show as I made sure not to charge it with more than a mild stinging sensation. I aimed for Trent's stomach and unloaded. He darted to avoid it and like a glowing meteor, it disintegrated into the earth.

Trent yanked my ankle, pulling on it until I lost my footing and fell. I braced myself for the impact and just as I rolled over, he jumped on me, pinning me down with his weight. Trent wasn't a huge guy but he was lots bigger and stronger than I was.

"I always wanted you in this position," he said.

I just smiled, manifesting a handful of sand that I threw into his face, giving me enough time to create another energy ball, this one full strength. I could feel the energy tickle the ends of my fingers as I hurled it into his chest and he fell over, landing with a great thud on the ground. Maybe it had been a bit more charged than I intended but it served him right for his stupid comment.

"Nice!" Christa yelled.

Trent wasted no time and hopped to his feet, his lips pulled back into a snarl as he charged me. I imagined a heavy silver dagger and once in hand, lashed out with it, missing his abdomen by a mere inch. And that miss was not due to my miscalculation, it was due to Rand grabbing Trent's arm and yanking him out of harm's way.

"Bloody hell!" Rand yelled. "You weren't paying close enough attention! Don't let your personal issues get in the way."

"I have no issues with Jolie," Trent spat out.

I didn't respond but shrugged while he glared at the silver dagger in my hand. With a quick glance, it disappeared into my palm. Although I hadn't really planned on hurting him, I guess I'd come pretty close. It wouldn't have killed him—I would have had to bury the dagger to the hilt in his heart for that to happen. But it would have hurt and taken a long time to heal so good thing Rand intercepted.

Trent, apparently miffed that I'd prevailed, trudged off while John patted me on the back with his mitt-like hand. "Nice going, Jules," he said with a laugh. "I didn't realize you were so good."

"She's better than good," Christa said, beaming. "I didn't doubt you for a second."

I smiled gratefully and turned toward Rand. Sinjin threw me a raised brow, as if mocking my victory.

"I want to fight Sinjin," I said, knowing I had to train with a vampire if I had any hope of defeating Ryder. And for me, killing Ryder was top priority.

Sinjin stepped forward and his eyes narrowed as a mischievous smile formed on his lips. "Nothing would please me more," he said.

"Jolie," Rand started. "Sinjin is centuries old …"

"I don't care," I said with renewed determination and walked the ten feet to the sparring arena. I braced myself and motioned to Sinjin that I was ready to take him. He laughed and appeared instantly in front of me, about two inches from my face. I couldn't help but gasp.

"I will not go easy on you."

"I'm not asking you to," I countered, my legs suddenly feeling like Jello. Sinjin was stronger than Ryder and when I'd sparred with Ryder, he'd thrown me around like a rag doll …

"Very well."

I knew he had more than enough tricks up his sleeve so I envisioned a safety barrier, hoping it would protect me, hoping my defensive magic would work against him. Witchcraft is useless against vampires but I could only hope that rule was reflective only of offensive magic, not defensive. Guess I'd find out.

He materialized behind me and pulled me into the hard plane of his chest. "Your magic does nothing to deter me."

"Then how do I defeat you?" I asked breathlessly.

He smiled. "You do not."

Then he nudged me with a strength so intense, I tumbled onto my back, the wind knocked out of my lungs. The stars above me appeared to move in a dizzying whirl, suddenly interrupted by Sinjin's handsome face. This time there was nothing mocking in his gaze. Just regret. It took me a second to inhale and the air burned my throat. Sinjin offered me a hand but I declined it.

"Sinjin!" Christa reprimanded. She started forward but I held her back with a wave of my hand.

"I'm okay," I muttered.

"I apologize," Sinjin said.

Rand leaned over me and offered a consoling smile. "He's just too strong."

I nodded but didn't make any motion to stand up. "How is anyone supposed to defeat them?"

Rand's lips tightened as Sinjin stepped forward. "Only the oldest and strongest can battle against us, poppet."

"So that means everyone else is doomed?" I protested and propped myself up on my elbows, still feeling too winded to stand.

"Not exactly," Rand said, rubbing the back of his head.

"The other creatures have been drinking our blood," Sinjin answered nonchalantly, crossing his arms against his broad chest.

"What?" I demanded.

"It's the only way we can fortify our strength to fight them," John answered, sounding defensive.

"Your blood?" I asked Sinjin, having difficulty with the idea that he would willingly allow anyone to drink from him.

"Of course not," he answered, clearly insulted by the idea. "I am a master vampire and I do not share my blood."

Hmm, so I guessed it was the lower strata of vampires that were suckling the minion. What a gross thought. Then it occurred to me that maybe Rand had done the same?

"Rand, have you …"

"No!" he said, affronted. "I don't need it."

I reached out a hand to him, suddenly thinking he'd be the best subject with which to spar. What better way to prove I could handle my own than tackle Rand? He took my hand and I envisioned a huge gust of wind billowing behind him which landed him on his ass.

He smiled. "Is it like that then?"

"Come on, warlock, let the apprentice parry with the master," I answered. While we'd been talking, I'd been visualizing healing white light, allowing it to circulate through me. It had taken away the pain and now I felt as good as new. I jumped to my feet. I'd had a win with the wolf and a loss with the vamp. I couldn't afford a tie.

I heard Sinjin's laugh but my attention was on Rand as he stood up and faced me, a smile still visible on his lips. Chances were that Rand would make mince meat of me like Sinjin had but it was a chance I was willing to take. I had something to prove …

You will regret that. His voice intruded into my thoughts.

So come and get me.

He made no motion to approach me but I suddenly felt myself hovering above the ground and gliding backwards, slowly. Rand, smiling smugly, walked behind me while I struggled to extricate myself from his power. I closed my eyes and concentrated on dropping from the air but that failed. There was nothing I could do to stop Rand's power. I felt my back against the bark of a tree about twenty feet from where we'd been standing. And then I was completely immobile, as paralyzed as I'd been after my fight with Dougal, the fairy.

I watched him address the others who looked as astonished as I felt.

"Get back to work, all of you."

John and Christa left arm in arm and Odran had apparently grown impatient with our staging earlier as he was nowhere to be seen. Sinjin wore an expression I couldn't read and paused for a second before he disappeared into the air.

And as for you … Rand's words echoed in my mind as he faced me.

You never taught me how to paralyze someone, I responded, trying to wiggle my toes which proved impossible.

Rand was standing in front of me now but made no motion to do anything. His jaw was tight and his complexion appeared incredibly tan against the white of shirt. His eyes lit with passion as they roved me from head to toes.

"There's a lot I haven't taught you," he said in a low voice, interrupting the chorus of night insects.

"So do you plan to keep me stuck to this tree all night?"

He shrugged. "I could." He ran his fingers down my face and neck and I shuddered involuntarily. "It might be fun …," he said as his finger continued to draw a line into my cleavage.

"Aren't you supposed to be commanding the troops instead of teasing me?" My voice came out breathless, wispy.

"Yes," he said simply.

Kiss me, I thought.

Rand wasted no time in planting his mouth on mine. There was nothing tender in his kiss; it was ravenous, hungry. His tongue mated with mine in a passionate dance and when he pulled away from me, there was fire in his eyes.

"Guess it doesn't take much to get you excited," I said with a laugh, pulling my knee playfully up to his erection to emphasize the point. "Ah, I'm no longer frozen."

"It doesn't take much to get me excited around you," he answered. There was a sincerity in his gaze that warmed me to my core.

I threw my arms around his neck and he pulled me toward him. "Rand, when was the last time you actually slept?"

"A week ago. I plan to sleep this evening."

"Come to my bed tonight," I said coyly.

He shook his head. "You come to mine."

~

I did go to Rand's bedroom later that evening, after shaving my legs and washing my hair. Then I lathered up in my favorite scent of all time—Benefit's *Touch me then try to leave cream* (ah, how fitting).

I sorted through my jammie collection and settled on some blue and white striped cotton short shorts with a matching white camisole. My boobs strained against the material which met my needs perfectly.

I intended to have sex with Rand tonight.

I walked the few feet to his bedroom, my heart drumming in time with my steps. The door was closed so I knocked. After receiving no response, I opened the door a touch, only to find Rand's room empty. I glanced over the hunter green room, bedecked with rich mahogany wood furnishings and inhaled Rand's spicy scent. There wasn't a thing out of place. No dust bunnies either—like it was never lived in. Now what to do with myself … I sat on the bed and noticed a book on one of his night tables. It was *Great Expectations* by Charles Dickens. I sat cross-legged and opened the book, turning to where Rand had left his bookmark.

I was in no mood to read though, no offense to Mr. Dickens. My mind was too consumed with thoughts of tonight. Rand's invitation earlier must have been an invitation for sex, right? Or had he only planned to sleep together, in the true sense of the word? He had said he was sleepy.

"How do you like Dickens?" he asked, suddenly appearing in the doorway.

"AH!" I screamed, jumping about two feet off the bed. I grabbed my chest, trying to calm my heart down. "You scared me to death!"

He chuckled and locked the door behind him, then approached the bed and looked me up and down. "You look delicious."

"Thanks," I said, heat flushing my cheeks.

Rand nodded and took the book from my hands, carelessly dropping it back on the night table. I moved closer to him, intending to drape my arms around his neck but he backed away.

"I need to shower. I'm disgusting."

Disgusting was an overstatement. As for showering, he could have magicked himself clean without water, but it never quite worked as well as the real thing.

I subdued my disappointment. "Okay, I'll just be right here," I said, settling into the downy comfort of his ample pillows.

He smiled and pulled his dirty t-shirt off, revealing the taut muscles of his abdomen. Rand's chest was nothing short of awe inspiring. Every muscle was chiseled as if by the hand of an artist, but he wasn't at all beefy like those body builder guys. He was perfect. I'd asked him in the past if he'd magicked himself to look like he did and he was offended I'd even considered it.

Nope, Rand was the real deal.

"God, you are so gorgeous," I whispered.

He smiled at the compliment and reached out, running his fingers down the side of my face. "No, Jules, you are the gorgeous one."

It was the first time he'd used my nickname.

"I'll just be a second," he said and slipped into the bathroom. I heard the water come on and then Rand humming something. It took me a minute to realize it was *Norwegian Wood.* I smiled as his pitch dropped and he struggled to reach a high note.

The water stopped and minutes later, he emerged with wet, uncombed hair, bare-chested and beautiful with a white towel wrapped around his middle.

"Have you been listening to my Beatles CD again?" I confronted him.

He just smiled.

Unable to wait another minute, I stood up and rested my head against his chest. He was so incredibly hot, I mean temperature wise. It suddenly dawned on me that I could never enjoy holding Sinjin in such a way, not when he was ice cold. It was a weird thought that had sort of ram-rodded my mind and I pushed it away. What the hell was I doing thinking of Sinjin?

Rand tilted my chin and kissed me as he scooped my submissive body into his arms and laid me on the bed, climbing on top of me.

"Rand, make love to me," I whispered.

He hesitated momentarily, pausing for a split second before a wide smile took his lips. Fire burned in my stomach as he kissed me, placing my arms above my head. He started at my fingers and ran his hands down my arms until he lifted my camisole up, his mouth tonguing my nipples. He sucked on them as I sighed, running my fingers through his hair.

"I don't know how long I can wait," he whispered. "I'm not feeling especially patient."

"We've already waited too long." Yeah, about six months too long.

He removed one hand from my breast, moving it down my stomach and paused above my thigh. He pushed my shorts to the side and with no warning, pushed a finger inside me. I bucked against the intrusion, arching my back as a groan escaped me. A second finger joined the first as he pushed them in and out in rapid succession.

"Rand," I moaned and he suddenly stopped.

I opened my eyes to find his clenched shut.

"Are you okay?" I asked.

He opened his eyes at once and forced a smile, "I'm more than okay."

But he didn't look more than okay. He looked like he was in pain. He resumed sliding his fingers in and out of me again as if to prove his point and I arched underneath him, trying to encourage him to push deeper inside me. I ran my fingers down his taut back, reveling in the feel of his incredible body. Shivers raced over his skin.

"Rand, I need you now," I pleaded.

He hesitated slightly and then yanked the towel away from his midsection and nestled himself between my open legs. I could feel his erection just skimming my opening. I pushed up against it, encouraging him to thrust into me.

"Don't tease me," I begged, wondering what was stopping him from taking me.

At his resistance to enter me, I opened my eyes to find his clamped shut again, his fists clenching the duvet cover. He didn't look like someone about to have sex—he looked like he was on the receiving end of finger nails being ripped off or hot pokers up the ass.

"Rand?"

He stood so suddenly, he nearly lost his balance and gripped his head, as if he'd just been plagued by the mother of all migraines. "You have to go now, Jolie," he said in a low voice.

I sat up in shock and felt my heart drop, like it was free falling from the sixtieth floor. "What?"

"You just … you just have to go," he said and disappeared into the bathroom. As he closed the door, I heard the shower come on.

Okay, what the hell was going on? Amidst the throes of passion, he gets up to take a cold shower? WTF? I stood up, pulling my camisole back down and pushed open the bathroom door, trying to decipher whether I should be livid or concerned.

"Rand, are you okay?" I took the concerned route.

Both hands bracing himself against the shower wall, he leaned into the water as it splashed off his head and flowed over his body. His erection was now kaput.

"We almost bonded." His voice was thick, deep.

"Bonded?" I repeated, suddenly remembering what that meant—that when witches bonded, it was their way of marriage for lack of a better word. But while I wasn't sure if bondage encouraged tax breaks, what it did encourage was death or insanity should something happen to separate the bonded parties.

And the fact that we'd just come so close to bonding was a shock in and of itself and it scared the crap out of me. I loved Rand, of that I was sure. But whether I wanted to take this step, especially when in the wake of an Underworld war? Not so much. Regardless, I was beginning to think I was destined for the convent.

"How?" I insisted.

"I just couldn't restrain myself …," he said and sighed, still supporting himself with the shower wall. "The bonding pheromones were coming off you so strongly and my body was aligned with yours. I tried to resist …"

"And did you?"

"I think so; I don't feel bonded now." He turned the shower off but stayed inside the glass stall, heaving as if he'd just run a marathon.

"Rand, are you going to be alright?"

He glanced at me but immediately glanced back down again. "Can you return to the bedroom? I'm afraid of what might happen if I look at you right now."

Unbelievable! Why was it impossible for me to get laid? Recently it seemed the most action I'd gotten had been at my last pap smear. I shook my head in disbelief and returned to the bedroom, dropping myself and all my despair on his bed.

"And what's so bad about bonding with me?" I asked, wanting to play devil's advocate.

"If we're bonded and I don't … survive this war, it could kill you."

"I understand that part; I mean in the future," I said, ignoring the part about him not surviving the war. That was something I refused to consider and another reason I'd resolved to fight—I had to keep Rand, and Sinjin, safe.

"I don't know."

"Then where does that leave us?" I persisted and started to get annoyed. Really, I was more annoyed with the situation than anything. If there were such a thing as blue balls for women, I had them bad.

Rand just shook his head as the bubble of anger growing in me burst. "Why did you even ask me up here tonight?"

"Because I wanted to be near you and thought I could restrain myself."

I nodded and closed my eyes against the whirlwind of confusion blowing through me. I mean, on the one hand I understood his concerns—as always, he was just looking out for me. But on the other hand, this put us right back where we always were—in a perpetual state of inaction and it was beginning to be too much for me to bear.

"I don't know how much longer I can deal with this, Rand," I said in a small voice.

He emerged from the bathroom in a blue robe that ended at his knees. I focused on his shapely calves, dusted with a covering of dark brown hair. Even his freaking legs were sexy. I glanced up and noticed he was handing me a white terry cloth robe.

"Do you mind covering yourself with this dressing gown?"

I grabbed the robe and dropped it on the floor. Going from steaming hot to ice cold wasn't something that was in any way fun. I had to remind myself that I was relieved about us not bonding because all I could really focus on was our situation—how it never seemed to progress.

"I can't do this anymore," I announced, starting for the door.

"Jolie …"

I turned on him and the tears broke through. "I'm done, Rand. Either you want to be with me or you don't."

"Jolie, if something happens to me, it could kill you—do you understand what I'm saying?"

"Yes!" I blared. "I'm not an idiot!"

He shook his head and glanced down. "I'm not willing to risk your safety."

"I'm talking about when the war is over," I persisted. "What then?"

"Either of us could be imprisoned or dead …" he began.

"Let's say we win. Then what?"

He shook his head and dropped his gaze to the floor, pausing entirely too long. "I don't know, Jolie. The idea scares me to death." He looked pensively into my eyes. "Bonding nearly killed me once before. I don't know that I want to enter into it again."

I shook my head at the futility of the conversation—I'd thought his angst was due to the fact that the war was nearly upon us; I had no idea that he never planned to bond again, and even though I couldn't say I was in love with the idea either, it still hurt. He reached out as if to console me but thought better of it and dropped his hand.

"If you aren't willing to allow things to progress naturally to where they seem to be headed, where does that leave me?" I demanded, tears threatening my eyes.

He ran his hands through his hair as water droplets sprinkled onto the neck cuff of his robe. I couldn't hold the tears back anymore and they came streaming down my cheeks but I didn't care. I was too preoccupied with the fact that nothing would ever be what I wanted it to be where Rand was concerned. It was a hard pill to swallow.

"Don't think of it like that, Jolie," he started.

"And how should I think of it?" He went silent again. "You won't answer my question so I will—it leaves me in the same place you always leave me … with nothing!"

"Jolie …"

I held my hand up to silence him. "This isn't fair to me, Rand. I need to get over you and I need to move on."

"You should also realize it's difficult for witches to … procreate."

I shooed him off with a wave of my hand. "I already knew that. Mathilda told me. But I would have sacrificed that if it meant we could be together."

"It would eventually destroy me if I wasn't able to give you a baby."

I turned toward the door again and twisted the doorknob. "I just can't do this anymore, Rand."

"Jolie," he said as the door refused to budge. "Don't leave."

"Open the door," I demanded, the need to escape suffocating.

He was on me almost instantly. "God, don't you see this is just as difficult on me?"

"Difficult on you?" I scoffed, jerking away from him. "You're the one who won't give in to the possibilities, not me. So no, I don't see that this is in any way as difficult for you."

"I haven't said no to bonding … in the future," he corrected in a small voice.

"But you aren't exactly welcoming the idea either." I paused and wiped the tears from my eyes. "And that's not good enough for me."

"I thought our relationship was coming along nicely; why can't we just go back to how it was?"

"Rand, we can't have sex. What kind of relationship is that?"

"Perhaps …"

"There's no point in discussing this anymore."

He slammed his hand against the door, his frustration palpable. "Unless I commit to bonding with you?"

"Yes, well no!" I yelled. "I don't know, dammit." And that was the truth of it. I wanted a relationship with Rand. Did I want to bond? I didn't know. But did it have to be all or nothing? Rand seemed to think so. Hmm, would I risk bonding to be with Rand? Yes, I would.

"If we attempt anything sexual, it will bond us."

I dropped my fingers from around the doorknob and faced him. This is what it came down to—I wanted him to choose me over his fear of bonding. I wanted him to love me enough that bonding would be an inconsequential issue.

"You need to decide if I'm worth it to you."

"Even though the war …"

My hands fisted. "Screw the war; I'm talking about after the war—about our future together. You need to think about what will happen between us if we survive the war, because I won't want to go back to how it is right now."

"Is that an ultimatum?" he asked, his jaw clenched.

"Yes. I'm tired of waiting around for you. Yes, there's a probability we will bond ourselves but that's a chance I'm willing to take but if you aren't, I need to … get over it." I paused and faced him with all the determination of a saint. "Now, open the damned door."

He grabbed my hand and pulled me into him, moving like he was going to kiss me but I jerked my hand from his grip. I couldn't allow him to touch me or my intentions would be out the window. I noticed he'd released the doorknob and I threw the door open, disappearing into the hall.

SIX

Three days went by and I crossed off each day on my calendar with a bold, black line like I was in prison. Otherwise, the days would have melted into the drab pool my life had recently become. It was like we were stuck in a perpetual holding pattern otherwise known as the lead up to the war with Bella.

"How is everything with you relationship wise?" Christa asked as she stuffed a wad of bread into her already full mouth. She rested her elbows on the table in Rand's enormous kitchen and watched me, her expression too knowing.

I glanced away and gulped down the reluctance that always visited me whenever I thought about my relationship status, or lack thereof. I hadn't told Christa about my most recent disappointment with Rand. I just didn't have the strength to suffer through it again. In fact, I'd been doing my damndest to lock it into a secret vault in my head, where it could never see the light of remembrance again.

"I've sworn off anything that has a penis," I said as I walked my half-eaten plate of shepherd's pie to the trash.

Christa frowned and downed a few swallows of milk. "What about when you got to second base with Rand?"

Second base? Were we in third grade? And speaking of idiotic sexual synonyms, Rand had gotten a lot farther than second base. But that was also something I didn't want to think about.

"There's nothing to tell where Rand is concerned," I said with finality, rinsing off my plate and stacking it in the dishwasher.

"What about Sinjin?"

"Sinjin nothing," I snapped, maybe a little too emphatically.

Christa spooned the last of her peas into her mouth and stood up. "Yeah right. He's really freakin' cute and I bet vamps are nasty under the sheets."

She handed her plate to me and I rinsed it, entirely too curious about sex with Sinjin. "I wouldn't know."

"Well, as I see it, you have two options where men are concerned." She leaned against the black marble counter top and held up her index finger. "One is Rand and I'm betting on him, but if that doesn't work, you have Sinjin." She flicked up finger two. "And he's number two."

"Rand isn't an option anymore," I said, shaking my head as I started loading the dishwasher with the plethora of dishes lining the kitchen counter—all of which belonged to Christa. She seemed to harbor an aversion to cleanliness. "And neither is Sinjin. They both have penises, remember?"

At the thought of Rand's and Sinjin's male equipment, heat spiraled through my stomach.

Christa flicked up a third finger. "And another could be Odran, even though I can't understand a word he says. But you guys seem to communicate pretty well."

My mouth dropped open at the mere contemplation of anything sexual with the king of the fae. An image of his fairamours lounging on my bed met me like a blade through the eyes. "Oh my God, Chris, Odran is a walking STD petri dish. SO not going there!"

She looked puzzled. "Do fairies even get STDs?"

It was a good question and one I'd never considered. "Hmm, I don't know." I reached under the sink for the box of *Finish* powder detergent and poured it into the dishwasher dispenser.

"Probably not, huh?" she asked, still mesmerized. "I wonder if any supernatural beings get STDs. I mean, when have you ever heard of a werewolf with gonorrhea or a vampire with syphilis?"

"The vampire is not susceptible to syphilis," Sinjin's voice interrupted and I stood up so fast, I banged my head on the kitchen counter.

"Dammit, Sinjin!" I yelled, rubbing the back of my head while magicking the pain away. Dressed in his usual dark attire, he was every inch as sexy as he was dangerous.

"I apologize," he said with the beginnings of a smile. "I have come to fetch you as we have received Bella's declaration." I started to worry about how much of our conversation Sinjin had overheard, but his announcement of Bella's declaration wiped the concern clean out of my head.

"Bella's letter of demands?" I asked.

Sinjin nodded. "Randall has called a meeting in the library and I imagined you wished to be present."

A chill ran over my body and I wasn't sure if it was a reaction to Sinjin or to the fact that Bella had sent her declaration.

"Thanks for letting us know," I said and threw the dishwasher door closed, pressing the button for extra hot wash (Christa had a tendency not to rinse her dishes) and started for the library, Sinjin leading the way.

"Hmm, so can vampires get gonorrhea?" Christa asked.

"No," Sinjin responded as he appeared to glide up the stairs.

"What about colds or the flu?" she continued.

"No and no," Sinjin finished and offered me a cock eyed expression.

We were spared further incessant questions when we entered the library. Even though a fire burned in the hearth, there was a persistent chill in the room, like it was occupied by ghosts. Rand, Odran, Nigel, and John gathered around the fireplace. None of them were seated, so with a shrug, I took a seat on the chaise closest to the fireplace. Christa sat next to me.

"Sorry, we were finishing up dinner," I offered with an embarrassed smile that was lost on Rand. In fact, he didn't even glance up when we entered the room. Instead, he just tapped a letter against the palm of his hand. As I regarded the letter, I had no idea what to expect and the feelings of anxiety and foreboding made me feel like throwing up.

Instead of delving into the letter right away, Rand merely clutched it, gripping it so that his knuckles turned white.

"What are we waiting for?" I asked when I couldn't stand it any longer.

Rand faced me, expressionless. It was the first time we'd seen each other since our last … encounter. I could read nothing in his face and the blank wall of his emotions forced me to drop my gaze. I just couldn't look at him, couldn't keep myself from wondering what was going through his mind.

"Trent."

"Start without him," Christa said, nervously shaking her leg as she tended to do when agitated.

"Everyone must be present," Rand said with finality.

No sooner did he finish his statement then Trent strolled into the room and threw himself into a wing-back chair opposite Christa and me, offering no apology. He definitely operated under the assumption of his own self-importance. I noticed the frowns on everyone's faces, but no one said anything.

Except for Rand.

"Promptness is a virtue, Trent."

Trent feigned innocence with an open-mouthed "what are you talking about?" expression. Rand, shaking his head, slid a letter opener under the red wax seal and slit open the letter. He unfolded the ecru parchment and scanned the letter before clearing his throat.

"'To Whom It Concerns,

'As outlined by the Doctrine of the First Coven, should our side triumph, our doctrine is as follows:

'As regards Bella Sawyer:

'Bella Sawyer will become queen of the Underworld and leader of all factions of vampires, wolves, demons, fairies, and witches. All creatures will be divided into covens and covens will be assigned to regions as decided by the queen. All ownership of land will revert to the queen and covens will live upon Crown property. All Crown Tenants will show fealty to the queen in the form of rent.'"

"What?!" Trent asked, bashing his balled up fist into the arm of his chair. "None of us can own property?"

"Apparently," Rand said, throwing Trent a scowl.

"Do you think her soldiers know about this?" I asked, wondering how anyone on her side could have agreed to such a proposition.

Odran shook his head. "Nay, I doona." Then he faced Rand again. "Read oon."

Rand nodded and resumed reading. "'As regards any and all supporters of Rand Balfour, including those who are not specifically designated below:

'You will be subjects of the queen. Each of those loyal to Balfour shall be given to the queen's legions to do with as they see fit.'"

"Slaves?" Christa asked, her mouth agape.

John draped his arms around her and nibbled on her ear. "Don't worry, babe; I'll keep you safe."

Christa smiled up at him and nestled against his broad chest. I ached as I looked at them, wishing I could find the same happiness. I shot a glance at Rand and noticed he was doing his best to ignore them … and me.

"Yes, as decreed, we would become slaves to Bella's soldiers," Rand said.

"I had imagined as much," Sinjin responded with a yawn.

"We can't let her win," I started, tears filling my eyes. It was a stupid thing to say, elementary at the very least, but it suddenly dawned on me how much we had to lose. If our side didn't prevail, our lives would become intolerable; if we weren't dead, that is.

Rand glanced at me and held the letter against his chest, regarding me sympathetically. "Perhaps the ladies should retire before I continue?"

No, I thought indignantly, worried my voice would betray me. *This involves all of us. Keep reading.*

Jolie, Rand started.

I'm fine.

"What's going on?" Trent asked, glancing at Rand.

"They're talking with their thoughts," Christa answered and glared at him, apparently still annoyed with his tardiness.

Rand didn't respond but resumed reading after taking a moment or two to figure out where he'd left off. "'As regards Rand Balfour:

'You will be appointed as servant to the queen. Your property will revert to the queen and you will exist solely to do the queen's bidding.'"

His face was stoic and revealed nothing. Without so much as a pause, he continued. I had such a lump in my throat, I couldn't find my voice. I wanted to reach out to him, to touch him and tell him he'd be okay, but I couldn't move.

"'As regards Odran, king of the fae:

'You will be mated with the queen, and act as her second in command.'"

"I willna mate that hideous creature," Odran said, balling his hands into fists at his side. "I would rather die."

It surprised me only momentarily that Bella would match herself with Odran, but then I realized it was a political decision—if Bella could control the fairies, she really would dominate all the Underworld creatures. Without a strategic fae alliance, the fairies could still exist outside the law. I mean, it was impossible for anyone to find a fairy village unless they were invited. So in order to maintain control over the fae, this made total sense.

"'As regards Sinjin Sinclair: as a traitor, you will be put to death.'"

"Sinjin!" I gasped.

If I was outraged by the decree, Sinjin seemed unconcerned, as he did with most things. He merely smiled and raised his hand as if to say I shouldn't be concerned either. "Continue, Randall," he said stonily.

Rand didn't even respond to the hated nickname and continued reading the letter. "'As regards Jolie Wilkins …'"

I was still so flabbergasted by the fact that Bella had ordered Sinjin dead that it took me a moment to realize Rand had spoken my name. He glanced over at me and I gulped down the anxiety now climbing up my throat.

"Read it," I croaked.

He dropped his eyes and continued. "'You will be in the in the employ of the queen and will reanimate the queen's dead and aid the queen in her search for the prophetess.'"

"The what?" Trent asked.

I sighed, not even knowing where to start. "When Bella kidnapped me, she tried to make me bring back some witch whom she claimed was a prophet."

"What does that mean, a prophet?" John asked.

"Bella believes the prophetess can alter history," Varick finished, his orange hair brilliant against the light of the fire.

I nodded. "Well, the woman wasn't the prophet Bella was looking for so I guess she's still looking for her."

"Who is this prophet?" Odran demanded.

I shrugged. "No one knows."

Odran scratched his chin, as if in deep contemplation. "This is the first I've heard ah this."

I wasn't sure if any of the fairy elders knew of the prophet but I stayed quiet. I wasn't even sure a prophet actually existed.

"What else do you know?" Varick inquired nonchalantly but I could see his body tuned to my response, like a hawk watching a field mouse.

I shrugged. "I don't know anything other than what I've said."

Varick nodded and appeared to accept my answer. I glanced back at Rand and signaled for him to start reading again with a wave of my hand.

"'When you are deemed no longer useful to the queen, Ryder …'"

Rand stopped reading and scanned the letter in silence as my heart plummeted. "Rand please!" I begged.

He shook his head and continued reading. "'Ryder will retain full custody of you to use as he deems acceptable.'" He reiterated the final words "as he deems acceptable" with resigned solemnity. His lips were tight as he studied me and his eyes burned with hatred.

I felt as if some part of myself had withered inside by the thought of Ryder maintaining custody of me. Ryder would kill me.

"Jolie!" Christa cried.

"He will never touch a hair on your head," Rand pledged between clenched teeth and his hand tightened around the letter's pages as if they were Ryder's throat.

"You have many eager guardians, poppet," Sinjin said with the devil's smile. "You may count me among them."

"We will fight for you, Jolie," Trent offered and even though I couldn't stand him, I smiled my thanks.

I looked back at Rand as another letter freed itself from the ream of papers in Rand's hand and sailed through the still air, landing on the hardwood floor as lightly as a feather; but its contents held the weight of a bomb. Rand appeared to be in slow motion as he reached down and picked up the letter.

"It's addressed to you, Jolie," he said solemnly but made no motion to hand it to me. If nothing else, Rand was protective.

"You read it," I whispered, fearing I'd be unable to touch it, let alone read it.

"Very well," he said although his voice belied the fact that he wanted nothing to do with it. This time he didn't bother with his letter opener and instead, tore through the letter with vehemence.

"'Jolie, I will own you.'"

It was from Ryder.

"'You will be mine in every way. I will use your body when and where I want.'"

Without realizing it, a gasp had escaped my mouth. I suddenly felt incredibly hot, as if I'd been submerged in boiling water. My heart jack-hammered in my chest as I glanced up at Rand.

"I won't read anymore of this rubbish," Rand said and threw the letter down in disgust.

But like the inability to turn your eyes away from a horrible accident, I had to know the entirety of the letter. Even though I was now sick to my stomach, I was driven by the need to finish it. I eyed the letter and pictured it in my hand. It scuffled across the floor before jumping into my hands like an eager lap dog. I decoded the chicken scratch that could only be Ryder's penmanship, as horrible as the vampire himself.

"'I will feed on you. If you deny me, I will kill you.'" My voice was hoarse, thick. "There's a post script," I whispered. "'Enjoy this memory.'"

Once I uttered the last word, a beam of light shone from the letter, projecting to the center of the far wall of the room. Various colors emanated from the light and after a few seconds, the lights morphed into images like a film reel on a projector.

There appeared a room with a cot and a chair. On the cot was a woman, lying prostrate. It took me a moment to realize the woman was me. I was restrained on the cot with my wrists handcuffed to it and I was in my training outfit—a sports bra and Lycra stretch pants. I was alone for the time being.

The door opened and Ryder entered. My stomach flopped at the sight of him. He was dressed in black, the thudding of his biker boots matching the thudding of my heartbeat. Ryder's face was wide and hideous. He had a Hells' Angels sort of dangerous look. My attention dropped to the tray of food in his hands. It was like déjà vu as I watched him leave the tray next to my bed and approach me, a sandwich in hand. He held up the food and taunted me with it, knowing how hungry I was. I watched myself refuse the food and knew only too well what would happen next.

Ryder yanked my head to the side as he inhaled deeply, cupping my mouth with his hand. He ripped part of his shirt and gagged me. I watched myself strain against the cuffs as I kicked against him and nailed him right in the face. Furious, he ripped my pants, thrusting his head into the junction of my thighs as he bit into my groin. As I watched it, my thigh started aching, like it had its own memory of the attack.

But this was virtual reality and in it, Sinjin never called for Ryder which meant one thing … Ryder could see his intentions to fruition.

But I wasn't about to watch him rape me. And I definitely wasn't about to watch it with a group of spectators.

"Enough," I said, a lump in my throat.

I dropped the letter on the floor, the light beams dancing across the hardwood. Rand smashed it with his shoe and the light began to dim until it was impossible to make out what it was.

"I … I have to go," I said, feeling the sting of tears give way to a deluge. I stood up and had to steady myself against the chair, suddenly feeling dizzy and uncomfortably hot. I rushed from the room and headed down the hallway.

"Jolie!" Christa called after me but I couldn't stop. All I knew was I had to get as far away as I could.

I started running, hurling myself down the stairs until I reached the kitchen. Throwing open the kitchen door, I felt my lungs sting as I inhaled the frosty night air. I shot out the door and turned to avoid the warring soldiers, tearing as fast as I could in the opposite direction. When I couldn't catch my breath and tears were blurring my vision so much that I couldn't see, I forced myself to stop.

The trees around me began to spin and I leaned against an elm as I trembled in the freezing night air. Images of Ryder burned in my mind, images that would never leave me.

"Jolie," Rand said, grabbing my elbow and pulling me into him. I collapsed into his outstretched arms, heaving with sobs. He kissed the top of my head and squeezed me tightly, breathing in my ear. "I will never let Ryder near you, I promise."

And for one moment I actually felt safe. One brief moment. But I knew it wouldn't last. "There won't be anything you can do if she wins."

"I will always protect you. No matter what." He held my head between his hands and pulled me away from him so he could look into my eyes. "Why didn't you tell me what that bastard … did to you?" The moonlight shone on his handsome face. A face full of concern.

"I did tell you," I started and then realized what he was hinting at. "He didn't rape me, Rand; Sinjin stopped him. The film was a promise of what could be."

Rand's lips were tight. "I will never let him touch you."

I closed my eyes, trying to catch my breath, trying to clear the images of Ryder from my mind.

"Jolie!" Christa yelled as she threw her arms around me. "It's okay!" she whispered exhaustedly.

But it wasn't okay. It was far from it and for the first time in a long time, I was completely and utterly terrified.

SEVEN

I had to find Sinjin to explain my reasons for going to battle, that's all there was to it. Rand clearly wouldn't help me so I could only hope Sinjin would. After our horn-locking incident, Sinjin had proven in no uncertain terms he could easily snap me in two. The only way I'd ever be able to overpower him was … by drinking his blood. It was the only way I could defeat Ryder, so it had to be done.

I slept all day, and now it was well into night. Stretching, I stood up, carefully avoiding Plum who slept undisturbed at the foot of my bed. I slipped into a pair of jeans, a sweater, and my down jacket, and finished by pulling on my sneakers. I was about to walk out the door but decided to check myself in the mirror.

My hair was a mess. With just a thought, the sleep-induced frizz was replaced with sleek and shiny locks with only the most natural hint of bounce. I blinked and my lips flushed with baby pink lipstick, my cheeks turned rosy and my eyes outlined in coal grey, while my eyelashes darkened to a velvet black. So I wanted to look nice, so what?

Without a minute more to waste, I hurried out of my bedroom door and ran down the stairs, aiming for the back entrance of Pelham Manor. As usual, Rand's legion was busy with training and finding Sinjin would be akin to finding the proverbial needle in the haystack.

A fairy passed me and I reached for his hand.

"Excuse me, but I'm trying to find the vampire Sinjin. Have you seen him?"

"No," he said, briskly yanking his hand from my grasp while he kept walking. Jerk.

The best chance I had of finding Sinjin was by searching through the soldiers, so I decided to follow the rude fairy back into the faux battle. At the mouth of the battle, I paused. There was no way in hell I was voyaging into it—it would be too easy to accidentally get nailed by some stray fireball or get in the way of an overzealous wolf … the list went on. Instead, I stayed on the sidelines until I spotted a vamp who looked somewhat familiar.

"Excuse me!" I shouted. Casting me an irritated glance, he restrained his opponent with a raised hand.

"I'm looking for Sinjin," I said, offering an embarrassed smile.

"He's feeding," the other vamp informed me.

"Where?"

"Back at camp," the first vamp replied. "Back at camp" sounded so boy scouts on a jamboree—so completely weird to be coming from a fanged mouth.

I thanked him with a wave and scurried back up the hill, towards the vampire pits. Sinjin was feeding … I wasn't sure why the news didn't sit well with me, but it didn't. I knew there were humans here for that purpose, but for some reason, I hadn't actually envisioned what that meant. Of course Sinjin would also have had a human to feed on.

When I reached the vampire pits, they looked deserted. I made my way closer and couldn't see beyond the horizon of the tents set up for their human inhabitants. The tents were butted up against one another so there wasn't a way to breach the vampire encampment. I continued around the perimeter, hoping to find a break so I could locate Sinjin. I finally found a small pathway etched between two tents and entered.

Along the perimeter, torches provided some illumination but inside it was as dark as … the inside of a coffin. I tripped over a casket, trying to accustom my eyes to the dark. The canopy of trees overhead eclipsed the moonlight so I couldn't even rely on that. I scanned the area, trying to find any hint of life … or the undead. Failing that, I continued forward, having to inch my way along the caskets. I heard the sound of voices and could see the profiles of two people in a nearby tent, backlit by the torches. Maybe it was Sinjin.

I slowed down to decipher if one of the voices belonged to Sinjin. If it was, what would I find upon entering? I wasn't sure I wanted to know. And furthermore, how did one announce one's arrival? It wasn't like I could knock or ring a doorbell. I stood just outside the tent listening, but couldn't make out a damned thing.

"And what might you be doing?" a voice sounded from behind me.

I leaped about three feet and turned to confront a man, er, vampire, I'd never seen before. His glowing eyes endowed him with a certain monsteresque quality.

"I, uh, I'm looking for Sinjin … Sinclair."

"I bet you are. Are you his snack for the evening or are you the main course?"

I narrowed my eyes. "I'm neither."

"Pity for him. Perhaps you'd like to share that luscious body with me? I haven't fed yet this eve."

He ran an ice cold finger down my cheek. I backed up until my ankles bumped against another casket.

"I'm not on the menu," I snarled.

"Feisty," he grinned, his fangs protruding over his lower lip. "I like my food spicy."

Then he lunged for me. I pushed against his chest, lost my footing and fell through the opening of the tent I'd been eavesdropping on. I didn't have a chance to apologize to its inhabitants because the vampire was on me, burying his head in the crook of my neck. I felt the scrape of fangs and thrashed against him.

"Get off me, you son of a …"

"Stephen!" It was Sinjin's voice. "Remove yourself from the lady immediately."

The vamp surged to his feet and with a deep bow of reverence, backed up until he was at the entrance of Sinjin's tent. I waited for my heart to slow down and then rolled over and stood up. Sinjin nodded to the vamp who immediately vacated the tent.

"So he attacks me and you're just going to let him walk away?" I demanded.

Sinjin was sitting in a chair opposite me, but all I could focus on was the redhead in his lap with blood streaming down her neck onto her bare breasts.

He smiled. "He sensed your humanity, love, and humans in this encampment are considered fair game."

"Real nice," I said, pressing my fingertips to my neck as I realized how close I'd come.

"Now, tell me why you have come, poppet; possibly to join us?"

I dusted myself off and gave him a glare. "No."

He cupped the woman's breast in his large hand. "Then why have you come, pet?"

I braced my hands on my hips. "It's private."

He nodded and faced the now irritated woman. "Candy, will you excuse us?"

Candy? Really?

She glared at me but the glare morphed into a sensual smile once her attention returned to Sinjin. I just dropped my gaze to the floor, not wanting to focus on the blood dripping down her body. It resurrected unwelcome images of Ryder.

"But we just started; you can hardly be full."

"I am not satiated, darling, but if Jolie needs me, she is my priority."

Thank God for that. I stepped aside as Candy stood up and offered Sinjin a kiss on the lips. And it was a loud one, sounding like a toilet plunger mid plunge. He accepted it but then tapped her on the butt which happened to be in the shortest skirt I'd ever seen and turned her around, sending her on her way. She glared at me again as she left the tent but I just smiled, not knowing what else to do.

"I'm sorry I interrupted you," I started. "You should have told me to leave if you … hadn't finished."

He shook his head. "I would much rather spend my time with you, love. Perhaps you would care to provide my dessert? Your blood was the best I have ever sampled."

I shook my head. "Sorry, but no."

"Very well. What can I do for you, poppet?"

I sighed. "I need your help, Sinjin."

He closed his eyes and smiled. "Words I love to hear from your lips." He opened them again and studied me. Standing up, he took the four steps separating us, until I was uncomfortably close to him. I backed away, butting up against the side of the tent. I glanced up and noticed his black button down shirt was half undone, revealing taut pectorals with the lightest dusting of black hair. I gulped.

"How can I help you?" he whispered.

"Before I tell you how you can help, I want to preface this by saying I'm going to have to trust you, Sinjin. I can't turn to anyone else."

"I am intrigued, poppet."

I nodded and thought about the best way to deliver my appeal. Best to just come out with it. "I want to go to battle."

He nodded and didn't seem fazed at all by my request. "Why?"

Why was better than no. Maybe we were making headway.

"For two reasons. The first is that I personally want to kill Ryder. When he nearly drained me and then tried to force himself on me, I made a commitment, Sinjin. I promised to kill him to make up for what he did to me and what I'm sure he's doing or will do to other women."

Sinjin nodded. "I had planned to kill him myself for those exact reasons."

I shook my head. "It needs to be me, Sinjin. Not you and not Rand. It's my revenge."

He nodded. "And your other reason?"

I dropped my gaze and attempted to take a step back but found myself pre-empted by the tent wall again. I could just make out Sinjin's grin in the glow of the torchlight. The reasons why he didn't allow me any room weren't lost on me … Sinjin, next to Odran, was probably the randiest of Underworld creatures.

"Well, my other reason might seem stupid to you …"

"Nothing about you strikes me as stupid, pet." He leaned into me until we were uncomfortably close. Close enough to kiss.

I swallowed hard. "I want to make sure you and Rand will be okay."

He chuckled but there was a strange expression in his eyes. Something deep, something serious. "I can take care of myself, poppet, and Randall is a very strong warlock."

"I know, but that doesn't change the fact that I want to make sure you're both okay."

"I do appreciate the concern. If something were to happen to either of us, you could just bring us back, no?"

I had thought of this. "I don't know. You're already dead for all intents and purposes so I'm not sure I could bring you back."

He nodded. "Very good point, poppet. And Randall?"

"Every time I've brought someone back from the dead, Rand has helped me do it. I believe it's a blend of our magic. I couldn't bring that witch back when I tried to with Bella. Maybe that's because my magic only works when it's melded with Rand's."

"Another good point. You have thought this through from all angles, it appears."

"Yes, I have. The risks are too big to take. And knowing what Bella has in store for you …"

Sinjin smiled. "I appreciate your concern, poppet. It is …" He leaned closer to me until we were an inch or so apart and breathed into the crevice of my neck. "Satisfying."

I closed my eyes against the feel of his breath as it sent shivers up my spine. "Will you support me?"

He pulled away, thank God. "I have always supported you."

I guessed that was a "yes." Relief was sweet. "Thanks, Sinjin."

"And what does Randall think of you going to battle?"

"Rand forbade me from any participation."

"Ah."

"You can't tell him about this, okay?"

"Of course, love, of course." He paused a moment and then smiled down at me. "Do you expect to go to battle as unprepared as you were when we sparred?"

Hmm, Sinjin was astute. "No," I started.

"And how do you plan to remedy that, then?"

I swallowed. This was the part he probably wouldn't like. "Well, there are two things. Prior to my kidnapping, Rand had hired Ryder to train me in the art of self-defense. But because you're so much stronger than Ryder is, I'm sure you could do a better job."

"I like this plan," he said, appearing to ponder it. "You said there were two … things, though?"

I nodded and focused on the shadows that appeared to flicker and dance along the tent walls according to the burning patterns of the torchlights.

"Yes, the other is that I need … I need to drink your blood."

He paused for a second and then threw his head back and laughed, distancing himself from me.

"It's really not that funny," I said, starting to wonder if the old Sinjin I knew was surfacing. I'd anticipated the fact that this couldn't be all smooth sailing. He turned his back on me and walked to the other side of the tent before facing me again.

"Poppet, I am a master vampire. Nobody feeds from me."

I sighed. "I understand that, Sinjin, but you're the only vampire I could turn to and the only vampire I trust. That, and you're the strongest."

"Varick is the oldest and strongest."

"But he won't help me and I wouldn't want his … blood anyway." I mean, hey, I'd just met the guy.

"I would lose all respect if any of my kind learned I had allowed a human to feed from me."

"I'm a witch."

He crossed his arms against his broad chest and eyed me, as if sizing me up. "Yes, you are a witch, pet, but human all the same."

"I won't tell anyone," I said, beginning to sound desperate. I'd guessed he'd be difficult but I'd hoped his affection for me would stop him from rejecting me outright.

"Do you know what my blood would do to you?" he asked, sidling up to me again, his muscular chest begging for attention.

I shook my head. "No."

"But you are well aware what my saliva did to you?"

"It healed me."

"My blood is much stronger, poppet." The idea of drinking his blood suddenly struck me as something … sensual, and I wasn't sure what I thought about it. Yes, Sinjin was a babe and a half but …

"Would it make me stronger?" I asked.

"Yes, of course."

"Could I defend myself against Ryder?"

"Yes."

"Would I be strong enough to kill Ryder?"

He cocked his head, considering it. "Perhaps."

"Then it's a bet I'm willing to take."

He laughed and leaned into me as if he were about to kiss me. I closed my eyes—I just couldn't help it, it was like an automatic response.

"I have not yet agreed, love."

I opened my eyes. So he hadn't meant to kiss me? Now I just felt like a dumbass. "I would protect you, Sinjin, against Bella," I blurted haplessly, embarrassment staining my cheeks.

He smiled. "I do not need your protection. I am stronger than any in Bella's legion."

Okay, there was nothing I had to offer him that would in any way equal what I was asking for in return. So … sometimes you just have to beg. "Please, Sinjin …"

"There is one thing," he said with an infective smile and I had to gulp down the thrill that invaded my stomach.

"I've sworn off men and I'm not into casual sex," I interrupted, almost more as a reminder to myself.

He chuckled, not in the least bit offended. "Why have you sworn off men, pet?"

"Because they are a pain in the ass and they've brought me nothing but misery. I've decided to become celibate."

"Pity, poppet; you are such a lush little package," he said, eyeing me from head to toe. "Much as I would enjoy making love to you, my thoughts had run along a different course."

"Which is?" I paused for a brief moment, suspicion getting the better of me. Who knew what desires frequented his mind. The real question was, would I agree to anything?

"I will train you and we will meet every night. But in return, you will attempt to locate the prophetess each evening."

I narrowed my eyes. Why was Sinjin suddenly interested in the prophetess? Hmm, whenever I started to think Sinjin might actually possess a magnanimous bone in his body, something laced with selfishness always reared its ugly head.

"I have no idea who she is or how to find her. I don't even know if she is really a she and for that matter, I'm not even convinced there is a prophetess."

"You have psychic abilities, do you not, love?"

"Yes, but they are unreliable."

He nodded. "That is good enough for me."

"And if I'm not able to find the prophetess, what then?"

"No harm done."

I eyed him, trying to solve the riddle of why he was interested in the possible existence of the prophetess. Of course he'd never admit his reasons to me but I wondered about them, all the same. "Did Varick put you up to this?"

He shook his head and reached for my hands. His were ice cold and I fought to pull mine away. "It will be yours and my secret, agreed?" he asked.

I nodded—what other option did I have? "Does this mean you'll give me your blood?"

He didn't say anything but brought his wrist to his mouth and smiled with a great show of fangs. He bit into his wrist and didn't even flinch. Dark blood trailed out of the wound and down his forearm.

"Lick it," he whispered.

I pulled my hair back and grabbed his arm. "Will it turn me into one of you?"

He chuckled. "No."

With my fingers wrapped around his wrist, I paused. Could I really do this? I mean, I barely ate red meat ...

"Look at me," he said. "I want to watch you."

So he was getting off on it—that was okay, I guessed. I kept my gaze fixed on his and licked the blood from his elbow. It was salty and metallic and horrible. I licked up his arm, trying to keep myself from gagging. He clamped his eyes shut and threw his head back as I licked the two fang marks.

"Enough, poppet," he said and opened his eyes, pulling his arm away from me. His breathing was belabored. "How do you feel?"

He brought his wrist to his mouth and licked the two open wounds. Instantly they closed up and the skin looked as good as new.

I shrugged. "No different."

"Sit," he said and motioned to the portable chair he'd been occupying before I interrupted his feeding with Candy.

"I feel fine, Sinjin."

"You will need the chair, love; just humor me."

I shrugged and took a seat.

"You must never allow anyone to know what we have just done, do you understand?"

"I promise, Sinjin. I'll never say anything to anyone."

Hmm, there was something starting in my stomach—a fluttering like a million butterflies. "I feel something," I started, pressing my palm to my belly.

"Pain?"

I shook my head. The fluttering of the butterflies was becoming stronger until it felt like an insistent buzzing from somewhere deep within me. I suddenly felt warm and … elation coursed through me, feeling like a warm breeze on a cold day.

"I feel … amazing," I said, a smile stealing my lips.

"Tell me more, pet," Sinjin said, kneeling down in front of me.

"It feels like," I closed my eyes, trying to describe the feeling. "Like I'm flying."

Bliss enveloped me and I couldn't help laughing. The butterflies clustered within me and when I opened my mouth to laugh again, they escaped on my breath, floating out of me in an array of colors. I gazed at them in awe. "Do you see the butterflies, Sinjin? They're beautiful."

He chuckled and the sound was so infectious, I giggled with him.

"You are hallucinating, pet."

"You just can't see them, Sinjin, but they're here, all over this tent." I said, watching them as they swirled around the tent, settling on the fabric walls. I attempted to stand up, to walk over to them, but Sinjin's hand on my knees stopped me. I relaxed back into the chair, noticing Sinjin's hand as it moved up my thigh.

"You feel so cold, Sinjin."

"Poppet," Sinjin said and touched my chin. I glanced at his face and gasped; his eyes were ice blue and glowing.

"Your eyes!" I said. "And you … you are beautiful, Sinjin."

"Thank you, pet. Now focus; why have you sworn off men?"

I shook my head, not wanting to focus on anything other than the ice blue of his eyes.

"Answer me, love," he insisted.

"Because my feelings are hurt," I answered, just as an incredible orange and black butterfly landed on my hand. It beat its gossamer wings as if showing off for me, prancing along my arm, just as proud as any show dog.

"Why are your feelings hurt?" Sinjin continued, stroking my hair. "Who hurt you?" His voice was laced with anger, possessiveness.

"Rand," I responded absently, admiring the beautiful monarch as it reared up and spread its wings, clearly impressed with itself and showing off.

"What did he do to you?" Sinjin demanded.

"Nothing, that's what the problem was," I said, my voice sounding far away. "I wanted to have sex with him and he refused me."

At the mention of the word "sex," Sinjin gripped my thigh tighter. "Why could he not do it, love?"

I shook my head, uninterested in the conversation. My little monarch had flown away, having grown bored with me, and joined its brethren along the walls of the tent. Then, as if my little friend had whispered to them, they fluttered from the walls of the tent and surrounded me, their paper-thin wings tickling me. They were nothing short of wondrous.

Sinjin tilted my chin, forcing me to look at him, instead of the butterflies. "Why would he not make love to you, poppet?"

"He was afraid we'd bond."

Suddenly, the butterflies scattered, having grown impatient with Sinjin's questioning. Damn him!

Sinjin stiffened beside me. "Are you and Rand bonded, Jolie?"

But I wasn't concerned about bonding or not bonding. I was only focused on getting the butterflies to come back. "You scared the butterflies away. I don't know where they went."

"Love, it is very important you tell me if you and Rand are bonded."

"Why does it matter so much?" I asked, annoyed.

"Because if you are bonded, I should never have given you my blood and you should not be here now."

"We aren't bonded," I answered, still searching the tent for any sign of the butterflies but they'd disappeared just as quickly as they'd arrived.

"Are you certain?"

"Yes, he stopped before we had the chance to bond."

Sinjin nodded and offered me a relieved smile. "Good, I am happy to hear it."

I yawned and leaned back into the chair, snuggling against his hard chest and suddenly became dizzy. "Why do you care so much, Sinjin?"

"If you and he are bonded, you and I can never be a possibility."

I laughed at the thought of Sinjin and I together although I couldn't put my finger on why it was so funny. Instead, I tried to stop the room from spinning. "It's funny sort of," I said, gripping the chair as the room started settling back into place.

"What, pet?"

"I can't get laid. No matter how hard I try." I covered my face as I giggled, finding the situation increasingly hysterical.

"I would not have failed you," he said, smiling and rubbing his hands up and down my thighs.

I took off my jacket, throwing it on the ground as I reclined back into my seat. "Your blood makes me feel so good, Sinjin. Why didn't you tell me it would make me feel like this?"

"I did not know it would."

I glanced at him again and traced the outline of his face with my finger. "Do you think I'm attractive, Sinjin?"

He nodded. "Beautiful."

I rested my palms against his chest. "And you would have had sex with me?"

"Say the word," he answered, gripping either side of my waist in his large hands. The cold of his touch penetrated through my sweatshirt and I shivered.

"So what's wrong with Rand?"

Sinjin sighed and dropped his hands from around my waist, as if the last thing he wanted to discuss was Rand. "Bonding involves a new set of rules, poppet." He paused, standing up as his attention fell to the ground. "You do not want to bond yourself, do you understand? It is dangerous."

I shook my head. "I've heard all that—I could die if something happens to him, blah! Do you know what I hate, Sinjin?"

Another bout of happiness welled up within me and I had to close my eyes to keep it all in.

"No, poppet, tell me."

"I want more of your blood."

He chuckled. "You had enough, love. Tell me what you hate."

"All the rules in this Underworld. Why are there so many rules?"

"It is just our way," he said and started for the mouth of the tent. "I must feed, Jolie; it is becoming too difficult to be near you when I am hungry."

I pulled up my shirt and bared my stomach. "Bite me, Sinjin. You gave me your blood so I'll give you mine."

In an instant he was on top of me, gripping both sides of my waist as he leaned into me. He moved down the length of my body and brought his face to my stomach, inhaling as he rested his head against my skin and closed his eyes. "No, poppet, I have just given you my blood. It would be a waste for me to take it back."

I closed my eyes against a bout of exhaustion that warred within me and ran my hand through his hair which was rabbit fur soft. The feel of his lips as he kissed my stomach tickled my skin and brought an aching need to the pit of my belly.

"But you must feed?" I asked.

He kissed my stomach again, his fingers massaging my sides. "Yes."

"Are you going back to Candy?"

"Yes."

"Are you going to have sex with her?" I wasn't sure why the question slipped from my mouth. I hadn't even been considering it. But once it was out, I realized how much I needed to know the answer. I opened my eyes and found Sinjin studying me intently.

"Not if you request me not to."

"I don't want you to," I said and suddenly felt extremely tired again. I pushed him away and stood up, intent on starting the short trip back to Pelham Manor where I could crawl into my bed and give in to the incredible desire to sleep. "I have to lie down, Sinjin." As soon as I took one step, my knees buckled and I collapsed. Sinjin caught me and gently laid me on a mattress in the corner of the tent.

"What's wrong with me?" I asked, fear lacing my voice.

"Shh, my love, it is my blood bonding with yours. You will be fine." He then craned his head out of the tent. "Dragos!" he yelled.

Moments later a tall and light-haired vampire materialized at the tent's entrance and faced Sinjin expectantly. So the master vampire had servants at his beck and call? Interesting ...

"I need to feed," Sinjin informed the vampire. "Watch her and make certain no one enters this tent besides me."

"Yes," Dragos answered. "Have you not fed on her?"

Sinjin stood up so quickly, I never saw him move. He grabbed Dragos by the collar and levitated him.

"Let no one touch her, do you understand? If she bears any marks or if she tells me you touched her, I will destroy you."

The younger vampire trembled. "I understand."

He let go and Dragos landed on both feet, seemingly no worse off after having been reprimanded in mid air.

"I will return momentarily, once I finish supping on the human's blood."

"I hope you enjoy your supper," Dragos said, his neck bowed in subservience as he walked backwards, bowing all the while and disappeared outside the tent.

Sinjin glanced at me and the fierceness of his expression bled into a warm and gentle smile. "I must leave you now, love, but Dragos …"

"Don't leave me, Sinjin," I said, amid a bout of yawns.

"I must, little poppet, much though I do not want to."

"Wait," I started, but Sinjin's index finger against my lips silenced me.

"Dragos will be your sentry while I am gone. You will be safe, my love." He leaned down and kissed my lips while I nodded and instantly fell asleep.

EIGHT

Part one of my plan was complete—getting Sinjin to train and share his blood with me. Now it was time to put part two into motion—and it wasn't like I had a lot of time left; the battle was just over a month away.

It was six a.m. and the sun had started its ascent across the sky, dappling Pelham Manor in hues of warm yellow. As usual of late, I wore my jogging pants, a sports bra, and a sweatshirt. My alibi in case Rand spotted me? A morning jog. But exercise couldn't have been further from my mind.

I needed to visit the oldest and wisest of the fairies, Mathilda.

My only problem with visiting Mathilda was that I didn't have a clue how to find her. The only way into a fairy village was with a personal invitation and I definitely didn't have one. Each of my previous meetings with Mathilda had been orchestrated by Rand. But I had a plan up my sleeve. The distasteful part was that it included Odran.

I jogged the two miles to my old abode, stopping over ten times to catch my breath like a three-pack-a-day smoker. Arriving at the front door, I knocked a few times and then doubled over, straining to inhale more air.

When no one answered, I knocked again, this time with more urgency. I heard shuffling and someone bumping into something, followed by cursing before the door swung open to reveal an indignant king of the fae.

And he just happened to be as naked as the day he was born.

"Lass," he yawned and then frowned while he rubbed his sleep-swollen eyes. I didn't have the chance to find amusement in the fact that even the most magical of the magical also succumb to morning face. Instead, I was doing my darndest not to look down.

"Can you please cover yourself?" I pleaded, my head craned upward in an uncomfortable angle like a woman in a Picasso painting.

I heard him chuckle and dared to glance back to find he'd magicked himself into a blue and purple kilt. His broad, impressive chest remained bare in all its glory, but that I could handle.

"Thanks," I grumbled.

"Lass," Odran started, no doubt about to inquire as to why I was on his, er, my front doorstep at six a.m. His stomach muscles tightened as he leaned against the door, looking like God's gift to women. Funny, but he did nothing for me. I was getting to know him too well.

"I'm sorry to wake you up so early, Odran," I interrupted. "It's just that I need to visit Mathilda and I don't know how to reach her."

He stifled a yawn and raked back his thigh-length, golden blond hair. "Ye what?"

"Can I come in? It's pretty cold out here," I said, eyeing my home wistfully.

"Aye," Odran said, holding the door ajar just wide enough that I had to turn sideways to enter. Odran didn't move, but smiled when I brushed up against him. I just rolled my eyes. Being in camp with a bunch of horny guys was wearing thin.

As soon as I entered my little house, I wanted nothing more than to crawl into bed and go back to sleep. But that feeling fled when I peeked into my bedroom to find Odran's two lovers naked and sprawled out on my comforter. Vo-mit. Note to self—*Get a new bed and linens.*

I glanced back at Odran and shook my head at his smug smile.

"Do ye want ta join us, lass?" he asked with a mischievous sparkle in his eye.

"No!" I said quickly. "I, uh, I'm fine, thanks."

The truth was, I'd never been more okay with my newly appointed abstinence.

Odran plodded into the kitchen, sitting down at my kitchen table. He looked ridiculously large in the me-sized chair, which he dwarfed. He waved at the empty chair next to him and I took the one across.

"I need you to take me to Mathilda," I blurted.

Odran rubbed his chin and frowned. "An why do ye need me ta do this?"

I had previously decided not to trust Odran but now I was left with no other option. I needed him to make my plan work but that didn't mean I had to fill him in on the whys and hows of it. Either he wouldn't keep my secret to himself or else he wouldn't approve, either of which I couldn't afford.

"I can't tell you."

He chuckled. "Why should I help ye, if ye willna tell me?"

I'd already imagined this scenario a few hundred times and in my head, I was ready for his line of questioning. Now I just had to wait and see if Odran would go for the bait.

I leaned my elbows on the table and stared directly into his eyes. "If you help me, I'll grant you a favor."

"I doona need favors from ye, lass. I am the king." He sounded slightly disappointed, like he was hoping I had something better up my sleeves. Well, I'd prepared for this response too.

"Think about it, Odran; I'd be obliged to you and you could collect any time for any reason."

He was quiet as he considered it, stroking his chin like Thinking Man. "An this favor … can it be anythin'?"

I shook my head; I did have some caveats. "Nothing sexual," I said, sliding a glance to the open doorway where I could see his two fairamours in my bedroom. "It seems you aren't in need of sexual favors anyway."

"Ye fault me fer this, lass?" he asked smiling. "I am king; is it ma fault women want ta lay with me?"

I guess it wasn't his fault but that didn't mean I had to partake. "No, but I'm not one of them and I'm not on the table."

His shoulders drooped a bit as he pouted for sympathy, a ploy that did nothing but tick me off. "Give me a break, Odran; you get plenty of sex."

He crossed his arms over his chest until his biceps bulged exaggeratingly. He was so muscular it was almost laughable, like I was sitting there and chatting with He-Man.

"Aye, lass, boot not with ye an' I still want to."

"Moving on …," I said firmly to let him know the subject was closed. "The favor can't be something like joining your fairy village, or living with you, and it can't be a favor that lasts too long."

He sighed, long and loud and interrupted me, "I find this conversation boring, lass."

I leaned forward, not caring if he was bored. Too much of my future weighed on his acquiescence. "Think about it, Odran. I can bring back your dead and that's just one of the many ways you can benefit from my magic."

He tapped his long fingers against the tabletop. "Ye'll be bringin' back all those oon our side who die in the battle regardless."

This was the second time someone referred to Rand's plan to reanimate the casualties of our legion. Yet he still hadn't discussed it with me! I made a mental note to confront him about it once I had the chance.

"I could place your fairies in top priority," I said, worrying he wouldn't go for it.

He stroked his chin again and nodded. "I doona need ah favor from ye, lass, boot I will accept yer offer an grant ye the favor ye seek."

I was surprised. Odran had never struck me as the charitable type. And as soon as the surprise wore off, I realized this favor would one day come back to bite me in the ass, but I couldn't think of that now. There were more important matters pressing.

"Can you take me to see Mathilda now?"

Odran narrowed his eyes as he analyzed me. "Why have ye noot asked Rand?"

Guilty heat shot to my cheeks. Hmm, Odran knew Rand could contact Mathilda whenever he needed to. "I don't want Rand to find out."

"Why noot?"

I debated whether or not to be honest, since I was such a terrible liar. "Rand won't give me what I want so I'd rather leave him out of it."

He smiled. "Ye should ha told me this sooner, lass, an' I would 'ah agreed sooner."

I cast him my prettiest smile, eager to visit Mathilda and get my plan underway before Odran changed his mind or Rand realized what I was up to. Odran approached the door with me on his heels. The bright sunshine forced him to shield his eyes.

"Go on, you big baby," I said, pushing him forward.

He chuckled and grabbed my hand, trying to pull me out in front of him. As soon as he touched me, I was seized by a vision.

It was of Odran in what appeared to be a field, surrounded by his compatriots as they fought using magic, weapons, and ugly words. It was a vision of the war. I couldn't make out who Odran was fighting. I could only see Odran in the midst of hurling a fairy concoction at his opponent. As quickly as it came, the vision vanished.

"Lass," Odran started, no doubt wondering why I'd suddenly gone quiet.

My heart was racing so fast that I had to stop walking and give it a chance to wind down. "I just had a vision," I said breathlessly.

"Ah vision? Ye 'ave them?"

"Sometimes. I'm psychic," I said, hoping that was answer enough.

"What was this vision?"

"It was the war and you were fighting."

Odran humphed, as if he wasn't impressed. I reacted with a glare. "I have no control over what I see and some visions are more meaningful than others." He didn't answer so I motioned to the road ahead that disappeared into the forest bordering Pelham Manor. "How far is it?"

"It isna ah matter o' distance, lass," he started. "Ah fae village can be accessed anywhere, through magic."

He stopped walking in front of a large pine tree and put the flat of his hand against the tree, closing his eyes as his lips twitched. He appeared to be reciting a chant or incantation of some sort.

When he opened his eyes, the miles of endless trees were replaced with a bustling village, peppered with fae children running through unpaved streets, tending to their livestock. The same enormous and brilliantly colored flowers I'd seen in the fairy village in Glenmore Forest, Scotland, impressed me all over again.

White-washed houses lined each side of the street, complete with thatched roofs. Each plot was separated by a white picket fence and it even seemed as if the sun shone a little brighter here. But maybe that was just my imagination.

"Wow," I said with a smile, always impressed with anything involving the fae.

Odran smiled proudly. He took my hand but quickly dropped it, probably remembering what had happened last time he touched me.

As Odran led me into the village, the scent of fresh dew peppering heady lilies and roses met my nose and closing my eyes, I inhaled deeply. We passed a young boy playing in the middle of the dirt street with a smaller boy. The smaller boy glanced up quickly only to return his attention to the hole they'd been digging. But the other boy's mouth dropped open as he recognized Odran. He bowed low, elbowing his comrade with a terse "it's the king." His playmate quickly attempted an unpracticed bow and nearly lost his footing.

Odran's hearty chuckle made them both smile as they continued to stare, as if in disbelief.

"You don't come here much, do you?" I asked.

Odran shook his head. "Nay, I doona care to. Ma home is in Scootland."

As we walked further down the lane, everyone reacted the same as the boys had, repeating in awed voices "the king." Odran nodded, smiling graciously and I felt a little important as their eyes settled on me, his human sidekick. Even though Odran made me crazy at times, he was still the king. And nothing exemplified that as much as watching his people's reactions.

We arrived in front of the last cottage on the lane, separated from the others with a much larger yard, trimmed with a rainbow of flowers. Odran knocked on the heavy wooden door. In a few seconds, the door opened and Mathilda stood there in all her silver-haired beauty.

At our first meeting, Mathilda informed me that everyone saw her as they wanted to—her fairy magic allowed her to be whatever one chose her to be. To me she appeared as an older woman who was undeniably beautiful in her age-old wisdom. My view of her was entirely different from Rand's. To him, she was more along the lines of an old, weathered tree stump.

Upon recognizing the king, she started to bow but Odran stopped her with a hand on her shoulder. "Nay, doona bow, Mathilda, boot I thank ye all the same."

She smiled and when she saw me, her smile widened. "My child!"

I hurried past Odran to hug her even though I wasn't sure if it was fairy custom. She hugged me back so it must have been okay. I did notice, though, that Odran raised an eyebrow to show his disapproval, but I didn't care. I was too happy to see my friend.

"Come in, come in," Mathilda welcomed us, holding the door wide.

We entered her small cottage and Odran had to slump in order to avoid smashing his head into the hay-stuffed ceiling. The cottage boasted a living room type area with a humble kitchen and a short hallway to a tiny bedroom. The floors appeared to be an untreated pine, dull with wear.

"To what do I owe this great honor?" Mathilda inquired in an English accent that tinkled through the room like wind playing chimes.

Even though Odran was Scottish, not all fairies were of the same heritage, and Mathilda was English. I'd learned there were numerous fairy villages scattered throughout England, Scotland, and Ireland, but their headquarters, for lack of a better word, was in Scotland.

"The lass has business with ye, Mathilda," Odran said simply.

Mathilda faced me inquisitively.

"I need your help," I offered as a gentle breeze sang through the window, ruffled Mathilda's curtains, and brought the smell of heavily blooming lilies to my nose.

Mathilda smiled brightly at me. "How do you require my assistance, child?"

I regarded Odran with a frown. "Could we have some privacy?"

"Jolie!" Mathilda said in a scolding voice as she glanced up at Odran. "She does not intend to offend …"

Odran waved away her concern. "Aye, tis joost how the lass is."

Slightly embarrassed by my faux pas, I took Odran's hand and led him outside, pausing underneath an arbor of red roses. Seemingly still unnerved by my vision, he yanked his hand from mine and rubbed it with his other hand, as if I'd pinched him or something.

Hallelujah and praise God, I'd finally found a way to ensure Odran kept his hands to himself! This was turning out to be a good day.

"I apologize if I was rude, Odran, but my reasons for visiting Mathilda are private. And I'm running out of time—Rand can't realize I'm gone."

Now that I thought about it, Rand definitely wouldn't believe I'd just gone running. He knew how much I abhorred exercise. That meant I'd need to finish up my business with Mathilda and get back before Rand suspected anything.

"I oonderstand," Odran said and paused momentarily before turning away and starting back down the lane.

"Odran," I called after him and said as an afterthought, "thank you."

He just smiled as I faced Mathilda's house. Mathilda waited by the door, her face drawn with concern and disapproval. The face of a disappointed mother.

"You should not treat the king with such ill manners."

"Odran and I have always had a different relationship," I started.

"He is a great king, descended from a line of great kings centuries old," she finished, wrapping her aged white shawl closer around her spindly shoulders.

"I'll tell him I'm sorry later," I offered and meant it. Maybe I took Odran for granted but it was only because he regarded me as nothing more than a bun for his hot dog.

She stepped out of her house and neared me, moving past a cropping of coneflowers. "Why have you come, child?"

I paused as I wondered how she'd react to my request for her help. "I'm sure you're aware of our impending war?"

She nodded. "Of course. All our menfolk have gone off to join Rand."

That would explain the lack of men in the streets. The fairy village had seemed pretty desolate, now that I thought about it. The idea weighed on me and I hoped all those fathers, husbands, and brothers would return to their families. And if they couldn't, I promised myself I'd do my damnedest to bring them back.

But that wasn't why I was here. What I needed to focus on now was persuading Mathilda to help me go to battle. My reasons were pretty simple—I had to kill Ryder. That and I wanted to protect Rand and Sinjin ...

"Rand has forbidden me to go."

"To protect you." She said it matter-of-factly, like I shouldn't be concerned with men going off to war and instead, should focus on my knitting.

"Yes, I know, but I also know my witchcraft can help him. It's not fair that I should be prevented from going just because Rand wants to protect me." I paused. "I'm the whole reason behind this war anyway."

She paused near a yellow rose bush and began tending to the dead and dying blooms, massaging the new blooms encouragingly. "You are hoping I can persuade him?" she asked.

I shook my head. "You won't be able to persuade him. He's the most stubborn man, er, witch, I've ever met."

She smiled knowingly. "Perhaps that is one of the reasons you love him?"

Surprise shot through me. Did her fairy magic allow her to be so perceptive or was I was just so obvious? Well, either way, there was no use in lying to a fairy, especially one as old and wise as Mathilda.

"Yes," I answered reluctantly. "Anyway, Rand won't change his mind, so I'm here to ask you to help me change my appearance."

Adopting the appearance of someone else was the only solution I could think of. If Rand saw the real me in battle, he'd undoubtedly hide me somewhere or worse still, jeopardize his concentration on the battle which could risk his safety. And as an added benefit, if incognito, I could take Ryder by surprise.

Yes, I could alter my appearance by way of magic, changing such things as my hair or eye color. Once I'd given myself a mole like Marilyn Monroe's and I'd removed the freckles from across the bridge of my nose and cheeks. But those were just short term spells—I could never maintain them and I'd never been able to change my appearance well enough nor long enough to pass as someone else.

"You intend to deceive Rand by pretending to be a stranger so you can fight alongside him?" Mathilda asked.

That was the long and the short of it. "Yes."

She nodded, a smile curling the ends of her lips. "I see."

"I must fight, Mathilda. I can help. I know I can. Rand says I'm a young witch and my powers aren't what they will be someday, but …"

"You are but a fledgling, child," she interrupted. "And I do understand Rand's reservations. He only desires what is best for you, but of course, much of his reasoning is selfish."

"Selfish?"

"Yes. He could use your assistance but he cares more about protecting you."

I glommed onto the fact that Rand could use my assistance. Now that I'd heard it verified from someone I respected, it only hardened my decision to go to battle. "Don't get me wrong, I appreciate all he's done for me but I want to protect him in the same way he wants to protect me."

She nodded, her stare penetrating. I tried not to wither under her stringent gaze and found it difficult. The fae were definitely not an easygoing crowd.

"So will you help me?"

She took both my hands in hers, closing her eyes as she did so. It seemed as if the entire garden hung on her response, the birds stopped singing, the droning hum of the insects now silent.

"Ah, yes, of course …" she whispered, responding to something only she could see.

She opened her eyes and dropped my hands. "Yes, you will fight in the war. It is as dictated by providence."

I frowned. "You mean I'm supposed to go?"

She nodded. "I have seen it and it is so."

At her words, I was reminded of the search for this so called prophetess. Could the prophetess be standing before me? "Mathilda," I started. "Are you the prophetess?"

She laughed. "Goodness no. The prophetess can see the future and change it."

"But you can see the future?"

"I see how the future will unravel in the way it is supposed to. Whether or not what is meant to happen happens, is another story altogether."

"Oh," I said. "Is there a prophet then?"

She nodded. "I believe there is though I have never had any proof, but sometimes one's belief is proof enough."

I smiled. "So you will help me?"

"Yes, you are meant to join the battle, Jolie. I do not know why nor if you will meet your end but I do know you are meant to go."

I swallowed hard. I could meet my end. It wasn't as if I hadn't been aware of this fact already, but hearing it out loud and hearing it from Mathilda seemed to cement the fact even more. But I'd made up my mind. I couldn't think about the what ifs now. I had a plan to see to fruition.

"Will you teach me how to transform myself?"

"If that is what is required. Perhaps I should speak with Rand and tell him I have seen the will of Nature and she dictates …"

"He won't let me go," I interrupted. "I don't mean to be rude but I know he won't let me go, no matter what you saw."

She smiled as she weighed the options. "Perhaps you are correct, little one. He is a most stubborn witch."

I laughed. "Yes, he is."

She started for the cottage door. "Then we must begin soon. It will take a great amount of magic to alter your face and it will last no longer than a fortnight."

A fortnight was two weeks. Well, I could only hope the war wouldn't last that long.

"You will come to me every day, Jolie. I will build up my magic reserves each night and feed them to you by day or the magic will not be strong enough to sustain."

"Okay, but I don't want to transform until the night of the battle." It wouldn't do me any good to be walking around Rand's house as a complete stranger, lest I be mistaken for a burglar or Robert Downey Jr.

"Of course. The magic will not take shape until we instruct it to. But we will have to build it up, all the same."

"Great." It was going to be tough finding ways to steal away every day, but I could make it work. I'd have to make it work.

"You will need plenty of nourishment and rest, child. I cannot do the spell on my own; it will require your help."

"Okay," I nodded.

"First, you must find an image of the person you wish to become. Bring me that image tomorrow eve and we shall begin."

I planned to rummage through Christa's magazines which currently consisted of about five million stashed all over her room. "Okay, that's easy."

"You will deceive all Underworld creatures with your guise except for the undead."

"Vampires?"

She nodded. "They recognize you by the scent of your blood and that is impossible to alter."

Dammit, that meant taking Ryder by surprise would be out. Hmm, I'd have to be that much stronger in my offense. I could only hope I was up for the challenge.

"Okay, when do we start?" I asked with a smile.

NINE

We had finished drawing up our doctrine and it was now in the mail, en route to the Wicked Witch of the West. To say our doctrine was the nicer, more forgiving of the two would be an understatement. Rand, a warlock full of morality and ethics, had composed a pact even the Founding Fathers would have been proud of.

Rand's demands precluded the existence of a monarchy, since all creatures were endowed with the freedom of choice. Similar to Bella's demands, the covens would remain in existence, but they would be free to govern themselves. Additionally, coven members would be able to pick the coven to which they belonged and coven magistrates would be elected. Rand delineated a panel of thirteen elders, each elected by a coven as their representative. These leaders would meet monthly to discuss problems and find solutions. Rand's demands were based on equality and liberty so he also specified that coven meetings would be held in rotating locations so each coven had a chance to host them.

All employment opportunities would be approved by the coven head and voted on by the entire coven. The document was well-planned and comprehensive and I had nothing to do with it. And I had no issues with having nothing to do with it.

It was now a mere two weeks until we would meet Bella's army at Culloden, and the stone of dread in my stomach seemed to be expanding. Every night I woke with heartburn and worried the stress was burning a huge hole in my stomach lining. Good thing I could heal myself.

One night I woke with my heart racing and it had nothing to do with heartburn or worry about the war. Nope, it had everything to do with an X rated dream about … Sinjin. Mortified, I forced myself to get up and tried to eradicate the explicit images from my mind. I was shocked my subconscious had concocted such erotic images about someone whom I still wasn't sure how I felt. Despite my sense of growing affection for Sinjin since he'd now saved me twice (once at Bella's from Ryder, and twice, from becoming canine), those feelings were nothing compared to what I felt for Rand … or the feelings I was in the process of attempting to bottle up for Rand.

Speaking of Sinjin, I'd drunk his blood each time before practice and luckily, I'd grown somewhat used to it—now I didn't hallucinate, but it always gave me a slight headache that faded after about twenty minutes.

Also, at each meeting we attempted to locate the prophetess. Sinjin would take my hands in his as I sought her out with my mind's eye, using astral projection. So far, we had no clue as to her whereabouts or identity.

Running late for my next training session with Sinjin, I opened the rusty iron gate that scratched like the cackle of an old witch. Guided by a beam of moonlight, I found my way into the garden, inhaling the sweet scent of roses. Rand wasn't a gardener, he hired laborers for that, but he dictated which roses to plant. And for some reason, I thought the fact that he'd ordered roses of every hue was romantic.

The garden was not huge—a stone fence approximately two hundred feet by two hundred feet surrounded the rainbow of roses. A lone bench sat in the middle of the square and from it you could not only view the garden's beauty, but also the forest at the east end of Pelham Manor which was graced by a seasonal creek.

"My lovely poppet," Sinjin said and I turned to find him leaning against the wall, outlined in shadows.

"Hi, Sinjin," I responded and joined him in the umbra of darkness.

Sinjin smiled and his hair was so shiny black in the moonlight, it looked like spilt oil. He bit into his wrist and held it out to me. I latched onto it with my mouth, trying to ignore the metallic taste of blood which totally grossed me out. I closed my eyes and sucked until he forced me to stop.

"You are getting a bit overzealous," he said with a smile and licked his wound until the skin closed over and healed.

"Maybe your blood is addictive," I retorted, wiping my sleeve across my mouth. "Do you know that I can run five miles now and not even have to rest?"

"This does not sound like much of a feat, pet."

"You don't know how much I abhor exercise," I laughed. And that wasn't all I could do. I could easily lift over one hundred pounds and could move as fast as I could think. I still couldn't materialize like Sinjin could but I was faster than any otherworldly creatures.

He crossed his arms over his chest and regarded me with amusement. "What else have you noticed?"

"My magic is much stronger," I started, feeling like I had to prove myself. "And I can focus on things more clearly. What used to take me minutes to accomplish now takes seconds."

I didn't want to mention the fact that I'd had a sex dream about him and imagined his blood had something to do with that too. Even though I couldn't deny I was attracted to Sinjin, I was firmly resolved not to get involved. The wound from Rand was still open and weeping … but only when I thought about it, so I resolved not to.

As to Rand, he was avoiding me. Whenever I entered a room, he always seemed to find some reason to leave. That was fine by me. I'd meant it when I said I'd sworn off men. And the more I thought about it, the more I decided that if we did prevail at the end of the war, I was out of here and totally done with this lifestyle. I didn't know where I'd go yet, or what I'd do, but I was done all the same. And that thought offered relief as well as sorrow.

"I am pleased to hear it, love," Sinjin said.

"Has anyone noticed you've been disappearing from the battle each night?"

He shook his head. "If anyone noticed, they have not said. But training is useless for me—practice does not make me a stronger vampire, only time does."

I nodded and examined a velvety rose petal, not wanting to look at him, lest images from my dream revisit me. And I really didn't want to admit that those images created a fire in the pit of my stomach, an ache.

"Are you ready, pet?"

I nodded and offered both my hands. His grip was cold and sent a chill down my body. I closed my eyes and descended past the inky blackness of my eyelids in order to see into another dimension that might offer a hint of this so called prophetess.

Nothing.

"This is a waste of our time," I said.

"Let us try again next eve."

As I started to release his hand, I was struck by a vision so lucid, it was like I was right there—in the freezing snow surrounded by pine trees. There was nothing else in sight—just thousands of acres of forest. I looked down to find the snow up to my knees. I crunched through it, cringing as the icy cold penetrated me to the core.

"What is it?" Sinjin asked.

The vision immediately vanished and I let go of his hands. "Just a blur of trees and snow," I said, shrugging. "No prophetess."

Sinjin offered me a smile and backed up a step. "Shall we begin our lessons, love?"

I nodded, taking off my jacket and dropping it to the ground. I strolled toward the center of the garden square. The bench was blocking us until I telekinetically moved it to the corner of the garden, simply using my mind. I could have done it before I'd feasted on Sinjin's blood but it wouldn't have been as quick or as easy.

"Impressive execution," Sinjin said, approvingly.

"Thanks. See what I mean about being able to move things a lot more quickly? I used …" I couldn't finish my sentence because he was suddenly on top of me.

He threw me onto the ground and I landed on my stomach, breaking my fall with my hands. My palms stung but that was about it—I'd managed to protect my chest and stomach, just like Sinjin had taught me. He instantly pinned my neck to the ground with one hand and tried to incapacitate me with his weight. As he pinned me, I managed to push against the ground and flip myself, landing on my back, but still beneath him.

He smiled, aiming for my jugular but I was a good student and hastily karate chopped his neck before he could touch mine. The blow momentarily stunned him (or maybe he was acting), but either way, it gave me enough time to regain my balance. When I glanced up, he was gone. I jumped to my feet and braced them shoulders width apart, listening for him. His blood allowed me to hear him on the wind, so I knew precisely where he'd materialize. As soon as I heard a slight swoosh, I turned to my right, kicking hard and planted my foot right where I wanted to, in his midsection.

He was thrown back about five feet and landed on the hard stone ground. It must have hurt like an SOB.

"Oh my God, Sinjin! Are you okay?" I asked, running over to him and bending down.

He was flat on his back and just as I reached out to touch him, he grasped my ankle and pulled until I lost my footing and fell alongside him. I landed on my butt, but managed to reach down, just below the small of my back to pull out a stake. From our first lesson, I learned I should arm myself with a stake since I couldn't create one, my magic being useless against vampires. I rolled over and onto his stomach until I was straddling him, and whipping out the stake, I held it just above his breastbone.

"Bam," I smiled. "One dead vampire."

He grabbed hold of the stake and tossed it aside. It clattered against the cobbled stone, before settling uselessly near the bench. "Very well done, pet."

"Were you going easy on me?" I eyed him speculatively, suddenly very aware that I was straddling him. His muscular body felt incredibly cold below me, like a statue. Although I knew I should get up, I just couldn't bring myself to move.

"No, poppet. You are learning quickly, it seems."

At the feel of something stirring at the junction of his thighs, I started to stand but he held me in place.

"Do not move," he whispered. "Your heat feels incredible."

"Sinjin," I reprimanded. "I didn't sign up for sex talk."

He sighed. "I am aware, my little warrior, and you are sticking to your oath."

He meant my celibacy oath and yes, I was sticking to it.

"I apologize, love; I have not supped as yet and it makes my attraction to you that much stronger."

"Whose fault is that?" I asked, suddenly feeling a bit dizzy again. I stood up and took a few steps, only to stumble. Sinjin materialized behind me, grabbing my arms to steady me.

"I think I drank too much of your blood," I said, holding onto him for balance.

"Perhaps we should rest?" He assisted me to the bench.

"Good idea," I answered and closed my eyes to stop the spinning. Would I ever get accustomed to Sinjin's blood? I guess this reaction was better than hallucinating but it was still a close second. I needed to change the subject, to focus on something other than the queasiness currently residing in my stomach. I decided to ask Sinjin a question I'd been wondering about for a while. "Why aren't you worried about Bella's terms?"

"Why should I be?"

I glanced up at him in surprise. "Um, I would be. That whole part about putting you to death for treason, I think it was?"

He shook his head. "Her vanity was crushed after she threw herself at me and I played her for a fool."

"Well, fool or not, she clearly wants you dead."

"Does that bother you, love?"

I frowned. "Of course it does!"

He chuckled a low, rumbling sound. "Do not let it concern you. The good always prevail, do they not?"

I laughed. "You sound like an excerpt from Jane Eyre or something. Who talks like you do? You are in the twenty-first century, you know?"

"It is my way, love. This is who I am."

I nodded and held my head with my hands, wishing I could be so sure of myself, so unapologetic. It was something I admired about Sinjin—he was who he was and made no attempts to apologize for it. "I didn't mean to tease you."

"I enjoy it when you tease me," he said with a sultry smile. Something about the way he said it brought my dream to light. I quickly stood up, not wanting to be so close to him. I needed to distance myself.

"Do you think drinking your blood could make me more attracted to you?" I inquired and started pacing, something I do when I'm in an uncomfortable situation. And this was uncomfortable. Mostly because I didn't want to feel anything for Sinjin.

Sinjin laughed. "And why do you ask this question?"

Here was the embarrassing part and like I've said before, I'm a terrible liar—lying just isn't an option. "I just feel …" Out with it. "Strangely … attracted to you, like I'm still a little bit drugged." Yep, just call me Honest Abe.

"Is it so impossible to imagine you might harbor … feelings for me?"

I shook my head and riveted my gaze on my hands, too embarrassed to look into his eyes, even though we were in the dark. Vampires possessed excellent night vision, though, so he could probably see the hot blush permeating my cheeks.

"No, it's not but it just seems unnatural, that's all … like forced."

"Well, to answer your question, I do not know." He paused. "Poppet, I have a question for you," he said before interrupting himself. "Please stop pacing, you are making me nervous and that is a difficult feat for someone as old as I."

He latched onto my hand and pulled me to the cold stone bench again. Surprised, I merely folded my hands in my lap as though I was about to be reprimanded. I'd never seen this serious side of the vampire before. Sinjin joined me on the bench and I could feel the coldness of his body radiating outward. It was an odd feeling—not in the least bit welcoming. No, more like sitting next to a talking ice cube … a really sexy talking ice cube.

"What is your current affiliation with Randall?"

"He's my employer," I said, imagining where this conversation was headed.

Sinjin chuckled. "I am not a fool, love."

"What do you want to know?" Irritation crept into my voice.

"Are you in love with him?"

I swallowed hard, never imagining this question would come from Sinjin. Course, my feelings for Rand had never been a subject I'd ever really considered discussing with anyone aside from Rand, himself, or Christa.

"Yes."

Sinjin nodded, as if weighing the information. "And does he love you?"

I almost laughed. That was the fifty-million-dollar question. Since our recent tryst, Rand had made it clear that sex between us would invariably lead to bonding which he didn't appear to want any part of, so I guessed the answer was probably "no."

"I don't know," I said simply.

Sinjin shook his head and clucked his tongue in admonition. "Not a very nice situation for you, now is it?"

"How is this any of your business?" I turned on him with a great show of anger. It was okay for me to realize the futility of a relationship with Rand but hearing it from someone else, especially Sinjin, really irked me. I wanted to leave his ice cold ass in the ice cold garden but his hand on mine stopped me.

"I did not intend to offend you, love," he said, smiling. "I share a common interest with Randall."

I watched him warily. "Which is?"

"You."

I always knew Sinjin was interested in me but I could never truly gauge what his motivations were—whether genuine or merely as a means to an end. He obviously wanted to have sex with me but that didn't mean much to me right now. In fact, it meant diddly squat.

"Sinjin, I want to keep our relationship purely platonic."

"What are your feelings toward me?"

"I don't know," I said, turning away from him. "But I do know I don't want to have this conversation anymore."

He nodded. "Do you love me?"

"No," I said quickly.

He didn't take any offense, which was good because I hadn't intended to offend him.

"Do you find me … attractive?"

That was easy. I'd have to be blind not to find him attractive. "You know I do, but ..."

"Then what is the problem?" he asked with a boyish grin.

"The problem?" I repeated. "There are a couple of problems, first that we're on the verge of a war. Second, I'm in love with Rand even though I'm trying to get over it."

"All surmountable issues, love," he said, drumming his fingers on the iron of the bench. "I am not concerned with this war. I have lived over six hundred years and in that period, the creatures of the Underworld have never lived together harmoniously."

"Have they ever declared war against one another?"

"No, but they have come close. Now as to your love for Rand, that is a small problem. I suppose we shall have to wait and see what his intentions are?"

That was basically what I'd been doing since knowing him—waiting and seeing. Well, with my new resolution of moving away once all this war stuff ended, I could leave it all behind. But I kept my decision to move away to myself. As far as I was concerned, this Underworld lifestyle would soon be behind me, with the exception of Christa, of course, and my cat.

"I guess so," I answered.

"Do you suppose you could develop feelings for me, poppet?"

Hmm, another good question. I didn't want to develop feelings for Sinjin. I didn't trust him and feeling anything for him would be a bad idea. This coming from my logical brain. As far as my idiotic heart was concerned … hmm, I didn't even want to go there.

"I don't want to answer these questions, Sinjin."

"Poppet, humor me, please."

"I don't know if I could. You are a hard person to trust."

He surged to his feet, his jaw tight—as if my statement had impaled itself into his heart. "What must I do to prove my feelings for you, Jolie?"

It was the first time he'd actually used my name instead of calling me poppet, pet, or love. It was weird—like he was suddenly all seriousness, something I wasn't prepared for.

"I have saved your life … twice," he continued. "I would think that proof enough for you to trust me."

Okay, all good points but they didn't change the fact that there was something missing—some piece of the puzzle that wouldn't fit. "It just doesn't make sense. You've been around for … ever it seems like. Why would you be interested in me?"

"You do not appear to hold yourself in very high regard. What reasons are there for me not to be interested in you, as you say?"

I scowled while he continued. "You are beautiful and strong minded. You are good—a nuance that certainly intrigues me. And you have a talent I have never seen before."

"Aha," I said. "That's it. You want to control my … talent. Whether you're aware of it or not, there's always an underlying motive for everything you do."

"You sound as if you know me well," he said, straightening his posture. He seemed angry, I could see it in the straight lines of his spine.

"I'm sorry if I upset you, Sinjin."

He shook his head. "I am not upset, though, I did not realize you thought of me in such unflattering terms."

I closed my eyes to the onset of another headache. "I don't want you to think I'm ungrateful for what you're doing for me, Sinjin, or what you've already done. I just don't know what to think right now between the war and Rand … it's too much for me to deal with."

"I did not intend to cause you chagrin, poppet," he said, reaching for me.

I took his outstretched hands and barely had a chance to gasp before he pulled me into him, planting his mouth on mine. My shocked mind took a second to register what was happening as I began to relive my dream all over again. His mouth was cold, incredibly so, but his lips were full and soft. I closed my eyes while his hands toyed with my hair. At the feel of his tongue in my mouth, reality bitch slapped me. I shoved my hands into his hard chest, taking a few steps back, not daring to look at him. I couldn't do this. I was too afraid that if we continued kissing, I wouldn't be able to stop. And it just felt wrong. In the back of my mind, was Rand. Always Rand.

"Jolie," Sinjin said, somewhat surprised.

"I, uh, I have to go."

I spun around and started for the haven of Pelham Manor.

"I did not intend to take advantage of the situation …" he started as he wrapped his fingers around my wrist, pulling me to a stop. "I have no ulterior motives, Jolie," he finished with a tired voice.

"I have to go," I answered and tried to wrench my hand from his grasp.

"Again, I apologize," Sinjin said, releasing my hand.

I didn't say another word nor did I look back as I started forward, the urge to escape the garden and Sinjin of prime concern. I headed for the safety of Pelham Manor and my private little bedroom where I could abandon all my worries. My only desire now lay in the comfort of my cozy bed, downy pillows, and one very sweet cat.

TEN

I sat and stared in the mirror that hung above my desk and practiced my concentration. Mathilda's instructions precluded me from doing anything but concentrating. I had to learn to eclipse my own face with my new identity, and once I could achieve that, I'd done my homework for the day.

This was my fifth day of practicing my magic. Every morning after I finished doing my homework, I'd meet Mathilda who reinforced my magic with her own. She'd hold her hands an inch or so away from my face, palms facing my cheeks. After studying the model in the *Vogue* picture, she'd close her eyes and visualize my new identity. Then she'd take whatever invisible magic she'd created and hold a tiny seed within her palm as she shut her eyes again, endowing the seed with her magic. Eventually, I was supposed to take the seed-pill prior to my transformation.

The new identity I'd chosen was a very attractive woman from one of Christa's *Vogue* magazines. She had short black hair and bright green eyes, a full mouth, and cheekbones you could cut yourself on. So she happened to be gorgeous ... it wasn't like I had much of a selection to choose from—*Vogue, CatWorld,* or *Men's Fitness* (Rand's). Needless-to-say, I didn't care to be a feline or a man.

As I poured my concentration into the mirror, I watched my hair sprout what appeared to be an oil leak at the roots and black poured over the blond, the long tresses disappearing until I had a shorter boy cut. A warm tan burgeoned from my cheeks and consumed my entire face as my freckles dissolved into a landscape of perfect homogeneity. My cornflower blue eyes lightened into teal before settling into an emerald while my lips inflated like two balloons. My nose tilted as my eyebrows darkened and drew a perfect arch.

Now I was no longer me. Well, my body hadn't changed but that was only because it would take too much magic to transform me entirely. And hey, who would recognize me by my body anyway? It was a chance I was willing to take. I'd just whip up a new outfit the old me wouldn't be caught dead in and I'd be good to go.

I placed my hands up and over my face and head, imagining the magic emanating from me in rays of light. I captured the special light in my hands and watched it mutate into clear droplets. I released the glittering drops onto a rose petal. At the touch of the drops, the rose's red hue increased to a deep crimson. Later, Mathilda would crush the magic petals and transfer their essence into her seed-pill.

I assumed it was due to Sinjin's blood that I was getting better and faster with my magic. My first attempt to turn into my *Vogue* counterpart had taken over an hour, but today it took a mere fifteen minutes.

Speaking of Sinjin, our sparring continued despite the uncomfortable kiss. He never tried anything else, and kept our relationship as professional as was possible for the vampire. How I felt about it, I wasn't sure. On the one hand, I was relieved—I mean, it wasn't right to be in love with Rand and yet yearn for Sinjin's touch. It was an uncomfortable thought and I pushed it to the recesses of my mind.

The blend of Sinjin's blood combined with his personal instruction had made me undefeatable during my defense training. My offense, on the other hand, still left much to be desired. It wasn't bad, but it was nothing compared to my defense.

I still hadn't managed to uncover any sign of the prophetess but Sinjin acted like he didn't care, which made me again question what his motive was in all of this. There had to be something ...

"Jules?" It was Christa.

I quickly glanced at the rose to see if it showed any evidence of my magic but relaxed when it collapsed limply as any other cut flower from Rand's garden.

"Hi, Chris."

The door squeaked open. "Rand asked me to bring you to the library. He has something he wants to discuss with us."

I hadn't talked to Rand in over a week. He was doing his damnedest to avoid me and that was fine by me. I figured if he didn't want to resolve our issues, then why should I? It still stung but it helped strengthen my determination to get over him and move on with my life … if moving on was even an option. The war was now just a week away and everywhere in our encampment you could feel the buzz of anticipation. There were surges of activity constantly, all day and night. Fights kept breaking out amongst the troops because everyone was so tightly wound.

"Hmm, okay," I said, standing up. I followed Christa down the stairs and into the library, where Rand sat behind his desk, studying some papers. He glanced up when we walked in and offered a quick smile.

"Christa, do you mind pulling the door closed behind you?" he asked.

"Sure," Christa said and did his bidding.

I took a seat in the leather arm chair furthest from Rand, trying to force myself not to inhale the air which was heavy with his clean, masculine scent. He didn't even glance at me and I had to suppress the tide of disappointment as it wafted through me.

"I've made preparations for the two of you," he started. "To ensure your safety, I've arranged for you to live in Australia until this war is settled."

"Australia?" we chimed in unison.

"But," Christa started, "John told me all the nonparticipants are staying in a fairy village in Scotland near Culloden."

Rand nodded. "A foolish decision."

"Why?" I asked.

He didn't look at me but stood up and started to pace toward the logless fireplace, leaning against the mantle as he kicked one of the burnt coals with the toe of his shoe.

"If Bella prevails, it will only be a matter of time before she has all the fairy villages under her thumb. Anyone who finds herself in one will be in for a surprise."

Christa stood up as if the chair had just bitten her. "John promised the fairies would send a warning to their families and loved ones to tell them to escape way before Bella could ever get to them."

"It's not a chance I'm willing to take."

"Well, maybe it's a chance we're willing to take," I snapped, pissed off. I was mostly annoyed that Rand refused to look at me. I thought his professionalism would dictate that he at least be polite.

He ignored my comment and continued as if I hadn't even spoken. "I've ordered your airline tickets and you depart in three days."

"Three days?!" Christa squawked as my heart began palpitating. This unforeseen deportation to Australia might make my plans more difficult to pull off …

Rand never missed a beat. "I've also arranged for a hotel in Sydney."

"But I don't want to leave John," Christa argued.

"If this battle doesn't go as planned, all of us will be doomed. I don't want that for you … or Jolie."

He started to look my way but apparently thought better of it and let his gaze fall to the floor.

"And how will we find protection in Australia?" I asked, still in shock. Well, I was mostly in shock for Christa. I had other plans for myself and they didn't include Australia.

"You'll live under Bella's radar with a new identity, making it very difficult for her to find you."

"Unless she takes Ryder with her and then he can just track me," I said, noticing the big gaping hole in his plan.

He finally looked at me with complete indifference. "I will kill Ryder. I won't stop until he's dead."

Well, Rand and I finally had one desire in common.

"And I've gone to extremes to ensure that neither of you will be found. Your flight and hotel reservations are in aliases. I have new personal documents for each of you as well." He walked to the desk and handed each of us a manila envelope. Inside were birth certificates, passports, drivers' licenses, and social security cards.

"How did you manage to get us Australian passports?" I asked, impressed.

"I have friends," he answered, still refusing to look at me.

"So that means we're now Australian citizens?" Christa asked.

He nodded. "Yes, you both have dual citizenship between Australia and the United States. You'll be able to go back to the US, should you ever need to, although I would advise you to stay in Australia."

Christa opened her passport and a credit card fell out, landing in her lap. "What's this?" she asked and held it up.

"It's a duplicate check card to my account. Should anything happen to me, I'm leaving everything to you both."

"Rand," I started but he shushed my concern with a wave of his hand.

"Don't worry about the financial aspects—I've already executed the necessary papers."

"But it's in another name—John Grant?" Christa asked, reading the card aloud.

Rand nodded. "I've put all my possessions in the name of John Grant so Bella won't be able to access them. If something happens to me, you'll need to act quickly to get my assets. I've hired a lawyer whose information is also within those documents."

My stomach dropped as overwhelming sorrow washed through me. If something were to happen to Rand, it would be my undoing. Even though we'd had our fair share of pain and frustration, he was a good man. And nothing reinforced that fact more than tonight.

"Australia might be fun," Christa said sadly, offering me a small smile.

I returned the fake smile although I knew she was withering inside. She was worrying about John—I could see it in her eyes. "Everything will be okay, Chris," I whispered and reached for her hand, squeezing it.

She nodded and batted her eyelashes a few times to force back the tears.

"Here are your flight details and your hotel reservations," Rand said and handed a neat pile of papers to Christa.

"Thanks," she said meekly.

He smiled, pausing for one long moment as if he had something to say. And damn it all, I wanted him to say something, anything. Tell me he'd missed me, that he cared.

He straightened his posture. "If you don't have any questions, I'll excuse myself as I have much to attend to."

Christa stood up and neared the door, me on her heels. Once outside the door, I paused and turned back around. "I'll be back in a second," I said and she just gave me a smile and nod of understanding.

I shoved my way back into Rand's office and closed the door behind me. Rand glanced up from behind his desk, immediately dropping his attention once he saw it was me.

"I'm busy, Jolie," he said.

"I know," I started, walking up to him. "I just wanted to thank you for everything you've done for us."

He nodded. "You're welcome."

"Are you that worried about this war?" I asked, taking a seat in one of his leather chairs.

He glanced up, irritation etching his angular face. "Jolie, I'm preoccupied."

I tried to quell the angry tide rising within me, trying to understand why he seemed so pissed off. I mean, I knew we were in a tough situation with the whole bonding scenario and granted, I'd been avoiding him just as much as he'd been avoiding me over the last couple of weeks, but this wasn't called for. Unable to defeat the anger within me, I stood up, bracing my hands on my hips. "What is your freaking problem?"

His attention fell back on the papers littering his desk and I thought he'd just ignore me. After a moment or two, he looked up and his face was flushed. "I don't have a problem."

"Bullshit. You're about to explode, your face is so red."

He stood up and approached the door, opening it wide. "I don't have the time nor interest in discussing this subject right now."

"I'm not leaving," I said, taking two steps nearer him and kicking the door shut. "Not until you tell me why you're acting like such an asshole."

The door slammed and reverberated through the whole house. I'd have to be more careful with my newly acquired vampire strength, lest Rand get wise to my activities of late.

"You …" he started and then stopped, running his hands through his hair. Apparently he hadn't noticed my superhuman strength. Phew …

"You know," I continued," I had no problem avoiding you after all this bonding stuff but what you're doing now is a little much."

"This has nothing to do with bonding," he sputtered between clenched teeth.

"Then what does it have to do with?"

He finally gave me eye contact and I could see he was livid. "It has everything to do with the fact that you don't give a fuck about me or my feelings."

"Whoa … what?" I asked, completely floored.

"Don't pretend, Jolie; everyone knows you're a terrible liar."

I wasn't sure if I wanted to hit him or cry. "Before you accuse me, I have a right to know what's got your panties in a bunch," I protested.

He paused and then faced me, incensed. "I saw you and Sinjin."

My heart dropped and I had to steady myself against the wall. He'd seen us sparring? That meant he knew I'd been planning on attending the battle all along and there went my carefully constructed plan. There was no way Rand would allow me to fight now, which meant all my efforts were basically fruitless.

"I can explain," I started, wondering where the hell I should start. Was my cover totally blown or could I still salvage some of it? My mind started racing with excuses; I could say we'd been practicing for the mere sake of practice? Hmm, no that wasn't believable.

"I don't want your explanations, dammit," he said and his face contorted with ire. "It's bad enough I had to witness you kissing Sinjin."

Kissing Sinjin? Then I remembered … the kiss that Sinjin had stolen from me. "Clearly you didn't stay to see the denouement," I said, annoyed but relieved at the same time.

He snapped, "And tell me why, in my right mind, should I have wanted to see more?"

"Because you would've seen me push him away and leave."

He shook his head and walked back to his desk, feigning interest in his papers again. "Your relationship with Sinjin is between you two but I would have appreciated it if you could have been a bit more delicate where I was concerned."

"You can really be a dumbass sometimes, Rand."

His jaw clenched and his hands fisted. "You can show yourself out."

"Sinjin kissed me, I didn't kiss him. And if you'd spied a bit longer, you would've realized that."

"Whatever happens between you two is none of my concern."

"Don't give me that crap," I snapped and obstructed his view of his precious papers by landing my palms on the top of his desk.

Rand's eyes narrowed. "What were you doing in the rose garden with him in the first place?"

Hmm, so he hadn't seen us training? This was the best news yet—an inconsequential kiss I could explain but battle training was beyond explanation. And as to what we were doing in the rose garden—I'd have to lie. It was my only resort now that he'd backed me into a corner.

"I wanted some alone time and he followed me." I riveted my eyes to his and tried to play poker face. Hopefully it worked. Rand didn't respond and his silence irritated me more than his false accusations had.

"What does it matter to you anyway? You clearly aren't interested in me. You said so yourself." It hurt to say it out loud.

"Don't put words in my mouth."

"You fought the bond," I insisted, playing a card I really shouldn't have. I mean, I knew we weren't ready to bond and I'd been relieved just as much as he had that we hadn't gone through with it. But it was the only card I had, so I played it.

"I wasn't prepared to bond with you now, before this war. As to the future, I said I was undecided."

Okay, he had me there. Though "undecided" usually meant "uninterested" in my experience. "So you saw me with Sinjin and decided to spy on us? How noble," I started. "What were you doing spying on me anyway?"

"I wasn't spying," he said, angrily. "I just wanted to know where the hell you were when I couldn't find you in the house."

"So all this time you've been avoiding me was completely unnecessary because you could have just asked."

He stood up. "What would I have asked, Jolie?"

I shook my head. "Oh, I don't know, maybe: hey, are you and Sinjin dating? Or if that's too big a mouthful, how about—what's up with you and Sinjin?" I sighed. I was so tired of arguing with him. Maybe it was just time to give up?

"I didn't think it my place to interfere."

"So instead, you ignore me and act like a total asshole." I shook my head. "Sometimes you infuriate me."

He narrowed his eyes. "I could say the same of you."

"Well, good thing we aren't dating."

"Jolie," he started.

"I'm sorry you saw Sinjin kiss me but it wasn't what you thought."

He exhaled and dropped his gaze to his hands. "I understand." He paused and glanced up at me again. "And I apologize for jumping to conclusions."

I had to stifle my surprise. I was prepared for a stronger defense, so I was slightly taken aback by his apology. Some of the fury began to dissipate and I exhaled the rest. "Truce?" I offered and extended my hand, with the hint of a smile.

He studied my hand for a second or two and then shook it, a smile teasing the corners of his mouth. "Truce."

"Next time you catch someone kissing me, why don't you ask me about it before avoiding me like the plague?"

He nodded. "I hope there won't be a next time."

I cocked my head. "Probably not, considering I've sworn off men."

"Sworn off men?" he repeated. "And why is that?"

"Because I'm tired of being disappointed when they don't live up to my expectations."

He sighed. "I'm sorry to hear that, Jolie and where I'm concerned, I hope you will change your mind."

I didn't know what to make of that so I didn't make anything of it at all. Instead, I stood up and yawned. This conversation had taken everything out of me.

"Well, I'll leave you to it," I said and started for the door.

"I mean it, Jolie. I hope you change your mind about giving up on men … on me."

"Until I'm given a reason, I don't see why I should change my mind," I said and rested my hand on the doorknob.

"Duly noted," he offered with a self-assured smile.

I just shook my head and left.

~

"Jolie!" It was Christa, screaming my name.

I tore out of my bedroom with my heart pounding. Screaming is never a good thing. She panted at the bottom of the stairs, holding the banister to steady herself.

"Chris, are you okay?" I demanded.

She nodded. "You've gotta come now. Rand and Sinjin are fighting."

"What?!" I yelled, nearly tripping down the stairs in my haste. "Where are they?"

"Outside," she croaked hoarsely, as we raced across the grass and headed for the sparring fields.

"What happened?" I yelled to her.

She shook her head, out of breath but resolving to keep up with me, impelled herself forward. "They were practicing … like normal." Huff. Huff. "Then, Rand just came out of the blue and sucker-punched Sinjin, Jules. It was like Rand went crazy—like he went psycho or something!"

"What the hell is wrong with him?" I asked, dawning realization suddenly making my heart plummet. This had to be about the kiss between Sinjin and me.

Christa started panting again and grabbed my arm. "How the hell are you running so fast?"

Damn, Sinjin's vampire strength had almost betrayed me again. I'd have to be more careful. I slowed down to a jog and glanced back at her.

"Just drank a Red Bull." Did they even sell Red Bull in the UK? Hopefully Christa wouldn't know.

We made it to the crest of the hill. Just below us, I could see our entire legion forming an audience around Rand and Sinjin, who were raining blows on one another.

"Oh my God, they are such assholes," I said as I caught Rand throwing a punch which Sinjin dodged by dematerializing. Not wanting to observe any more of this lunacy, I pushed through the throng of spectators until Rand and Sinjin were directly in front of me.

"What the hell is wrong with you both?" I screamed, but neither paid me the slightest attention. Instead, Sinjin thrust Rand's chest violently which sent him flying until Rand magically stopped himself in midair. He simply landed on his feet and ferociously charged Sinjin. Rand's strength could easily be compared to Sinjin's, so this was a fight that would last all night ... something I had no interest in waiting around for.

"I hope you have something better than that, you boffin," Sinjin taunted.

The only other time I'd ever seen Sinjin this angry was when Ryder had nearly raped me. Sinjin had a vehemence that was terrifying and now that vehemence was aimed at Rand. Rand feigned as if he would charge Sinjin, but at the last minute, jumped to the side of him and hammered a blow right into Sinjin's temple. It sent the vampire toppling to the ground.

"Rand! Stop!" I screamed.

He ignored me and leapt onto Sinjin. He pummeled another blow to Sinjin's head, while Sinjin used both hands to pry him off and sent Rand helplessly into the onlookers, who weren't making any motion to disrupt the fight. Men ...

"There goes your bet on Rand." It was Trent and he nudged the were standing next to him, who just snickered.

"You're sick," I said, shaking my head. What had I ever seen in him? God, he was such a dick.

Rand climbed back up but didn't make any motion to attack Sinjin. Sinjin stood up, ready for more action, although his footing was slightly unbalanced. He brushed himself off, his smile revealing fangs on his handsome face. Debris littered his clothing and his hair was disheveled, but other than that, he was just as sexy as ever.

"I have been waiting for this moment for a long time, Randall."

Rand took two steps nearer Sinjin and I could see his chest rising and falling. He was exhausted. "I warned you to keep away from Jolie, you bastard," Rand said.

Great, the fight was about me. Sensing my opportunity to intervene, I grabbed Rand's arm, pulling him backwards. My strength was such that he couldn't help but take notice. I really wasn't able to disguise it very well.

"Have you lost your freaking mind?" I screamed and stepped in front of Rand and positioned myself between the two opponents, hoping they wouldn't attack one another with me in the middle. I grabbed Rand's upper arm.

"My mind?" Rand repeated and glared at Sinjin. "I'm not the one who took advantage of you!"

So it was about the kiss. Great. "Why couldn't you just leave it alone, Rand?" I demanded. "I can take care of myself."

Sinjin's expression was hard to read—maybe it was one of betrayal. He didn't make any motion to attack Rand, though, so at least that was over, or so I hoped.

"Poppet, you told him of our kiss?"

I suddenly felt sick, especially because my private life was being broadcasted in front of everyone. I really didn't want to be in the middle of this. "He saw it," I corrected.

"If you thought I had acted inappropriately, you should have said so yourself. Not sent this todger to tell me."

Rand resisted my hold as if to punch Sinjin and I pushed against his chest, forcing him to stop. "I was handling it myself," I yelled, glaring at Rand. "It was none of your business!"

He frowned and pulled away from me, all his fury now aimed at me. "Then why did you tell me?"

"Because you were acting like a jealous idiot, that's why!"

Sinjin chuckled and Rand pushed me to the side, lunging for him. Sinjin punched him in the stomach and Rand doubled over, collapsing painfully on the ground. I kneeled down and placed my hands over Rand's stomach, imagining his pain draining away into the damp ground. Once Rand could breathe a little easier, I glanced up at Sinjin.

"And you're no better!"

"He attacked me, poppet; I had nothing to do with this."

I stood up and pushed Sinjin away, not wanting him anywhere near Rand. Sinjin grabbed my upper arms and pulled me into his broad chest as I struggled to release myself. But Sinjin was like trying to release yourself from manacles.

"Randall, you aren't man enough for her," Sinjin snickered.

"Let go of me!" I seethed, glaring up at him.

He ignored me, his ire aimed at Rand.

"If you don't let go of her, you'll regret it," Rand said in a low voice, approaching us cautiously.

Sinjin just laughed. "When I am given the chance to warm her bed, I will not fail her as you did."

I forced myself from Sinjin's grip, anger welling up inside me until I wanted to burst. Of all the rotten, horrible things with which to belittle Rand, he'd chosen the one subject that would cut any man down. The subject of failing a woman in bed.

"You asshole!" I spat and backhanded Sinjin across the face. He stumbled back, his hand on his cheek.

But I didn't care about Sinjin at that moment. Frantic, I faced Rand. He was pale, his breathing harsh—he looked shell shocked. He paused a moment or two before turning around and walking back up the hill, his pride shattered, lying in fragments at my feet.

ELEVEN

"Rand!" I yelled after his retreating figure.

The sound of a door slamming echoed through the house. I ran the distance separating me from Rand's closed door but before I could reach it, I bounced off an invisible barrier he'd magicked outside. I pushed against the rubbery blockade but it just undulated like jelly. There was no way I was getting through it. Thinking I could break it with my own magic, I sent a bolt of electricity through my fingers but the energy just sizzled futilely against the invisible barrier, emitting plumes of white smoke that danced like ghosts. Dammit!

"Rand, just let me explain!" I yelled, my voice desperate.

No response. He was pissed, that was for sure. I could practically feel his anger through the door. And I couldn't blame him. It had definitely looked like I'd blabbed about our bedroom issues to the one person he most disliked and distrusted. But in all fairness, I hadn't been in my right mind at the time, hallucinating on Sinjin's blood. I wasn't going to let myself off easy though. This was my fault.

Rand, please just talk to me, I thought, hoping he might be willing to communicate telepathically.

Nothing.

Please don't ignore me!

After another few minutes, it was pretty clear I was on his shit list. With a defeated sigh, I turned around and took the five steps to my bedroom, feeling like my chest was caving in on itself. Closing the door behind me, I collapsed on my bed.

I couldn't keep the tears at bay as I realized the weight of the situation. I'd royally screwed up. It seemed like no matter what, nothing was ever easy between Rand and me. There was always some force working to keep us apart—most recently there was the bonding situation as well as the war. And as if those weren't enough, I had to go and spill my guts to Sinjin.

God, I'd had enough. Even though this most recent event was my fault, it pushed me past my ability to cope. My resolution to leave this lifestyle behind me was now stronger than it ever had been. I just couldn't take it anymore. Every time I started to think I could make things work with Rand, something else happened that pushed me farther and farther down the line of wanting to retreat and lick my wounds.

I lay back on my bed and curled into a ball. But if I were to take off, what would I do and where would I go? Although I wasn't sure, at this point I didn't really care. All I knew was the need to escape was stifling. If we defeated Bella and the US was deemed safe, I'd probably just move back there and hopefully leave this whole mess behind me.

And to all those people who say you can't run away from your problems? I'd say to them: just watch me.

A knock sounded on the door and I stumbled from the bed, relief tickling my stomach where previously nausea had been tenant. God, I hoped Rand had decided to give me another chance ... Granted, he was stubborn, but hopefully he'd realized that in a matter of days, we'd say farewell and who knew what would happen?

I pulled the door open, mentally rehearsing what I'd say to him but the sight of Sinjin dissolved the words right off my tongue. "You're the last person I want to see right now," I snapped, attempting to shut the door in his face.

"Jolie," he started, wedging his hand between the door and the wall.

I turned around and glared at him. "What do you want?"

"I came to apologize."

"It's a little late for that."

"May I come in?" It wasn't like as a vampire he had to ask in order to gain entrance, he was just being polite. Or as polite as the jerkwad could be.

I felt like telling him to get lost when it occurred to me that he was asking of me the same thing I'd been asking of Rand—to be heard. Damn my conscience! I moved away from the door and sank onto my bed, nodding my okay to enter. He smiled appreciatively and closed the door behind him, approaching the foot of my bed. Since the fight with Rand, he'd changed his clothing and now looked as dapper as usual in black pants and a dark grey button-down shirt.

For one long moment he merely stared at me while the emotions within me fought for control—anger, hurt, compassion, forgiveness. This was Sinjin, a man who constantly charmed me with his smile and witty repartee, and now? Now I felt as if he'd betrayed me. "You really can be an asshole sometimes, Sinjin," I began. "Just when I thought you weren't so bad and you might actually be a good guy, you had to go and mouth off."

He nodded. "I should not have disrespected your trust in me and for that, I apologize."

"So why'd you do it then?"

He cocked his head. "The words came out of their own accord."

"What a load of crap," I said and folded my arms against my chest, trying to quell the ire that suddenly raged in me. "Do you really expect me to believe that? You knew exactly what you were doing and you did it to humiliate Rand."

Sinjin gazed out my window as if outside it were raining O Positive. "Yes, that is so," he offered and sighed with frustration, something I'd never observed in him before.

I narrowed my eyes and glared at him. "Wow, well now that we've gotten that out of the way, what a great apology, Sinjin."

"I could not help it, pet," he said, his eyes finding mine again. "I wanted to hurt him." His jaw was tight and his normally ice blue eyes radiated with a whitish glow. I had to talk myself out of being intimidated.

"Why? What has he ever done to you?"

He arched a brow. "He possesses your heart."

"Oh my God," I said and started to laugh at the idiocy of the whole situation. "This is all because you were jealous?" Hmm, why did a feel a moment of joy at his admittance?

"Am jealous, love."

"Well, that doesn't make it okay," I snapped. I'd never imagined two men fighting over me—that was something reserved for romance novels that make you envious of relationships that don't exist. Well, now that I had two males fighting for my affections, it wasn't sexy or exciting. Instead, it basically sucked.

He nodded. "I am aware of that, pet."

"And now he won't talk to me."

"He will come around."

I shook my head. "I doubt it." If Rand was anything, it was stubborn.

Sinjin smiled in that way of his, like he was aware of something I wasn't and reached into his pants pocket. He produced a sealed envelope and tapped it against his fingers twice before handing it to me.

"I brought you a peace offering."

"What is it?" I asked, making no motion to accept it.

"Flight details," he answered simply.

"Flight details?"

"Yes, for Culloden."

I quickly glanced at the door, hoping we didn't have any visitors. Worried that someone might overhear us, I stood up and closed my eyes, imagining a sound-proof barricade surrounding the room. I tested my work by humming "do re me" and blew the notes into the boundary. The notes could be heard on the air until they hit the barricade and immediately fizzled into nothing.

Sinjin cocked his head and smiled. "Impressive."

"Tell me about the flight details," I ordered.

"I imagined you had not already booked your flight since Randall announced only last eve what our itineraries would be."

No, I hadn't made any arrangements for myself and was trying to figure out a way to do so without piquing Rand's interest. Now that problem was solved, or so it seemed. I reached for the envelope and opened it, reading the printed flight confirmation. Sinjin had routed me from Newcastle airport, which was a mere thirty minutes from Pelham Manor, to Aberdeen, Scotland.

"Is Aberdeen near the Clava Cairns?" I asked.

Sinjin shook his head. "Aberdeen is perhaps two hours from Inverness."

"And Culloden is in Inverness?" I asked, thinking it sounded familiar.

"Yes," Sinjin answered, his eyes roving over me like he was hungry.

"Stop looking at me like that."

"I apologize, pet."

I frowned and returned my attention to the printout. "So I guess I'll have to rent a car in Aberdeen," I said, albeit none too happily.

"I thought we might ride together, but before we broach that topic, have you considered what Randall will do should he encounter you at the airport or on the flight?"

"Of course," I snapped. I hadn't exactly planned my mode of transport to the battle but that didn't mean I was totally unprepared. I could feel irritation bleeding into my eyes. "I'm magicking myself a new appearance so he won't recognize me."

"Very good," Sinjin said and nodded. "I have been contemplating your situation as well, love. I believe it best if you pose as my human."

By his human he meant his blood bank. "Why?" I asked, scrutinizing him.

"If you appear as a stranger, Randall will not recognize you, which offers the potential for problems."

"There's no way Rand could know all of our soldiers," I argued, shrugging off his concern with a flick of my wrist.

Sinjin nodded and returned his attention to the window. I couldn't help but wonder what the hell was out there that was so interesting. As far as I could see, there was nothing beyond the velvet black of night. He must have been avoiding eye contact with me.

"That is true but he also possesses a master list of identities. I learned that we are due to be charmed tomorrow eve in order to gain access to the fairy village in the Cairngorms."

"What fairy village?" I asked, this information unbeknownst to me.

"We are to take refuge in a fae village, pet, prior to the battle."

"And how will Rand charm the vampires? I thought our magic didn't work on you."

Sinjin smiled. "It does not, poppet. The undead will be supplied with keys."

Fae keys are nothing like regular keys. I only had one experience with them and the key basically acted like a dog of the pointer persuasion. It led

Rand, Christa, and me to a tree, where it then lodged itself, granting us entrance into the fairy village where I'd first encountered Odran.

And without a fae key or Rand's magical charm, I wouldn't be getting anywhere near a fairy village anytime soon. Good thing I had Sinjin on my side, even though he was still in my bad books.

I nodded, thinking the pieces were beginning to fit. If I were Sinjin's human, it would make total sense that Rand wouldn't know me because he couldn't be bothered with the vampires' human luggage.

"That could work, then," I said, chewing on my lip as I digested the information.

"In order to be successful, love, you will have to act the part of my human," Sinjin said, looking me up and down again. He must not have fed because he was entirely too interested in my body. I scowled at him, not wanting to give him any ideas. Just because I'd agreed to his plan didn't change the fact that I was still pissed.

"What do you mean by that?" I asked.

"It means you must dismiss this anger towards me. My humans desire and fear me, pet; they do not harbor anger against me."

I refolded my arms across my chest, feeling uncomfortable under his scrutiny. And as to his humans desiring and fearing him—I wasn't a normal human; I was a witch. "Well, I'm still mad at you, Sinjin," I started. "And I'm not afraid of you."

He chuckled. "You are aware I could kill you quite easily?"

I shrugged. "Actually, no I'm not. Ever since our sparring, I can hold my own." He smiled lasciviously so I quickly changed the subject, lest he call me on my bluff. "I'm just agreeing to be your human because it makes the situation significantly easier on me. As far as I'm concerned, you're still a jerk."

He nodded and didn't seem the least bit offended. "Then you will have to act well, poppet, if you do not wish to draw attention to yourself."

"I guess so."

The blackness of night was now evaporating into a dark grey as night prepared to hand over its throne to day. "I must return shortly, love; dawn is coming."

"In two days, Christa and I are supposed to be boarding a plane for Australia. Our flight departs an hour before your flight to Aberdeen."

The fading moonlight broke through the clouds, bathing Sinjin in milky white. I swallowed hard, not wanting to admit, even to myself, the fact that Sinjin was pretty damned hot.

"I will meet you at your departure gate," he said. "Have you informed Christa of your intentions?"

I shook my head. "No."

"And ..."

"That's for me to figure out and doesn't involve you," I interrupted. I'd have to charm Christa into boarding the Australia flight on her own, that's all there was to it. And it wasn't a reality that pleased me—influencing one's best friend via the powers of witchcraft definitely wouldn't win me any friendship awards.

"Very well," Sinjin said quietly and started for the door before apparently remembering something and turning back around. "What of our sparring?"

I shrugged. "We have two days left before we leave for battle. I don't think I need any more practice."

He nodded. "You will drink from me prior to the battle. And you will need to double your dose."

I nodded, thinking he made a good point. "We can plan for that at a later time."

"Very well, poppet. I will see you at the airport."

He opened the door and was about to shut it before it occurred to me that he'd have no idea who to look for as I hadn't shown him the picture of my alternate identity.

"Don't you want to know what I'll look like?"

Sinjin smiled in that way of his. "I will know you by your scent, love."

~

It had been a day since the fight between Sinjin and Rand and I still hadn't seen Rand. The barrier to his room remained in full effect and all of my attempts to reach him telepathically went ignored. I might have been concerned about his personal well being but Christa had said she'd caught him in the kitchen, noshing on an apple. So he was just ignoring me. Fabulous.

Now, as I walked into the forest bordering Pelham Manor, I couldn't escape my sadness and desperation to make things right. The war was looming closer and closer and time was slipping through my fingers like sand. Even though I'd be fighting alongside Rand, I wanted to set things straight before I boarded the flight to Aberdeen. But now that wasn't going to happen. I wondered if Rand would even say goodbye.

Oh well, I had to shelve such thoughts for the time being—now I had to focus on completing my transformation into my *Vogue* counterpart.

I stepped over a rotted tree trunk covered in verdant moss and stood in front of a massive pine tree. It was the same tree I'd been using to enter Mathilda's village. I imprinted my palm on the tree and closed my eyes, imagining the passage leading to Mathilda's house. I opened my eyes to find the trees had disappeared, revealing the now familiar dirt path leading into the village.

I started the quarter-mile walk that would take me to Mathilda's doorstep. No one was in the village and that depressed me even more as it reminded me of the fact that very shortly many of this village's inhabitants might never return. Upon reaching Mathilda's cottage, I knocked once. She opened the door and greeted me with a placid smile. I tried to offer my own happy greeting but couldn't disguise the fact that I wasn't happy.

"Hi, Mathilda," I said.

Her smile fell. "Jolie, what is the matter?"

"Everything," I grumbled and entered her house, the smell of brewing tea welcoming. I took a seat at the wooden kitchen table. It was really the cross section of a tree, supported by four smaller stumps.

I reached inside my coat pocket and handed Mathilda the rose drenched with my magic. She reached for a mortar and pestle residing on her kitchen counter, placing both on the table before me. Plucking the petals from the rose, she dropped them into the bowl, grinding them until they were reduced to a red pulp. Then she faced me and held her palms up to my cheeks, closing her eyes as she did so.

"Do you care to explain, child?"

I needed a shoulder to cry on. Christa spent all her time with John and I didn't dare confide in Pelham—the ghost was the biggest gossip around. So I could use some female advice.

"It's Rand," I said with a sigh.

Mathilda opened her eyes long enough to offer me a knowing smile before closing them again. "What is the problem between you two this time?"

"I broke Rand's trust by confiding in Sinjin who betrayed my confidence and now Rand won't speak to me."

God, it sounded like an episode from 90210 or something. Had my life really been reduced to a Tori Spelling soap opera? I didn't want to answer that question.

"And have you learned your lesson?"

Yeah I had learned it—don't talk about boy problems with the competition. And more importantly, never trust Sinjin again. I actually felt pretty stupid about the whole thing —what reason did I ever have to believe Sinjin could actually be trustworthy and not out for himself? Jealous, my ass. Sinjin probably just wanted me because he couldn't have me.

"Yes, I have," I answered.

"Then the event proved good for something," Mathilda said. She didn't open her eyes, but continued feeling around my face, chanting inwardly as she did so.

"I guess," I grumbled, trying to see it more positively but failing.

"You must not focus on petty squabbles, Jolie. Not while you have much larger issues to face. Your focus must be on this war."

I sighed. "I know."

She opened her eyes and balled each of her hands into fists, as if she'd captured something. Opening each hand above the mortar, several opaline drops fell from the ends of her fingers into the mortar. Mathilda's magic drops erupted into a display of flashes and spatters of multi-colored light as they fell upon the remains of the rose petals infused with my magic. She used the pestle to grind our magic together into a pink paste.

"I had a vision, child," she said very matter-of-factly.

I stiffened. "You did?"

She nodded but appeared to be putting entirely too much effort into grinding the pestle. Something had to have been bothering her. "Yes. I want you to carry something with you into battle."

I didn't have the chance to respond as she opened a drawer and pulled out what appeared to be a piece of amber. It was about the size of a quarter, but square rather than round and the thickness of my thumb. When she handed it to me, it warmed my palm. Unlike other pieces of amber, there wasn't anything fossilized in it. It was just a pure honey color.

"What is it?" I asked.

"Amber."

I frowned. So it was just a piece of amber? I'd imagined it was some magical fairy stone or at least something more impressive than what it actually was. Well, maybe this was just a lesson in looks being deceiving. It had to have magical powers if Mathilda owned it. Maybe it contained the essence of a mighty dragon—like the one I'd fought when I was at Odran's court. Or maybe it could turn the enemy to stone by chanting a charm over it. Or best of all, maybe it was a protection amulet!

"Will it protect me?"

"No."

"Is it magical?"

"No."

"What does it do, then?" I asked, finally giving up.

"Nothing."

I glanced up at her in question. "Nothing? Why do you even have it?"

She shrugged. "It was given to me many moons ago."

Hmm, Mathilda didn't appear to be the type to believe in talismans. "Why should I carry it in battle if it doesn't do anything?"

She shook her head. "I know not, child. But you possessed it in my vision and therefore, it must be necessary though we know not why."

I shrugged and put it in my pocket—if she wanted me to take it, I'd take it. Maybe it would turn out to be lucky—like the Underworld's version of a rabbit's foot. Thankfully it wasn't as gross. "Okay."

"It will be of use to you."

"Yep," I said before changing the subject. "I'll have to transform myself tomorrow night." Tomorrow evening Christa would be flying to Australia and I'd be destined for Aberdeen.

"Our magic will be ready," Mathilda responded.

"All I have to do is swallow the seed?" I asked, eyeing the seed pod that had doubled in size since the last time I'd seen it. "It's way bigger now."

Mathilda nodded. "Of course, it has more magic within it."

Interesting. "So once I swallow it, will it work right away?"

Mathilda nodded again. "Once it enters your blood stream, the magic will begin."

"And how long will that take?" I'd have to be sure to time my metamorphosis just right.

"Perhaps thirty minutes."

"And my new likeness will last two weeks?"

"Yes."

Suddenly it dawned on me that even though my outer appearance would be altered, my aura would still give me away with its otherworldly blue, pointing to the fact that I was a witch. "My aura," I started.

"Will appear human to any creatures capable of viewing it," Mathilda interrupted.

I nodded, mentally filing all the information. The finale to my battle overture was nearing its end. Soon the night of reckoning would be on me. And that meant I'd be up against Ryder. A cold feeling of dread twisted in my stomach. Suddenly, the thought of Mathilda's vision in which she saw me carrying the amber talisman reentered my mind. "This vision you had, did it reveal anything else?"

Mathilda seemed slightly agitated. "Snow."

I was reminded of the vision I'd had when I'd touched Sinjin while attempting to locate the prophetess. "I had a similar vision. What do you suppose it means?"

Although England was admittedly chilly at times, at present there wasn't any snow nor would there be for at least the next three months. We were still in summer.

"I do not know, child."

She spooned the magic rose concoction into another bowl, this one with the seed pill resting in it. Then she emptied both the pill and the rose concoction into a pot of boiling water and the seed double in size again as it absorbed the last of our magic.

"I can't swallow that. It's too big."

"You are not meant to swallow it. Just put it on your tongue and it will dissolve."

Hopefully it tasted good.

TWELVE

Christa and I had made it through security at Newcastle Airport, with no one the wiser to our false identities. Now, we waited for the flight that would take us to Heathrow airport in London. Well, Christa waited for it. I had other plans.

"Do you think we'll see kangaroos and koalas?" Christa asked as we sat in uncomfortable chairs and she perused a Lonely Planet guide on Australia.

"Probably," I answered, still trying to control the ache in my stomach due to the fact that I'd have to bewitch my best friend. Well, it also had something to do with the realization that I'd soon be transformed into another person while I hoped Rand wouldn't suspect anything. And as if that wasn't enough to turn my stomach sour, I was also well aware that in a couple days' time, I'd be in battle. Although I felt prepared, thanks to Sinjin's training and his blood, it didn't alter the fact that I was as nervous as a virgin on prom night.

Christa's eyes narrowed as she continued to study the guide. I had to applaud her; she was handling the whole situation really well. I mean, if I'd been in her shoes and soon to be thousands of miles from John while a major war raged that would determine our future, I'd be a wreck. Don't get me wrong, Christa had been emotional about it—her goodbye to John at the airport rivaled the death scene in Titanic. But all in all, she was handling it amazingly well and I was proud of her.

"What exactly does it mean to 'put a shrimp on Barbie'?" she asked.

I couldn't help my smirk which turned into a frown as amusement morphed into heartache. I blinked away tears as I wondered if this would be the last time I'd ever see my best friend. If Bella won, would she keep me alive? Bella's doctrine had alluded to the fact that she wanted me alive in order to bring back her dead but who really knew for sure? And furthermore, I could die in battle. So all in all, there was a very probable chance this could be the last week of my life. I was suddenly overcome with the urge to escape, to accompany Christa to Australia. The feelings raged through me like an angry elephant. But I couldn't give in to such thoughts now. Not when I needed to fight.

Glancing at my watch, I realized I was quickly running out of time. So as I choked back a sob, I did what I had to do and grabbed Christa's wrist, feeling like I'd explode if I didn't get through this quickly. "Chris, I think I have something in my right eye, can you check and see?"

She nodded and dropped the Lonely Planet guide into her lap, innocence etching her features. If she only knew what I was about to do to her ...

"Sure, just look up at the ceiling."

I stared at the corner of the ceiling but the tears felt as if they'd bust through any minute so I clenched my eyes closed to restrain them.

"Are you okay, Jules?" Christa whispered.

I bit my lip and just nodded. My hand instinctively went to my neck, searching for the piece of amber Mathilda had given me. I'd magicked the amber into a pendant, suspended on a chain. I wasn't sure how else to keep it safe. I rubbed the warm talisman and tried to talk myself out of the tears that already glistened in my eyes.

"Everything is going to be okay," Christa said and took my hands in hers. "We won't be in Australia long. Before you know it, Rand will fly down and pick us up and take us back to Pelham Manor."

God, I hoped it would turn out to be true ... well, the part about everything being okay anyway.

"I hope so," I said bleakly.

Knowing I still had to bewitch her into boarding the plane, I squeezed her hands and pictured a flurry of energy leaving my body and surrounding hers until she glowed as if in the embrace of an ethereal being. I opened my eyes and found Christa's eyes riveted on mine. There was no emotion or expression on her face; she was now a blank canvas.

I ignored the guilt and continued with my plan. "Christa, you are going to travel to Australia by yourself. I'll come to get you in maybe a week or so," I started. "And you won't be afraid."

She just nodded dumbly.

"When you arrive, you will get a taxi and take the taxi to the hotel, okay?"

She nodded again.

"I will come back to get you as soon as I've finished my business here. Where are your documents and where is your hotel confirmation?"

"In my purse."

The charm was done. I released her hands, heaving a sigh as I began to consider the rest of my plan. I rechecked my watch and was shocked to find twenty minutes had flown by. I had to get going.

Christa looked a little dumbfounded but not suspicious. She stared at me with an addled expression as if trying to replay our last conversation. Getting bewitched is like being drunk since you lose track of conversations and sometimes time.

"Did you see anything in my eye?" I asked, hoping to prod her memory.

"Oh, um no." She exhaled and her whole body seemed to deflate with the effort. Then, as if she didn't have a care in the world, she let go of my hands and grabbed her Lonely Planet, picking up where she'd left off.

"Okay, well thanks for looking," I started. Now it was time to test the charm. "Are you okay to sit here alone and wait for your flight? I should get going."

She glanced up and the breath caught in my throat. Would she go for it? Hopefully my magic had been strong enough and hopefully my visualization hadn't left anything important out.

"Yeah, I'm good. I wish you could come with me though."

Phew, the charm had worked. Thank God. "I do too, but I'll see you soon enough." I stood up, mentally checking off everything else I still needed to do before I could calm down. "Okay, so you've got everything, right?" I asked, sounding like a mom sending her ten-year-old on her first solo flight. Actually, now that I thought about it, this was Christa's first solo flight. Ergh … I wouldn't make a very good mom.

"Yep. I'm good to go," she chirped.

I leaned down and hugged her like I'd never hugged her before. Whatever happened to me, I took solace in the fact that my best friend would be safe. And if something did happen to Rand, John, and me, I doubted very much that Bella would waste any time in coming after Christa. That was a relief in and of itself.

I pulled away from her and chewed my bottom lip, trying to remember if there was anything else I needed to tell her, anything else I might be forgetting. "Christa, do you remember what Rand told us about his bank information? Do you have all that stuff with you?"

She nodded. "Geez, Jules, you're going to see me in a week or so, everything will be fine."

I prayed she was right.

~

After leaving Christa, I had to go through check in and security all over again, but this time my flight details would take me to Aberdeen, Scotland. Check in and security had taken longer than I'd anticipated and now I only had thirty minutes left to take Mathilda's pill, transform, and find my departure gate. Talk about cutting it close.

Once through security, I hightailed it to the nearest restroom, nearly bowling over an old lady as she came through the door. Luckily, there wasn't a line so I charged into the first stall, reached into my jeans pocket and pulled out the seed-pill. Now was the time of reckoning.

I opened my mouth and plopped the pill on my tongue, waiting for some hideous flavor to reach out and accost my taste buds. But the taste wasn't half bad—maybe a mix of mint and berry. I'd have to thank Mathilda later ... well, if there was a later.

It didn't seem as if the pill was dissolving but I continued sucking, all the while manifesting the new outfit that would take the place of my jeans and t-shirt. My sneakers melted into Birkenstocks, which I'd ordinarily never be caught dead in, but I was going for an ensemble that in no way resembled my wardrobe. My jeans transformed into a tie-dyed mini skirt while my white t-shirt bloomed into a blousy peasant top to match the blue of the tie-dyed skirt. I looked very ... groovy.

Now that my outfit was accomplished, I ran my fingers over my face, trying to feel for any transformations, but I seemed to be the same old me. I couldn't detect any voices in the restroom, so I peeked out of the stall door and found myself peering back in the restroom mirror. Hmm, maybe the pill needed a little more time ...

I timed another five minutes during which the pill had completely dissolved but, still, my hair remained long and blond. The acid taste of panic started in my gut. Maybe Mathilda had missed a necessary step of the magic? Maybe I hadn't focused enough? If the pill was a dud, my whole plan was blown. I thought about altering my appearance by means of my own magic but I didn't think I could keep it up for more than an hour.

As soon as the thought left my mind, I felt a slight tug at the nape of my neck and the heavy mass of my hair started to recede. I reached for the back of my head and found my hair was now short. A slight numbness overtook my face and I peeked out of the stall again to watch my transformation in the mirror.

My hair was now short and black. And my face—my skin blanched white before a tan began climbing from one side of my cheeks, waging a war against my paleness until it had usurped the entirety of my skin. That was when I realized my face didn't match the rest of my body. I looked like a caramel lollypop on a white stick. Dammit!

I glanced down to assess my lily-white legs and magicked myself into some red tights. Then I turned to address my peasant blouse which openly exposed the expanse of white skin flowing across my chest and shoulders. I imagined the peasant blouse morphing into a light-weight cotton turtleneck. Then I faced the issue of my white ass feet and with a thought, watched my Birkenstocks give way to brown cowboy boots. Thank God there wasn't such a thing as the fashion police.

Glancing back at the mirror, I exhaled a sigh of relief—my metamorphosis was complete. I was easily the most beautiful woman in the airport wearing the ugliest outfit. *C'est la vie*! And now I had just five minutes before my flight departed. Craptastic.

Hurrying from the bathroom, I checked my ticket and noted I was at Gate 22. Luckily, Gate 22 was just two gates from the restroom. Well, at least that was easy! I jogged to the gate, weaving through the hordes of people all desperate to make their flights on time. I started to freak out again when I noticed there wasn't one person in the waiting area. When I checked the boarding screen, the words "Flight 3453 to Aberdeen, Scotland, moved to Gate 1" nearly made me wet myself. Gate 1 was all the way at the other end of the airport. Double Dog Dammit!

Well, this was where Sinjin's blood would serve me well. I didn't have a moment to debate whether or not I should use his extreme speed as I was surrounded by humans. But I was about to miss my flight. So I ran, although it would probably be more fitting to say I flew because in a matter of seconds, I was standing in front of Gate 1, right as the airport attendant closed the gate doors. And as far as I could tell, I'd moved quickly enough that no one had noticed.

"I'm on this flight!" I called and rushed the elderly woman who glared down her nose at me.

"You're too late."

"I can see the plane," I argued, hoping she wasn't going to be difficult.

"Once this door is closed, it's closed for good and as you can see," she glanced at the door, "it's closed."

I didn't have time for this. I looked at the woman and once I had her attention, used my powers of reasoning. "I have to board that flight so open the door."

My powers of persuasion work almost like hypnotism—basically using suggestion to persuade someone to take whatever action I desire of them. The woman merely nodded and opened the door, holding it wide for me. So she'd turned out to be all bark and no bite. I ran down the platform to find Sinjin standing with the flight attendant who was attempting to close the door but unable to do so with Sinjin blocking it. Of course, she didn't look ticked off in the least. Quite the contrary, they appeared to be playing a flirtatious game—her trying to close it and him sidestepping her every chance he got.

Sinjin glanced at me and a huge smile beamed across his face. Even though I didn't want to admit it (he was still on my shit list), his smile made me weak in the knees.

"Ah, there is my little poppet now."

So he could recognize me by the scent of my blood because there wasn't a thing about my appearance that even slightly resembled the old Jolie.

The flight attendant stepped aside as I walked aboard and threw me an irritated expression, like I'd just made off with her catch, which, in a manner of speaking, I guess I had. Course, if she knew the real Sinjin was a self-centered, infuriating, jealous, albeit incredibly sexy, vampire, maybe she'd thank me.

Sinjin locked my arm in an ice cold grip and eyed me from head to toe, only to suppress an amused chuckle—probably at my outfit. He escorted me onto the plane which was chock full of our legion from front to back. The plane was ablaze with auras of every color except, of course, for the vamps, because they have no auras.

No one paid me the slightest attention, which was good.

"What a bizarre getup, love," Sinjin whispered in my ear.

"I don't have the energy to respond," I muttered, wanting only to find my seat and take a nap. I needed to purge all the stress that had been building up in me before I exploded.

"Here is your seat, pet," Sinjin said and pointed to an aisle seat just before us. I allowed him to take the window and then started to take my own seat when a shadowy figure obstructed my view. A shiver of awareness washed over my skin, and I spun around to watch Rand walking down the aisle, only to sit directly across from me. Perfect, just perfect.

I practically dove for my seat, huddling down low and tucking my chin to my chest. "Thanks for seating me here," I muttered, fully aware that Sinjin had orchestrated it on purpose just because he enjoyed stretching my limits. Before I could sit down, Sinjin smiled up at me devilishly. It was a smile that could lead to nothing good.

"Randall, meet my human," he said and I could've punched him.

Rand glanced at me apathetically. He offered his hand but I was scared to take it, lest he somehow detect who I really was. But when he didn't pull his hand away, I accepted it and shook it limply.

"Pleased to meet you," he said, smiling. "And I'm Rand, not Randall, despite what some people would lead you to believe."

I offered him a quick smile, hastily yanking my hand from his. "I'm …" Crap! I hadn't invented a new name and worse, I was talking in my own voice! My entire brain went into a meltdown and I just sat there like a moron. Sinjin reached out and patted my hand.

"This is Tallulah," he said in a mocking voice. "I have just feasted on her blood, thus she is quite scattered."

Tallulah?? WTF?? I swear Sinjin existed merely to piss me off. I exhaled a long breath and tried to contain the hurricane of anger that was currently plowing through me. Regardless of what Sinjin did or said, I had to maintain my composure. There was just too much riding on my ability to dupe Rand. So that's what I focused on.

I managed an embarrassed smile to which Rand reciprocated before returning to his *Economist* newspaper. Well, at least he had no clue who I really was. And as for Sinjin … how I would survive the flight to Aberdeen, not to mention the two hour drive to Inverness, was beyond me.

"Love," he whispered and put his hand on the highest point of my thigh, just underneath my skirt. "Remember you are my human and you only live to worship me. You are not quite acting as well as you should."

I leaned into him and whispered, “Get your hand off my thigh or I’m going to stake you.”

He chuckled and instead of removing the offending appendage, he massaged the inside of my thigh with the pad of his thumb. I didn’t want to admit it, but something like liquid lava erupted in my stomach and went due south.

“I can smell your desire, love,” he whispered with a sibilant hiss.

A bolt of embarrassment coursed through me at the thought that Rand was sitting so close. Not wanting to draw attention to us, I merely gripped his hand, dug my nails into his skin and returned his property to his lap. “Are you trying to piss me off more than I already am?” I snapped.

“I find your anger … sexy.”

“I don’t have the patience to deal with you right now.”

“Ah, Tallulah …” he chuckled.

This was going to be a long flight.

~

One long, long hour later, during which Sinjin relentlessly pushed all my buttons, we landed in Aberdeen. As we exited the plane, Rand stood next to me while Sinjin moved down a few rows to get his bag from the overhead. Luckily for Rand and me, we didn’t need any luggage since our magic meant we could create whatever we required.

“I couldn’t help but notice you … arguing with Sinjin,” Rand started as my stomach plummeted. God, I hoped my rebellious sparring with the impossible vampire hadn’t jeopardized my disguise ...

“Oh,” I started, but remembered I was speaking in my own voice again. Luckily, Rand didn’t seem to notice.

“I would be more than happy to share a ride with you if you’d like,” he said with a boyish smile. It was just like Rand to offer help to the damsel in distress. I could think of nothing I’d rather do than share a ride with him but as myself, Jolie, not as Tallulah the hippie cowgirl.

I cleared my throat and in the split second decision required to change my voice, I could only think of Dolly Parton, go figure. So my voice came out soprano high, southern, and completely weird. “Thanks for the offer but Sin … and I were just havin’ a … lover’s quarrel.” Not only was my voice ridiculously high, but my accent was worse, a cross between a redneck in *Deliverance* and Scarlett O’Hara. Still, ridiculous or not, it didn’t appear Rand was in any way wise to my deception.

He just smiled and nodded. “I understand.”

“Thanks all the same … shugah.” Ugh, this was just embarrassing.

He turned and started down the narrow aisle, his body taking up the entirety of the small space. His relaxed dark jeans cupped his ass beautifully and contrasted against the white of his t-shirt and the navy blue of his … jumper as he called it. God, he was just beautiful.

Apparently the flight attendants concurred, as they both watched him and once he'd departed, one turned to the other, and whispered. "Holy shit, was he hot."

I didn't have a chance to see their reactions to Sinjin because he was several people behind me but I'm sure it would be the same. Despite being surrounded by incredibly handsome men, it didn't take away from the fact that they were equally frustrating.

~

Sinjin told me to wait by the curb in front of the *Hertz* Rent-A-Car while he retrieved our rental. As I stood there, the members of our legion dispersed throughout the myriad of rental car agencies. It made me proud to be among them, to be fighting for the same goal.

I watched Rand depart from the *Europcar* rental counter, dangling keys from his fingers while searching for his rental from among the hundreds. His eyes eventually found mine and he smiled and waved.

"Good luck!" he called and I smiled, feeling like I wanted to cry.

I lost track of Rand as he disappeared into the deluge of rental cars which was just as well because watching him only depressed me. I didn't ponder it any further because a black Mercedes pulled up. The windows were tinted so dark, I couldn't see who was driving. The door opened and a smiling Sinjin stepped out, walking over to open my door.

My mouth dropped. This was like no Mercedes I'd ever seen before—two doors with the overall look of something closer to a Viper. No, this was an SLS AMG and the only reason I knew that was because I read it off the back of the car. "Hertz rents these?" I asked, amazed.

Sinjin chuckled. "No, love. I own it and arranged to have it sent here. I thought you would enjoy driving to Inverness in style."

Style could mean lots of different things. And I would've been fine in a Chevy Malibu … I shrugged and climbed in, sinking into the red leather bucket seat. The entire interior (seats, dash, doors) were red leather, in contrast to the shiny black dash. This vehicle was Sinjin to a T.

"So you own this?" I asked, once we were on the road and his navigation aid finished chirping directions in a female British accent.

"Yes. Do you approve?"

I didn't really know if I approved or not and was overcome by the realization that I really didn't know much about Sinjin. I mean, I didn't know where he lived or what he did when he wasn't preparing for war, the list went on. And how in the hell had he orchestrated delivery of this vehicle to Aberdeen in the first place?

"Do you live in Scotland?" I asked.

"No, pet."

I frowned when it appeared he wasn't going to expostulate. "Okay, so where do you live?"

"I have made my home all over, love. Most recently in Paris."

"So how did …"

"Enter next roundabout and take first exit onto A96," the navigation aid interrupted me. Sinjin downshifted as we took the roundabout and then double clutched, revving the engine once we were out of the turn and onto the highway. With the scenery melting into a blur amid a black canvas, I couldn't even guess how fast we were going. I hadn't realized I was gripping the door handle until Sinjin glanced over and chuckled.

"I am a very good driver, love." He turned up the volume of the CD player and I couldn't say I disliked the song. It wasn't loud or too fast paced but there was definitely a beat. The male singer's voice was soft, moody almost. Once I heard the lyrics, it made more sense as to why Sinjin was listening to it …

"… but resistance is futile … and I am gonna drink your blood … give you eternal life …"

"So not only are you a vampire but you listen to songs about vampires?" I asked incredulously.

Sinjin smiled and didn't seem in the least bit embarrassed. But he never got embarrassed, so it wasn't surprising. "It would appear so."

"What are we listening to?"

"Indie music." He reached into a consul in the middle of the car and handed me a CD. The cover was pink with some sort of robot on it. The band was *Say Hi to Your Mom*. I flipped the CD over and found the song—*Blah Blah Blah.*

"Can we listen to it again?" I asked, needing something to focus on, something to pull my thoughts away from the impending war.

Sinjin raised an eyebrow but didn't say anything, merely hitting the back button on his steering wheel and *Blah Blah Blah* started up again.

I relaxed into my seat, watching the lights of the small Scottish burgs vanish as we raced by. The velvet black of the sky was punctuated with millions of twinkling stars and I couldn't help but feel attracted to my vampire driver. I glanced over at him and noticed his eyes were frozen to the road ahead of us. Intermittently, he glanced over his shoulder so he could pass whoever happened to be slowing our progress.

Blah Blah Blah ended and another equally great song took its place. The CD player screen read *Digitalism—Pogo*. Somehow Sinjin's choice in music gave me a window into his personality I'd never seen before. And his indie music choices impressed me far greater than his car did.

"Are you still angry with me, love?"

Was I still angry with him? The answer was pretty obvious. "It's difficult to stay angry with you." And it was the God's honest truth. There was just something about Sinjin—something innocent and honest which so contrasted with who and what he was. At any rate, I wasn't angry with him anymore.

He smiled eagerly. "Good, I do not like it when we quarrel."

I continued staring out the window, studying the passing lights and feeling an emptiness that depressed me. In a night's time, we'd be in the throes of battle. And there was so much riding on the outcome of this war. My stomach cramped violently and I suddenly felt as if I'd be sick. Anxiety climbed up my chest and lodged in my throat, cutting off my breath. As the panic overcame me, I grabbed the hand rest, leaning forward as I started hyperventilating.

"Jolie?" I couldn't see Sinjin's reaction, but the concern in his voice was obvious.

Tears started in my eyes as I tried to calm myself and tried even harder to breathe. I was hyperventilating to such a degree, I couldn't control it. "I … I can't breathe."

I felt the car pull over and come to an abrupt stop. Sinjin's door opened and the cold air enveloped me in a welcomed hug. My door flew open and Sinjin fumbled with my seat belt before hauling me out of the car and into his arms.

"Breathe, love. You are having a panic attack."

A panic attack? Yes, I imagined a panic attack felt just like this, although I'd never had one before.

"Jolie, look at me," he said, holding me at a distance. "Focus on the black of my eyes."

His eyes glowed in the moonlight but I couldn't focus on them, I was so petrified by the fact that I couldn't breathe. "I … I …"

He shook me. "Focus on the black of my eyes!"

I forced myself to look into his eyes.

"Just breathe. You and I are going to get through this, do you understand?"

I nodded dumbly, wondering if he was referring to this particular situation or the war in general. My breathing became more regular but I wasn't sure if Sinjin was bewitching me or just using the power of persuasion. Then I remembered he couldn't bewitch me, so I guess I had my answer.

"Take another breath for me, love," he whispered. "There's my good girl."

Finally calm, I inhaled deeply and collapsed against Sinjin's chest, wrapping my arms around him. I just needed to be close to him, to be comforted. Sinjin held me while I cried, rubbing my back in large circles, reassuring me.

"What is the matter?" he crooned against my ear.

"I'm so afraid, Sinjin."

"There is nothing to be afraid of; I will not allow you to come to harm."

It was the same thing Rand had told me. But what neither seemed to remember was the fact that if Bella won, there wouldn't be a damned thing anyone could do for me or for themselves. And that's what scared me the most—the what ifs. I couldn't face that now though. Instead, I took comfort in Sinjin's strength, in the feel of his arms around me.

"Thank you," I whispered, suddenly overcome with the realization that Sinjin had always been there for me. Maybe I'd taken him for granted? I mean, I'd always thought of him as the hot vamp who wanted to get into my pants but figured it ended there. Was there a chance I'd been wrong? Maybe there was more to him than met the eye?

He pushed away from me and wiped my tears with the pad of his finger. "Your breathing has slowed."

I nodded and couldn't tear my attention from his incredibly handsome face, from the deep angles of his cheekbones, his Roman nose, and the squareness of his jaw. How his impossibly light blue eyes leant him the look of some mythical creature, someone designed by the Gods themselves.

He chuckled. "Poppet, you almost appear as though you like me."

His comment surprised me. Did he really think I didn't like him? That I just put up with him? Hmm, maybe I'd made it seem that way? I gulped hard as a dawning realization hit me—I'd been hiding my feelings for Sinjin, hiding them from him as well as from myself. And now, as he stood before me in the moonlight, I couldn't keep my feelings at bay.

I looped my arms around his neck and pulled him closer to me, gazing up at him. Shock usurped his expression, melting the smile right off his face. He swallowed hard and wrapped his arms around my waist, not making any motion to take things further. So he was going to leave it to me, was he?

I didn't even have to ask myself what my intentions were. There was no regret, no second thoughts as I stood on my tip toes, my eyes never leaving his. I leaned into him and brought my mouth to his lips which were freezing cold but so soft and full. I closed my eyes, relishing the feel of his arms around me. His grip on my waist tightened and he pulled me even closer, the chill of his body radiating through me. His kiss was delicate, almost shy, allowing me to take control. It was a side of Sinjin I'd never imagined seeing—so different to the cocky and confidant vampire I'd grown to … deeply care about.

But that side of Sinjin wasn't far behind, and when I opened my mouth and slipped my tongue into his, a groan escaped him. He lifted me and carried me to the car, depositing me on the hood as he leaned into me, meeting my tongue thrust for thrust. His hands splayed through my hair, tugging slightly on the nape of my neck. He angled my head back and pulled away from me, gazing down at me with a mysterious smile.

Without a word, he dipped his head and the feel of his lips on my neck caused the breath to catch in my throat. I angled my head back further, offering him free reign. Somehow, I knew he wouldn't bite me, wouldn't take it to that level. This was just a warning, a tease of what he was capable of. Fire burned in the pit of my stomach and moved south until I yearned for more. Desire exploded within me, hinting to the fact that I was dangerously on the brink of wanting more and not being able to stop.

"Sinjin," I said in a breathless voice. "We have to stop."

"Why?" He didn't look up from his assault on my neck.

"Because, I won't be able to stop if we keep going."

His hands fisted and his breathing was shallow, rushed. He pushed away from me and met my eyes, his glowing white. His fangs crested his lower lip and I gasped, not out of fear but intense passion.

"You have no idea how much I care for you," he said in a raspy voice. "How I desire you."

And I knew at that point I had to be honest with him, I had to admit to what was in my mind, pulsing through my veins. I didn't want him to go into battle thinking he meant nothing to me. "I care for you too, Sinjin, and … I want you too."

A devil's smile spread across his full lips. "Then what is stopping us?"

"Rand," I said in a small voice. As honest as I'd been about my burgeoning feelings for Sinjin, I also had to be honest about my feelings for Rand.

His smile fell and he stepped away, his jaw tight.

"I'm sorry," I whispered and jumped to the ground, watching him approach the rear of the car. His back was to me but I could see the frustration boiling through his body—it was in the tightness of his shoulders, his fisted hands.

He turned around and refused to look at me, just started for the car door and opening it, deposited himself in the seat and turned the engine on. I opened my door and sat down, not saying anything as I buckled myself in.

There wasn't anything more to say.

THIRTEEN

An hour and a half later, we arrived in Inverness. I was exhausted, both physically and emotionally. Luckily, I didn't have another panic attack, although the one I had gave me cause for pause. I'd been completely unable to control myself. I felt like I'd been sinking fast and there was nothing I could do to save myself. If not for Sinjin, I'm not sure what would've happened.

And speaking of the vampire, after giving me the silent treatment for about twenty minutes, he'd reverted back to his normal self and acted as if our kiss was a thing of the past, forgotten as quickly as it happened. I, myself, didn't know what to make of it. I loved Rand, yes, but I couldn't help the fact that I also cared about Sinjin … a lot. But I resolved to push the confusing thoughts aside, seeing as how I had no answer for them.

"What time is it?" I asked, in search of a clock in the Batmobile but failing to locate one.

Sinjin took a corner a little too fast and the tires squealed in protest. "Five past two."

I gripped my seat and glanced at him, at his perfect profile and suddenly was consumed with the need to touch him, to kiss him again. God, I hadn't realized I'd been suppressing my feelings for Sinjin, pushing them out of my conscience. The thought frightened me—what if Sinjin was only interested in sex? Or what if he was just as opportunistic as I'd originally imagined and only wanted me for my otherworldly powers? I gulped as I realized my heart was now on the line.

"How much further is the fairy village?" I demanded, trying to focus on other subjects.

"Just off Culloden road, poppet. We shall be there momentarily."

It suddenly dawned on me that staying in a fairy village alongside the battlefield might not be the best of ideas. I mean, if Bella were victorious, would it be to our advantage to be so close? "Isn't it kind of dumb that we and our loved ones are staying in such close proximity to the battle?"

Sinjin shook his head. "The village is not truly in Culloden, pet. This is merely the easiest access point. The village itself is buried deep in the Cairngorms forest."

"How far away is that?"

"Perhaps an hour by automobile."

Hmm, I remembered Odran accessing Mathilda's village from a remote tree near Pelham Manor. A tree that was miles from the actual fae village. So maybe this little bit of fairy magic extended even farther than I'd assumed?

I nodded as my eyes settled on the navigation screen which informed us to stay on B9006. According to the female voice, we'd arrive at our destination in seven minutes. I thought it strange that there were a multitude of modern houses and subdivisions off Culloden road ... odd because such an ancient and respected site should somehow be off limits to such spec developments. Oh, well, I guess people had to live somewhere.

We exited onto a road that didn't appear to have a name because the navigation announced we were "off road."

"Are you sure it's down here?" I asked dubiously.

"Yes, love, quite."

I shrugged and resolved not to be a backseat driver, or passenger seat driver as the case may be. We turned a corner and on either side of the road were rows of cars parked along the shoulder. So it seemed we'd found our destination and these were the rental cars belonging to our legion. Sinjin pulled the Mercedes onto the lip of the road and turned off the engine. Now it seemed there was no going back, the battle looming ever nearer like a nightmare. How much blood would be shed? How many of our legion would make this their last stand?

The car lights came on as Sinjin opened his door and faced me with a wide grin. Hmm ... As if my hopeless situation with Rand weren't enough, now it seemed I could add Sinjin to that sentiment. How had I managed to be digging two men at the same time?

"We are here, poppet."

In an instant, he appeared on my side of the car and opened my door, acting like the perfect gentleman. I smiled hesitantly and stood up, inhaling the clean air. Dark, low clouds interrupted the milky glow of the moon as thunder sounded from the heavens. A soft, cool breeze blew through the trees and caressed my face. I watched Sinjin retreat to the trunk, where he pulled out his overnight bag. He rifled in his pocket and produced a skeleton key which was maybe the length of my thumb. It was different to the key Rand, Christa, and I had used to access the fairy village in Glenmore but I imagined it worked in the same way.

"Have you used one of those before?" I asked, watching Sinjin hold it between his thumb and forefinger, looking like he was using a divining rod to locate water.

"No."

"Finally, there's something I can do that you can't." I reached for it and grabbed it out of his grip with a self-satisfied grin.

"I am certain there are many subjects in which you excel, poppet," he said, looking like he was about to touch me but instead, dropped his hand. I wanted to grab his hand and hold it, just to feel his skin but instead, returned to the subject of locating the entrance to the fairy village. I laid the key flat on my palm, stretching my arm out in front of me and took a few steps nearer the tree line of the forest.

"It is not doing anything, love," Sinjin said, suddenly appearing right next to me. The chill of his breath sent shivers over my skin and I was reminded of the last time we were in the forest together. When I'd escaped from Bella's House of Horrors, Sinjin had tracked me the entire way. At the time, I'd thought he was allied with Bella and Ryder, but even then, I couldn't deny my attraction to him and the way my heart sped up whenever he came too close. I never knew whether it was fear or attraction. Even now I sensed a tinge of fear regarding the vampire. It must have had to do with the fact that I never truly trusted Sinjin; there was always something that warned me not to get too close to him. And there was always the possibility that he could break me like a twig.

"You are too quiet. What is consuming your thoughts?" he inquired, grabbing my arm and forcing me to face him.

The moon broke through the clouds and painted him in an eerie glow of luminescence. In his black pants and black cashmere sweater, he appeared every inch the sinister vampire. I gulped down a ray of fear that appeared from nowhere.

"Poppet, you look frightened."

I tried to smile. "It just occurred to me that I put entirely too much trust in you."

"It is a little late for thoughts such as those, no?"

"Probably." What was it about Sinjin that was just so … arresting? I couldn't put my finger on it. Maybe it was the thrill of his unpredictability—like walking a precipice, knowing you could fall off any minute.

He chuckled deeply. "And what do you suppose I plan to do with you? Drink you? Molest you?"

I shuddered involuntarily at the words "molest you" and killed thoughts of Sinjin's touch. "Mostly drink me."

He smiled and ran his index finger down my neck. "You do not know me at all well, pet. I would far rather touch you."

"Well, I guess I'm just glad you're a good guy and on my side." It was more a question than comment.

"It is not wise to trust blindly, love."

Before I had the chance to respond, the key appeared to sense my disquietude and pitched itself forward until it was hovering an inch or so above my hand, pointing to the right.

Sinjin chuckled. "Ah, very good, little poppet."

I didn't respond but followed the direction dictated by the key, stomping through the undergrowth and God only knew what on the forest floor. At least it wasn't raining like it had been in Glenmore. I lost my footing and started to stumble when Sinjin grabbed my waist with both his hands, righting me. He didn't let go and instead, pulled me into him, breathing down my neck until my entire body shivered with cold. I couldn't pull away though. I just stood there, like an idiot.

"Watch your step," he whispered and pushed me forward.

The key leapt from my palm, buried itself into a nearby tree and cranked to the left, making the bark of the tree transparent. I ran my hand through the transparency which felt like lukewarm water and walked through it. As I came out on the other side, I blinked against the glow of numerous torches that lit the otherwise dark dirt pathway leading into the village.

Sinjin stepped through the tree, warily gazing around. I took his hand; why, I wasn't sure … maybe because he looked like he needed guidance. I led him down the dirt path, following the torchlights as they curved around a corner. The commotion of laughter and singing filled the night air as we approached an open courtyard.

Ten or more female fairy dancers fluttered this way and that, their bodies barely covered by flowing silks in all colors. My eyes moved from the fairy dancers to the audience which was comprised of our entire legion. Hmm, maybe my little meltdown had cost us a lot of time because it appeared we were the last to arrive.

Our soldiers perched on bales of hay set around an amphitheatre in the courtyard where the dancers entertained them. A wooden banquet table lit by candelabras was piled high with a smorgasbord of foods, ales, and meads. And as with the fairy village in Glenmore, at the end of the table, Odran's gold lionhead throne sat vacant.

"It looks like we are just in time for a festival," Sinjin said and pulled me close to him. "Remember to play your part, love."

I nodded; this time I wouldn't screw it up. I couldn't alert Rand to my appearance, especially this close to the battle. Speaking of the hardheaded warlock, I searched the now familiar faces, trying to pick his handsome face from among the crowd. Instead, I found Odran, sitting atop a bale of hay between two fairies, but not his usual fairamours who lived with him at Pelham Manor. Tonight he was between a blond and redhead; his hand was up the blond's skirt while he fervently kissed the redhead. Well, maybe that's an understatement; it looked like he was trying to strangle her with his tongue. Just as I was about to turn away, Odran suddenly pushed the blond down, climbed on top of her and mounted her right there! In front of everyone!

"Oh my God," I said in disgust.

Sinjin's eyes fell to the rutting Odran and he faced me with a coy smile. "Quite vile."

Thank God Rand had warned me about the mead tainted with a love spell Odran had insisted I drink when we'd first met. Otherwise, if I'd slept with the king of the fae, I don't think I ever would've forgiven myself. Odran gave Hugh Hefner a run for his money.

I shook my head and my growling stomach grabbed my attention. How long had it been since I'd eaten? I couldn't remember. One thing I could say about hanging out with Sinjin, opportunities to eat were never plentiful. I grabbed a wooden plate and piled an ample serving of bread, cheese, grapes, half a pomegranate, and two sausages.

Sinjin observed my plate with a twinkle in his eye. "What army are you planning to feed, love?"

"Ha ha, very funny. I haven't had a freaking thing to eat all day, so zip it."

"You will certainly have enough sustenance after that feast to last all week."

I took a seat on a nearby bale of hay and started in on my dinner, not caring what Sinjin thought. He remained standing.

"What may I bring you to drink, love?"

Hmm, I'd been so hungry, I'd completely forgotten about a beverage. "Anything, I don't care. Well, no mead," I added, suddenly remembering I still had to take my daily allotment of Sinjin's blood. "When will I drink from …"

"Before morning comes."

Then our sleeping arrangements dawned on me. "Where will I be sleeping?"

"With me."

My stomach dropped. Behind closed doors with Sinjin … As much as I didn't trust Sinjin, I also didn't trust myself. And the more time I spent with him, the harder it was to convince myself I wasn't *that* into him.

"Is that the best idea?" I started.

"You are my human; it is only natural," he interrupted with a knowing smile before he sauntered over to a huge tankard of what appeared to be ale and poured me a generous glass. Sitting, he handed me the glass and I thanked him.

"Poppet, I will need to feed this eve," Sinjin whispered. "Especially if I am to give you my blood."

I nodded although my stomach fell at the idea that he would need to become so intimate with someone else. "I understand. I'd offer you my blood but …"

"I would not feed from you. Not when you need your strength."

Even though I piled a piece of bread high with Swiss cheese, I wasn't hungry anymore. The thought of Sinjin feeding on a woman had sent my hunger packing. I dropped the sandwich on the plate with a sigh. Swallowing some of the ale, I watched Sinjin stand.

"I find myself growing increasingly hungry. Would you mind if I left you momentarily?"

I shook my head, although the truth was that I did mind. But I couldn't tell him that; I *wouldn't* tell him that.

"Once you requested me not to make love to my donor," Sinjin said, his eyes glowing.

I swallowed hard. "Were you … planning on doing … that?"

He chuckled. "It heightens the experience."

I nodded and suddenly felt like being sick, like keeling over right there and depositing whatever I'd managed to intake all over his shoes. Was sex so casual for him? Apparently. And I couldn't help but wonder if I fell into that category. Not that I ever imagined we would have sex but just to play devil's advocate, would I end up another notch on his bedpost?

"Then do whatever you … want to," I hadn't intended my voice to sound so acerbic.

He reached forward and grabbed my hand, covering it with both of his. "What is your desire?"

"I have no right to ask you not to," I said in a small voice, reminding myself of the same thing. "You and I aren't in a relationship."

The intensity of his gaze burned me. "That is not what I asked. Are you desirous that I make love to my donor … or not?"

I didn't want to get involved in his sex life. I mean, with thoughts of Rand consuming my brain at any given moment, it didn't seem right that I should keep Sinjin from … enjoying himself. I laid no claim to him. The mere thought of Rand stirred warmth inside me and I knew it wasn't right for me to ask anything of Sinjin. Not when I was in love with Rand.

"I'm not in the position to …"

"Yes or no."

"No!" I said sharply, surprised to hear the word come from my mouth. I slumped forward and exhaled the pent-up air in my lungs. I dropped the mostly uneaten food on the hay next to me as I tried to figure out what the hell was wrong with me. Was I in love with Sinjin? I didn't think so—the feelings I harbored for Sinjin weren't the same as those I felt for Rand.

"Very well," Sinjin said, wearing the smile of someone who'd just won an argument. "I shall return shortly."

"What if someone sees you?" I asked. "Won't it seem weird you aren't feeding on me, when I'm your human?"

"No. Our humans require time to rebuild their blood supply so it would not appear strange in the least. All the same, I will shun any audience."

I stood up, intent on refilling my cup of ale and more so, departing Sinjin's company so I could interrogate myself regarding my feelings for him in private. Sinjin grabbed my hand, pulling me into him. I braced my hands against his chest, my heart thudding.

"Your answer pleased me," he whispered.

I pulled away from him. "Well, at least it pleased one of us."

He chuckled and strode off into the darkness as I returned to the task of getting more ale. As soon as I reached the banquet table, I noticed the noise around me dying off and people shushing one another. I glanced up and watched Rand stroll out to the middle of the courtyard amidst applause and calls of "Speech! Speech!"

Rand laughed and quieted them with his raised hand. He was nothing short of beautiful in his dark jeans and chocolate brown sweater. His hair looked as if it had been freshly cut, somewhat shorter than I was used to but it suited him all the same. He had one of those classically handsome faces that would suit any fashion.

"This won't be a long speech," he started while the legion echoed "boooo" in unison. Rand quieted them and continued. "First, drink and be merry. You deserve it. When you are ready to retire, you'll find a tankard of sleeping potion next to your bed. It will allow you to sleep off your inebriation." A round of laughs ensued and Rand laughed with them. "I'll be sure to down it myself." He inhaled deeply as the smile vanished from his mouth. "I want to thank you for your hard work and dedication. I have a short speech to share with you, so without further ado, I'll get to the point." He smiled again and then became more solemn. "We are in this together; we're all united in our defiance of Bella and her followers. We are united in our moral obligation to one another and to the humans who share our world. Tomorrow eve we will find ourselves in a long and arduous night of struggle and suffering. Many of us will die, many will be wounded. I promise you, if we are victorious, Jolie and I will not rest until we have resurrected every one of you." He paused and cleared his throat. "What each and every one of us is fighting for is freedom. We will fight against the tyranny of Bella with all our might. We will fight for honesty, for morality, and for justice. In the words of brave Sir Winston Churchill, 'Come then, let us go forward together with our united strength.'" He lifted his tankard and there was a round of cheers and applause. "To all of you. Victory is ours!"

He downed the tankard and everyone stood, cheering and singing. Rand gracefully accepted the cheers and pats on the back with an elegance that was unique to him.

His speech had basically torn me apart. I secretly wanted nothing more than to run to him, throw my arms around him and tell him how much I loved him, how I was here to fight alongside him, to share his victory. But I knew that was an impossibility. All I could do was love him in anonymity. Tears spilled from my eyes, splashing into my cup and I furiously batted them away.

I started walking blindly, seeking some alone time, wanting to get my emotions under control without an audience. Instead, I walked headlong into Rand's broad chest. "Oh my God, I'm sorry," I said, remembering my

Southern accent about halfway through my sentence. He must have thought I was a total idiot, and I basically agreed with him.

"No worries." He paused and seemed to be reading me. "Are you well?"

I nodded and looked down, embarrassed.

"It appears you've been crying? Did Sinjin …"

"No," I laughed halfheartedly and wiped away a few errant tears. "It was yer speech. I thought it was very touchin'."

"Oh, well thank you."

I nodded and didn't know what else to say. Rand seemed uncomfortable as he nodded back and then started to walk away. But I didn't want him to leave. I tried to resist the urge to stop him but my feelings were suffocating me. I grabbed his hand and he turned around, more than a little surprised.

"Can I stay with you tonight?" I blurted the words before I had a chance to even consider them and after considering them, talk myself out of them.

Rand was visibly shocked, but he responded with a warm smile. "Thank you, but …"

"I apologize to y'all. I … I mean, I shouldn't have said that to y'all," I started, desperately trying to sound southern but suddenly realizing y'all was plural. Son of a ...

"I thought you were with Sinjin?" Rand asked, somewhat confused. Was he interested? Although I ached to be with him, the fact that he might return my interest not knowing I was me was something I wasn't prepared for. My heart felt like it dropped out of my chest.

"Oh, well, I am but …"

He shook his head. "If you wish to be free of Sinjin, I'm more than happy to help you. But if you are asking merely to be … with me, I have to … politely refuse."

"I understand," I said, beaming with relief.

"I … I appreciate your invitation and you are very beautiful …" he began in an embarrassed tone "I … I … just, well, my heart belongs to someone else."

My own heart swelled in the hope that I was his someone else. Me, the old Jolie. The one that wasn't quite as pretty as the new Jolie but the one who dressed a hell of a lot better and didn't have a two-toned neck. "I understand, shugah. Is she here tonight?" Inwardly, I cringed. My acting was just … revolting.

"No," he smiled. "I won't let her fight although she argued every step of the way." He shook his head and smiled. "She can be difficult."

Okay, it probably wasn't right to pry, especially when Rand had no idea I was trying to find out about how he felt towards me, but seriously, how could I not? And since Rand refused to talk to me before my big move to Australia, what better way to know if he was still mad at me?

I laughed nervously but continued, "Where is she?"

His eyes took on a sad, faraway expression. "Aboard a plane, headed to Australia."

"Well, I hope she realizes what a lucky gal she is."

He became quiet and nodded, then the warmth of his eyes blanched into ice and his jaw tightened. I felt cold arms around my shoulders and didn't have to look up to realize Sinjin had returned.

"Tallulah, my love, I was looking for you."

"Sinjin," Rand's voice was anything but friendly.

"Ah, Randall, I understand I just missed a most glorious speech given by you."

"You didn't miss much." Rand gave me a hurried smile as he turned from Sinjin and started walking away.

Without any warning, Sinjin grabbed me and kissed me. His kiss wasn't tender; it was almost angry. I wanted to pull away but knew I couldn't. I didn't want to blow my cover. Luckily, Sinjin withdrew on his own.

"Poppet ..." he started.

But he never finished his sentence because Rand suddenly whirled around and started coming back toward us, anger radiating from him. He pushed Sinjin away from me impulsively and then stopped himself. "Damn you, Sinjin," he fumed.

Sinjin wiped his shirt and smiled sarcastically. "Randall, what have I done to offend your delicate sensibilities now?"

Rand's face was red and his aura steaming purple as it glowed in the night. "You disgust me."

"And why, pray tell?"

"You vie for Jolie's affections and yet when you're away from her, you switch direction like the wind ..."

"How poetic, Randall," Sinjin said with a laugh. "Bit of the green-eyed monster, is that it?"

"You are scum and you don't deserve her."

"What would you have me do?" Sinjin scoffed, his anger suddenly becoming visible. That was when I realized Sinjin was easily as angry as Rand, only he controlled it better.

"Stay away from her," Rand seethed.

"And if she desires me above you?"

Beads of perspiration appeared on Rand's brow. "I hope she doesn't. But if she falls for your game, and you hurt her, you'll have to answer to me."

"Poppet," he said and laughed in my direction. "Observe the drama."

But I wanted nothing to do with the drama, confusing thoughts ramrodding my mind. I loved Rand but I couldn't help my feelings for Sinjin. Was it right to love Rand and yet be so attracted to Sinjin? No, the answer had to be no. Suddenly, I was overwhelmed with the need to retreat, to run away. The kicker of the whole stupid situation was that I couldn't say one word! But what I could do was walk away—I could absolutely play the part of jealous second as far as Sinjin was concerned and it wouldn't seem odd. So that's exactly what I did.

I walked as quickly as I could and was relieved when Sinjin didn't follow me. Maybe he realized I needed some alone time. I neared the blackness of the forest and collapsed next to an immense, gnarled tree trunk, sobbing. What a way to spend what could be the last night of my life!

Jolie.

It was Rand. I couldn't find the strength to respond right away. I was still trying to control the flood of tears choking me.

Can you hear me? he persisted.

Yes, I can hear you.

Good ... good. I wanted to ensure you and Christa were safely aboard the flight to Sydney?

Yes, we are. God, I didn't like lying to him but what choice did I have?

Very good. I ... also wanted to apologize for not saying goodbye properly.

I didn't know how to respond. There was so much to say but I didn't have any idea where to begin. *I wanted to apologize to you too,* I started.

Rand was quiet, finally allowing me to get the words out that had been bottled up within me.

Rand, I want you to know I didn't ... I didn't think Sinjin would say what he said to you. I never wanted to hurt you. I don't know how to explain it but I wasn't in my right mind when I told him about ... us. It just came out and I've regretted it ever since. I trusted him and I was stupid to trust him. I just needed someone to be there for me.

I am always here for you.

I needed to talk to someone other than you, Rand. I paused. *I'm sorry and I want you to know I have total faith in you regarding the battle tomorrow.*

He was quiet for a moment or two. *Have you been crying?*

Hmm, how had he figured that one out? I shrugged, imagining maybe he could pick up on my feelings through our mental connection. *Yes, I've been so worried and I couldn't stomach the idea of you going to war and being angry with me.*

I wasn't angry with you, Jolie. I was hurt.

I'm sorry.

There is something I've wanted to tell you for a while. I'd hoped to tell you before tonight and I could kick myself for my own bloody foolish pride ... but I want you to know there has never been a day I haven't thought of you. Sometimes I drive myself mad with debating over whether we should be together or not. I've never acted on my feelings because I've convinced myself I'm not in your best interests.

His comment amazed me. Not in my best interests? As if to say I was too good for him? *How could you not be in my best interest?*

Because you are special, Jolie. You're unique and someday you'll realize the extent of your powers. You're not like any Underworld creature I've ever seen before and I've kept you at arm's length because I feel such an incredible need to protect you.

Rand ...

It's my own foolishness that has made me unable to tell you, but now we might never see one another again. I ... I just want you to know ...

He paused for such a long time, I wondered if I'd lost him. I was about to prompt him, to make sure he was still there but he beat me to it.

I love you. I've always loved you.

FOURTEEN

I blinked and awoke with the feeling that something wasn't right. It was the silence. It took a second for my eyes to adjust to the pitch blackness of the room, so I blinked a few more times, rubbed my eyes and sat up. Still no good. Imagining a flame in midair, my magic acquiesced and the flame hovered in the middle of the room, burning orange with flecks of purple-blue. The fire offered enough light to show me I was in a room unknown to me, still in the fairy village.

So the fairy potion designed to sleep off any partying we'd done the evening before had worked like a charm. Haha, no pun intended. I turned to the bedside table, searching for the stake I'd brought with me which I'd laid next to the bed last night. Glancing down at myself, I noticed I was still dressed in my Tallulah outfit. Not exactly battle wear. With a thought I magicked myself into stretch pants, tennies, and a form-fitting t-shirt over a sports bra. A training outfit for the battle. The thought filled me with uneasiness and the fact that I was alone did nothing to soothe my agitation. I instinctively searched my neck for the amber talisman from Mathilda. As soon as I fingered the warm stone, it brought a rush of soothing comfort to me. I'm not sure why—it wasn't like the damned thing was good for anything. I grasped the stake and pushed it into the waistline of my stretch pants, at the small of my back. I had my amulet and my stake; I was good to go.

I stretched and wondered what the time was. There weren't any windows in the room, owing to Sinjin's vampiric reaction to sunlight. Speaking of whom, where the hell was the vampire? I moved the flame around the perimeter of the small chamber, only to find I was alone.

I sprang out of bed, suddenly fearing the worst: it was daylight and Sinjin was outside, probably cooking like a piece of well done meat. I bolted for the door and threw it open and was greeted by a sliver of moon in an array of twinkling stars. Judging by the navy blue of the sky, the sun had just expired. A cold breeze wafted through the otherwise still room and enveloped me, as if beckoning me to walk outside.

I stepped outside my door which slammed behind me as if a ghost had just locked me out. I wrapped my arms around myself, trying to figure out in which direction to go. I mean, it wasn't like I'd paid any attention when I'd come here last night.

Last night … the memory of my conversation with Rand radiated warmth throughout my body, shielding me from the bite of the cold night air. After confessing our love for one another, we'd agreed to try to make our relationship work, being careful to avoid the subject of the whole bonding scenario. And I'd been careful to shove any thoughts of Sinjin to the back of my mind.

At the end of our cosmic call, a glowing pixie appeared, telling me she was to lead me to my bedroom. Too exhausted to argue and still elated, I obediently followed the sprite to my pseudo hotel room, swallowed the tankard of fairy potion next to the bed and promptly fell fast asleep.

I took a step toward the dirt path leading from my room into the village, yellow floating torches lighting the way. I followed the torches down the winding, narrow passage, numerous one room bungalows sprouting off the pathway. Many of their doors opened, revealing members of our legion as they stepped into the moonlight. Their garments were varied—seemingly dependent on what particular magical race they were. A few weres were dressed in their everyday wear since they'd soon be reverting into their wolf forms, thereby shredding whatever they'd been wearing.

The air felt weighty, thick with emotion. It was almost like we were en route to a funeral, everyone so quiet and morose. A vampire I didn't recognize walked along the pathway beside me, sporting a metal breastplate and backplate. The only way to kill a vamp was to bury a stake in his heart so his defensive measures made sense. His face, as well as those of the other legion members, didn't reveal much but since this was the night of reckoning, I had to imagine their hearts were heavy. Mine certainly was. I felt like I was on auto pilot as I trudged along the path, consumed by my own anxiety. I couldn't stifle the worry concerning Sinjin's whereabouts. But beyond that, I resolved not to focus on whether the next few hours of my life would be my last.

I hurried past the soldiers as they made their way down the path. My only hope was that Sinjin had gone in search of food? Maybe he was in the throes of supping on Candy's blood while fondling her breasts. That thought brought a pinch of jealousy with it but I actually welcomed the spectacle over the alternative of finding Sinjin dead and unrecognizable, reduced to mere dust. He was over six hundred years old, so surely he'd had to seek shelter from the sun before? Probably so, but I found it hard to convince myself, nonetheless.

I followed the torches into the courtyard where more soldiers continued to exit their assigned rooms, heading for the mouth of the fairy village to take them to the battle site, I presumed.

"Poppet," Sinjin's voice and icy fingers dispersed my thoughts as he pulled me from the midst of our legion.

"Sinjin!" Relief consumed me as I realized he was absolutely fine, nothing fried or melted about him. "Where have you been?"

He chuckled. "I stepped out this evening, love, to feed." He pulled me into him. "Speaking of feeding, you were asleep last eve and missed yours."

"Crap!" I blurted, realizing I wasn't helping my odds of surviving this battle by missing even one opportunity to drink his blood. A panic attack loomed over me but vanished as soon as Sinjin took my hand. Somehow his touch soothed my fear and allowed me to breathe again. He led me off the path and into an alcove of elm trees. We walked down a small ravine and I glanced behind to make sure no one had followed us. I wasn't sure who was more uncomfortable with the bloodsharing, Sinjin or I. When his privacy was finally satisfied, he stopped walking, pulled me close to him and pierced his wrist. He offered the open puncture as though he was offering milk to a kitten.

"Where is your armor?" I asked, when I noticed he wasn't wearing a shred of protection. His usual outfit consisted of dark slacks and sweater or button down shirt but now he wore dark jeans and a black t-shirt.

He shooed me away with a wave of his unpunctured wrist. "I do not require armor."

I was ready to debate that but Sinjin wrapped his arms around me, bringing his wrist to my lips. "Drink, my love," he crooned, stroking my hair. "You will need it."

I closed my eyes, forcing myself not to gag and fastened my lips over his icy vein. After a minute or so and five swallows, I pulled away. The start of a blood headache began in my temples and emanated toward the back of my head.

Sinjin grasped the back of my neck and forced my mouth back to his sputtering vein. "You need more, pet."

I shrugged, but continued sucking, deciding more was better than less. I had to close my eyes, the sight of his blood making me nauseous. I couldn't get used to the metallic taste as it spurted into my mouth and I had to force myself to swallow. I wouldn't make a good vampire.

Without warning, Sinjin pressed me tightly against him, dropping his head back and exhaling deeply. I often wondered if my drinking his blood was in some way sexual for him and I guess I got my answer—it looked like he was ready to lose it right there. His free hand meandered down my back and cupped my butt as he pushed me onto his erection. I stopped drinking, dropped his wrist and threw myself away from him, shocked and angry.

"Sinjin!" I started but in an instant, he knocked me to the ground and pinned me in the dirt. His fiery eyes glowed white and his fangs were fully extended. Half of me worried he was going to bite me. The other half was riveted by his erection that was now ensconced between my thighs.

"Get off me," I gasped, trying to still my beating heart, trying to talk myself into being upset and not out of breath with excitement.

"This is your final self-defense lesson, love," Sinjin said, his eyes deadly serious. For a split second I feared he might attack me—there was an angry vehemence in his eyes I'd never seen before. He just appeared so … completely emotionless. And at that point, I realized I didn't know Sinjin as well as I thought I did. I'd trusted him naively but he was unpredictable and could turn on me at any instant. I wondered if that instant had arrived.

"We have to meet at the Clava …" I started in a hesitant voice laced with trepidation.

Sinjin didn't reply; he just leaned against me while his hands gripped both sides of my waist almost painfully. I braced my hands against his chest, my fear turning to anger and demanded, "What the hell has gotten into you? Have you lost your freaking mind?"

His hands left my waist, sliding underneath my t-shirt and further still. Before he could reach my breasts, my heels found traction against the loose earth and I shoved away from him. I got up so fast, my head fogged with blood and dizziness and I had to lean against a nearby tree for stabilization. Sinjin was instantly beside me, leaning into me, pushing me against the rough bark of the tree.

"The warlock is not right for you," he whispered, restraining my arms behind me with one hand. The other hand gently massaged my waist, moving lower until he ran his hand across my butt.

"Get your hand off me," I snapped as I attempted to buck against him, something which was futile. "Any feelings I had for you are in the process of being decimated."

He responded by pulling me closer to him, smothering me with his coolly masculine scent. "You will not admit it, Jolie, but you know I speak the truth."

Anger swelled inside me and I managed to pull one of my hands free which I used to lash out against him. I smacked his face with all my pent up rage. His neck recoiled with the force of the blow, surprising him long enough that he was temporarily off balance. I wasted no time in bolting in the opposite direction. Before I had the chance to run, he grabbed my hand and with an intense strength, whirled me back around and pressed me against the tree again, this time with my face against the rough bark.

"To think I trusted you," I spat, unable to move.

"You feel a deep connection to me, pet. Do not deny it, for you know it is true." I could feel his icy breath on my neck. His words seemed to melt all over my body. I closed my eyes and felt a surge of excitement that worried me. It was like his words could dictate my body's reaction. But that was impossible.

"The warlock cannot feed the passion within you. He is too good, too noble, and too concerned with morality."

"And I'm not?"

"You are different, poppet. You have a fire in you the warlock cannot satisfy."

I scoffed. "And you can?"

He returned my sarcasm. "You already know the answer to that question."

I frowned, not appreciating his comparison of me to himself. Despite all of my issues, I was nothing like Sinjin. I was much more like Rand than Sinjin was willing to admit. I suddenly realized most of Sinjin's actions of late had stemmed from jealousy. He couldn't have known what Rand had said to me the previous evening but it didn't change the tide of desperation in his words and actions. Desperation to keep me away from Rand.

And just like that, he let me go, leaving me to contemplate his words. But there was nothing to contemplate. Rand was noble, true, but it wasn't as though I was ignoble. And as for Rand satisfying my passions, he was definitely up to it and then some. I mean, even though he and I hadn't done the nasty yet, the promise was still there. So take that, you stupid vampire.

The coldness of the night air felt warm in comparison to the chill of Sinjin's body. I glared at him before trudging back up from the ravine, through the trees, and returning to the courtyard. I knew Sinjin would be beside me momentarily.

"You make it easy to dislike you," I seethed.

"The truth is difficult to hear, love."

"There is no truth in anything you've said. You're just trying to convince me because you can't stand the fact that you've lost."

"Lost?" he asked with a flirtatious smile—like he had information to which I wasn't privy.

"Yes, you've lost to Rand and you can't stand it."

"Love," Sinjin started.

"No more, Sinjin, I don't want to hear anymore." I held up my hand to end the conversation and tried to calm my racing heart. I didn't have time to spar with Sinjin, verbally or otherwise. There was a war on the horizon, and who knew what it would bring. All I did know was that I only cared about terminating Ryder and keeping Rand safe.

I didn't wait for a response from Sinjin and instead followed the throng of soldiers as they marched to the entry of the village, leaving Sinjin in my wake. I couldn't see over the wall of shoulders but soon realized they were dividing into two lines. Each line stood in front of a large and gnarled oak tree, probably as old as Sinjin. The soldiers at the front of the lines placed their hands on the tree trunk and vanished from sight. I walked the few paces that separated me from the last creature in line, a vamp, and shrugged off Sinjin's fingers as they drummed the nape of my neck and trailed my spine.

"Love, you are my human or have you forgotten?"

"Our charade is done," I spat, not daring to glance behind me. In an effort to escape him, I moved so close to the vamp in front of me that he turned around with an annoyed expression. I had to wrap my arms around myself to ward off the chilly air as I stood between Sinjin and his brethren.

"Jolie, dear Jolie, do not resent me for speaking an ugly truth." His fingers caressed my neck and throat as he whispered in my ear.

"I trust nothing that comes out of your mouth, Sinjin. Everything you do and say arises from your own self interests."

It was nearly our turn to go through the portal trees, so Sinjin pulled the skeleton key from his pocket—the same one we'd used to enter the fairy village. I wondered silently if it was a universal key to all fairy villages but wasn't about to ask. I was still too pissed off.

"Be that as it may, pet, we have larger issues on which to focus." Finally, he was thinking about the war. It was about damned time.

As he approached the tree, the key leapt from his hand and impaled itself into the bark, transforming the tree's center into a semi-transparent cloud. Without waiting for Sinjin, I stepped through the portal. It took me a second to adjust to my surroundings once I was on the other side because as soon as I stepped through, I walked headlong into … Trent. I quickly stepped to the side but not before I saw his flirtatious smile, highlighted by a beam of moonlight.

"Sorry," I muttered in my own voice, forgetting I was incognito. Not that it mattered because Trent clearly had no clue who I was—his eyes revealing no recognition. Instead, they consumed my face and body unapologetically. He was such a player—how had I never realized that before? Well, I guess I had realized it but dismissed the realization all the same. It was a mistake I'd never make again.

"No problem," he said with a wolfish glint in his eye. The sound of an owl hooting overhead caught my attention. God, what I wouldn't have done to switch places with it—to fly away and never look back. But thoughts such as those were useless.

Trying to reassess my surroundings, I wasn't able to take in much because the two lines of our legion began to move forward, so I followed. A road sign along the footpath grabbed my attention. It read "Clava Cairns"—something which was a bit difficult to make out in the dark, the clouds having obscured the milky glow of the moon. So we were en route to the ancient burial site. A pang of fear accompanied the realization that we'd soon face Bella's legion in a matter of seconds but I squelched it, knowing my fear would only be a liability now.

We trudged through a parking lot and continued following the road signs until the last one proclaimed "Balnuaran of Clava". We'd reached our destination. The skeletal trees surrounding me dotted a verdant pasture peppered with standing stones, some of which were as tall as me and others even taller. What captured my attention, however, were three strangely circular stone erections. They appeared to be perfect circles comprised of hundreds or maybe thousands of water-worn pebbles, stones, and boulders balanced one on top of another to form circles that were about three feet high and ten feet wide. The inside of the circle was empty—probably where the ancients had buried their kin. Two of the cairns had passageways allowing entry to the circles but one did not. Some of the larger boulders surrounding the cairns were etched with cup-like markings almost like ring indentations.

I ran my hand across one of the stones and felt a pulsating energy from deep within, as if the stone were alive. I could sense the stone's longevity in endless years, rendering it timeless. This place had witnessed so much. As I explored the rough markings decorating it, I withdrew my hand, discouraging any visions. I needed to focus all my concentration on my survival.

I stopped short as the soldiers ahead of me came to a halt. I couldn't see over their massive heights and was about to weave my way through to see what was happening but the icy clasp of fingers wrapping around my wrist stopped me. I turned to find Sinjin had caught up with me.

"Poppet, stay with me."

I just nodded. Granted, I was still pissed off but it didn't change the fact that I needed him. Having him by my side in battle was exactly where I wanted him. My chances of surviving this war had probably just risen.

"Remember your training," Sinjin continued and his gravity concerned me.

"I will." I sighed deeply and tried to subdue the fear that was beginning to spiral out of control. I had to keep my wits.

He studied me for a moment or two, without saying anything and then waded through the throng of soldiers, leading me by the hand. When we emerged from the crowd, my heart sunk as I watched Rand heading the legion and facing who else but Bella? She stood alone in powerfully confident defiance. She wore dark blue chinos and a forest green sweater with black boots. Her perfect figure combined with her long, massive mane of blackish-red hair arrested me. It seemed like the wind adored her, the way it breezed around her body, ruffling her hair and caressing her face.

"She is beautiful," I whispered, startled by the sound of my own voice. She was more beautiful than I remembered.

Sinjin sneered derisively. "She is hideous."

I stopped wasting my time on Bella's appearance. Instead, I thought about the fact that she was unescorted. It surprised me because I expected her legion to flank her in the same way we supported Rand. Apprehension suddenly pounded through me and my heart began palpitating, echoing the anxiety that was making quick work of my stomach. It was enough for me to bend over and throw up. But luckily for Sinjin, who was standing beside me, I didn't. Instead, I honed in on what she and Rand were saying.

"Do you accept our doctrine, Bella?" Rand called from his perch next to one of the ancient standing stones. His cadence was deep, strong, and sure. Even with his back to me, I could tell he was tuned to Bella's body language.

"I do," she replied, with a voice equally unwavering and strong. Her confidence frightened me more than a room full of hungry vampires could have. Why was she agreeing to our terms so easily? Was it just for show? Did she know something we didn't? Was her legion stronger than ours? I closed my eyes in the confusion of unanswerable questions. I started to hyperventilate, my breathing becoming harsh and irregular.

"Poppet," Sinjin reassured me in a strong, even voice. "I am here. You have nothing to fear."

I nodded, relishing the steadiness of his hand on my neck. I had to abandon my fear. I had to get through this.

"And do you still intend to wage war against us?" Rand demanded.

Bella didn't even pause. "I do." At her words, a circle of blue light surrounded her and Rand.

"What is that?" I asked.

"The magic seal," Sinjin answered. "Binding the battle pact, ensuring neither side will attempt to break the battle bond. It is also a failsafe to ensure neither side … cheats."

Hmm, well that was good to know. I returned my attention to the image of Rand and Bella before me. Rand's jaw tightened but he was quick to mask any anger.

"Very well. We shall meet you and your legion at Culloden." As he turned to face his army, the sag of his shoulders revealed his weary resignation. Did he really think Bella would retreat from our declaration of war? I couldn't imagine she would but who could say what went on in Rand's head. I had no clue as to what the warlock was thinking, or planning. But in that one moment of seeing him address his army, I felt incredible pride. Pride to know him and love him. Pride that he was so noble and honorable.

My adoring thoughts were suddenly interrupted by the sounds of hollering. At first the sound seemed to be distant but the more I listened, the more the yelling surrounded us, almost as though it was coming from the trees. Rand's face wore an expression of shock, no, anger. I rubbed the amber amulet around my neck and I prayed. Without knowing who or what I should pray to, I closed my eyes and prayed we would survive and that Bella's forces would not be victorious.

"Bloody bitch," Sinjin seethed, yanking me behind one of the freestanding boulders. He placed himself in front of me and stood, bracing himself as if for an attack.

"What's …?" I started.

"Bella has ambushed us," he said matter-of-factly, and no sooner had he announced it than Bella's soldiers emerged from the trees like ants defending their hole.

"Oh my God," I whispered, frozen with fear. "How?" The magic of the battle pact should have ensured that Bella not pull a fast one, right? Wasn't that what Sinjin had just said? Regardless, somehow Bella had broken it.

Our soldiers scattered. Some ran for cover in the trees while others hid behind the stones that stood among the cairns. In the frenzy of surprise and shock, I could think of nothing but Rand … praying he was prepared for whatever Bella was dishing out.

I scanned the horizon and couldn't help my gaze as it transferred past Rand to the sight of fifty or so weres descending on the battle scene, led by Grimsley. And true to his word, his wolves attacked Bella's soldiers and I couldn't help but smile. But smiling wasn't going to help me kill Ryder and that's what I intended to do.

"I can't fight if I'm wedged between you and a rock," I yelled, pushing against Sinjin.

"Stay where you are!" he hissed and pressed me against the rock.

I glanced to my right where hundreds of our legion met Bella's, the sounds of screams, clanking of metal, and bursting of magic interrupted the otherwise still night. Good thing we had a spell on the place so no humans could overhear or see what was really going on. To my left was empty forest—just the skeletal outline of trees. At the sound of hollering, I glanced forward and noticed three of Bella's legion descending on Sinjin and me. Based on their auras, none of them were vamps. Maybe two weres and a witch? I couldn't be sure—they were moving too fast.

"Crouch down!" Sinjin yelled and I did as I was told, leaning against the rock. "Dragos!" he screamed to the vampire who stood about thirty feet away. The younger vampire nodded and materialized directly beside Sinjin.

Our attackers were momentarily stunned by the appearance of Dragos, but to their credit, did not allow their surprise to betray them. The two weres dropped to their knees, while their clothes shredded and fell off. Their muscles rippled as their skin turned into fur. Dragos leapt on one of them and managed to wrestle him to the ground, descending on him like a rabid dog. He ripped into the wolf's throat with his fangs and reared up his head, fur and flesh hanging from his mouth. The wolf was very dead and lying on the ground, his blood moistening the earth.

The other wolf attacked Dragos from behind, knocking him onto the ground. He rolled over and I was unable to see what happened next since Sinjin suddenly appeared before me, taunting the last of the dreadful trio.

"Come, demon," Sinjin seethed.

Demon? I'd never seen a demon before, though I knew they existed. I curiously observed the creature which appeared as human as I, yet there was something very primitive and bestial in him. His eyes and skin glowed a crimson flush. When he opened his mouth, teeth that had previously seemed human tapered into sharp points until it looked like the mouth of a shark.

It dropped to the ground and a long red tail unfurled from its backside. Its back arched to accommodate a now bulbous rib cage. With incredible speed, it ran at Sinjin but the vampire did not back down. He met the demon with the force of a tidal wave, bowling the creature over, onto the ground.

Sinjin pummeled the creature with such ferocity, it amazed me. But it didn't even phase the demon which lashed out with its tail, on the end of which was a nasty barb. It caught Sinjin across his back, and I could see the blood gushing from the ragged wound. Sinjin winced at the pain but didn't falter. Almost immediately the wound began mending, sowing itself together as if with invisible hands. Sinjin opened his mouth to reveal his fully extended fangs and ripped into the demon's neck with a speed it never saw coming. And in that same critical moment, Sinjin wrapped his hands around the demon's neck and snapped it.

The lifeless demon carcass fell to the ground as I glanced back at Sinjin. He was eyeing Dragos and the were in combat. Sinjin approached them, grabbed a fistful of were-fur and threw the hapless wolf into a nearby tree. I winced when I heard the sound of the wolf's back breaking as it wrapped around the tree. Dragos stood up and semi-bowed with a nod of thanks to Sinjin. He walked over to the suffering wolf, leant down and with his fangs, eviscerated the wolf's carotid.

My hands were shaking; I wasn't prepared for this. My training with Sinjin had prepared me physically but not mentally nor emotionally. The horror of murder and death surrounded me—Underworld creatures tearing each other to raw flesh and bone. It was like watching the worst, goriest horror movie. But the real horror was this wasn't a movie.

"Love," Sinjin materialized before me and offered his hand. I remained crouched behind the rock and made no motion to accept it.

"We must find better cover," he continued.

It suddenly dawned on me that I was a coward. As our legion battled around me, many were dying. It wasn't right for Sinjin to protect me and it wasn't right for me to want his protection. I came here to fight and that's what I'd do.

"Sinjin, I won't go," I started and stood up. "I'm here to fight."

He shook his head. "I will not allow it."

"Sinjin!" I screamed just as a vamp descended on him. Sinjin swiftly sidestepped the vamp, throwing him to the ground and jumped on him.

"Here!" I remembered the stake in the back of my pants and tossed it to him. Sinjin caught the stake and in one deft act, buried it to the hilt in the vampire's chest. The vamp spontaneously turned into a pile of ash while a gentle breeze picked up his remains, littering them across the battlefield.

"I'm ready," I said and I meant it. "I'm ready to fight."

Sinjin shook his head. "I cannot … I will not lose you."

He didn't wait for my response but grabbed my hand and elbowed his way through the throng of battling soldiers, pulling me close to his hard chest as he did so. I had no clue where he was headed as there didn't seem anywhere to go. All around us creatures fought and fell.

I glanced to my right and caught the image of Ryder with an axe in hand, sneaking up behind Rand who was holding his own against Bella. My heart plummeted as I screamed to alert Rand. But I was too far away and in the sounds of battle, my scream blended into the myriad of screams and cries. I pushed away from Sinjin while he desperately tried to grab me. He lost his footing when I dodged him, my thoughts only of Rand. I ran like I'd never run before. I weaved through the battling legion, thinking of nothing more than shortening the distance between me and the warlock.

A were stepped before me and I shoved him out of the way, watching Rand hurling energy orbs at Bella. Behind him, Ryder was about to swing the axe. And in that split second, I used all the vampire strength I'd absorbed from Sinjin's blood and forced myself forward.

FIFTEEN

"Rand!" I screamed although I was still too far away for him to hear me. Then I remembered I was a witch and could use my magic against the axe in Ryder's hands. I envisioned the weapon sailing out of Ryder's grip and landing helplessly on top of one of the cairns. I didn't have the chance to see if it had worked and instead, pushed myself to run faster, my legs aching with the extreme speed. I rammed into Ryder, knocking us both over. When he got up, the threat of retribution was in his eyes. His bald head reflected the moonlight and his ensemble was exactly as I remembered it—black biker boots, dark black jeans, and a black t-shirt. This one had a white skull on the front with a red rose clamped in its mouth. The bull nose-ring between Ryder's nostrils was icing on the cake.

My stomach dropped at the sight of him and a scream sounded in the bottom of my stomach, never birthing itself on my lips. I felt like I couldn't move, like I was planted in cement. The vampire approached and started to sniff the wind for my scent. His smile broadened and I forced myself to stand. Instantly, Sinjin was beside me—I could tell by the icy chill in the air. He took one step in front of me, covered me with his body and braced himself for an attack. But Ryder made no motion to attack either of us, instead he continued staring at me and inhaling.

Ryder laughed and it was the most disgusting, sneering snort I'd ever heard. "Jolie, I almost didn't recanize you."

The sound of his voice grated against my nerves and I was reminded of the fact that I hated his diction almost as much as I hated him. I tried to sidestep Sinjin but he wouldn't allow me past him. "Sinjin, this is my fight," I seethed.

Sinjin never broke his gaze from Ryder, but whispered. "I cannot ..."

"If you really care for me, then let me do this."

Sinjin's body suddenly went soft and he nodded in compliance as I turned my attention back to Ryder. He just stood there, without making any motion to attack us. I glanced back at Rand and found he was still in a heated exchange with Bella, although neither looked the worse for wear. Rand had no idea we were just behind him as the three of us were ensconced in a frame of trees, blocked by standing stones which separated us from the battlegrounds.

Sinjin chose to act as sentry and barricaded the one section of our alcove which opened to the battlefield.

"Did you get my note?" Ryder snarled. Over the cacophony of the battle, his words were nearly lost.

"Yes," I answered, my heart pounding against my chest. I stepped forward and was surprised Sinjin allowed me to do so.

"You ready to give yerself to me or are you gonna put up another fight?" Ryder demanded.

"No, I'm here to kill you."

Ryder threw his head back and laughed as if I'd just landed an awesome punch line. In fact, his stomach shook with the effort, his chest muscles bulging under his arms. I'd forgotten how tall and muscular he was—but not in an attractive way. No, he was menacing and hideous. I had to swallow my fear. I wouldn't back down now; I couldn't back down now.

"And you?" Ryder asked, addressing Sinjin.

Sinjin gritted his teeth but made no motion to approach either of us. "I am merely an observer."

I suddenly felt such an inordinate surge of gratitude toward Sinjin—that he was allowing me to do what I needed to, that he wouldn't interfere. Naturally, my thoughts for Rand's safety were beginning to obsess me and when I glanced over to see how he was faring with Bella, both of them were gone. Fear started winding up my legs but I had to face the fact that Ryder should be my biggest concern. Kill him then I could search for Rand.

"Good, then you can watch me screw her," Ryder said as the smile melted off his face and he approached me with an ugly leer. His eyes glowed red and his fangs had already elongated.

Sinjin's jaw tightened, his fangs fully extending beyond his lips while his hands fisted at his sides. He was panting with ire but held his ground. I could see his jaw twitching with the effort.

I didn't allow myself to react to Ryder's comment as it wouldn't do me any good. Now, more than ever before, I had to focus everything on my training. If I was to prevail over Ryder, I had to be able to sense him even when he disappeared into thin air. I had to be able to calculate his moves before he did.

I started to walk toward him until we were about a body's length apart and motioned to him to come to me. His eyes narrowed as he snarled and lunged at me, throwing his bodyweight into the attack. I easily sidestepped him, using the speed of Sinjin's blood. Ryder nearly lost his balance but righted himself and turned around, an expression of confusion on his face.

"You been trainin'," he said and offered me an ugly smile. I didn't respond but watched him dematerialize and closed my eyes, knowing I would do better detecting him on the wind if I didn't have my eyesight to distract me. I sensed a slight heaviness in the air just beside me so I fingered the stake in the back waistline of my stretch pants and pulled it out, stabbing the air just as Ryder materialized exactly where I'd expected. I missed his chest by only a fraction of an inch.

"Good try," he said and snatched the stake from my grip, tossing it to the ground. I watched the stake bounce once and fall into the grass, completely useless.

Before I knew it, Ryder leapt on top of me and using his massive strength, dropped me to the ground while I tried to roll out from underneath him. Despite my best attempts, he had me pinned. He laughed as he held me, each of his hands holding my arms and his thighs pinning mine. I glanced up at Sinjin, to make sure he wasn't going to break his role of sentry but he stayed true. He was going to let me fight this battle. I imagined the gamut of emotions running through his mind—he didn't want to stand there immobile but restrained himself. I never appreciated him more.

I tried to thrust Ryder off me by using my hips but he just laughed and pushed his pelvis harder into mine, trying to draw my attention to the growing bulge in his pants. "We gonna have us an audience?" he asked, motioning to Sinjin.

"I guess so," I said, waiting for him to free up one of his hands. He'd have to unless his plan was just to pin me all night. When he moved his arm to cup my left breast, I managed to whack him on the temple with my fist. My hand ached once it came into contact with his head but he toppled over and instantly, I was on my feet.

Not appearing to have been severely impacted by the blow, he stood up and studied me, his eyes narrowed. "You've been drinkin' vampire blood."

I failed to respond but I didn't have to. Ryder's eyes moved to Sinjin who remained indifferently blocking our only exit.

"Your blood," Ryder said as he pointed to Sinjin. He laughed acidly, "You, a master vampire, sharin' blood with his stupid little whore."

Sinjin's fangs descended, his eyes livid, glowing white. "Apologize to the lady," he seethed.

"I ain't gonna do no such thing."

Sinjin made a motion to approach Ryder but I held my hand up to keep him back. "Sinjin," I said, a warning in itself. Ryder was just provoking him. He had to know that.

Ryder glared at Sinjin. "I'll never call you master again," he spat.

"You will not live another night to call anyone master," Sinjin answered icily.

"An who's gonna kill me?" Ryder croaked. "This bitch?"

"Yes," I interrupted, bracing myself for his attack. I wasn't as comfortable with my offense as I was with my defense so my plan was to let him make the first move. Then I'd take the asshole down. I only had one problem—my stake was still lying in the grass about five feet away and any motion I made for it would jeopardize my plan.

"So lemme get this right," Ryder started, glancing between Sinjin and me. "You're sharin' your blood with 'er in exchange for what?"

"Stop stalling and treat Jolie as a worthy opponent," Sinjin said in a monotone.

"I ain't stallin'," Ryder yelled. "I'm tryin' to understand how this slut was able to wrap a master vampire aroun' her little finger." He paused and then spat on the ground. "You ain't a master no more. You ain't shit."

"Sinjin?" It was Rand's voice. He shoved past Sinjin, pausing when he saw me. His hair was disheveled, sweat beading his brow. His shirt was torn, hanging open to reveal his incredibly muscular chest.

"I have everything under control," Sinjin said curtly.

Ryder snickered derisively as I eyed the stake, wondering if I was quick enough to grab it. No, I couldn't make my move just yet.

"You come to watch me screw the bitch, too?" Ryder asked.

Sinjin made no motion to allow Rand into the alcove, so Rand shoved his way through a narrow breach in the trees. "What the bloody hell is going on?" he demanded, looking at me.

"Jolie's gonna murder me, didn't you know?" Ryder asked facetiously.

Rand's expression went dark. "Jolie?"

Ryder threw his head back and laughed again. "This is too good. You didn't know the slut was Jolie?" His laugh echoed through the trees, momentarily interrupting the battle sounds. I wanted to kill him now more than ever before just to get him to shut the f up.

Rand's eyes went wide as he realized I wasn't who I appeared to be. Surprise quickly gave way to anger. His eyes narrowed, his hands fisting and I swallowed hard. Before I could stop him, he surged toward Ryder, but Sinjin latched onto his shirt, drawing him back with a quick jerk.

"He will slaughter her!" Rand screamed, struggling against Sinjin's grip.

I looked back at Ryder who was mesmerized by the situation, a smile still visible on his lips. While Ryder's attention was captivated, I decided to make a move for the stake. I dove for it like a shortstop going for a baseball and joyfully grasped the wooden handle. Just as I expected, instantly I felt Ryder on my back, hurling his weight into me until I felt like I was going to break in two.

Even though my magic was useless against Ryder, it could be used as a momentary diversion so I envisioned flames consuming the grass below us. The flames immediately surrounded us, a virtual fire that didn't harm either one of us but diverted Ryder's attention all the same. I took the opportunity to buck him off me. Fortunately, Ryder was caught off balance and I was able to roll away from underneath him. He was instantly on his feet but made no motion to attack me. He just glared at me.

I didn't have to glance at Rand and Sinjin to know they were still wrestling one another. I could hear their grunts and curses.

"C'mon, you little bitch," Ryder taunted me but I hesitated, I had to rely only on my defensive measures.

"You come to me, you big, stupid piece of shit!" I screamed, venting my anger. I had never hated anyone more than Ryder. Images of the video he'd included in his letter came back to haunt me and I had to force them aside. I couldn't let my anger get the better of me. I had to be cool and calm and focus on defeating him with my training.

Then it happened. He materialized directly before me and aimed a punch at my head. I ducked and went on autopilot and let my body react rather than my brain. It felt like I was watching Ryder move in slow motion as he impelled himself forward, trying to pin me down again. I deftly sidestepped him and came up from behind. The stake was heavy in my hand and the thought of impaling Ryder suddenly consumed me. As I lifted the stake to plunge it into his back, I felt like I was watching a movie. The hard coldness of Ryder's back met me as I drove the stake into his flesh with all the strength I could muster. For one moment he stood there, shock in his eyes. Then he suddenly exploded. I covered my face with my arms as his ashes rained over me.

I fell backwards on the ground as I let go of the stake and I could only stare up at the stars as I realized I'd done it! I'd killed Ryder.

"Jolie!" Rand screamed.

I shoved my elbows into the ground and sat up. Gwynn, the half vampire, half witch who belonged to Ryder, was suddenly before me. We were nose to nose. The hatred in her face didn't surprise me considering I'd just decimated her lover and maker.

I didn't have the chance to defend myself before I felt the sharp end of a dagger against my stomach.

~

I screamed against what I imagined would be blinding pain as Gwynn sunk her blade into my gut but … nothing. I blinked and blinked again before my eyes convinced my brain that what they were seeing was real. Snow … for miles. And pine trees for more miles. And as if that weren't enough for me to crap myself, no Rand, no Sinjin, no battle. I was on my own.

Okay, well this was definitely better than being run through by a blade, but it didn't change the fact that I had no idea where I was or how to get back. I was suddenly struck with that feeling of déjà vu. I'd seen this before in a vision—the unending snow, the umbrage of tree branches above me. And Mathilda had seen it too. I clasped the amber pendant in my freezing hand and tried to move forward which was difficult because I was up to my knees in snow.

So what in the hell had happened? The last thing I remembered was the feel of Gwynn's cold, steel blade and then, boom, I was suddenly in a winter wonderland, like a scene from Currier and Ives. Magic was involved, it had to be. Whose magic though, was the question. It couldn't have been mine because I was off guard and unable to escape the bitch's blade. Could Rand have transported me all these miles? Maybe so, but what about the snow? Maybe he'd mixed up his charms and accidentally added snow to my relocation efforts? Yeah, that sounded like a good explanation, so I'd go with it.

I shivered, the cold wind piercing my t-shirt and stretch pants. I envisioned thick, insulating pants, a turtleneck, and down jacket. But when that still wasn't enough to keep out the cold, I mentally fabricated an energy barrier of heat to envelop me which allowed me to create a path by melting the snow. Thank God for being a witch. I plodded through the snow, watching it melt away as I moved forward. I had to re-envision my blanket of heat over and over because my magic needed constant renewal. I wasn't sure how long I could keep this up.

I needed to get back to the battle and fast. Suddenly, I remembered Ryder was dead. A feeling hard to describe descended on me—one of infinite pride and relief, huge relief. All my training, every night of drinking Sinjin's blood had been worth it. Ryder would never harm another woman … or man again. His rampage was over. And at my hands. Then a sad thought began to form as I considered the fact that I'd killed. I mean, even though he'd had it coming and I didn't regret his death at all, death was now staining my hands.

It made me feel a little nauseous and reinforced the fact that I never wanted to experience it again. It wouldn't be an easy thing to live with and I almost felt tainted, different. Not wanting to dwell on such morose thoughts, I turned my attention to which direction I should take in order to find our legion. I'd been walking for maybe ten minutes with no change in scenery—just acres of snow and trees. And I couldn't hear the battle sounds to which I'd become inured. No matter, I continued moving. I had my magic to keep me warm, things could be worse.

Things got worse. About an hour or so later, I hadn't located another living creature and my magic was starting to fade. It takes a lot of concentration to keep magic going and the cold was little by little creeping into me. And still nothing but trees. If I didn't know better, I'd think I was just walking in circles. But I couldn't have been. I was just stuck in the middle of a huge forest. Thanks a lot, Rand. Well, I guess it was better than imminent death but still …

I nearly tripped over a tree root and felt a nasty pain radiating up my foot. Great, a twisted ankle. God freaking dammit. I leaned down to cradle the injured joint and focused healing white light onto the swollen area. Instantly, the pain subsided and I was as good as new. Except for the fact that my magic was dwindling. Keeping myself warm was about to become a tough order. Hopefully I'd find civilization soon.

I magically refurbished my blanket of heat and continued forward. How freaking far had Rand relocated me? Jeez, it seemed like miles. Maybe he was as navigationally challenged as I was. Then a thought occurred to me. If I could access Mathilda's fairy village from here, maybe she could transport me to the one in the Cairngorms? Then the Cairngorms fairies could help me get back to Clava Cairns? It wasn't a bad idea. I just didn't know if Mathilda's village was accessible from Scotland. Well, it was worth a try.

I approached a large pine tree and placed my hand on it, closing my eyes as I imagined the entryway to Mathilda's village. I opened my eyes. Nothing. Hmm, I tried again. Still nothing. Well, third time's a charm, right?

Wrong. Third time sucked as bad as the first and second. Guess I couldn't access Mathilda's village this far north. Dammit! And as for the Cairngorms fairy village, I couldn't access that at all because I'd never been invited and Sinjin still had the key. Double dammit!

I plodded along, the snow not melting as quickly so it was becoming harder to trudge through. Despite Rand's good intentions to protect me, it now it looked like I'd die in this snowy forest.

An hour later, my magic was basically useless. And I was freezing which made it even more impossible to create magic. For magic to work, one must be healthy and well rested. At this point, I was neither. My fingers were getting frostbitten and I'd stopped feeling my toes a long time ago. The crunch of snow underfoot was the only sound to greet my ears, aside from the intermittent howl of the wind as it coursed through the skeletal pine trees. My nose stung, the rest of my face having already grown numb. I wanted to cry but was afraid the tears would freeze to my face.

After what seemed like hours, I could make out lights maybe a mile or so ahead. I had to rub my eyes again just to make sure the lights were real and not a mirage. After further consideration, I couldn't deny the fact that there were definitely lights dotted intermittently between the endless miles of tree trunks and branches.

With renewed energy, I forced myself onward, hoping to ward off the cold long enough to reach the house. My stride had long since slowed, my teeth chattering nonstop and I wondered if I could even make it to the door. I tried to close my eyes and summon up any remnants of magic but it was futile. I'd have to continue forward using human strength.

About halfway to the house, my leg muscles completely froze and I could barely walk. I had to take baby steps which, given the knee-high snow, were reduced to fetus steps. My teeth were now chattering like a skeleton in a windstorm. I collapsed onto the icy ground and glanced up at the lights glowing through the trees. They were so close. If I could just go a little further … but my legs were useless.

I couldn't die out here! I grabbed hold of a low tree branch to drag myself forward, or at least tried, but my body was freezing and … dying. I pounded the earth with frustration as tears flooded my eyes only to freeze on my cheeks and litter the ground like diamonds.

The irony of surviving a battle with Underworld creatures only to die from the elements was not lost on me. It wasn't fair! I punched the ground again just to make sure I could and the urge to scream overwhelmed me.

"Rand, Sinjin!" The wind took my voice and the sound echoed against the trees, as if mocking me. A few birds scattered from a tree overhead but other than that, no response. Panic overtook me. I dropped my head to the ground and sobbed over the fact that my life had come to this. What a way to go … I wasn't in much pain—just the pain of intense cold which meant I wasn't completely frozen … yet.

"Goodness, you are nearly an icicle, miss."

Startled, I glanced up into the lovely face of a woman, a smiling and friendly face. Her beautiful green eyes radiated warmth as she kneeled down next to me, her long dark hair framing her stunning eyes and heart-shaped mouth. I tried to speak but she silenced me with a finger on her lips. She picked me up as if I didn't weigh a thing, hoisting me over her shoulder and started singing something I didn't recognize. Her body was warm against mine, so warm I wanted to sink into her, to close my eyes.

"How did you know?" I started, wondering why she'd been out in the snow and more so, if I'd completely lost it.

"I have been expecting you," she answered. It took my iced mind a second or two to grasp the strangeness of her comment.

"How have you been expecting me? Why?"

I watched the snow dissolve before she took a step, as if carving a pathway for us. Funny, but I hadn't noticed that her aura was in any way different than an ordinary human's.

"We can discuss it later. For now, we need to warm you up!" And that was the end of that. She continued trudging through the snow, humming a tune as if she didn't have a care in the world.

I didn't know how long we walked because I blacked out a few times. Coming out of my cold stupor, I opened my eyes when the woman carefully laid me on the freezing ground in front of a great doorway. From my vantage point, I couldn't make out much of the house—just that the entryway was grand and constructed of stone. The woman wiped her hands on her apron and reached for a rope attached to the overhang of the doorway. A deep bell sounded from within.

The woman glanced back at me. "You will be fine," she started. "We will take good care of you."

"Who are you?" I asked.

The woman smiled suddenly, as if just realizing she'd never introduced herself. "I am Mercedes Berg." She was probably in her early thirties, if I had to guess.

"I'm … Jolie," I started, suddenly realizing I was no longer cold. In fact, since the arrival of my friendly savior, I hadn't been bothered by the cold, the snow or the biting wind. Hmm … there was something … familiar about her. Perhaps it was the bizarre response of my dying body but I couldn't help the feeling that we'd met before. That somehow I knew her. It was her voice … but I couldn't put my thumb on how or where I knew her.

When the door remained unanswered, Mercedes lost her smile and pounded on it. Moments later, the door opened and revealed a youngish girl, maybe in her early twenties. She was wearing a funny hat—like a doily on top of a mass of red curls. And her dress was just as odd, floor length and a drab brown. It seemed to be a heavy fabric—something like wool and the white apron wrapped around her waist gave her a scullery maid sort of look. That was when I noticed the garb of Mercedes—the same long and drab dress that dragged along the ground, soaked by the melted snow. Hmm, I'd been saved by the Amish.

"What have ye got there, Miss Berg?" the girl asked in a thick English accent, her hands on her hips as she eyed me. Her expression was less than pleasant. To hear her, you might've thought Mercedes had just shown up with a flea-infested, dead rodent.

"Elsie, the lady is ill." Mercedes glanced at me with warmth in her stunning eyes. And that was when I realized Mercedes wasn't English or Scottish. Her accent was one I couldn't pinpoint, not European, maybe American? Actually, it was as if she possessed no accent at all, nothing that might hint to her beginnings.

Elsie muttered something with a frown, then positioned herself at my side and with the help of Mercedes, hoisted me up and carried me inside. I tried to smile my thanks.

"A lady?" Elsie asked in a facetious tone. "Don't look like a lady ta me. She's dressed like a man!"

I disregarded the comment, thinking to myself that the Amish certainly were judgmental. Mercedes didn't respond either and instead, she and Elsie placed me in front of a roaring fire in what appeared to be a kitchen. Just above the fire was what looked like a bread oven with a semi-circular brick opening. Pots and pans hung from beams on the ceiling and in the middle of the room was a large wooden table full of vegetables and a few dead pheasants.

"Go fetch one of your dresses, Elsie," Mercedes said as she bent down on her knees until we were eye level.

"My frocks? But I've only three and …"

"Go!" Mercedes wore an impatient expression, her eyebrows drawn in annoyance. When her attention returned to me, she smiled warmly. "We should remove this wet clothing from you."

I just nodded and tried to take off my tennies but my fingers were still too clumsy. Mercedes started humming her favorite tune again as she gently untied my shoelaces and pulled off my shoes. When she removed my socks, I gasped at how blue-purple my toes were and suddenly started freaking out when I attempted to wiggle them and nothing happened.

"Oh my God, I think I have frostbite," I whispered, imagining amputation at Amish hands …

Mercedes just shook her head and covered my toes with her palms as she closed her eyes. An incredible heat infused my feet, burgeoning from my toes and growing stronger as it climbed up my foot. When she removed her hands, my feet had regained their natural pink color, as if they'd never been in the snow.

"How did you?" I started. Hmm, there was more to this mystery woman than I'd supposed. But I couldn't get past the fact that, even in the warmth of the fire, her aura was still human. Impossible …

"The warmth of the fire, miss," she said and moved away as though she didn't want to discuss it further. She didn't have to because Elsie appeared in the doorway, holding a green dress—as shapeless as the dresses they both wore.

Mercedes wasn't shy as she pulled my off my jacket, followed by my damp t-shirt. I wrapped my arms around myself, glad I still had my sports bra on, and couldn't help but feel self-conscious.

"Stand up, miss," she said.

I did as I was told and didn't have the chance to react when Mercedes pulled my pants down. I felt myself starting to blush but willingly stepped out of them as Elsie dropped the dress over my head and shoulders and Mercedes started doing up the buttons in the back.

"We'll have to alert the master, Miss Berg," Elsie started.

Mercedes didn't glance up from the task of buttoning me. "Yes, Elsie, I am aware."

Elsie frowned and took her leave with a great show of annoyance, stomping out of the room.

"We *will* have to alert the master to your presence, miss," Mercedes said.

"The master?"

"Yes, the master is a very kind master and will not turn you out, miss."

"Turn me out?" I repeated. Jeez, turn me out in this weather and it would be my death sentence. It nearly had been.

Mercedes offered a small smile. "You just stay here, miss, while I go alert the master. I will return momentarily."

I nodded, not knowing what else to do, and watched her leave. Then I warmed up next to the fire and tried to figure out how I was going to return to the battle. Since these people were humans, they'd have no clue about an Underworld war even brewing. Hmm, so how to get back? As soon as my magic was restored, I could just bewitch the master to drive me to the Clava Cairns ... Not a bad idea.

I didn't have the chance to further plan because Mercedes suddenly reappeared in the doorway. "The master will see you now, miss. He is waiting in the drawing room and you are in luck, he has his good friend with him. Both of them are very kind, miss, so please do not be anxious."

"I'm not anxious."

Mercedes led me out of the kitchen and through a long, dark hallway that emptied into a foyer. The high ceilings, hardwood floors, and crown molding reminded me of Pelham Manor. And with the pine boughs decorating a great chandelier and red and white bows entwining the balustrade amid sprigs of holly, it looked like Santa Claus was due any second. Mercedes started up the grand staircase, me on her heels. The walls on either side of the staircase were bedecked with oil portraits of women dressed in exquisite gowns, their male counterparts looking off into the distance in apparent indifference. When Mercedes arrived in front of a doorway, she paused, curtseyed to the room's occupants and then started back down the stairs. I hadn't approached the doorway yet, not really sure what I should do. I glanced at Mercedes and she cued me to enter the room with a wave of her hand.

I approached the doorway and observed a man standing before a roaring fire, a wall of books behind him. I entered the room, and noticed another man reclined in a great leather chair next to the fire. I smiled and was about to thank them for Mercedes having saved me when they both turned to face me.

"Rand?" I asked, in complete shock.

It was Rand standing before me, leaning against the fireplace, and although I knew it was Rand, he didn't look like he had when I'd last seen him. No, instead he was dressed in a dark grey waistcoat, cut straight across the front with a wide, velvet collar, deep cuffs and lapels. The white of his stiff shirt peeked out through the coat and contrasted against the black tie knotted into a bow around his neck. My gaze traveled down to his form-fitted pants that finished in high black boots. His long side chops and tidy mustache, which was the width of his lips, completed the look.

Rand appeared to be in total confusion and glanced toward the other man, as if searching for a solution to his confusion. I followed his gaze and felt my stomach drop.

"Pelham?" My voice didn't even sound like mine, it was so constrained with shock. And the shock wasn't due to the fact that Pelham was strutting the same strange fashion as Rand because as a ghost, he was always dressed like that. No, the shock was due to the fact that Pelham was no longer a ghost, he was as much flesh and bone as Rand and I.

My gaze returned to Rand who looked bewildered. "Who the bloody hell are you?"

Fuck.

SIXTEEN

I felt like I stood there looking like a complete and total idiot for a few minutes, although it couldn't have been more than a few seconds. While I might have looked like a big dope, without a thought in my eggshell head, inside my head the wheels were turning. Thoughts spun through my mind, colliding with one another until I developed a massive headache.

I was faced with a fact that was difficult to swallow. Somehow, Rand had managed to send me back in time. Despite how ludicrous it sounds, I couldn't fathom how else it was possible—how Pelham was alive and Rand looked like Sherlock Holmes … but above all, how neither one had a clue as to who I was.

"How do you know our names?" Sherlock demanded.

I couldn't find my voice.

"Perhaps Miss Berg told her," Pelham answered, appearing the calmest of us all.

"What year is it?" I barked, surprised by the harsh sound of my voice.

Rand glanced at Pelham but Pelham just shrugged, a smile lighting up his eyes. "Perhaps the cold has made her wonky."

Irritation burned my stomach. "I'm not wonky. Just … please answer the question."

Rand faced me again with no expression. "1878."

I grasped my throat in shock, fingering the amber amulet which in some small way was a relief to know it still existed. Like somehow this reminder of Mathilda would help get me through the fact that now I could add "Time Traveler" to my resume right next to "Detail-Oriented Witch" and "Resuscitator of the Dead."

"She looks a bit pale," Pelham said, his brows drawn in concern. He stood up and approached me while Rand continued studying me from the fireplace. Both of them were becoming blurry, weaving in and out of focus. "I believe she is about to faint, Balfour."

~

When I awoke, I found myself wedged into a bed with a mountain of pillows forcing me upright. I blinked a few times as the realization that I was living in the past, in 1878, dawned on me. I shook my head in amazement, glancing around the room and was struck with familiarity—the angles of the beams, the wood burning fireplace and marble mantel. I marveled at the view outside my window of a grove of elm trees pierced by a flowing stream and realized I was in my own room at Pelham Manor except now it was one hundred thirty-three years earlier.

"Miss?" Mercedes's soft voice grabbed my attention and I turned to find her sitting right beside my bed with a book in her hand. After marking her place with a blue ribbon, she thoughtfully closed the cover and placed it back on her lap.

"How is this possible?" I asked aloud, more to myself than to Mercedes. "Maybe I really have lost my mind."

Mercedes shook her head. "No, miss, you are quite well."

Then the strange words Mercedes had uttered when we'd first met in the snow and she'd hoisted me over her shoulder like a sack of potatoes revisited me. Hmm, apparently there was more to Mercedes than met the eye. "What did you mean when you said you'd been expecting me?"

She didn't seem concerned as she fiddled with the satin of her ribbon bookmark before meeting my gaze again. "I have been expecting you, Jolie. But I do not want to start that conversation just yet. You have come a long way and nearly met your end. You must rest."

Her tone was different now—none of that servant vs. employer stuff. She was much more matter-of-fact. And her words did nothing to dispel my disquietude. "But I need to know …"

She stood up and patted me on the head like I was a favored dog. "All in good time. For now, just rest."

And as if obeying her order, my body suddenly felt like it was sinking into the quicksand of exhaustion. My eyes drooped heavily and it was a battle to keep them open. I couldn't fight the battle any longer and succumbed.

When I came to, there was a new visitor in my room. She wasn't dressed in the dowdy attire of Mercedes or of Elsie. Instead, she wore a red and green velvet dress fringed in white lace around her décolletage and along the bottom of her sleeves. She was probably in her early twenties and in her beautiful dress, looked like something right out of a museum.

She sat in a chair just beside my bed and smiled at me warmly, her skirts so massive, I couldn't figure out how she was able to fit into the chair, let alone comfortably. Her hair was pulled back at the sides with a great show of light brown ringlets at the top and bangs bisecting her forehead, which only drew attention to her green eyes, high cheekbones, and lovely face.

"Hello, miss," she started, somewhat shyly.

"Hi," I said, rubbing my head as the throbbing between my eyes started again. Maybe time traveling was hard on the body. Hmm, well now would be a good time to decipher if my witch abilities were still with me. I focused on the pain and imagined it fading away into nothing and bam, my magic complied. Thank freaking God!

"Are you feeling better?" she asked in a soft German accent.

Her German pronunciation threw me for a second or two but I dismissed it and turned to responding to her question. Was I feeling better? Yeah, a damn lot better now that I realized I possessed my magic. Course, I was still stuck in 1878 with no idea how the hell to get back to my own time. So all in all, I wasn't much better.

"I'm okay," I said softly, feeling the threat of tears.

"Miss Berg said you nearly expired."

I nodded. "I'm so lucky she found me. Are you …" I started, when I suddenly realized I could persuade this girl to answer any questions I had. While it might sound less than honest, I needed information and I didn't have any alternatives to get it.

I focused on her eyes and imagined a cloud of energy surrounding her, washing her mind and priming it for the invasion of my questions. A few seconds later, her gaze was blank, her big green eyes resting on the foot of my bed. "Who are you?" I asked.

"I am Christine Trum Pelham, the lady of the house. My brother, William, is master of Pelham Manor."

"And Rand?"

"Mr. Balfour is our guest. We usually reside in London but William's health has been poor of late and Mr. Hodgins, our doctor, who is really a lovely man, advised William to live in the country." She took a deep breath and I wasn't sure how she'd managed all that on the one breath she'd just taken. My head was still spinning. Pelham had a sister and more so, she was German?

"How are you German if Pelham is English?"

She swallowed. "Our father, rest his soul, upon his travels was indiscriminate and I was born out of wedlock. Once our father passed and William's mother had passed long before, William arranged for me to live with him."

What a good brother. "How long ago was this?"

Christine appeared thoughtful for a moment. "Perhaps ten years."

"How long will you and your brother stay out here, in the country?" The last thing I wanted was to be relocated. Well, that is if Rand and Pelham weren't already making arrangements for me elsewhere. What were the parameters on finding someone in the snow in 1878?

"This has become our permanent residence; Mr. Hodgins's orders."

I nodded, pleased to hear it. Living in Pelham Manor, even it if was over a hundred years in the past, consoled me. At least I had something that was familiar. "And will Rand stay with you?"

"Yes, he has become our constant guest as he looks after my brother. Mr. Balfour is more family than friend."

So Pelham's health was failing. I knew he died from cholera but how far he was into the disease was anyone's guess. He couldn't have been too far into it though, because cholera was a quick killer.

The charm started to fade so I surrounded Christine with a burst of blue light, mentally reciting the words: *Christine, you and I are good friends. You must do everything you can to see that I remain in Pelham Manor, no matter if Rand or your brother wants to send me away.*

It probably wasn't a bad idea to persuade Pelham as well. Better to safeguard my chances of remaining in my haven that was this house. I didn't expect I could influence Rand.

"Nice to meet you," I offered, trying to probe Christine out of her zombie like stupor. "I'm Jolie Wilkins."

"What a lovely name!" Christine beamed, seemingly not having missed a beat. "And you, miss, you are an American?" She looked hopeful and it suddenly dawned on me that she was stuck out here in the remote country, uprooted from what had to have been a lavish lifestyle in London. Now the only people to keep her company were Rand, her brother, and the house staff. And the lady of the house would not have kept company with the house staff.

"Yes," I answered, wondering how much information I should divulge.

"What state …" Christine started, hints of her German roots sliding in and out of her accent.

Was California even a state back then? Duh, of course it was. "California."

Christine beamed. "Gold mining, *wunderbar*!" I knew enough from high school German to know "*wunderbar*" meant "wonderful." She clapped her hands together as if today was her lucky day. "We are a long way from California! How did you arrive here, freezing in the snow?"

Hmm … good question. I was battling some vampires, weres, an evil witch, and had just been introduced to demons. Yeah, maybe not. "I don't know."

"You have lost your memory!" She exclaimed and I could see the excitement building in her eyes. This could be her very own mystery to unravel, an actual living, breathing mystery. Like playing Clue in 3D.

"Miss?" It was Elsie. She popped her head into my room and focused on Christine.

"Yes, Elsie?" Christine responded in a friendly manner.

"Master Pelham is callin' for ye."

Christine stood up and gave me a huge smile. "I will return momentarily." She started for the door but seemed to remember something and turned to face me again. "Please do not worry, Miss Wilkins; we will find out how to get you home again."

I just smiled, watching her sashay through the door, a mass of velvet skirts, flat in the front and drawn up like a Christmas bow in the back. After a few minutes, I threw off the bedclothes and stood up, noticing I was now clad in long underwear. I plodded over to the chair, grabbed the drab dress Elsie had leant me and struggled to pull it over my head, yanking the scratchy, miserable fabric until it was in place. Realizing I couldn't do up the back without the help of magic (and I was trying to be inconspicuous), I craned my neck out the door and eyed Elsie.

"Elsie!" I whispered, trying not to alert the whole house. "Can you help me with my buttons?"

"Aye," Elsie muttered and took her sweet ass time walking down the hall. Once she entered my room, I turned my back and she started on my buttons.

"Thanks," I said.

Feeling her fingers on the last button at the nape of my neck, I turned around, offered her a quick smile and approached the door. I had to find Rand. Of all the people I needed to talk to, he was at the top of my list. In 1878 he would have been thirty-five and hopefully well into his warlock training. I could only hope so because I needed him to help me get back to my own time. I crossed my fingers, hoping and praying that Rand was at least aware of the fact that he was a witch and would be willing to help me.

"Miss, ye shouldn't be traipsin' around. Ye should be in bed," Elsie admonished.

I continued out of the doorway and down the hall, calling over my shoulder "I feel great."

Without waiting for Elsie's response, I hurried to the library which was empty. Dammit! I continued down the corridor, heading for the stairs when I heard voices downstairs. I followed the voices and found myself in an entryway of a living room, complete with a piano and floor to ceiling windows that revealed the icy coldness of winter at Pelham Manor. An enormous Christmas tree dominated one corner of the room, its glass ornaments reflecting the burning glow of a hearth-side fire. I could see Rand reading a newspaper on the settee beside the fire, so I entered.

He glanced up with little or no excitement. Granted, he probably thought I was nuts. Despite his ennui, I was more than elated to see him. My heart raced and I nearly melted when I gazed into his warm brown eyes. And even though I'm not into facial hair, his neatly trimmed moustache actually suited him.

He was the only one in the room, but from the voices I'd heard earlier, someone must have just left. Realizing my opportunity and knowing I had little time, I decided to inform him of my plight immediately.

But where to start? "Um, hi."

Rand dropped the newspaper into his lap and regarded me with indifference, or maybe more irritation than indifference. "Good afternoon."

"I really need to speak with you, Rand."

He folded the newspaper and stood up, warming his hands by the fire. He seemed perturbed. "How is it that you know who I am and I haven't the foggiest notion of who you are?"

Well, crap, that wasn't an easy answer. "Because … you know me very well; you just don't know it yet."

He laughed but there was nothing happy about the sound, it was more biting and acerbic than anything else. "What are you after? Pelham's fortune, perhaps mine?" Then he seemed to lose his composure and rushed me in an instant, his face only inches from mine. "Let me warn you not to attempt to blackmail me. I do not know why you're here but I will not stop until you are out of Pelham's home and back to whatever place you came from."

Well, I guess we had that in common. But as to blackmailing him or extorting money from him, that was the last thing on my mind. "I'm not interested in your money or anyone else's," I said firmly.

"Then what, pray tell, are you interested in?"

"I need your help."

He cocked a brow. "My help?"

"Yes, you sent me here from the future so you've got to send me back." There, I'd said it.

He hesitated before allowing his laugh to echo through the room. "The future, you say?"

"Yes," I answered, unable to share his humor. Shouldn't a warlock be a bit more understanding of these things? Maybe he wasn't a warlock yet? That could be a big problem. "Are you in training yet, Rand?"

He shook his head at my apparent lunacy. "In training for what?"

"Becoming a witch."

And the smile was wiped clean off his face. His expression became as unreadable as a blank piece of paper and I had my answer. He was a warlock, after all. This was the response of someone who was floored. Hmm, now I didn't seem quite as crazy, did I?

"H … how … what would make you say such a ludicrous thing?" he stammered, crimson overtaking his cheeks.

I had him. "Because, as I told you earlier, you and I know one another and as you are a warlock, I'm a witch."

He glanced around the room, appearing worried about eavesdroppers. "Such preposterous allegations do not put you in my favor."

"You can deny them all you want, Rand, but I know the truth and I need you to help me return to my own time."

Then it suddenly occurred to me that if I were returned to my own time, did that mean I'd last for maybe a second before Gwynn shish-kabobbed me on her blade? Hmm, I'd have to make provisions for a little extra time once Rand sent me back; that way I'd be prepared for the bitch.

Rand was spared the chance to respond when Christine sauntered through the doorway, giving me an askance expression only to clap her hands together in a great display of glee. "Oh, dear! Miss Wilkins, I mistook you for the maid for a moment. That frock will not do at all!"

"It's really fine, Christine." Both she and Rand glanced at me quizzically and I realized my mistake. "Er, Miss Pelham."

She picked at my offensive garment as if it were the very definition of filth and then stepped back, measuring me with one eye. "I believe you will fit into my gowns quite nicely."

"Really," I started but Rand beat me to it.

"Christine, I would not …"

Christine waved away our concerns. She'd made up her mind—I was going to be her living Barbie Doll. "Miss Wilkins is my friend, and as such, she should be dressed as a lady. Come, Miss Wilkins," she said and offered her hand.

What choice did I have? I took her hand and followed her through the hallway to the bedroom at the opposite end of the hallway from mine. It was bedecked in silk wall coverings with a large canopy bed covered in an elegant velvet quilt. She went to the armoire and opened the doors, revealing rows of wools, velvets, and silks.

She glanced back at me and with one eye closed, seemed to be studying me. "With your lovely blue eyes, I believe my blue organdy would be most appropriate." She pulled out the chosen gown and handed it to me. I accepted it, noting it felt like it weighed twenty pounds, and waited while she called for Elsie.

The disgruntled maid arrived momentarily and her frown deepened as soon as she eyed me with Christine's beautiful gown in my hands.

"Elsie, we need to change Miss Wilkins out of your frock," Christine said while she rummaged through her wardrobe, extracting a white undershirt and long lace-trimmed muslin capris, followed by something I was less than enthusiastic about.

"A corset?" I asked, eyeing it dubiously.

"Of course, Miss Wilkins," Christine started.

"Please, call me Jolie," I said.

"Then you must call me Christine," she said with a bright smile, as if we'd just become the best of friends. Well, a friend was exactly what I needed.

Elsie had already begun unbuttoning me and once I was free of her itchy dress, she reached for my underclothes but I grabbed her hands. "Can't I just keep these?"

Elsie frowned. "I haven't many, miss."

Christine dispelled Elsie's concerns as she handed her a pile of white undergarments. "You can keep mine, Elsie."

Elsie's smile broadened. "Oh, thank ye, Miss Pelham. That is very kind o' ye." Elsie wrapped the corset around my middle and started to lace it up. "Hold the bed rails," she ordered curtly.

With my hands locked around the canopy post, she yanked on the laces so brusquely, I let out a yelp. Christine giggled while Elsie continued to tug on the laces, cinching my waist until I couldn't breathe.

"This is too tight," I gasped, feeling like all the blood was being pushed out of my center.

"I barely pulled on ye," Elsie said.

"Barely pulled on me?" I repeated. "I feel like my liver's now wedged in my throat!"

Christine cupped her mouth as she fought to get her laughter under control and walked around me, as if admiring a horse at auction. "Your figure looks quite nice," she commented. Then she faced Elsie again. "Elsie, where is the bustle from Mrs. Marseille's?"

Mrs. Marseille must have been a seamstress or a boutique proprietor, if I had to guess. Elsie muttered something undistinguishable and disappeared into Christine's armoire, returning with what appeared to be a straight jacket. Rows of baleen ran up the sides to the back of the contraption giving it structure. Elsie pulled my arms up until they were perpendicular to my body and started securing the contraption around my waist. Christine looked on approvingly, as if enjoying my transformation. I, myself, couldn't enjoy it and was instead visited by images of Hannibal Lecter.

She grabbed a mound of muslin trimmed in lace. "And her petticoats, Elsie."

Elsie accepted the garments and carefully arranged them atop the bustle until I looked like my waist was all of two inches wide but my ass would stretch from here to Scotland. Scotland … the thought made me twitch with panic. What was I doing playing dress up when I should be in battle? God only knew what had happened to Rand, not to mention Sinjin. Then I suddenly had a thought—maybe the future was standing still now that I was in the past? I could only hope so. But regardless, I had to get out of here; I had to convince 1878 Rand to help me.

"Am I nearly ready?" I asked, albeit breathlessly.

"Your hair," Christine started and motioned for me to sit down in front of her vanity. I could barely walk in all my new garb and sitting could only be more difficult. But as much as I wanted to complain, I couldn't let Christine know I wasn't used to wearing this type of getup. After all, in California in the 1800s, as a wealthy woman, I probably would have worn the same thing. So I sucked it up and sat down. Christine lifted my elbow length hair and secured it into a bun at the top of my head.

"That will have to do for now. Dinner will be served shortly."

I glanced at myself and didn't know what to think. With the top knot, I looked like some old school marm but the dress really was lovely. The rich blue matched my eyes perfectly. And I definitely looked well off with the lace billowing from the neckline and tight jacket narrowing over my waist with equally tight long sleeves ending in more lace.

"Thank you, Elsie," Christine said with a smile as the maid curtseyed and left.

I turned to the task of standing up and didn't want to alert Christine to the fact that I wasn't practiced in Victorian fashion in the least. I attempted to stand and once accomplished, I tried to walk gracefully but the circumference of the dress turned it more into a hobble. Christine eyed me suspiciously, her smile about to give way to amusement.

I took baby steps until I joined her at the doorway and together we hobbled down the stairs. She led me into the dining room where Rand sat beside Pelham, who looked pale or rather, green. Christine obediently took the chair beside her brother and I sat next to her. Actually, it would be more fitting to say I sort of flopped into the seat and rolled back up into a sitting position.

"Are you well, William?" Christine whispered, the smile at my ridiculous display vanishing from her face as soon as she eyed her brother's ashen countenance.

Pelham smiled warmly. "Yes, darling, I am well, merely vexed with a trifling cold." Hmm, could this be the beginning of Pelham's cholera that eventually killed him?

"Perhaps you should be," Christine started, her face highlighted by the yellow flames of multiple candelabras.

Pelham waved away her concern, then faced me. "In honor of our mysterious guest, I have asked Cook to marvel us with new treats from the kitchen!"

Rand grumbled something unintelligible, making me realize he probably wasn't going to help me. In fact, this Rand of 1878 was kind of an asshole. I frowned at Rand before turning to Pelham with a bright smile. At least he and his sister were friendly. Rand and Elsie could go screw themselves.

"Thank you, Mr. Pelham," I answered, settling my eyes on the white table linens. The sparkle of the crystal candelabras and glasses contrasted against the silver of the utensils, all erupting in a beautiful display of prismatic reflection.

"Please, call me William. My Christine says you and she have become friends."

Hmm, maybe I wouldn't have to bewitch Pelham after all—maybe the prospect of a playmate for his sister was enough for him. I smiled at Christine and before I could respond, I was interrupted by two servants carrying silver trays which they laid before us.

"And what is this, George?" Pelham asked.

George, who upon further inspection was the identical brother of the other servant, replied "For your first course, fillet of sole with anchovy sauce, cream of celery soup, mutton curry, and sherry."

While his brother announced the menu, George ~2 filled our glasses with pink sherry while I inspected the plate of fried fish before me cautiously. Celery soup sounded doable albeit uninteresting. I turned my attention to the silver platter of mutton curry which I thought might be more palatable. I was a big fan of Indian food, although I rarely ate lamb or mutton. George ~1 ladled the mutton into our bowls, followed by the celery soup, while George ~2 busied himself with filleting the fish.

Once the two Georges retreated to the kitchen, I waited for the others to begin eating, planning to emulate them. Instead, Pelham lifted his glass of sherry and the others (including me) followed suit.

"To the queen's health," he said quickly and swallowed a gulp. I thought it more fitting for him to cheers his own health, but there it was. We raised our glasses in toast and even though I'm not a big drinker, the sherry went down with no problem. I spooned a small portion of the sole and found it wasn't incredibly bad. The mutton curry, on the other hand, was like no Indian food I'd ever consumed. It was in a word—vile. The curry was sharp and left my tongue wallowing in discontent. So I concentrated on the sole and finished it quickly, only to find everyone's eyes settled on me.

Christine shifted uncomfortably and turned beet red while Pelham resumed spooning his curry. Rand continued to watch me with elevated brows and a slight smirk playing with his lips. So the bastard could smile; imagine that.

"Is there a problem?" I asked.

"Perhaps California is different," Christine started in a small voice, before flushing even more brilliantly red and focusing all her attention on her untouched plate.

"Okay, out with it," I said, becoming visibly irritated.

Rand met my eyes directly. "When a lady consumes her dinner with such voracity, it often displays a voracious appetite for other pursuits."

"Balfour!" Pelham reprimanded.

"*Du liebe Güte*!" Christine blurted. Hmm, my German wasn't good enough on that count so I thought I'd rely on my magic—it was worth a shot. I thought to myself: *translate* and almost instantly, the words "Oh my goodness" traveled through my mind.

Then I focused on what Rand had just said and it took me a second to realize he was talking about sex. Oh my God. I felt the heat of a blush suffuse my face but refused to look away. "Christine, as to your point, yes things are quite different in California."

Rand faced Pelham and there was anger in his eyes. "*Sie gehört hier nicht hin.*" The words "she does not belong here" rang through my mind, loud and clear. So Rand could speak German. Ha, well I could understand it.

"*Wo sind deine Manieren? Darüber sollten wir später redden,*" Pelham said and my mind translated the meaning to: "Where are your manners? We shall discuss this later." Then Pelham faced me with an embarrassed smile. "Apologies, Miss Wilkins."

I just nodded while he faced his sister and Rand again. "We will speak English only, please."

I smiled and relaxed into my chair, hoping my magical translation ability could not only translate but also create. Worth a shot. "*Keine Sorge; ich spreche Deutsch*!" I said, which meant, "No worries; I understand German."

Christine's mouth dropped open while Rand shook his head in irritation and dropped his attention to his plate. Pelham just chuckled.

So the Victorians were pretty freaking unbelievable. A woman with a healthy appetite meant she also had a healthy appetite for bedroom sports? Good God. I glanced at Christine's plate again and noticed only a mere indentation in her fish while her mutton was untouched. The two Georges rescued me from further embarrassment by removing our plates while a female servant began replacing them with new plates and glasses. Then the two Georges returned with something I will never forget as long as I live. And I don't mean in a good way.

"Second course," George ~1 began. "Boiled calf's head, brains in butter and herb sauce, citrus cranberry sauce, carrots in dilled cream sauce, tipsy cake, and claret."

V O M I T.

Well, thank God women were supposed to show restraint at the dinner table. I had no argument with that, although the tipsy cake sounded interesting. The boiled calf's head was absolutely repulsive and I couldn't help but notice Rand's avoidance of the nasty thing. Pelham, on the other hand, didn't wait for the two Georges to begin serving him and tore off a piece of the cheek revealing a toothy grin. George ~2 ladled up a spoonful of brains and butter sauce on my plate, a lump of cranberry compote, and a couple of inconspicuous carrots smothered in a white sauce before departing back into the kitchen. I immediately went for the carrots, being careful not to consume them too quickly, lest Rand think I was interested in a carrot of another sort.

After finishing my last carrot, I eyed the mound of brains amid bleeding butter as it ran the entirety of my plate. It seemed like minutes as I forked a very small bite and brought it to my lips reluctantly. The taste was horrid and I felt myself start to gag. I washed down the brains with a healthy gulp of claret and thrust my spoon into the cranberry, hoping it might soothe my thoroughly disturbed taste buds. The cranberry citrus goulash was as tart as biting into a lemon and I decided I was finished.

"You will sample the tipsy cake?" Christine asked. She cut me a piece no more than the width and length of my index finger and plopped it onto my plate. The cake looked alright but after taking a bite, tipsy wasn't a good description. There was no taste of alcohol at all and instead, it was dry and felt like I was chewing cement. What a disappointment. I washed it down with the claret and wanted to brush my teeth, the brain film still hanging onto my molars.

"Have you given more thought to Christmas dinner?" Pelham asked Christine.

Christine beamed and clapped her hands together ecstatically. "Oh, yes, I have completed the list of courses and I have even arranged for games."

"Christmas?" I started, downing another mouthful of claret.

Christine faced me with a large smile. "Oh yes, Miss …"

"Jolie."

"Jolie," she corrected with an embarrassed smile that gave way to an excited smile over Christmas planning. "Christmas at Pelham Manor is just lovely. It is a true German celebration. You will so enjoy it. I am terribly sorry you cannot be with your own family but we will try to make it as enjoyable for you as we can. Won't we, brother?"

Pelham smiled. "Yes, of course we will."

"Really, William," Rand started, throwing an angry look in my direction.

Pelham silenced Rand with his hand. "It is the Christmas season, Balfour; you might learn from Dickens' example."

Maybe he was referencing Dickens's A Christmas Carol. If I could remember correctly, Dickens wrote in Victorian times and seemed to be mostly concerned with the plight of the have nots. Hmm, more importantly, when the hell was Christmas? I really wasn't planning on staying that long, if I could help it. I needed to get Rand to use his warlock abilities and get me the hell back to my own time—with a few seconds to spare me from Gwynn's blade. And I also needed to do a bit of research into Mercedes. The more I thought about her bizarre words and abilities, the more I thought she might be able to help. So no offense to Old Saint Nick, but Christmas didn't enter into my plans.

"When is Christmas?" I asked.

Christine faced me, wide eyed. "Why, in half a fortnight."

That was just one week away.

I gulped the remainder of my claret, eyed the forlorn calf's head, and resolved to get on the next train out of 1878 ASAP.

SEVENTEEN

The next morning, after tossing and turning all night, thinking of and refuting ways to get back to my own time, I awoke to find a ray of sun struggling to get through my drawn curtains. I yawned, stood up, and yanked the curtains back. The sun's brightness assaulted me as it reflected off the blanket of snow covering the trees, bushes, and grounds outside Pelham Manor.

My heart sped up. I didn't belong here; I had to get back to my own time. Yet, insofar as I could see, there was no way to get there. Rand had clearly demonstrated his aversion to helping me and he was my only hope. My heaving chest felt like it might cave in on itself so I closed my eyes and inhaled deeply, focusing on my exhale. My heart's palpitations slowed and a wave of refreshing calmness washed over me. I had two goals: first to find out more about Mercedes; and second, to persuade Rand I wasn't after his money, but his help.

I opened my weary eyes and gazed out the window again, trying to appreciate the beauty of the sparkling snow. The tranquility of the moment was interrupted when Rand and Pelham appeared, Pelham sporting a thick blanket around his shoulders. He took such small steps that Rand basically hobbled next to him. Hmm, I would've loved to have been a fly on the wall for their conversation because I was convinced it had everything to do with me. Obviously Rand didn't want me here.

Well, while I might not have been able to magick myself into a fly (ew), I was able to assume the shape of the fox. I turned away from the window, observing my floor length nightgown. Not wanting to take the time to magick myself into the height of Victorian fashion, I decided to venture outside in my nightie, despite the fact that it would be considered indecent to be seen in my undergarments. At this point, I didn't care. Besides, once I became a fox, my clothes would be destroyed anyway.

I checked the empty hallway outside my bedroom which only emphasized the early hour by the fact that the entire house was silent with not even the sounds of maids stirring the coals. I crept down the stairs into the short hallway that linked the back entrance of Pelham Manor. Once there, I opened the door, only to find Rand and Pelham just twenty feet ahead of me. I tip-toed into the snow and closed the door behind me as carefully as I could.

Noticing a skeletal bush covered in downy snow, I hid behind it and closed my eyes, calling my fox. I envisioned the creature flooding my body with a spry quickness I could feel through my blood. Shape shifting is not painful; your head begins to cloud, like you're about to pass out and *voila*, you're on all fours.

I scampered out from behind the bush and scurried the distance separating me from Rand and Pelham. I had to be careful to remain covered by the bushes so neither would notice me—I mean, wasn't fox hunting a national pastime in England?

"Thank you for assisting me outside, Balfour," Pelham started. "I am not quite so hot now."

Rand merely nodded and grabbed Pelham's arm when Pelham misstepped and nearly fell over. Pelham heaved a frustrated sigh and gratefully allowed Rand to support him. Then his body went still and he fought to catch his breath with only his contorted face revealing his agony. Guilt suffused me—I could heal Pelham; I could take away his pain and sickness. At the same time, though, was it right for me to do so? Was I in a position to make such a decision? I didn't think I was.

"Where does it hurt, Pel?" Rand asked, his expression full of concern.

Pelham sighed. "Pain is a general theme of the whole of my body."

Rand said nothing but maneuvered Pelham to a wooden bench overlooking the grove of elm trees. Rand swept the snow from the bench and supported Pelham's upper arms as the weaker man attempted to seat himself. Rand placed Pelham's blanket around his shoulders before positioning his hands above Pelham's head. Then he closed his eyes and his aura amplified its blue radiation. When Rand opened his eyes, Pelham glanced up at him with a smile.

"I do not understand how you are able to do that, Balfour, but I thank you all the same."

"Let us leave it as one of the world's unsolved mysteries," Rand said with a laugh.

Hmm, so Rand had already mastered the ability to remove pain. Although it wasn't the be all end all, neither was it something relegated to an intermediate. Maybe Rand *was* more advanced in his magic than I'd presumed. I hoped it was far enough advanced that, once blended with mine, we could send me home again.

"Pelham, would you be averse to discussing Miss Wilkins?" Rand asked, standing before Pelham with a worried expression marring his otherwise perfect face.

Pelham shook his head and looked incredibly tired, almost achingly so. "What is worth discussing?"

"She does not belong here, Pel," Rand started.

Pain and anger shuddered through my fox body. How could he be so cold, so uncaring? Hadn't he understood when I said I was a witch? What would it take to convince him I wasn't after his fortune? Maybe I hadn't done enough to prove my powers ...

"And what shall we do with her?" Pelham retorted. "Throw her into the cold?" His voice cracked and he closed his eyes, looking as though he would fall asleep right there.

Rand frowned, turning around to face the grove of elm trees as he crossed his arms against his chest. "There are places for people like her—people with dementia."

Before I had the chance to squeal my protest, Pelham beat me to it. "I hardly think her mad, Balfour. She nearly met her death in the snow—it seems perfectly acceptable that she would be a bit … delirious."

God, at least someone was supportive. Thank you, Pelham! Rand continued to shake his head, apparently hell bent on believing my marbles were lost. "Pel, you must admit, if only to yourself, the fact that you enjoy Christine having a playmate. You know I love nothing more than seeing your sister happy …"

"Christine has not been happier since Miss Wilkins' arrival. The vivacity she now exhibits has replaced the sullen and withdrawn creature she once was."

Rand continued staring at the horizon, his jaw tight, making his features hard. "Yes, but that is not to say that Miss Wilkins might harbor ill intentions regarding you and your fortune." Pelham laughed as Rand faced him with an expression of surprise.

"And what of your fortune?" Pelham asked, his chin tipped in defiance. "Your fortune is far more sizeable than mine."

Rand raised his brows and nodded, shifting a pine cone with his shoe. "I have not rejected that thought either, Pel. I do not believe Miss Wilkins cares whose fortune will be pillaged as long as she can get her grubby little hands on someone's."

Grubby little hands? Seriously? God, the more I saw of this 1878 version of Rand, the more I disliked him. If ever I thought the Rand I knew so well was a little uptight and old fashioned, he was nothing compared to this Rand.

Pelham sighed heavily and the anger in Rand's face dissolved into concern for his friend. "Are you well?" he asked in a small voice.

Pelham nodded slowly. "Yes, although I find day by day I become weaker." He was quiet for a moment. "If I should meet my end …"

"Do not say such things," Rand interrupted, pain visible in his eyes. "You thought it merely an insignificant cold?"

Pelham shook his head. "That was for Christine's sake, Balfour."

"Perhaps I should send for Mr. Hodgins," Rand started. Hmm, I had to wonder at the fact that Rand didn't heal Pelham himself. Maybe his magic wasn't yet strong enough.

Pelham shook his head. "No, I will not see the doctor." He paused for a moment, feigning interest in his fingernails. "Shall we change the subject?"

"Pel, if you are merely being headstrong ..."

"Say no more of it; I am well." Pelham's jaw was tight, his lips pressed into a straight line, signaling the fact that he wouldn't discuss the topic any longer. "What became of that vile creature who set his eyes on my Christine?"

Rand's hands fisted at his sides and he took a few steps forward. "Sinjin received his just rewards, Pel."

My ears perked at the mention of Sinjin. Could this be the same Sinjin, my Sinjin? I couldn't imagine it could be any other. How common was the name Sinjin anyway?

"Have you located him, then?" Pelham asked.

Rand nodded and continued pacing back and forth, his jaw clenched. "Yes, I did not want to inform you until your health had improved, but Mr. Sinclair is no longer welcome in the upper circles of London, Yorkshire, Derbyshire, and the Midlands."

"Thank you, my good friend."

Rand stopped pacing and patted Pelham's shoulder, a sad smile appearing on his face. "Anything for you and Christine, Pel. You are all the family I have left."

Pelham covered Rand's hand with his own, patting it consolingly. "Then perhaps you will allow me one more request, Balfour?"

"Of course."

"Please allow Miss Wilkins to stay."

Rand pulled his hand away and sighed. "William," he started.

"At least through Christmas. I could not turn her away during this season. Perhaps by the time the holidays are over she will have regained her memory?" He became thoughtful. "And she is quite lovely."

Rand chuckled, a deep, harmonious sound that echoed through the trees. "Ah, your ulterior motives have surfaced." The smile melted into a frown again. "Lovely or not, I cannot ignore my suspicions."

Pelham cocked his head and an amused smile lit his lips. "Balfour, always looking out for us. It is my hope the mysterious Miss Wilkins will grow on you, old man. Perhaps she will change your opinion dramatically."

Rand remained serious. "Do not conceive any matchmaking notions in that head of yours."

Pelham's smile widened, making him appear incredibly young, only his pallor the reminder of his ill health. "Tell me you do not find Miss Wilkins quite fetching?"

Rand appeared to be having a mental conflict, his eyebrows knitted and his lips pressed into a rigid line. "I would be blind not to notice her beauty," he said in a small voice, as if trying not to admit it to himself, let alone Pelham.

Pelham nodded. "I can now die a satisfied man, Balfour," he said and attempted to stand, looking like a wobbly newborn giraffe. Rand was instantly by his side, taking his arm and helping him to his feet.

"Shall we retire inside?" Rand asked, stepping slightly away to allow him the dignity of walking unassisted.

Pelham just nodded.

I began to experience the lightheadedness inherent in my magic whenever it begins to wane, so I scampered back to my snowy bush. I allowed the fox to leave my body, and watched as she trotted off to join her natural world again. The raw cold of the snowy air slapped me back to attention. I glanced down at myself, remembering my nightgown which was now ripped along the breast area and soaking up the snow. Well, so much for that. I closed my eyes, trying to ward off the cold and imagined a pair of thick and insulating pants, and an oversized sweatshirt. The clothing suddenly enveloped me like a warm hug. Not wanting to waste any more time to magick a pair of shoes, I hurried back up the snow covered path to Pelham Manor and opened the door as quietly as I could. The last thing I wanted was to draw attention to myself in my current getup. The house was just as quiet as it had been when I'd first descended the stairs. I tiptoed to my bedroom and once safely ensconced in my room, behind the locked door, I relaxed.

So Sinjin was once involved with Christine. Intrigue piqued my curiosity. Hmm, this little situation had to be the reason for all the bad blood between Rand and Sinjin—it had to be. Absentmindedly, I magicked off my clothes and tried to remember the style of the nightgown I'd been wearing. Grasping a picture of it in my mind, I felt the lightweight fabric materialize as it skimmed my knees and flowed over my shoulders. I wrapped my arms around myself, still chilled to the bone and opened my bedroom door, glancing down the hallway to ensure I was still alone. The coast was clear so I ran the long corridor separating me from Christine's room and knocked on her door.

"I am asleep, Elsie!" she called.

"It's Jolie," I whispered but didn't wait for her response. I opened her door and entered, carefully closing it behind me.

Christine sat up in her canopy bed and rubbed the surprise from her eyes. "Jolie, are you ill?"

"Yes, I mean no." I took a seat on her bed. The fire was still flickering in her fireplace, making the room almost too warm. Hmm, it wasn't lost on me that Elsie had allowed my fire to go out. What a …

But on to more important subjects, such as the situation between Sinjin and Christine. I didn't imagine Christine would willingly discuss Sinjin, seeing as how we'd basically just met, but maybe it was worth a try. Being stuck in a house with only two men for company would definitely make me yearn for some estrogen. And if natural coercion failed, I could always charm her, much though I didn't want to.

"I overheard your brother and Rand discussing someone named Sinjin?" I initiated.

Christine nodded and her gaze fell to her fidgeting hands as a blush suffused her cheeks. "Yes."

"Tell me about him," I started, taking her hand and offering what I hoped was a consoling smile. I mean, despite my burning curiosity about Sinjin, I really did care for Christine and if I could help her with any pain she was harboring, I was happy to do it. Think of it as killing two birds with one stone.

"I prefer not to; my brother has forbidden his name to be mentioned in this house." Her wide eyes met mine, belying the fact that she did want to discuss the subject of the charming vampire.

"Christine, I will not tell another soul, I promise." I even crossed my heart but didn't hope to die. I'd come close enough already.

She seemed to be considering it, cocking her head as if deep in thought. Then a huge smile overtook her face. "Oh, Jolie, Sinjin Sinclair is … the most handsome and irresistible man I have ever met." Well, I could concur with her on that one. Sinjin definitely was handsome, and the irresistible part? Check. Her smile vanished as her lip began trembling. "I have so desperately attempted to forget him, to stay angry with him."

"Why would you be angry with him?"

She glanced away, shutting her eyes tightly against her tears. "My brother says he courted me merely to spite Mr. Balfour." Her German accent was thicker now, as if the purging of her emotions encouraged her natural state.

"Why would he do that? You're beautiful, Christine, and you have a lovely personality."

"You are very kind." She sighed. "As I understand, Mr. Balfour and Mr. Sinclair had known each other previous to Mr. Sinclair's and my introduction. I believe they had a business deal that went sour and my brother believes Mr. Sinclair was retaliating when he sought me out. Retaliating in order to upset Mr. Balfour."

Hmm, Sinjin and Rand in business together? That didn't seem to ring true. I mean, it wasn't that farfetched but what business could Rand and Sinjin possibly have in common? No, that must have been a cover up. The truth of the matter had to be more closely aligned with the Underworld, and if so, of course Christine wouldn't be aware of any of that … right? Did Christine even realize Sinjin was a vampire? Over six hundred years old, in 1878 Sinjin would be well into his blood diet. "So did you allow Sin … er, Mr. Sinclair to court you?"

She nodded and nervously picked at her coverlet before returning her glassy green eyes to mine. “Yes, I was foolish, Jolie. And I cannot blame my foolishness on youth. This occurred in September, merely three months ago. And I also cannot wipe the images of Mr. Sinclair from my mind, try as I might.”

I offered her an understanding smile. I knew all about trying to forget about disappointing men and unluckily for me, I had two to commiserate over. As if one wasn’t enough. “Okay, so let’s go back to Mr. Sinclair for a minute. How did you meet him?”

She bit her lip, as if trying to arrange her tempestuous thoughts into some sort of fluidity. “Yes, I should have started from the beginning.” She sighed, long and deep. “Mr. Balfour, my brother, and I were at the Furvish’s for a harvest festival. Mr. Sinclair happened to be attending the celebration as well. As fate would have it, we were introduced and Mr. Sinclair entertained me with tales of his travels abroad. During the course of the evening, he danced with me three times! Can you imagine?” A flush lit her face.

“Wow, three times,” I said, not knowing what else to say. It didn’t sound like much of a milestone to me but what did I know about Victorians and harvest festivals? Not much, apparently.

Christine’s eyes took on a faraway glaze, as if she were reliving the events as she told them. “That very evening when I retired, I heard the sounds of pebbles on my window and found Mr. Sinclair outside.” She smiled nostalgically. The poor girl was absolutely head over heels in love with Sinjin. And if the Sinjin of 1878 was anything like the Sinjin I’d come to know, I didn’t imagine being in love with him would be a good thing, whether in 1878 or the twenty-first century.

“Go on,” I said, smiling encouragingly.

“I know I should not have, Jolie, but I sneaked downstairs to meet him.” Her lip started trembling again and I gripped her hand, as if to say I was there for her and she could get through this. She nodded and wiped her eyes. “He told me of his undying love for me. How we should always be together.”

Yep, good ol’ Sinjin, the rake. I’d have to give him a ration of crap for this one, that is, if I ever got home again. The thought of home deflated my entire being so I pushed it to the back of my mind. I’d get home. Somehow. “So I imagine this courtship continued?” I prodded.

“Yes, Mr. Sinclair swore me to secrecy, that I would not inform my brother or Mr. Balfour. And like a silly fool, I never uttered a word.” She glanced away, biting her lip again as if doing so would keep her tears at bay.

“It’s okay, Christine.”

She faced me again. “On our last meeting in the courtyard, Mr. Balfour must have overheard us because he suddenly appeared and a horrid fight erupted between the two, Jolie. And … I never saw my Mr. Sinclair again!” She lost it at that point and collapsed into a teary heap on her bed.

Hmm, a fight between Sinjin and Rand over a girl … it sounded oddly familiar.

So what was Sinjin planning? To elope with her? That didn't seem like him. Had he truly been in love with her? Rand apparently didn't seem to think so. But what did 1878 Rand know of love? Then it occurred to me that maybe Sinjin merely intended to deflower her to ensure she was damaged goods? If nothing else, that would have destroyed her chances to marry well. Hmm, if Sinjin had done that then he was a bigger asshole than I'd ever imagined.

"Christine," I started and tilted her chin up, wiping away her stray tears with the pad of my thumb. I wasn't sure how to ask this question, seeing how completely personal it was. And she'd probably be mortified I was even asking … Crap! I was mortified, myself. "Were you ever intimate with Mr. Sinclair?"

She blushed until she was the color of me after I've been in the sun too long. The decision of whether or not to tell me played out on her face like a bad movie. Then she shook her head. "No, thank goodness. Though I believe it was just a matter of time, Jolie. I was so foolish, I would have done anything for him, even given him the prize reserved for my husband." Hmm, and knowing Sinjin, he would have greedily accepted.

Then she fell onto the bed again with renewed anguish, so I held her, crooning in her ear and rocking her back and forth as if she were a colicky infant. My mind raced with thoughts of Sinjin's involvement with this girl. There had to be more to it than a business arrangement gone wrong. And I intended to find out exactly what had transpired between Rand and Sinjin that ended with Rand abhorring Sinjin for over one hundred years.

~

For the remainder of the day, I searched for Mercedes, after deciding she was my most important contact. But she managed to elude me and I couldn't prevent the anxiety that was now stampeding through me. I had to get out of 1878 but I had no clue how and anyone who seemed a likely assistant either refused to help or had gone MIA. I paced my room, trying to think of another plan. If I could just get Rand alone again, maybe I could convince him I really was a witch and not a gold-digger. I mean, when I'd tried earlier, it hadn't exactly gone well but maybe if I tried again—if I performed some of my witchcraft, maybe he might believe me?

Anxiety spiraled up my throat and I had to sit down on my bed and close my eyes, trying to rein in the panic attack that was looming. If only Sinjin were here so I could gaze into the abyss of his beautiful eyes. The thought made my stomach ache as I wondered if I'd ever see my infuriatingly charming vampire again.

Tears flooded my eyes and I didn't bother wiping them away. Maybe I needed a good cry, a soul cleansing. The panic in my stomach had dissipated just at the remembrance of Sinjin's eyes but now my focus was on my miserable plight. What if I couldn't return to my own time? Could I even survive in 1878? What would become of me? If Rand had any say so, I'd be shipped off to the local loony house never to be seen or heard from again.

Now the tears were streaming full force and I let them come, quickly blotting them once I heard a knock on my door.

"Jolie?" It was Mercedes. Thank God.

I leapt off the bed and threw the door open, not caring that my eyes were red and swollen. "I am so happy to see you," I croaked.

She entered and once I closed the door, approached me, her arms wide, as if to hug me. The offer surprised me momentarily but I needed a shoulder to cry on so I collapsed into her outstretched arms.

"There now," she crooned in my ear. "We will find a way to send you home."

I pulled away from her and dried my tears, needing to understand how much she knew and more so, *how* she knew it. "How do you … how did you … what did you mean when you said you were expecting me?"

She sat on my bed, patting the coverlet beside her to indicate I should also sit. I did so as she took a deep breath. "You are Jolie Wilkins and you were in the midst of battle before I found you in the snow. Prior to being thrust into 1878, you were in the process of being stabbed by Gwynn. You had just defeated the vampire Ryder, and before you could blink, you ended up here, freezing in the snow."

I just gawked at her, wide eyed. "How can you know that? I mean, your aura is human."

She smiled, a wise and knowing smile. "I am a witch, as you are a witch, Jolie. And as to my aura, I shield it so as not to expend energy uselessly." To prove her point, she ran her hands over her head and down to her waist. As if unzipping her aura, it blasted out of her in a rainbow of colors. I gasped as the colors vacillated this way and that, a glow that lit the entire room. Holy freaking crap. She was like the mother of all witches, a mega witch.

"Oh my God," I said in awe.

Mercedes just laughed and ran her hands back up her waist and head and her aura disappeared as if it had never revealed itself to begin with.

"Unbelievable," I said, my mouth still hanging open. Trying to shake myself out of my stupor, I focused on her stunning green eyes, a gold ring circling the irises, like cat's eyes.

"Thank you," she said proudly. With an aura like that, I would've been proud too. I shook my head and tried to focus on the facts before me—that Mercedes was a witch, well, more fittingly, an uber witch. "You must be powerful enough to send me back?" My voice was hopeful.

She lost her smile, her lips twitching slightly as if she wasn't sure what to say. "Yes and no. My magic is very powerful, yes, though there are laws of nature which I am unable to alter alone."

"Maybe we could do it together?" I asked desperately. I couldn't stay here—I just didn't think I could ever get used to calf's heads, no cell phones, 1878 Rand, or corsets.

Mercedes laughed again and patted my hand. "Do not fret, Jolie. I have a plan where you are concerned. Let us start from the beginning. Do you know how you arrived here?"

I nodded. "Rand's magic." As soon as I said the words, I wondered how familiar Mercedes was with Rand. "Wait, you do know Rand is a warlock, right?"

"Yes, though he is barely into his apprenticeship with the fairies."

So she knew about the fairies too, which meant they existed in 1878 as well. Thank God because I was beginning to feel like a mental patient. "Yeah, so at the moment Gwynn stabbed me, Rand yelled and the next thing I knew, I was here. So I just figured he sent me."

She shook her head. "I brought you."

"How?"

Mercedes was silent for a moment, as if deciding how to explain. "I had been attempting to bring you back multiple times previous to the battle but your subconscious barriers were too high, too strong. Your magic is incredibly powerful, Jolie, though you do not realize it."

I was trying to grasp what she was saying, trying to understand what she meant but finding it difficult. "So I like, kept you out?" Ergh, I hadn't meant to sound so … valley girl.

"Yes, I could not break down your inhibitions. But everything changed once I had a vision of the battle. I knew at the point that Gwynn stabbed you, your barriers would be down long enough for me to pull you back, so I did."

Then it was Mercedes who'd saved me? That was twice now. If I hadn't liked her before, I loved her now. But warm and fuzzies didn't explain why she'd brought me back. "Why did you relocate me here, to this time?"

Mercedes stood up and sighed deeply, walking to my window as she took in the view. "As with the laws governing nature, there is a path we must take in the present to create an intended outcome in the future."

"What does that mean?" I demanded. "Why was it so important for you to pull me back to this time?"

She faced me. "Your fate and my own require us both to return to the battle."

"Your fate?" Why did it suddenly feel like there was more to this story than I'd previously imagined?

"Yes, I am coming with you."

I stood up, half in shock. "So that's why you brought me here? Not to save me but because you … needed me to give you a ride into the future?" I couldn't think of how else to say what I was feeling and didn't mean for the words to sound so … dumb.

"I brought you here because providence dictated it. If you and I do not travel back together, I will be murdered in less than a fortnight and will not be able to end this foolish war between the Underworld creatures."

"Murdered?" I repeated. "Who … who kills you?"

"Lurkers," she said and there didn't seem to be any emotion in her voice. It took my frazzled mind a moment or two to fully grasp her response. Lurkers … then I remembered. Lurkers were human half-breeds, caught between vampires and humans. They had been killing the otherworldly little by little for hundreds of years. But since relocating to England and being so involved with the war with Bella, I'd pushed concerns about Lurkers out of my mind.

"They kill you?" I whispered. Mercedes just nodded. "So how are you here now if they've already killed you in the past?"

"I simply repeatedly relive the time before my death."

"You mean, like reliving the same day over and over?"

Mercedes shrugged. "Something similar, yes. Though not just one day. I can relive any of my nine hundred years."

"Nine hundred?!" I gasped. Damn, she gave Sinjin a run for his money. He was just a baby at six hundred. I calmed myself down and tried to grasp the facts, tried to understand how what Mercedes was telling me was possible. "So how do you really know you'll die if you haven't lived to that point yet?"

"A vision," Mercedes answered succinctly. "And I do not care to test it." She smiled broadly and I smiled back. Touche.

As if the proverbial lightbulb went off over my head, it suddenly dawned on me as to why Mercedes had first seemed so familiar. Her voice pulled at some latent recollection deep inside me. "Your voice," I started, still in awe. "I knew I'd heard it before but couldn't put my finger on how. Now I know. It was when I was battling Odran's fairy, Dougal, and I was dying. I heard your voice, you saved me."

She faced me and shook her head, dropping her attention to her small hands. "I did not save you, Jolie; I merely gave you the positive reinforcement you needed to find your own magic."

I didn't know what to make of that. All this time, I'd thought it was someone else's magic that had saved me. But it had been my own all along. Maybe I was more powerful than I'd ever imagined. The thought pleased me, made me proud to be who I was, not to mention what I was.

I glanced at Mercedes and noticed she was just watching me patiently, allowing me time to come to terms with everything she'd said. And man, was there a lot of it. But somehow I couldn't get past Mercedes and her powers. This was the first I'd ever seen a rainbow aura and I'd never heard of anyone being able to time travel. Suddenly, something occurred to me. "Are you the prophetess?"

She laughed and her voice carried through the room like an echo. She walked back towards me and I sat down on my bed again, feeling like I needed to sit in order to let everything sink in.

"I have been called many things throughout the ages. Prophetess seems to be the most recent."

"Oh my God," I started, dumbfounded. "The prophetess is real."

"Quite so."

I shook my head, as if to clear any residual delirium. There *was* a prophetess and she just happened to be standing in front of me. Wow, Mercedes was the real deal. "So all that time that Bella had me searching for you to bring you back to life again, I couldn't find you because you were never really dead."

"Yes."

"How did Bella know about you?"

Mercedes's eyes narrowed. "I do not know. Perhaps lore that had been passed down through the centuries."

I nodded, I guess it made sense. I mean, Bella really had no clue whom she was searching for and had me trying to bring back some old bag twice who had nothing to do with the prophetess. It was sort of funny, actually. But I didn't have time to focus on Bella.

"Okay, getting back to business, how are we going to send me, er, us back?"

Mercedes's lips formed a straight line. "Unfortunately it is not quite as easy as you make it sound. Sending us back will require the magic of more than just you and me."

"But how were you able to bring me here?" I demanded, refusing to accept the fact that getting back to my own time was going to be difficult. Mercedes was the prophetess; how could her magic be limited?

"As I said before, your magic guard was down, otherwise I would not have been able to reach you at all." She shrugged. "Incidentally, even with your magic defenses down, it took an inordinate amount of my own magic. It took me all night and well into the next day to recuperate. I simply cannot break through your barriers alone."

"Then who can?" I asked immediately, half guessing what her response would be as my stomach started to sink.

"We need Rand, Jolie. We require his assistance."

I shook my head. Yep, I figured Rand would enter into the equation. Dammit! "He hates me."

She smiled but the smile didn't quite reach her eyes. "He distrusts you, which is natural to his disposition. You must win him over, Jolie."

I sighed, thinking how futile her suggestion was. Rand had already demonstrated that he wanted nothing to do with me and worse, was probably devising ways to get rid of me. "I've tried and failed. I don't know what else to do."

Mercedes sat next to me again and patted my knee, as if realizing I needed reassurance. But what I really needed wasn't reassurance, it was a time machine.

"We require the assistance of two people who know you in this year and who knew you in your own time."

Great, I was going to be stuck here forever. It was hard enough to woo Rand to my side but now I needed one other person? Looked like it would be the loony ward for me. I felt tears welling up in my eyes and I dropped my head, trying to subdue them. "Rand is the only one who knows me from both times," I whispered.

"Are you certain?"

Then it dawned on me. Rand wasn't the only one who knew me. I glanced up at Mercedes, my eyes wide. "Pelham?"

Mercedes shook her head, dashing my hopes into tiny shards of frustration. "I'm afraid both parties must be of the magical persuasion."

My shoulders slumped forward as the tears returned. This time I didn't hold them back, letting them fall freely down my cheeks. "Then I'm going to be stuck here forever. There is no one else."

Mercedes stood up, giving me an expression I couldn't read. "We must return to your own time, Jolie, and we must do so quickly."

"Look, I want to go back just as much as you do," I snapped, wiping the tears from my face.

"Then find the two people who knew you in your time and know you in this one."

I nodded dumbly, still feeling sorry for myself. Mercedes offered me a raised brow expression and I couldn't help but find amusement in the fact that she was like the chief of all witches and dressed in the outfit of a scullery maid. "So why are you a maid?"

She laughed. "I am not truly a maid. I had to ensconce myself in Pelham Manor, Jolie, to ensure that I would be here to save you when you came through. This was the easiest persona to assume." Mercedes approached me and squeezed my shoulder reassuringly. "Tonight Rand will venture into the woods. It would behoove you to follow him." Her tone let on to the fact that she wasn't going to reveal any more than that. What was it with the magical that they felt the need to riddle like the sphinx?

"Okay," I didn't know what else to say before thoughts of the forest led to thoughts of the fairies which, in turn, brought me to thoughts of Mathilda. I faced Mercedes in shock. "Mathilda! She's the second person who knew me in my own time and could know me in this one."

Mercedes just smiled and I stood up, staring out my window and feeling as if the weight of the world was on my shoulders. And really, it was.

EIGHTEEN

It was pitch black outside, the moon eclipsed by thick and unyielding clouds until its glow was no more than a haze. I'd have to use my magic to enable night vision. I closed my eyes and concentrated on my pupils dilating, allowing my magic to penetrate them. I blinked and everything was tinted an eerie green. Now I had to turn to more important matters, such as finding out where the hell Rand was.

I'd followed him outside into the freezing darkness after playing lookout from my window for forty-five minutes. I finally caught sight of him stealing away from Pelham Manor and checking behind him more than once to ensure no one had followed. Then he disappeared into the forest. In my rush not to lose him, I'd nearly tripped over myself to get down the stairs and out the back door. Now here I was, with no Rand in sight, just the outline of a myriad of trees, their skeletal branches swaying in an icy breeze.

I hurried past the tree line, looking left and right, hoping to catch a glimpse of Rand. I faintly made out the image of a man in an overcoat as he disappeared behind a tree to my right. It was Rand, less than a hundred feet away. I paused behind a giant willow to allow him more of a lead, and when it looked as if I might lose him again, I started forward. Why was he venturing so deep into the forest? Didn't he know he could access Mathilda's from any nearby tree?

My footsteps made a sloshing sound as I moved through the snow. A twig snapped underneath me and two crows scattered from the tree overhead, squawking their displeasure. I dove behind a maple tree, holding my breath. Silence settled around me. After another few seconds, I dared to peek out from my hiding place. Rand was gone. Dammit! I surged forward, leaping over a fallen log, my heart pounding. I couldn't lose him! Too much depended on me reaching him, convincing him that I was as much a witch as he was. I ran for maybe a minute or so, glancing frantically from left to right but found nothing. It was as if he'd disappeared into thin air. Then it occurred to me that he'd probably already found whatever tree he was searching for and was now inside Mathilda's village. Dammit Dammit!

Before I could further ponder that idea, I was suddenly crushed by an incredible weight that pushed into me and knocked me over. I landed on my ass and before I could get up to defend myself, someone thrust himself on me, pinning me to the ground.

"Let me go!" I yelled.

"What the bloody hell?" Rand demanded, once he recognized me. "I mistook you for a man."

It made sense considering I'd magicked myself into a pair of comfy jeans, a turtleneck, and a sheepskin jacket. I probably looked like a lumberjack.

I didn't answer because I was trying to wiggle out from underneath him which proved impossible. Straddling me, he held my arms to the ground and appeared as though he wasn't going to release me anytime soon.

"Why are you following me?" he demanded.

"I'll explain if you get off me."

He narrowed his eyes. Then, apparently realizing I posed no threat, he let go of me and stood up, dusting the forest debris from his waistcoat and vest. He didn't offer to help me up but I wasn't expecting it. I stood and took a deep breath.

"I'm following you because I need your help."

"This again?" he grunted, running his fingers through his hair and freeing a few dead leaves in the process.

"Yes, and since you still don't believe I'm a witch, I'm going to prove it to you."

Boredom etched his features. "Amaze me."

Okay, he'd asked for it. I braced myself, placing my feet a shoulder's width apart and raised my hands up, palms facing skyward. Then I closed my eyes and envisioned a series of energy orbs of all colors emanating from my hands. When I opened my eyes, the orbs sailed up into the sky, in green, blue, red, pink, and purple. They morphed into various ovoid shapes and circled Rand's head, whose eyes narrowed.

"You could be a master of guile," he said with tight lips.

Hmm, maybe he meant a magician. "You've got to be kidding." But his expression said he wasn't. Not by a long shot. Crap and a half, he was stubborn.

I frowned and the energy orbs dissipated into nothing, exploding with tiny pops. I placed my hands on my hips. "Okay, then what about this? You seek the council of Mathilda, one of the oldest fairies and you are on your way to her village right now."

He moved a few steps closer to me and grabbed the lapels of my jacket, pulling me to him until we were nose to nose. My breath caught in my throat as I inhaled the spicy scent that was uniquely his. He just glared down his nose at me, close enough to kiss me. "How do you know this?"

My lust collapsed into irritation as I realized I'd already explained the whole witch deal to him more than twice. At what point would he believe me?

I pushed him away and smoothed my lapels back into place. "How many times do I have to tell you? I'm a witch."

"And your connection to Mathilda?"

"Mathilda was one of my fairy teachers along with Gor."

His eyebrows arched at the mention of Gor but he didn't say anything. Maybe he hadn't completely bought my story, but at this point, I didn't care. I was more interested in testing whether or not my open invitation to Mathilda's village was still in effect. I approached the nearest tree, an oak, the trunk of which was easily the width of a car and placed my hand on it, closing my eyes as I envisioned Mathilda's village.

"What are you doing?" Rand demanded.

I didn't open my eyes. "If you won't believe me, maybe Mathilda will."

I opened my eyes when I felt a switch in energy, as if a breeze had just blown right through the trees and into another dimension. The snow-covered dirt path to Mathilda's village lay before me and I glanced back at Rand who regarded me with even more suspicion than he had before.

"How did you know …" he started.

"Really? This is getting old, Rand."

He grabbed my hand. "How can I be certain you aren't here to hurt Mathilda?"

New, er, old Rand was really starting to annoy me. "I guess you'll have to take my word for it."

I pulled away from him and took two steps forward but he easily caught up with me. I didn't say anything and instead, focused on the cottages that lined the snowy path. Mathilda's village hadn't changed at all in over one hundred years, the whitewashed cottages still occupying their same places along the dirt path. Enormous flowers of every persuasion lined the road, dusted with white flecks. The smell was just as sweet as it always had been—something between lilies and roses, refreshing in the arctic air.

When we reached Mathilda's door, Rand grabbed my arm and pushed me behind him, cautiously knocking. So he still didn't trust me and wanted to protect Mathilda. Okay, that was understandable. She opened the door and upon seeing me, her smile vanished. She faced Rand angrily.

"Why have you brought a stranger?"

I took a few steps forward, still blocked from Mathilda's doorway by Rand. "I'm not a stranger. I'm Jolie Wilkins and I'm a student of yours … from the future."

It suddenly struck me as odd that both the Mathilda and Pelham of my own time acted as though they hadn't previously known me upon our introductions. But they had to have known me, right? I mean, they'd met me in 1878. It was a question for Mercedes.

Mathilda backed away and there was extreme ire in her features. "A fairy village is a secret place, Rand."

"She located it herself, using her palm to open the passage," he answered in a flustered tone.

Mathilda's body suddenly glowed with blue light and I realized she was protecting herself. "I'm not here to hurt you or anyone else. I'm here because I need your help and Rand's," I said, attempting to get around Rand but he side-stepped me and grabbed hold of my arm.

"She should not be here," Mathilda said in a scolding tone.

And that was enough for Rand to turn around and push me away from the door, his anger billowing out of him as his aura raged purple.

"Wait, Mathilda!" I screamed, desperate to get them to understand.

Mathilda said nothing but her lips were drawn tight. She didn't trust me either—son of a … As Rand grabbed me, set on getting rid of me, an intense heat broke out on the V of my neck, a sting like an insect bite. I grasped the amber amulet Mathilda had given me. Of course! Now it made total sense as to why the Mathilda of my time had entrusted it to me.

"Wait!" I screamed again and yanked the pendant from my neck, breaking the chain as I held it up in the air. "I have your amber amulet."

Mathilda's gaze fell on the object in my hand and her eyes widened, her mouth dropping open. "Rand," she said in a constricted voice and he released me. I glared back at him and edged closer to her, holding the amulet out as if to remind her not to turn on me again. When I was right in front of her, she opened her palm and I dropped the amber into it.

"How did you get this?" she demanded.

"You gave it to me when I was in my own time because you had seen me with it in a vision. You told me to carry it with me into battle."

"Battle?" she repeated.

Rand shoved his way between us, still playing protector. "Mathilda, what is it?"

She faced him. "It is my amber pendant given to me centuries ago by the only … man I ever loved. It is the only object I possess which means anything to me."

Wow, the modern Mathilda had loved a man? Hmm, sounded like a chapter for another day, not a stressed out, I-need-to-get-back-to-my-own-time day. Mathilda continued staring at the pendant until something made her withdraw into her house. Hurrying into her kitchen to open a drawer, she searched for the amulet and when she came up empty-handed, she had to face the fact that I was who I said I was.

"Come in," she said with a gentle, apologetic smile and held the door wide.

Rand's perturbation was evident as he ran his hand through his hair and stood in the doorway, watching me settle myself at Mathilda's tree stump table. "How do we know she is who she says she is? Amber is plentiful."

"No," Mathilda shook her head. "Not this one." She glanced down at the pendant in her palm and closed her fingers over it. "This belongs to me."

Rand shut the door behind him and though Mathilda took a seat at the table next to me, he remained standing. Mathilda smiled and reached her hand out to grasp mine. "You said you are called Jolie?"

"Yes," I nodded.

"Tell me about this battle," she began.

And I told her about the battle, about Bella, about nearly being impaled by Gwynn's blade and ending up freezing in the snow, in 1878. Pretty soon that recollection necessitated others and after two hours, I'd told Mathilda and Rand my entire life story, starting from the moment Rand had walked into my tarot-reading shop and changed my life forever.

As I explained, Rand's face didn't change. He maintained a placid, poker faced expression that prevented me from reading his emotions. And I still couldn't tell whether or not he believed me. But at least one thing was clear, and that was Mathilda did believe me, which was a huge relief. If I could win over Mathilda, I could win over Rand. Of that I was convinced.

"So that brings me to where we are today," I finished. "Mercedes told me I must find two people who knew me in my own time and who know me in this one and those two are you and Rand."

"Ms. Berg is a witch?" Rand scoffed as Mathilda stood up and entered her kitchen, reaching into a cupboard and taking out three clay cups. Her hand hovered over each cup and in response steam rose up from each one. She brought them to the table, offering one to Rand and me. I inhaled what smelled like chamomile tea and took a sip, relishing the heat of the liquid as it warmed me from the inside out. Then I turned to respond to Rand regarding Mercedes. I was really getting sick of him and his inability to believe anything I said.

"Yes, she is," I said simply.

"Not only is the prophetess real but she lives in Pelham Manor, as an unassuming housekeeper," Rand asked with a great show of sarcasm.

Tears welled in my eyes as I faced Mathilda. "Why won't he believe me?"

Rand pounded his fists on the table, anger burning in his eyes. "Because nothing you have said can be proven. Yes, you know about Mathilda and yes, I believe you to be a witch, but that is not to say you do not have evil intentions, that you are not here for reasons you have failed to reveal."

"But my amulet," Mathilda started.

"She could have stolen it from you, Mathilda," Rand said while I swallowed hard. "Nothing she has said can be tested, none of it can be proven. Are we to endow her with our blind faith?"

"It's true," I demanded and stood up, approaching him. "It's all true but you are so freaking stubborn, you refuse to see it."

He took the two steps between us until we were only an inch's width away. "I do not trust so blindly."

"Children," Mathilda said, rising as she pulled Rand's arm, forcing him away from me. "This situation is easily resolved."

"How so?" Rand demanded, never taking his eyes from mine.

"By way of magic," Mathilda answered.

"Can you perform a Liar's Circle on me?" I asked. Why hadn't I thought of this before? Rand tended to make my sense of logic and reason dissolve into heated anger or intense lust.

"I can do one better than that," Mathilda said with a smile before facing Rand again. "Rand, if you consent, I will cast a charm on you that will not only prove if our mysterious guest is telling the truth, but it will also allow you to feel the emotions you possess toward her in her own day."

"I do not understand," Rand started.

I couldn't say I fully grasped the concept either, but thought we should give it a shot. What other choice did I have? "You mean you can make this Rand know me in the same way my Rand of my time knows me?"

Mathilda shook her head. "No. Magic will only allow me to enable Rand to feel the emotions that the Rand of your day feels towards you. He will not have the memories associated with those feelings but he will have the feelings all the same. If the Rand of your time did not trust you, those feelings will be passed to Rand now."

"I will feel the emotions of myself in the future?" Rand asked.

"Yes," Mathilda responded.

"I do not see how that will prove whether …" he started.

"If she is telling a falsehood and you do not know her in the future, you will realize that based on your feelings towards her. You will not have any. Similarly, if she wronged you in the future, you will know it based on your emotions towards her now. And if she is telling the truth, you will know that as well."

"Why can't you just recreate his memories?" I asked.

Mathilda shook her head. "That is beyond the scope of my magic, child."

Okay, well this was second best. If we could instill within Rand his feelings towards me, it would make this a hell of a lot easier. More than anything, I needed him to trust me and it sounded like this charm would do exactly that.

"I'm game," I said and faced Rand who was studying me with a strange expression.

"Rand?" Mathilda started.

"Very well," he said indifferently.

"Please have a seat," Mathilda said and we both watched him try to accommodate his large body into the small chair. I stifled a smile as Mathilda sat down next to him and took up one of his large hands in her own. "Jolie, please take his other hand."

Rand refused to look at me but I didn't care. I sat down on the other side of him and picked up his hand. There was no shock of electricity coursing through me, something I'd become accustomed to every time Rand touched me. Maybe he was too young a witch to have mastered the energy exchange. I watched Mathilda close her eyes.

"Do I need to do anything?" I asked.

Mathilda shook her head. "No, stay connected with your hands so we can establish the link between you both. I will handle the rest."

I just nodded and glanced around the room while Mathilda chanted something undecipherable, her mouth twitching with the effort. I brought my attention back to Rand and found he'd been staring at me all along. And when I faced him, he made no motion to drop his gaze, but just studied me intently. I lost the stare down and felt as if I couldn't bring my eyes back to his, afraid I'd wither underneath his stringent gaze.

Suddenly Rand's grip tightened and I looked up to find his eyes fastened tightly shut. He was trembling and I had to hold onto his hand with both of mine to ensure he didn't pull away. I glanced at Mathilda and noticed she was doing the same thing, holding his other hand in both of hers as she recited the chant.

I didn't want to say anything, afraid I'd break Mathilda's concentration, but Rand was shaking so much, it seemed like he was having a convulsion. His eyes remained shut tight and his face was bereft of emotion. It was like he was undergoing a shock from the outside in. Then, before I could think another thought, Mathilda opened her eyes and dropped his hand.

"It is done."

I glanced at Rand and noticed he'd stopped shaking but his eyes were still clamped shut and he appeared to be sleeping. I dropped his hand and glanced at Mathilda. "Is he okay?"

She nodded. "Awake, Rand."

He opened his eyes and studied Mathilda for a moment or two, confusion in his gaze. Then his eyes moved to mine. "Jolie?"

I smiled and felt the hot sting of tears in my eyes. "Yes, Rand, yes it's me. Do you remember me?"

"He won't remember you," Mathilda said. "It is all emotions he is feeling towards you."

He stood up suddenly and grabbed his head as if it were throbbing, his eyes never leaving mine.

"Rand," I started and stood.

He shook his head and moved away in the opposite direction, leaning against the door as his chest heaved with his exaggerated breathing. He reached for the doorknob and turned it, without glancing back at either of us. "I … I must leave."

I started after him but Mathilda grabbed my hand. "Let him go," she warned.

"But …" I started, feeling my stomach sink as Rand disappeared out the door and the frozen darkness chilled Mathilda's house. It hadn't worked! Tears began in my eyes as I swallowed my frustration.

"He is confused and needs to be alone to understand what has happened to him, child," Mathilda said. "He is overcome with emotions he does not understand."

"Then the spell worked?" I asked as I wiped my tears away. Suddenly, it occurred to me that maybe Mathilda still didn't trust me. I mean, it didn't appear that Rand's feelings towards me were good ones.

"I would say it did."

"And do you believe me?" I asked. Mathilda merely nodded with a sweet smile. Well, at least I had Mathilda on my side, even if Rand hated me just as much as he had.

~

In his usual form, Rand disappeared for the whole of the next day and I was left not knowing what to think. Had Mathilda's charm worked? She certainly thought it had. But if it had, what feelings did Rand harbor towards me now? I mean, his actions didn't seem like those of someone who had amorous feelings for me in any way. Hmm, so what did that mean regarding modern Rand's feelings for me? It was a question I didn't want to answer.

"Jolie?" It was Christine's voice, accompanied by a timid knock on the door. I sighed and pulling it open, pasted on a fake smile.

"You will be late for dinner," she started, smiling shyly. "And we have company."

"Company?" I repeated, following her.

"Yes, the Furvishes have come to dine with us."

I remembered the name Furvish from the harvest festival Christine had told me about when she'd first met Sinjin. At the thought of Sinjin, a deep hollow feeling engulfed me, as if my stomach were as empty as a dry old well. I suddenly felt dizzy and had to catch my balance against the banister.

"Are you alright?" Christine asked and reached out, as if to prevent me from fainting.

I nodded and closed my eyes to dam the surge of tears that were just waiting to escape. *I would get back home. I had to get back home.* Once I'd regained control of myself, I opened my eyes, giving Christine an apologetic smile and we started down the stairs. Christine reached for my hand and held it tightly in her own as we entered the drawing room.

I first saw Pelham sitting on a settee, conversing with an older woman beside him. Rand leaned against the fireplace mantel, resplendent in dark brown breeches, a matching waistcoat, and shiny, knee-high black boots. I felt my stomach start to ache. I loved this man, whether in my own time or now. I loved him and yet it appeared as though he still didn't know me. And as if that weren't awful enough, he was smiling warmly at a young, beautiful woman which gave me cause to throw up.

Her black hair was arranged into a heap of perfect ringlets, complementing her long, graceful neck and piercing blue eyes. Upon our entrance, she looked up at us indifferently. I noticed Rand feigning extreme interest in the crackling fire. The woman's eyes darted from Christine to me as she looked me up and down, as if trying to detect my social status. She smiled so maliciously, she might as well have stabbed me.

I returned the smile, taking in her white billowing skirts and bodice, trimmed with baby pink lace and bows until it looked like a cupcake complete with white frosting and pink sprinkles was in the process of swallowing her whole.

"Miss Wilkins," Pelham announced without rising. Hmm, he was getting sicker. I wanted to help him, to heal him, but I knew deep down that I couldn't do it. It wasn't my decision to make.

"Mr. Pelham," I said with a smile as Christine accompanied me into the room.

"It is my pleasure to introduce to you Mrs. Furvish," Pelham continued while the older lady offered me the same rotten smile her daughter had.

"I understand Mr. Pelham found you in the snow?" she asked, her nasal tone as frosty as the falling snow outside. Her dull grey hair was pulled into such a tightly strained bun, she appeared to have a receding hairline. Her eyes were the same shade of dull steel and too close together. With her hooked nose and beady eyes, she looked like an eagle. It was impossible to see what her figure was like considering the layers of garments she wore compared to those of her daughter. The only difference was her choice of colors: lilac and baby blue.

"Yes," I said, smiling broadly and amused by the fact that I'd figured out this charade in less than five seconds. Mrs. Furvish was desperate to see her daughter wed and both she and her daughter had their eyes on Rand. And as for Rand? Hmm, I couldn't tell what he was thinking … as usual.

"This is my daughter, Victoria," Mrs. Furvish interjected and the pink and white cupcake offered me an insincere curtsey, to which I offered another apathetic smile.

"Dinner is served," one of the Georges announced, so formal and stiff it was as if he were walking on stilts.

Rand approached Pelham, offering his arm and not even glancing in my direction. Apparently, the task of convincing him I was a witch was going to be even more difficult than I'd imagined. I followed the others into the dining room and wasn't surprised to see Victoria seat herself beside Rand while her mother occupied the chair on his other side. Pelham sat at the head of the table and Christine and I sat opposite Rand and the Furvish doilies.

George ~1 (I believe) entered the dining room carrying a silver-domed tray and laid it on the table, proclaiming, "For your first course: potato croquettes, pigeons a la Duchesse, French beans, and claret."

Thank God animal heads weren't on the menu. I watched the Georges fuss and fidget around the table, while Victoria Cupcake fingered her ringlets, cocking her head in completely unnatural angles, and laughed a high-pitched ringing sound. It was a wonder she wasn't summoning all the dogs in the area.

And Rand? Hmm, I still couldn't read him. Despite his smile and amity, he didn't seem smitten, and he certainly didn't eye drool all over Victoria the way she did over him. Course, in 1878 he was a completely different person so who knew what he was really thinking.

"Please do tell us more about your mysterious guest, Mr. Balfour," Victoria started, smiling up at Rand before glancing at me, her expression souring as if she'd just gotten a whiff of vomit.

Rand's eyes met mine but he didn't say anything.

"Our guest is an American," Pelham interrupted.

"From California," Christine chimed in with a pretty smile as she caught my eye. I downed my glass of claret, not concerned with propriety and smiled broadly at Victoria.

"Yes."

Victoria seemed perplexed. "And how did you manage to wind up in the snow out here of all places?"

I tilted my head, trying to mirror the ridiculous angle of hers. "I don't know."

She frowned. "You leave us at a disadvantage, miss."

George refilled my claret.

"I guess I don't have much to say," I offered.

Mother Cupcake glanced at Pelham, her eyebrows drawn into a tight knot in the middle of her forehead. "I imagine our generous host was quite surprised to find a Colonist on the grounds?"

I nearly choked on my claret. "A Colonist?" I laughed. "Really?"

The old woman said nothing as she frowned at me. Her squinty eyes narrowed even more until she looked like she didn't have any eyes at all. Christine thumped my thigh underneath the table but I could detect a smile forming at the corners of her mouth.

The Georges returned and cleared away our untouched plates. I noticed Victoria and her mother had not only refused to eat, they hadn't even bothered to shift their food around to pretend they'd eaten something. Yep, they'd come here with one goal in mind—to marry Victoria off to Rand. I could only wonder if he knew of their ulterior motives.

"For your roast course," George ~2 interrupted. "Partridges with truffles, snipe heads, snipes on liver toast, and champagne."

God, what was it with the Victorians and animal heads? And furthermore, what the hell was a snipe? Well, I soon found out. Snipes were small birds with incredibly long beaks. I reached for my glass of champagne while I watched the Georges make the rounds, serving up our "roast course."

"Do Americans enjoy spirits?" Victoria asked with her shrill tone, bringing attention to the fact that I was quickly becoming inebriated.

I finished my champagne and placed the glass on the table. "I would say so."

She glanced at her untouched food and made a huffing sound. "Well, Miss Wilkins, since you prefer spirits to conversation, perhaps we should address Miss Pelham."

Christine blushed and looked down, not wanting to attract attention. She mindlessly played with the snipe heads as if she were playing finger croquet, avoiding everyone's eyes. "I have been practicing piano, caring for my brother, and amusing myself with Miss Wilkins," she said in a small voice.

"Yes, you must entertain us later with your piano playing, dear," Mother Cupcake commanded. "Miss Pelham really is quite a delight at the pianoforte."

Christine blushed even deeper crimson as her brother offered her an encouraging smile. "Yes, Christine, we would love to hear you play."

Christine just nodded. Feeling uncomfortable, I glanced up to find Rand staring at me. As quickly as my eyes met his, he averted them to his glass of champagne which was just as empty as mine.

"I believe Mr. Sinclair was spotted in town just recently," Victoria said in a casual tone after an uncomfortable silence which only garnered another uncomfortable silence. Christine's attention fell from Victoria's face to her plate where it remained. I grasped her hand underneath the table and squeezed it.

"We're not concerned with Mr. Sinclair," I said in a stiff voice, glaring at Victoria.

Victoria smiled coquettishly at Rand but his attention remained on me.

"Oh? Silly me! I had thought otherwise," Victoria continued. "If I recall, at our last harvest festival, Mr. Sinclair danced with Miss Pelham at least three times."

Hmm, maybe Victoria wasn't aware of what had transpired between Christine and Sinjin ...

"I heard Mr. Sinclair has become something of a pariah in most respectable households," Victoria continued and I realized she was just fishing, hoping to know the real story. So somehow she had found out about Christine's tryst with Sinjin.

Well, despite her aversion to me and her stuffy old goat of a mother calling me a Colonist, when it came to injuring Christine, I wouldn't allow it. I pretended to drop something under the table and closed my eyes, clouding the vision of everyone at the table with the exception of Victoria. She needed to see what I had in store for her.

"Are you ill, miss?" Victoria demanded as I sat up again.

"I thought I dropped an earring."

She frowned as she noticed I wasn't wearing earrings but turned to Rand, offering him a dazzling smile. "Mr. Balfour, when shall we go riding again?"

Before he had the chance to answer, I focused on one of the snipe heads sitting untouched on Victoria's plate and imagined my energy suffusing it, blanketing it with magic. It turned its mini head in the direction of Victoria and opened its beak. It took her a second to bring her attention from Rand to the snipe head as its beak opened up and down, its dried eyes seeing nothing.

"Hi baby," it said in a high-pitched, nasally Brooklyn accent. "Youse gotta kiss for Daddy?"

Victoria gasped and surged from her chair, stumbling backwards. Everyone around the table looked at her askance.

"Daughter, are you well?" Mother Cupcake demanded.

Victoria, realizing no one else could see the talking snipe, dumbly nodded. "Yes, I am well," she said in a small voice as she settled back into her chair, her trembling hands kneading the white linen napkin.

I glanced at the snipe head again and smiled.

"Pucker up those juicy lips!" it said and Victoria clenched her eyes shut, biting her lip. She opened them again, as if to prove to herself that the decapitated bird head wasn't really talking to her.

"Gimme some shugah, baby!"

Victoria pushed herself away from the table and leapt up, tears streaming down her face. "Do you see it?" she demanded, pointing at it in horror.

"See what?" I asked, noticing Rand was staring at me again. There was mirth in his eyes and a slight smile teased his lips. So he'd seen the snipe's antics and my magical buffer hadn't worked on him? Rhetorical question.

"What is the matter, my love?" the old woman demanded, her eyes furious with Victoria's display.

"I ..." Victoria started, grasping her head as if she might faint. "I believe we need to return home, Mother. I am not feeling at all well."

"Shall I call for Mr. Hodgins?" Pelham asked.

"No, no," Mother Cupcake said, waving off Pelham's concern. "She has merely had too much excitement today."

"Don't go, my little coquette!" the snipe head wailed out.

Victoria screamed and tore from the room, her mother right behind her. I turned to look at the rest of the diners and held up my glass, noticing Rand's intent gaze.

"Cheers," I said.

NINETEEN

As I retired that evening, Elsie helped me into my nightgown and assisted me with building a fire then left me to my solitude. I wasn't sure what time it was but I couldn't sleep. I paced back and forth, reminding myself that the dark shadows cast about the room were merely caused by the burning fire and not some demonic night creatures come to spirit me away. Settling at my window, I watched the moon illuminate the grounds of Pelham Manor in a silver glow.

The entire house was quiet, except for the wind rattling the incredibly old windows. Everyone had retired to their bed chambers hours before, after the outburst at dinner. The thought of Victoria and the talking snipe head brought a smile to my face and I couldn't help but giggle.

A strident knock on my door pulled me from my reverie. Christine must have come to gab about Victoria's strange reaction at dinner. But when I opened the door, I wasn't greeted by Christine at all, but a very flustered Rand. He didn't say anything at first; just stood there staring at me. He seemed anxious, running his hands through his hair while attempting to start a sentence and then clamping his mouth shut again.

"Rand? Are you okay?"

"May I come in?" he blurted.

I merely stepped aside, allowing him entrance. He stormed into the room, the epitome of frazzled nerves and frustration. As I closed the door behind us, I wondered if I was about to be reprimanded for scaring the death out of his intended. The thought that Victoria was someone he might be romantically interested in was enough to cause my stomach acids to come up my throat. Luckily for me, they didn't.

I sighed deeply and turned around, only to find him directly in front of me. Before I could speak, he embraced me tightly and planted his lips on mine. His kiss wasn't gentle; rather it was demanding, almost angry. Then, just as quickly, he pushed me away and fisted his hands at his sides, pacing to the window.

Holy crap! I hadn't seen that one coming! It was like I'd just been blindsided by the Rand love train.

"I apologize," he started, shaking his head and dropping his gaze to his shoes as a scarlet blush blossomed along his cheeks. "I should not have come."

He started for the door again but I blocked him. Still startled by his kiss, I was about to reach out to him when he whirled around and clasped his hands behind his neck. Walking back and forth, the sound of his footfalls echoed the frenetic beating of my heart.

"I do not understand it, Miss Wilkins."

"Jolie," I corrected.

"Jolie," he said and finally brought his eyes to mine. "I cannot fathom how it can be so, but whatever charm Mathilda put on me has addled my mind."

"Addled your mind?" I repeated, wanting nothing more than to touch him, to hold him tight and kiss him, to reassure him everything was going to be alright.

He nodded emphatically. "Yes, I cannot … stop thinking about you."

I smiled and it was a smile that was not only on the surface but extended into the depths of my soul. Finally! Finally Rand had reached the realization that I was who I said I was. "Then Mathilda's charm worked?"

"I suppose so," he said and dropped into an arm chair in the corner of the room. "I came to ask you questions to … better help me understand my feelings towards you."

"So Victoria …" I started, about to ask the nature of their acquaintance.

"Means nothing to me," Rand answered. "Truth be told, I am pleased to be rid of her and her nosy mother."

"Oh," I commented, trying to conceal my happiness.

"As to you and me?" Rand began again.

I sat on the end of my bed, my feet only inches from his. "Ask me anything you want."

He looked me up and down, his cheeks flushing. "I should not be here, in your bed chamber alone with you. It is quite indecent of me."

He started to stand up but I beat him to it and pushed him back into the armchair. "It is not indecent where I come from."

He eyed my hand where it rested on his chest. Then he grasped it and glanced up at me. "I do not know what to make of these emotions. I cannot sleep, I cannot think of anything other than you." He sighed. "And my thoughts are quite improper."

I swallowed hard—all my thoughts regarding Rand were improper and always had been.

"Would you describe our relationship in your own time?" he asked, his voice much softer and huskier than before.

I pulled my hand from his chest and inhaled, trying to regain control of my lusty feelings. Now was not the time for such unwholesome thoughts! Rand needed to understand our relationship, but more importantly, he had to understand why I needed him to help send me back. I took a seat on my bed again and nodded. "What would you like to know?"

"Are we lovers?"

His eyes burned as they searched my face, his jaw tight. The question made my stomach drop and goose bumps broke out on my skin. "No, not exactly."

He nodded and leaned forward, resting his elbows on his knees. Raising his face up, he glanced at me again. "Are we in love?"

"Yes." I didn't pause; I didn't have to.

He stood up and paced to the window, dropping his hands so they rested on the sill. His incredibly broad shoulders completely blocked the view outside and the fire cast highlights and shadows across his back. I had to gulp down the sense of foreboding climbing up my throat.

"I am not surprised. What I feel for you … it is most definitely love." He didn't turn around but continued staring out the window, looking like some brooding, Gothic hero.

"I'm sure this has been very hard for you—feeling such strong emotions for someone you don't know."

He faced me and nodded, sighing deeply. "Yes, I am still wondering if perhaps I am mad."

I laughed and shook my head, standing up. Walking over to him, I grasped one of his large hands in mine. "You aren't crazy, Rand."

He pulled me close and traced the outline of my face with his index finger. At his touch, I closed my eyes, remembering the Rand of my own time touching me in exactly the same way. Some things never change.

"Tell me more about us. If we are in love, are we married?" he whispered.

I opened my eyes and found his riveted on mine. "We aren't married," I said, my voice sounding like a foghorn in the quiet room. I preferred the soft cadence of his breathing complemented by the sputtering of the fire.

"And why are we not lovers?"

"You and I have had a difficult history," I began with a small, sad smile. "We've always loved one another but because of the circumstances, we've never acted on our feelings."

"Then I am a fool," he summarized and tilted my chin up. His lips were tender and his moustache tickled my nose. I closed my eyes and melted into the broad expanse of his chest. His hands fumbled through my hair as I opened my mouth to allow his tongue entrance. A groan sounded from within him and he pulled away from me.

"Have we made love?"

My eyes fluttered open and my heart sped up. "We came very close."

"How close?" he demanded and pushed me back on the bed, wedging his body between my legs. Removing his waistcoat, he threw it on the floor and loosened his necktie.

"Very close," I mumbled while unbuttoning my nightgown. A burning had started deep within my belly and was now an all out desire. Was this really going to happen? I couldn't suppress the current of excitement that tore through me. It appeared we were finally going to seal the deal.

He rose up to tear off his white long-sleeved shirt, and I marveled when his bare chest greeted me. Remembering the same smoothly defined muscles peppered with light brown, wiry hair, they could only belong to Rand. Without another word, he lay down on me, probing his tongue into my mouth. I moaned underneath him, wrapping my arms and legs around him as he eagerly sought my tongue. His hands migrated down my side, bunching my nightgown above my waist while his fingers traced my upper leg. Reaching the juncture of my thighs, his fingers moved to the crotch of my panties. I arched up, gasping my pleasure.

"Rand," I whimpered.

He made a throaty sound and raised up, watching my face while his fingers danced over my panties, teasing me ruthlessly. He brought his face to my neck and kissed the distance to my collarbone, steadily descending until he was stopped by the nightgown. He pulled it up, yanking it over my head. If I hadn't noticed the bulge in his incredibly tight trousers before, I noticed it now. I was unable to pry my eyes from it and he chuckled deeply, placing my hand on the crotch of his pants. He rubbed my hand back and forth while taking one of my nipples in his mouth. He sucked and teethed at my nipple while I moaned achingly underneath him. It suddenly dawned on me that if we did have sex, we might bond. But as soon as I felt his fingers on my panties, the thought was lost. He shifted them aside, running his index finger down the length of me. I clamped my eyes shut.

"You are incredibly wet," he whispered, plunging his finger into me as I bucked beneath him.

"I want you, Rand," I confessed

He slid my panties off and spread my legs wide, settling himself between them. The head of his erection perched at my opening. I blinked to find him gazing down at me, love and desire penetrating his stare. My breath caught as he drove himself into me. Gasping at the feel of his invasion, I wrapped my legs around him and he pushed harder into me. Every inch of my being was alive, tuned to the feel of him sliding in and out.

"I have wanted you for so long," I whispered. And, God, was it the truth. Now that the moment had finally arrived, I almost didn't believe it. I felt as if I had to pinch myself out of a dream.

Rand didn't respond but leaned down and kissed me again. It was a kiss like none other we'd ever shared. Our tongues mated as he pushed himself harder and deeper into me. He suddenly pulled out.

"Rand?" I asked, opening my eyes and wondering why he'd stopped.

He gave me a mischievous smile and rolled over next to me. Grasping my waist, he pulled me on top of him.

"I want to watch you atop me," he said.

I grasped his throbbing erection, positioning it barely inside me as I ground my hips in gentle circles, teasing him. He tried to thrust his hips upward but I easily outmaneuvered him.

"Tell me what you want," I said with a smile.

"I want to be inside you."

He sat up to take my nipple in his mouth again, grasping my breasts as I allowed him re-entry. I could feel myself growing wetter, hotter. I was going to come soon, I could feel it.

"I'm so close, Rand."

"Allow yourself," he said between clenched teeth, revealing that he, too, was very close.

I arched up on him and threw my head back, gasping as bliss reigned through me. At the same moment, he grabbed hold of my waist and forced himself in and out of me, before moaning deeply. And then? Then I'm not sure how to explain what happened. It was like an explosion within me, something emanated from the middle of my body and shook me to the depths of my soul. I fastened my eyes shut and screamed in pure shock when I felt a stifling heat flow through me.

I opened my eyes to see Rand's clenched shut. A thin, almost imperceptible white glow slowly emanated from me as the heat in my body flared. I embraced Rand and the intensity of his grip on my waist made me realize he was experiencing this also. We held one another, too frightened to move and just watched the white glow become blinding as it emanated through the room. In a blink, it was gone and we were alone, naked and holding onto one another.

Then I felt like I'd just walked into a wind tunnel filled with thoughts and emotions.

Fear. What happened?

Love. Pain. Sorrow. Loss.

What will become of us? How can I allow her to leave now?

I kept my eyes shut and covered my ears, hoping to force the thoughts out of my head. When I reopened my eyes again, Rand appeared to be experiencing the same thing, his eyes still tightly shut, almost painfully.

"Rand," I said, gripping his arm. "Rand!"

At the feel of my hand on his arm, he opened his eyes and faced me.

I love her.

The thought was clear in my mind, as if he'd just said it. And that was when I realized just what had happened. Rand and I had bonded. It was as obvious as the fact that I was now receiving all his thoughts, all his emotions and likewise, he was receiving mine.

I stood up and inhaled deeply.

"What … what happened?" Rand asked as he stood behind me.

I didn't turn around but just continued staring out the window as I felt his hand on my waist, caressing it. "We bonded, Rand. Do you know what that means?"

"No."

I offered him a small smile. "When two witches love one another, the ultimate show of their love is bonding which means they become one—they can hear each other's thoughts."

He nodded. "I could feel your fear and hear your voice in my head."

"Yes," I said, pausing for a moment as I tried to put all of this into perspective. "Our magic is bonded, as well. We are both more magically powerful now."

There was so much more to explain. I selectively omitted the part about dying when eternally separated from your lover because I didn't want to destroy the mood. And then, it dawned on me. I remembered when Rand told me he'd nearly been killed and driven mad by the death of the one woman he'd loved and whom he'd bonded with ... It was like slow motion as I realized that woman had been me. Even though I hadn't technically died, our eternal separation had been enough to nearly kill him. Mathilda had wiped all the memories of me from Rand's consciousness in order to save him when I had to leave, to return to my own time. The realization was one that brought tears to my eyes and my knees felt as if they'd buckle.

"Are you alright, my love?" Rand whispered while running his fingers down my waist. He lifted my leg up so it rested on the arm chair and I could feel his penis hardening as it lay against my thigh. I blinked the tears from my eyes and leaned back against him, relishing the moment.

"If we are truly bonded," he whispered, bringing goose bumps to my neck, "I want to know your feelings when I am inside you."

I didn't say anything but allowed my tears to flow, knowing I couldn't tell him what would happen—that he would nearly die because of me.

I responded to his finger inside me like a reflex. If there was to be any consolation, it was knowing that Rand would survive our separation; Mathilda would see to it. My breath caught in my throat as he positioned himself to enter me, pushing his shaft within me deep and hard. And sex had never felt like this—I was in his mind, feeling my tightness and wetness surrounding him and he was experiencing my own sensations. We were one, his thoughts meshed with mine, his emotions the same as mine.

When both of us came, our orgasms exploded into one, and I had to stabilize myself against the chair so I wouldn't collapse on the floor. It was a feeling I couldn't even begin to describe—just emotion, raw and limitless.

"I love you, Jolie," he whispered.

~

I awoke to gentle snoring. I tried to roll over but Rand's arm across my chest prevented me. I smiled as I recalled the events of the night before and I'd never been happier—having slept off a night of lovemaking, bonded to the one man I could honestly say I loved more than any other.

"Are you awake?" I whispered.

"I am fast asleep," he muttered, his face pressed against my breasts. He opened his eyes and smiled. "Hmm, but these tempting breasts might be reason to wake."

I laughed and he sat up, rubbing his eyes and stretching. "Good morning," I said.

"Good morning, my love," he answered, planting a kiss on my forehead. His fingers resumed tracing my already perky nipples. "What shall we do to amuse ourselves this glorious day?"

I reclined into the mound of pillows, enjoying the attention he was paying to my breasts. Then I was struck as if by a lightning bolt sent by the Responsibility God, to find Mercedes and tell her I'd convinced Rand I really was a witch. We could get started conjuring up the magic that would send me home. A feeling of emptiness lodged in my stomach as I realized I didn't want to leave Rand.

"We should talk to Mercedes," I said, my voice hollow.

He cocked a brow, his handsome face suddenly serious. "Why?"

"To tell her we can rely on your magic now, in addition to ours." Well, that is if he agreed to help us. I hadn't exactly asked him that. "You will help me?" I inquired doubtfully.

"Assist in sending you away from me?" he asked, his shoulders rigid and his mouth a mere straight line, revealing no emotions. But I could read his feelings like an open book. He definitely had reservations when it came to sending me back. I had to wonder if some of those reservations weren't me just realizing my own feelings.

I dropped my attention to my hands, realizing what I'd just admitted—that I would leave him. A feeling of desperation welled up inside me at the very thought of it. I knew the Rand of my own time would have no recollection of what had happened between us in his past. No recollection of the fact that he'd been bonded to me.

"Yes," I whispered.

Rand looked outside the window and his eyes took on a faraway gaze, as if he wasn't really seeing the scenery outside. "When we were at Mathilda's and you were explaining how it was that Ms. Berg found you in the snow, you said you were in the throes of being … stabbed?"

I nodded, sensing where the conversation was headed. Rand stroked my hair and I closed my eyes, savoring his touch. Was it terribly wrong that I wanted to have him inside me again?

"Does that mean, then," he paused and I realized he'd received my lustful thoughts. His hands toyed with my nipples as he fought to regain his train of thought. "Does this mean you will be thrown into harm's way when you return?"

Since even I didn't know the answer to that question, I did my best to shield him from my own sense of doubt. I wasn't sure if it worked. "When I explained the situation to Mercedes, I told her I needed to return a few seconds earlier to spare me from Gwynn's blade."

Rand's face was stoic, as if chiseled out of stone. He stopped playing with my hair and I was aware his feelings ran counter to wanting to help me, feelings that, instead, wanted only to protect me.

"You do not know for certain the situation will unfold as you wish it to."

"No, not for certain." I shook my head; there was no use in lying. I didn't know what would happen, what to expect. All I did know was that I had to return and that I'd have to take Mercedes with me—to end the Underworld war.

He was quiet for a long minute, and when I tried to read him, I encountered a wall. So he *could* block his thoughts from me. Interesting.

"Can today be ours alone?" he started. "Must you seek Mercedes?"

I shook my head, wanting only to remain here with him—holding him, touching him, loving him. "It can probably wait another day."

He smiled down at me and looped my hair around his thumb and forefinger, wetting his lips with his tongue.

"What did you have in mind?" I asked, my stomach buzzing with excitement.

"I require nothing more than a day with the woman I love," he started before a sinister smile engulfed his face, "in bed."

I giggled. "And what of Pelham and Christine? What will we tell them?"

He shrugged and leaned down, kissing me. I closed my eyes to enjoy every second of him, every inch of his soft lips and the way his sensations to our kiss reciprocated through me. I wasn't sure I'd ever get used to this bonding thing, but it was fun to try.

Rand pulled away and began playing with my hair again. "We will tell them nothing. It is none of their business."

"And when they come looking for us?" I continued, playing devil's advocate.

"They will not," he replied with raised brows and a deep smile. "We will use our magic to prevent them from even thinking of us."

Hmm, didn't sound like a bad plan, actually.

I toyed with the corner of the blanket covering us when it suddenly occurred to me that I'd never gotten the full story regarding Sinjin.

"Rand?" I started.

"Hmm?" he responded, glancing up at me with a smile as his hand found the inside of my thigh.

"What really happened with Sinjin Sinclair?"

The happy expression on Rand's face fell and I almost regretted asking. Rand sighed and pushed himself into more of a seated position beside me.

"Sinjin Sinclair is a vampire," he said.

"Yes, I know."

Rand flashed me an expression of surprise. "You are acquainted with him?"

I nodded. "I've always wondered why you hated him so much."

"Well, there is not much to describe regarding the beginning of our liaison. Sinjin, being the opportunistic bastard he is, desired that he and I should become a team, separating ourselves from the Underworld community. He possessed high hopes of using our incredible strength and powers to force the other creatures, and humans as well, to bend to our rule. As you can well imagine, I refused, wanting nothing to do with him. But rather than leaving the situation well enough alone, Sinjin went after Christine."

"He attempted to seduce her to get back at you for refusing his offer?"

"Yes," he sighed deeply and dropped his attention to the window. He was quiet for a moment before facing me again. "That is all there is to tell of Sinjin."

I nodded, finally understanding Rand's anger towards the vampire. And I couldn't say I blamed him. By every angle, Sinjin certainly appeared the villain. I had to wonder, though, could people change? Or was he, deep down, the same person he always had been?

~

Later that evening, Rand left me to my seclusion. There was a carefree joy inside me that had never been there before—a feeling of fullness and gratification. We had consummated our love so many times I'd lost count, but that wasn't even the best part. Knowing Rand loved me and I loved him, that he'd given himself to me in the way I'd always wanted him to—that was the best part. Even though this wasn't the Rand of my time, it was Rand all the same.

Then, as quickly as the incredible sense of happiness surrounded me, it was eclipsed by extreme sorrow. I had to leave him; I had to return to my own time. And who knew what that would mean—would I be able to escape Gwynn's blade or would I be sending myself back to experience my own death?

I forced the thoughts from my mind. I had to return; that's all there was to it. There was no use worrying about the what ifs.

I stood up and stretched, taking my nightgown off a nearby chair. I pulled it over my shoulders, all the while watching the moon disappear behind the clouds. A glow of light from the ground diverted my attention. Mercedes was right below my window, in front of the grove of elm trees. The candlelight illuminated the contours of her face. I swallowed dryly and sighed, knowing I had to speak with her. All I wanted to do was to curl up in my bed and await Rand's return. Instead, I magicked myself into my lumberjack outfit and headed for the stairs. I met with no one along the way. When I opened the door and walked outside, only the icy cold of the air greeted me. I hurried around a corner, feeling along the stone façade of Pelham Manor.

"I wondered how long it would take you to come," Mercedes said, not glancing up from whatever it was she was doing. She held the white candle in her hand, which dimly highlighted her movements.

I remained standing with my arms crossed over my chest, and watched her draw a large circle around herself in the dirt, using a sword. As she drew the circle, she repeated: "north, south, east, west" followed by "earth" and she scooped up a mound of dirt, allowing it to fall on the ground again. When she uttered the word "water," a stream of clear drops fell from her palm, into the mound of earth. At the word "fire," her candle increased its flame tenfold, only to die down again. And when she said "air," a strong wind blew past us, dislodging plenty of leaves from the elms but never blowing the candle's flame out.

Then she held the candle with both hands and addressed the heavens, closing her eyes. "And the Goddess," she chanted.

Nothing changed with the mention of the Goddess. My teeth chattered as I waited for her to finish, but rather than interrupt her, I just observed. She clenched her eyes tight as she held the candle between both hands. The flame increased in height, then diminished again, as if ghosts were playing with it. Several minutes must have passed before Mercedes opened her eyes again and offered me a smile, blowing the candle out.

"What was all this about?" I asked.

Mercedes dropped the candle into her circle and it disappeared into the earth. She lifted the sword and closed her eyes, as it too disappeared from her grip. "I was calling on the Goddess to advise me when we should attempt our return to your time."

I nodded, unable to shake the feeling of dread. I didn't want to leave—that was now more obvious than ever. I wanted to stay here, with Rand. I hated the idea of leaving him to face his fate, knowing what that would mean—that it would nearly kill him. But I couldn't tell Mercedes. I didn't think she'd understand, especially since my staying in this time meant her demise. Ergh … talk about being stuck between a rock and a hard place.

"And what day did the Goddess decide?" I asked, ignoring my private thoughts for the moment.

"The twenty-sixth of December."

I felt my stomach drop. That was just two days away. I'd only have two more days of bliss with Rand. And then, Poof! It would be over.

"Are you sure that's the right date?" I mean, it wasn't like the heavens had opened up and a little Goddess figure had said: "Yep, you're gonna be gettin' outta here on December 26th."

Mercedes frowned as she destroyed her circle by muddying up the lines with the toe of her shoe. "Yes, I am certain."

"Well, it doesn't leave us much time to practice, does it?" I demanded, hating the idea that I had such little time left.

She shook her head. "This spell does not require practice. It only requires enough magic to make it plausible."

I had no answer for that so, instead, I watched her start walking in the direction of Pelham Manor and followed her, suddenly remembering a question I'd been meaning to ask her. "How is it that Mathilda and Pelham didn't know who I was when I first met them, considering I'd met them in 1878?"

Mercedes didn't glance back, but continued her hurried pace. "When we enter your time, magic will rinse the memories of everyone who knows you now."

I frowned, not completely sure I followed. "So Christine, Pelham, Rand, and Mathilda ..."

"Will not remember you."

"Why?" I asked, my stomach dropping.

"It is too dangerous to allow others to know we can manipulate time. As a precaution, we eliminate that knowledge."

"But Mathilda nurses Rand back to health when he nearly dies from our separation," I started.

"Yes, she does but she does not know the details of who you are. She just knows she must help heal him." She turned to face me, throwing her hands on her hips. "Does Rand know you are a witch?"

"Yes, he believes me now," I answered in a monotone, my stomach cringing at the very mention of it. It was a deep, hollow feeling of incredible sadness.

"And has he agreed to perform the magic with us?" Mercedes continued, glancing back at me as the moonlight reflected off her hair.

She might not like this part. I hadn't gotten Rand to agree to helping us or not helping us. I'd, uh, I'd been too busy shagging him. "Well, I don't know that I've completely persuaded him, but at least he realizes I'm a witch." At her raised brow expression, I felt my mouth run in diarrhea mode. "Mathilda made him feel the same feelings the Rand of my time feels towards me ... so that he would know me. Well, as well as he could know me considering this Rand never met me before." I took a deep breath.

Mercedes nodded. "Yes, I am aware of Mathilda's charm. But he has not agreed to participate?"

It appeared there was no end to Mercedes's omnipotence. I wasn't about to ask her how she knew about Mathilda's spell; I just didn't want to know. "He hasn't agreed to help us yet. I thought it was a pretty big accomplishment just getting him to believe me. Oh, and by the way, we bonded."

She didn't look surprised. "Yes."

"You knew?" Of course she knew. She was the uber witch, remember? Well, uber witch or not, I was suddenly pissed off. "So you knew all along that Rand and I would bond? And you also know that when I leave, it will nearly kill him?"

She stopped walking and faced me with little or no concern in her face. "Rand will not die. Mathilda will see that he survives the ordeal."

That wasn't my point. I didn't like putting him through it to begin with. It didn't seem right or fair. "I don't like playing a pawn in your game."

Mercedes's mouth was tight. "This is not my game and we are all pawns."

I frowned and wished I could bury myself in Rand's arms; I needed his comfort; I needed him. "What do you want me to do?"

"Rand must agree to participate; you must get his word that he will. Then you are to meet at the junction where the elm tree meets the willow at the far north corner of Pelham Manor. You will bring Rand and I will bring Mathilda. We will all meet there exactly ten minutes prior to the dawn of the twenty-sixth of December."

"You mean at 11:50 p.m.?" Hey, I just had to be sure …

"Yes." She started to walk away but came back to me again, taking my hands in her own. "This must be, Jolie. It is the hand of destiny, of the Goddess."

That didn't mean I had to like it and I didn't like it, not one bit. "Who is the Goddess anyway?"

Mercedes smiled and her face reflected the moonlight as her cat's eyes hinted at her incredible power. "She is destiny, she is nature. She is the natural order of things and fate. She is everything you observe around you."

"And she is going to send us back?"

Mercedes nodded.

I wanted to make a crack about the *Flux Capacitor* but refrained.

"Great Scott!" I said with a smile, clearly not able to control myself.

Mercedes just frowned.

TWENTY

Christmas day greeted Pelham Manor with a new blanket of crisp white snow. The house even smelled like Christmas: cinnamon, nutmeg, and clove. And while the season of mirth was upon us, I was not in any sort of mood to rejoice. Not while knowing the next day would rip me away from the only man I loved, was bonded with, heart to heart and soul to soul.

Speaking of whom, Rand had been gone all day. I awoke to find myself alone and now it was just moments before dusk. Tension gnawed at my gut. I still hadn't explained to him the part he would play in sending me back and worse still, that we were planning to attempt it tonight, just before midnight.

"Did Mr. Balfour inform you of his whereabouts?" I asked Pelham, as I strolled into the drawing room.

"No, the sly fox!" he said, somewhat unconcerned. A soft smile lit his pale face. For the first time in days he appeared almost well, as if the season had given him strength. We listened to Christine play "Oh Christmas Tree" on the piano. She sang a lovely rendition of the song in German, "*Oh Tannenbaum.*"

I stood beside the roaring fire and felt like crying. Over the past few days, I had never been happier, never felt like I belonged somewhere so much as I did now. And I was unable to concentrate on anything but Rand and the bliss we experienced while bonding. If soul mates existed, he was mine. But I suddenly missed Christa—she was the one piece that didn't fit into this puzzle. I expected to see her soon enough though, once I was zapped from this reality into my own. Along with Christa, much though I didn't want to admit it, I also missed Sinjin. I missed his rapier wit, his smile, and his friendship. I wouldn't allow myself to miss him more than that.

I sipped my warm *Glühwein*, a German Christmas wine of black tea, orange juice, rum, cinnamon, clove, coriander, and sugar. Smiling down at Christine, I leafed to the next page of her sheet music when she nodded the okay. She looked lovely in a grey, white, and black plaid dress, its collar and sleeves trimmed in lace. A few sprigs of holly decorated her hair.

"I wonder where our Mr. Balfour has disappeared to," Pelham commented from his place on the settee before the fire.

I offered him a warm smile. His health was definitely fading; he became progressively sicker as the days went by, but tonight he was in good spirits.

Somehow, his symptoms made me double guess whether or not he truly had cholera, as his regression seemed too drawn out. I closed my eyes, using my magic to learn what the symptoms of cholera were and was answered with: *intense vomiting, wrinkled hands, and sunken eyes*, none of which Pelham exhibited. Hmm, maybe he'd been misdiagnosed?

I previously decided I wouldn't, shouldn't, and couldn't use my magic to heal him. But now something pulled inside me. The pity I felt toward him wrenched my soul and I couldn't leave knowing I could have done something about it. Smiling at Christine, I walked toward the fireplace, taking a seat in the armchair opposite Pelham. I feigned interest in the fire and imagined healing white light surrounding Pelham, highlighting him in an aura of wellness. I did nothing but concentrate on healing him for a good five minutes, exhausting myself in the process.

After I finished, I melted into the chair and looked over at him to find he'd fallen asleep which was just as well. When he awoke, he'd be a new man.

Just then the front doors swung open, revealing the moonlight which illuminated the now dark sky accompanied by a howling wind. Rand entered the foyer, laden with packages, and Elsie hurried down the hallway, slamming the door shut behind him.

"Happy Christmas!" Rand yelled, causing Pelham to jump about a foot into the air, after which he feigned a heart attack and turned around with a great smile.

"Where have you been, Balfour?"

Rand's hair was peppered with snow, snow which followed him through the house as he carefully placed his packages under the Christmas tree. I smiled, trying to restrain the urge to throw my arms around him and kiss him. But I couldn't do that. Pelham and Christine didn't know about us yet. We'd decided to keep it a secret, since our future was now numbered in hours.

"The *Christkind* has arrived!" Christine said with a laugh as I gave her a puzzled glance. "The *Christkind* in Germany is a plump little angel, very fair, who brings Christmas presents to the children!"

I eyed Rand, noticing nothing *Christkind* about him in the least. Rand looked at me and his dimpled grin made me melt. "Miss Wilkins, you look ravishing, if I may say so."

I blushed profusely as I watched Pelham's shocked expression, his eyebrows reaching for the sky. He glanced at Christine who merely shrugged, wearing a huge smile.

"What has gotten into you?" Pelham inquired.

Rand tore off his overcoat and left it on a coat rack beside the hearth. He stood in front of the fire, rubbing his hands together. "The Christmas spirit, my good man," he answered and faced Christine. "Why are you not playing for us, Christine?"

She nodded and returned her fingers to the piano, belting out "God Rest Ye Merry Gentlemen."

"Are you feeling well, Pelham?" Rand asked.

Pelham nodded slowly, surprise in his eyes. "Yes, I have not felt so excellent in a long while, my friend. Perhaps we can attribute it to a Christmas miracle!"

Rand glanced at me. Hmm, he must have realized it wasn't a Christmas miracle at all but a Jolie miracle. Well, it didn't appear to upset him. Quite the contrary, I'd never seen him so happy. Maybe he'd wanted to heal Pelham himself but didn't have the power to do so?

"Shall we open gifts now?" Rand asked, barely able to contain his excitement.

"Oh, let's!" Christine answered and clapped her hands together like a jubilant child.

Rand nodded, and without further encouragement, he reached under the tree which now overflowed with packages beneath its bows. Rand picked up a promising gift festooned in bright red and green wrapping and handed it to Christine.

"I shall play Father Christmas tonight," he said happily.

Christine ripped off the wrapping and beamed when she saw her new hat. The brim was extra wide and made of straw, topped with a white egret feather attached to a bouquet of pink and white silk roses.

"*Ach, du lieber Gott*!" Christine exclaimed, which meant something like "Oh, my God!" She immediately put the hat on and beamed at Rand. "Thank you!"

Rand returned her smile as he tossed the next gift to Pelham who became the recipient of a pocket watch. Before he could offer his thanks, Rand was busy handing both Christine and Pelham more gifts and searching under the tree for yet another. He finally emerged with a small box which he handed to me. I was surprised, not expecting to exchange gifts in front of the Pelhams. For all they knew, we were still enemies.

I opened the package to find a ceramic bird statue, maybe a finch; its mouth appearing to be in the midst of song. I looked up to thank him but he was still sorting through the packages, tossing one after another to all three of us. By the time he was finished, Christine had received a hat, a riding outfit, the entire collection of Mozart and Beethoven sheet music, and a collection of ceramic cat statues. Pelham had received an assortment of wool scarves (which Rand claimed to have been imported from Scotland), the pocket watch, a gold compass, and a mahogany walking stick that featured a gold handle. I received not only the bird statue, but a silk covered journal, wooden fountain pen, and an emerald brooch. Christine then picked out her presents which she gave to all of us; wool mufflers in a variety of colors knitted by her own fingers.

When it was my turn to play Santa, for Christine I'd magicked my favorite perfume, *Flower Bomb* by Viktor and Rolf along with the entire *Black Dagger Brotherhood* vampire book series by J.R. Ward. The covers alone were suggestive enough to give her a heart attack, so I camouflaged them inside the entire works of Jane Austen. Once Christine opened them, she'd be in for a big surprise! For Rand and Pelham, I'd magicked two huge feather down parkas I remembered seeing in an Eddie Bauer catalog last Christmas. They accepted them suspiciously but soon embraced them once I said they were all the rage in France.

Then Rand faced Pelham with a twinkle in his eye. "Is it time, Pel?" he asked.

"It is," Pelham responded, standing up, while Rand hurried to his side. "I am fine, Rand," Pelham said. "No need to fuss over me. I will retrieve it."

Then he disappeared while Christine and I exchanged surprised glances. When he returned, he held a white box in his hands, maybe two feet tall by two feet wide which was wrapped in a red ribbon. He handed it to Christine, who happily accepted it and untied the ribbon. As soon as she released the ribbon, out came a long-haired, fluffy white and brown cat which meowed at her. With his baby pink nose, he was one of the cutest creatures I'd ever seen. Christine gently lifted him out of the box and I realized he was also the biggest cat I'd ever seen, definitely no lightweight.

"Happy Christmas," Pelham whispered, tears flooding his eyes which he furiously tried to blink away.

"*Ich habe mich in dich verliebt*!" she said to the cat, which meant "I've fallen in love with you!" She kissed his whiskered face before turning to her brother. "*Vielen Dank*, William!" Then she addressed Rand. "Thank you! This is the best Christmas!"

"What will you call him?" Rand asked, smiling with pleasure.

She studied the cat which was busy cleaning her kisses off and purring. "I shall call him Bruno."

One of the Georges burst through the double kitchen doors with a dour expression announcing dinner was served. Pelham, Christine, and Bruno started for the dining room. Before I could take a step, Rand grabbed my hand and pulled me next to him. Pelham glanced back at us, startled. Rand's cheeks flushed.

"We shall be along momentarily," Rand offered.

Pelham shook his head while mumbling something about Christmas miracles and disappeared into the dining room.

Before I could think to say anything, Rand dropped his head and kissed me. I wrapped my arms around him and returned his thrusting tongue, wanting to melt into him. He pulled away from my embrace and reached for his coat which he'd draped over the coat rack. Flakes of melted snow wetted the stone hearth. He fished inside the coat pocket and returned with a small gift, wrapped in silver foil. Shocked, I merely stared at it. Could it be what I imagined it was? No, this wasn't a *Lifetime* special with some farcical happy ending. It was just earrings. Yeah, I'd go with that.

He handed the gift to me and I reached out, accepting it. I tore the paper off, letting the silver foil fall to the ground. Rand lowered himself to one knee at the same time that I flipped open the box to find a ring. It was a brilliant sapphire encircled by white diamonds which reflected the fire light onto the walls, like a prism.

Tears blurred my vision as I gazed from the ring to Rand's hopeful face, suddenly aware what this meant, what he expected. "I love you, Jolie. And I want you to be my wife."

I shut my eyes to stifle the pain that suddenly overcame me. God, if only I could stay with him and play full-time homemaker. If only I could enjoy him warming my bed each night and sharing the rest of our lives together. But I knew it was useless. I couldn't stay here. Not when so much depended on my and Mercedes's return.

"Rand," I started.

He took the ring out of the box and slid it onto my finger. It fit … perfectly. "It was my mother's. And now I want you to wear it."

"It's beautiful, Rand, but …"

He stood up and kissed me again, erasing my concerns with his urgent lips. When he pulled away, his face was flushed. "No more talk of returning to your own time, Jolie. Not when you would be endangering yourself. I simply will not hear of it again."

"Rand …"

"If ever your safety is in jeopardy, that is enough for me to refuse."

"I can't stay here," I protested softly. Rand's attention focused on my hands which he clasped in his. I tightened my grip as I felt new tears rolling down my cheeks. "I have to go, Rand, and I have to bring Mercedes with me. There is too much at stake if I remain here."

"What is at stake aside from your safety if you return?"

I swallowed hard. "Rand, Mercedes will die if we remain."

He gazed with an expressionless face at the fire. He didn't answer but remained staring intently at the flames as they crackled and hissed. Then he turned to me with a face full of pain. "Then we could send her back alone," he started, almost desperate. "I cannot lose you, Jolie."

I shook my head. "Rand, Mercedes is the prophetess and it was my mission to come here and take her back with me. We have a master plan to fulfill and I can't abandon my responsibility."

"What master plan?" he demanded.

"Providence's," I said in a small voice, trying to recall everything Mercedes had told me.

"Jolie," Rand started when Pelham suddenly appeared in the doorway.

"Cripes, old man, are you joining us?"

Rand nodded, but continued to stare at me. "Momentarily."

Pelham returned into the dining room.

"Will you consider my proposal?" Rand asked.

I nodded and marveled at the ring on my finger as it gleamed, representing a life of happiness—the life I'd always wanted. Damn it all, for one moment I'd pretend this could really be. Just for one moment. "Yes, of course."

Rand held out his arm and I ran my hand over the fine material of his sleeve, allowing him to escort me into the dining room. Yes, I'd pretend that Rand and I really could be a couple. That Christmas was truly a time for miracles.

Silver linens covered the table, where a huge centerpiece of red roses, oranges dotted with cloves, and pine boughs dominated. Tall red tapers illuminated the great length of the table which contrasted with the snow plastering the window sills outside and the fire crackling in the hearth inside. It was a Christmas scene to end all Christmases, bar none. I sat opposite Rand, beside Christine, who seemed to be studying us intently. Once she caught sight of the ring on my finger, her grin grew exponentially. She picked up my hand and inspected it, suddenly addressing her brother.

"It seems congratulations are in order," she began while displaying my hand in the air for Pelham to see.

Surprise was his only expression and he thumped Rand heartily on the back, his smile beaming. "Balfour! You are a sly fox after all." He hugged Rand, eyeing me. "You will have the loveliest bride in the all the shires, old man."

Rand regarded me and nodded, his eyes deep pools of chocolate brown. "I am quite aware, Pel, I am quite aware."

One of the Georges interrupted my moment when he flew through the kitchen doors carrying a silver tureen, his brother at his heels with two serving trays. They laid them before us and George ~2 announced, "For your first course: brown Windsor soup, potato croquettes, baked cod's heads, and Negus."

I just shook my head. What was it with the Victorian proclivity toward just eating animal heads? All the excitement precluded me from having an appetite. So tonight, maybe I would be the perfect Victorian lady.

"What is Negus?" I whispered, leaning over to Christine.

"Goodness, do you not drink Negus in California at Christmas?"

"No."

She nodded and held her glass for George ~1 to fill. "It is a mulled wine, mixed with the flavors of Christmas—cinnamon, clove, and nutmeg. Then it is mulled before the fire."

"Oh," I said, comparing it to the *Glühwein*. I shrugged while watching the Georges serve our first course. Pelham lifted his glass of Negus in toast and we all followed suit.

"To another year of success. To the people I love most. To the future joy of both Balfour and Miss Wilkins. Cheers!"

"*Prost*!" Christine announced and took a sip of her mulled wine, glancing at me to see what I thought of it. I swallowed and couldn't say it was half bad—definitely Christmassy. I nodded my approval and she seemed satisfied.

Our second course consisted of roast goose and *bratwürste* with *sauerkraut*. I picked at the food on my plate but had no desire to eat anything. And this time, it had nothing to do with my suffocating corset. I was reeling inside with new emotions I couldn't control. This might prove to be the toughest thing I'd ever have to do—pry myself from the man I loved to return to my own time. Even though I felt sure Rand would survive our separation, it didn't soothe my anxiety. The Rand of my own time wouldn't know he'd been bonded to me. And furthermore, when he did find out, how would he react?

The Georges appeared again, removing our plates from the table only to return with an assortment of what appeared to be desserts.

"For your third course: plum pudding, Bird's custard, Furmity, and mince pies," one of them announced. I'd grown tired of trying to decide which George was which, preferring to just refer to them as the two Georges.

"And the *Bratäpfel,* George?" Christine asked.

"Coming momentarily, Miss Pelham."

Before I even had the chance to ask, Christine leaned into me and explained: "It is a baked apple stuffed with marzipan, nuts, and red current jam."

"Sounds wonderful," I said with a fake smile. I was too preoccupied by the fact that this might be the last time I ever saw Christine, Pelham (alive), and my Rand again.

"I do love a good pud," Pelham announced and encouraged one of the Georges to add a bit more of the Christmas pudding to his plate, something which looked like a dark brown circular block with a few raisins and currants trying to escape. The sprig of holly at the top did nothing to make the pudding appear any more appetizing.

After everyone enjoyed the holiday desserts, with the exception of me, our plates were cleared again and Christine clapped her hands together excitedly.

"Shall I retrieve the Christmas crackers?" she asked.

Pelham nodded and she hurried to the Christmas tree, her skirts swooshing this way and that. She returned with a box from which she handed each of us a wrapped cylindrical little gift, maybe twelve inches long. Each cracker was adorned by a small paper crafted Christmas tree. I watched

Pelham and Rand hold the cracker between each of their hands and copied them.

"Go!" Christine announced and we each pulled our Christmas crackers until they exploded with a small bang and the smell of gunpowder lay in the air. What surprised me were the few gifts that landed on the table after the crackers snapped. I unwrapped a crown and realized everyone was already crowning themselves. Not to be outdone, I unfolded the gold paper crown and fashioned it atop my head. Then I noticed a small slip of paper similar to what you'd find in a fortune cookie.

"What is red, white, and black all over?" Christine read, holding the cracker paper in her hands. We all shook our heads and a smile radiated across her pretty face. "Father Christmas after he has slid down the chimney!"

Suddenly the major event of the evening prodded me out of enjoying myself, and I remembered that I hadn't let Rand know what was going to happen this evening. More than anything, I had to convince him sending me back to my own time was not up for debate.

Rand?

He glanced at me and there was such love in his eyes, I felt myself choking on a sob.

Rand, Mercedes is meeting us tonight, before midnight with Mathilda.

The smile on his face dropped. *Why?*

So we can attempt the spell to send us back.

Jolie ...

I clenched my eyes shut and focused on my shaking hands. *Please, Rand. You must accept this. It is as it has to be.*

You have already decided then? His eyes revealed anger and hurt.

I want nothing more than to stay with you and be your wife but it isn't a possibility, Rand. I love you with all my heart but I must leave. I'm so sorry.

He finished his mulled wine, refusing to look at me.

"Shall we retire to the drawing room to watch the snow fall?" Pelham asked, observing both our wan expressions.

I smiled and stood up. "Yes, that sounds wonderful."

"And shall we sing carols?" Christine suggested.

I nodded. "That sounds even better."

She disappeared into the drawing room and began playing "Away in a Manger" for her first sing-along.

Before I could follow Pelham into the drawing room, Rand grabbed my hand and whisked me aside, closing the dining room doors for privacy.

"Jolie, please tell me you have thought this through thoroughly."

I nodded. "There is no way around it."

"Does my love for you mean nothing?"

I shook my head, biting my lip as tears welled in my eyes. I stared at the floor then clenched my eyes shut, hoping to control my emotions. But I failed.

I opened my eyes as a stream of tears escaped, rolling freely down my cheeks. Rand wiped my cheeks with his fingers and blotted the tears away.

"I feel your agony," he whispered hoarsely.

"I love you more than you'll ever know," I whispered. "But I can't stay with you. I have to return."

He didn't say anything for a few seconds, but pulled me into the warmth of his embrace and held me as I cried, kissing the top of my head. "I understand," he said finally.

I felt a suffocating weight lift from within me and realized I was channeling Rand's feelings. He had let go and was going to allow me to do what I had to do. He supported me and honored my decision even though he didn't entirely understand it.

"Promise me something, Jolie," he started.

I pulled away from him and noted the glassiness of his eyes. "Anything," I whispered.

"You must make the me of your time understand our connection. We are meant to be together; I know it as clearly as I know my own name."

I nodded. "I will do my best. I will tell you everything that happened here, now."

He smiled before kissing me. His lips were so soft and warm. I closed my eyes and relished the feel and taste of him before returning to the drawing room. Even though Christine and Pelham had no idea I would soon be leaving, I had to see them once more, thank them for their hospitality and tell them how grateful I was. I knew I would see Pelham again, as my ghostly friend of Pelham Manor, but this would be a final goodbye to Christine and the thought wrenched my heart.

~

At ten minutes to midnight, Rand and I awaited Mercedes and Mathilda at the junction of the largest elm and willow trees on the property. I was impervious to the freezing night air as I was cocooned in Rand's embrace. Not able to fight my tears, they fell freely.

"I see them," I whispered, observing Mathilda and Mercedes's colorful auras as they shone through the skeletal outlines of the trees. I wondered why Mercedes wasn't covering hers which radiated in a rainbow.

Rand tightened his grip on me and held me closer. As we watched them advance, the sinking feeling in my stomach increased. What if the spell didn't work? What if I could never get back? That very thought that had plagued me only days before, I now welcomed. But one thought I didn't welcome was the concern that Gwynn's blade might kill me.

"Do not think those thoughts," Rand said and I realized I should have been blocking my feelings. It wasn't right for him to know my private worries, not when there would be nothing he could do about them.

"Jolie, Rand," Mercedes said, greeting us.

"Ms. Berg," Rand started.

Mercedes smiled and said, "Please, call me Mercedes." She glanced around, observing the scenery, while she placed her hands on her hips. Nodding, she faced us again and held out her arms, just as a giant sword appeared. It was the same sword I'd seen her use to create her magical circle when last we'd met.

I watched her perform what seemed like the same ritual, outlining a giant circle in the dirt around all four of us. She called to the different directions again, and to the elements of the earth, using fire and water in her incantation. Then she turned to face us.

"Please join hands." We did as we were told. I reached for Rand's hand while Mathilda took my other hand.

"Wait," Rand started. "How can I be certain Jolie will not be in danger?"

I gulped, wondering this question myself.

"There is no guarantee," Mercedes started.

"Then I will not agree to this," Rand said, dropping Mercedes' hand.

"Rand," I started.

"Allow me," Mathilda said and pulled him aside. I couldn't make out what they were saying but Rand's mouth was tight and his body language showed reluctance to accept whatever it was Mathilda was telling him. He finally heaved a sigh and nodded. Whatever Mathilda had told him had worked. He returned to our circle, looking weary—as though he were supporting the weight of the world.

"This will require complete focus and projection," Mercedes resumed. "Rand and Mathilda, the force of the spell will come from you both. Rand, you must channel Jolie's magic through your bond."

And that was when I realized this whole bonding scenario was necessary for the magic to work properly, as Rand never would have been strong enough to perform it alone. It disagreed with me like a bad taste in my mouth and made me feel more like a pawn in the Underworld than I ever had before. Was our love true, real? Or was it just the means to power this charm? It certainly felt real …

Mercedes faced me angrily. "Never doubt the bond, Jolie. It is not something I could have fabricated. It is whole, pure, and cannot be manufactured."

I swallowed hard and nodded, silently happy to hear it.

"Focus," Mathilda said softly. "This will require a great deal of energy and power."

I closed my eyes and tightened my grip on their hands.

"Imagine a portal opening in your mind's eye," Mercedes said, her voice sounding melodic in the still night air. "Direct all your power into that portal, allow it to open and remain open."

Everyone became quiet as we imagined the portal opening, creating a passageway into my own time. After a few minutes, I opened my eyes and saw Mercedes's frown.

"It is not working," she said, eyeing each one of us. "You must put all your energy into making that portal real enough that you could touch it. The spell will not work if we cannot fully commit our intentions into it."

She closed her eyes again and we all followed suit. I pushed myself to the edge, imagining the portal opening wide, imbuing it with my magic.

Mathilda let go of my hand and I opened my eyes.

"She is too strong," Mathilda whispered.

Mercedes nodded and glanced at me. "Jolie, your barriers are stopping us and we cannot break them down."

I swallowed hard. "What does that mean?"

Mercedes heaved a deep sigh, which was something that left me feeling nothing but anxious. When she looked into my eyes again, there was nothing I could read in her expression.

"We must recreate the event in which I was able to break through your barriers."

It took me a second to realize what she meant and when I did, a bolt of despair and panic shot through me. "You mean …"

"We must stab you."

TWENTY ONE

Rand dropped both my and Mathilda's hands and stepped away, all the while shaking his head. "I will have nothing to do with this."

Well, I couldn't say I wasn't thinking the same way. I'd been nearly stabbed once and that was one too many times, thank you very much.

"We are losing time," Mercedes started, pacing back and forth as the full moon highlighted her long brown hair.

"I am finished. I cannot endanger Jolie's life," Rand said, running his hand through his hair in frustration. He moved to stand in front of me protectively, as if sheltering me from Mercedes.

"We will not endanger her life," Mathilda started.

"You?" Rand faced her and his voice betrayed his disappointment. "You comply with this absurdity?"

Mathilda nodded and brought her gaze to the cloud studded sky. She held her hands upward and closed her eyes, looking like some sort of human antenna ... well, fairy antenna. She reopened her eyes and let her hands fall, nodding. "It is the only way."

A cold wind suddenly swooshed through the trees, their skeletal branches swaying with the gusts. The wind howled, chilling us with its icy embrace. I wrapped my arms around myself more tightly.

"Jolie's protective walls are too impervious," Mercedes started, capturing Rand's attention again as she approached us. Her tone was level, informative. "If only we can break through her barriers, our magic will send her back."

"And if we fail to break through?" Rand demanded, holding me firmly in place behind him.

"Then I die," I croaked and stepped out from his protection. The moon almost blinded me with its intensity. It was like the God of Night was shining a spotlight on me.

Mercedes shook her head and it felt as if her eyes were boring through my soul. "Mathilda and I will not allow you to die, Jolie. You must trust in providence. You have a purpose to fulfill which does not include you dying here."

"I hope you're right," I started, wondering if the "fulfilling my purpose" stuff was all true or just a way for Mercedes to get me to do what she wanted. If nothing else, she was persuasive. She should've been a lawyer.

"Does this mean you agree to this insanity?" Rand asked, turning his anger and pain filled eyes on me.

"What other choice do we have?" I answered in a mouse voice.

His smile was as full of sweetness as it was sorrow. He grasped my hands and rubbed the tops of my fingers with his. "We can choose to forget this foolishness and share the remainder of our lives together," he started, his voice soft, lulling. "As husband and wife."

I tightened my grip on his hands, feeling an ache inside that spread like cancer through me. I started to cry and closed my eyes, dropping my attention to the ground in order to get my emotions under control. I didn't want Rand to see me cry; that would be too hard on him. Granted, he could feel everything I was currently feeling so he knew how depressed I was, but I didn't want to add to his pain.

"I want that, Rand, more than anything, but we can't have it here and now," I whispered. "We will have it in my own time, though, I promise."

"Jolie," he started.

"She cannot stay here," Mercedes interrupted sternly. "The Goddess dictates that she must return to her present time. Her destiny does not include remaining."

Rand wouldn't look at Mercedes and instead tightened his lips into a straight line, never removing his eyes from mine. I could read his love for me in his gaze like I was reading a book. His feelings surged within me so strong that my heart ached and I wanted desperately to agree to his proposal. He sighed deeply, as if expelling the sorrow building within him, and I knew he had come to accept the situation.

Finally, he addressed Mercedes. "Can you ensure me that your blade will not kill her?"

Mercedes nodded emphatically. "Yes, I can."

Rand shook his head and looked at me again. His smile was warm, sincere. As he gazed at me, he ran a finger down the side of my face. "Then it looks as if I have no choice but to participate."

"Thank you, Rand," I said, rubbing my sleeve against my face to dry away the hot tears that continued to fall down my cheeks. I was afraid and Rand was feeling it too. I trusted in Mercedes, but it was a wary trust as I knew she was only obeying the Goddess's bidding. Did I think Mercedes would lie to us? No. Did I think she had my best interests at heart? I couldn't be sure.

"Jolie," Mercedes interrupted and I turned toward her.

"Yes?"

"When Gwynn attacked you, where were you standing? Can you demonstrate please?"

I closed my eyes and tried to remember. An image of the battle entered my mind like a nightmare and I could see our little alcove, with Sinjin acting as sentry while Rand looked on in shock. I'd been facing away from Gwynn, looking at Rand. At Rand's verbal warning, I'd turned and Gwynn had plunged her dagger. But I'd only ever felt the cold steel of her blade on the surface of my stomach. Why? Because just then, Mercedes had intercepted and saved me. I opened my eyes again and took a few steps away from everyone.

"Rand, you were there," I said, pointing to a space just to the northeast of where I stood.

Rand nodded and with a heavy heart, walked to the location I pinpointed. I turned away from him, closing my eyes as I tried to recreate the scene in my mind, trying not to think of the gaping hole in my heart. Instead, I focused, focused entirely on staging the scene that had nearly killed me. I opened my eyes again and focused on Mercedes.

"Gwynn came up behind me," I said and stood beside her, turning toward Rand while trying to estimate the distance between Mercedes and him. I stepped away from Mercedes and asked her. "Will you play the part of Gwynn?"

She nodded. "Yes."

"I was facing Rand when he yelled to me to turn around and when I did, Gwynn buried her blade into my gut. At least that's what I thought happened but you rescued me before her blade could even penetrate my skin."

Rand's hands fisted at his sides and Mercedes settled her attention on him. "And I will rescue her again, Rand. Nothing to fear."

At the mention of "rescuing her again," I thought I should probably bring up the question of timing once more, just to be sure she hadn't forgotten. "So we will go back to my time with at least ten seconds to spare, right?"

Mercedes faced me and her mouth was tight. "It is very difficult to predict timing."

Not exactly the answer I wanted to hear. "But you were able to pull me back before Gwynn did any damage."

"That is not to say I can do it again."

I shook my head. That wasn't good enough. "So I could die?"

Mercedes's eyes were intense, powerful. "You will not die."

"But how," Rand started, determined steps bringing him closer.

"You must trust in providence," Mercedes interrupted and held up her hand as if to say she'd heard enough and didn't want to bother herself with the messy details. Not waiting for us, she turned around to ponder the scene before her. She took a few steps forward, only to rest her chin on her hand as if considering the best layout for our reenactment. She sidestepped me and then nodded.

"Mathilda, please stand beside Rand," she requested.

Mathilda nodded and approached Rand, holding his hand in her own. She smiled up at him, seeming to say she understood what he was going through, that she was there for him. I could only wonder if Mathilda knew what would happen to him after my departure. Since she was the all-knowing fairy, I imagined she must've been very familiar with what happened when one bonded party was forever separated from the other. Yes, Rand would have someone to look after him, someone powerful who truly cared for him. I was leaving him in the best possible hands.

Mercedes glanced at the moon and I followed her gaze, watching the clouds eclipse the great orb. With the wind blowing through the skeletal trees and scattering the light snowfall that had just started, I had to wonder why I wasn't cold. It was probably my own raw nerves keeping me warm.

"We must hurry," Mercedes said, looking back at us. "Rand and Mathilda, at the very moment I approach Jolie with the blade, you must envision the portal to Jolie's time opening wide. We must time it exactly or it will not work."

Mathilda nodded but Rand said nothing. His face was expressionless but I could feel his pain; it practically handicapped me.

"We will only have one chance to do this properly," Mercedes continued and stood behind me. "Are we ready?"

I nodded and turned away from her, facing Rand. I offered him a small smile and didn't miss the way his eyes filled with tears or how tight his jaw was. I memorized every detail of his face, how young and innocent he looked. How beautiful …

I love you, Rand.

And I you. He closed his eyes and I could see his grip on Mathilda's hand tightening as tears coursed down his face. *I will love you always.*

I gritted my teeth, wanting only to run to him and tell him I wouldn't go through with this, that I would stay with him forever.

But I never had the chance. Instead, my ears caught the sound of snow crunching behind me and I watched Rand's eyes open wide in alarm.

"Jolie!" he yelled, surging forward.

I whirled around at the same instant Mercedes plunged the dagger's blade into my stomach.

~

It was like time was standing still, only to go into fast forward. There was a bright flash of light and then utter blackness. I opened my eyes and blinked against the garish display of moonlight accompanied by the incessant twinkling of stars.

"Jolie!" It was Rand's voice screaming at me.

I turned to him in shock, noticing the familiar standing stones behind him, the cairns beyond the stones. We were back in the alcove of trees; Sinjin was standing there, staring at me. He looked as shocked as Rand. Wondering what the hell was going on, I spotted Mercedes standing just beside Rand.

And then it dawned on me.

Gwynn …

I whirled around and caught only the ire in her eyes, the anger in her tight-lipped expression. Then I felt myself thrust backward as an incredible burning in my stomach overcame me. I glanced down and screamed at the sight of her blade buried in my gut. It seemed like slow motion as I hit the ground.

A cacophony of voices sounded over the pounding of my heartbeat as it reverberated through my head. Rand was yelling, punctuated by the raucous sound of metal on metal and whooping of war calls. The battle still raged around me.

I'd hit the ground hard but never felt it. I was too consumed with the burning in the middle of my stomach. My heartbeat was suddenly slowing. I saw Gwynn standing over me and before I had the chance to do anything, Sinjin leapt on her, his fangs exposed. He tore into her neck like an outraged animal. Gwynn dropped and in an instant Sinjin grasped her by the hair and ripped her head off. Her carcass exploded into ash, her head dangling in Sinjin's grip. A few seconds later her head exploded just as her body had. I pulled my attention from Gwynn's ashes that now sailed on the wind and found Sinjin. His eyes were full of an emotion I'd never seen on him before—pain; it was the look of extreme loss.

And that was when I realized I was dying. Mercedes had lied to me. She'd promised I wouldn't die but it looked like that's exactly what was happening.

I felt the touch of warm, soft hands on my hairline and glanced up. Rand's face met my eyes. He looked like an angel, even with his hair mussed and the dirt mixed with blood that speckled his forehead and cheeks.

"Jolie, can you hear me?" he demanded. Tears fell helplessly down his cheeks, making tiny rivers through the dirt.

I tried to answer but had no voice. So I nodded, suddenly feeling like I was choking. I tried to inhale but couldn't take in any air. Panic started a slow twist up my body, amplified by the feeling of liquid rising up my throat. I tasted hot, metallic blood gurgling out of my throat and dribbling down my cheek into the moist earth below. Breathing in a wispy breath, I felt my lungs filling with liquid, with blood. The panic was little by little fading into oblivion and my eyelids were becoming so heavy.

"No," Rand cried and cradled my head in his lap. His tears flowed unrestrained and I wanted to reach out to him, to tell him it was okay, that I was not afraid. But I couldn't. I couldn't even feel my body anymore.

Rand hugged me tightly. As I lay in the warmth of his embrace, I took one last glance at the battlefield, hating the violence and carnage. Now I would never know the outcome of our battle. My thoughts were interrupted by a woman screaming. She was pinned by a tree behind her and in front of her, a snarling wolf. Her face was familiar. Her long dark hair and wide dark eyes tore at my memory. Anne. I had seen this vision once before, right down to the wolf growling at her. Behind this wolf, another wolf with a reddish coat suddenly leapt up and buried its teeth into the wolf threatening Anne. The creature fell to the ground while the attacking wolf bit into its throat, gnashing its teeth while the wolf bled out and died. The victorious wolf shape-shifted back into a man and I recognized him as Trent, my ex. Anne ran to him and he embraced her.

I couldn't help my smile. I felt a kind of lightweight happiness, the feeling of warmth penetrated me and I knew everything would work out. Just in watching Trent defend Anne, it was enough for me to trust in providence, to trust that everything would go as it had to go. And suddenly, I was okay with the fact that I'd played my part, the fact that I'd been a pawn in a game I'd had no control over. Rand, and Sinjin, were safe. That was really all that mattered.

Rand pulled me away from him and cradled my head between his large hands. I caught the image of Sinjin standing behind him. Blood stained his face and his mouth was set in a tight line. He gazed down at me with love and sadness in his eyes, extreme sadness.

I blinked and Sinjin was gone. He'd disappeared into thin air.

"Jolie?" Rand called. "Use whatever magic you have left and help me heal you."

I wanted to hug Rand and tell him it was okay, that he had to let me go. He knew I was dying—he just couldn't admit it. He closed his eyes and hovered his hands above my wound but it was no good. I was too far gone.

I tried to speak but no sounds came out. Then I attempted to use our mental telepathy but I was too weak even to form the words in my head. I suddenly felt very cold and so tired. I closed my eyes.

"Jolie!" Rand shook me.

I was too weak to fight. Instead, I melted into the black of my eyelids and was suddenly met with a stream of images—my mother's face when I'd fallen off my bike and skinned my knee. My seventh grade teacher. Anderson Lake in Washington State, my favorite vacation spot as a kid. And Christa … Christa in her pigtails in the third grade when we'd met. Christa and I getting ready for Homecoming. Saying goodbye at the airport to my closest friend in all the world.

Then there was Rand.

Rand walking into my shop and introducing himself with his dimpled smile. Rand teaching me to assume the likeness of a fox. Rand slow dancing with me. Rand's lips so soft and full against mine. Rand laughing. Rand sliding his mother's ring on my finger. A ring that was still in the same place.

I could feel the smile spreading across my lips and knew I could let go now. I could say goodbye.

I tried to tell him how much he meant to me, how I loved him and would always love him but no words came out.

~

It was like I'd been wading in the balmiest sea, warm water surrounding me. Then I felt a jolt and was thrust into ice. A bolt of pain shot through me at the change in temperature. The sounds of screams and clanking metal accosted my ears. My head ached as I opened my eyes frantically.

Rand was right above me, tears freely flowing from his eyes. And next to him, Mercedes. Her expression was stoic, her lips tight. Her hand was on my forearm, with a viselike grip.

"Jolie, can you hear me?" she demanded.

I tried to sit up, but Rand held me down. Fear spiraled through me as I felt a scream building from the bottom of my stomach. My stomach … I ran my hand up and down my waist, feeling for the hilt of Gwynn's blade but there was nothing there. My clothes were drenched with wet blood. I searched my stomach for any sign of the mortal wound but only felt my skin raised with goosebumps.

"How?" I started, my voice thick and rough.

"She brought you back," Rand managed, cocking his head in Mercedes's direction while he nearly choked on his tears.

I glanced at Mercedes in amazement. "You reanimated me?"

She nodded and her smile was broad. "Yes. Did I not promise you would not die?"

I had been dead and Mercedes had brought me back to life. The tables had turned. And it felt so strange to be on the receiving end of my talent. Not only that, but to know there was someone else who possessed the same power. The thought struck me like a bolt of lightning and ricocheted through me. I wanted to cry at the same time I wanted to laugh.

"Can you sit up?" Mercedes asked, her attention divided between me and the battle still roaring around us.

I nodded as Rand slid his arm around my waist, helping me into a seated position. Grasping onto my waist, he pulled me back so I rested against one of the standing stones. I took a deep breath and tried to steady my shaking hands.

"I feel okay," I said in a small voice, rubbing the back of my head as I attempted to understand what had happened. The urge to cry overcame me; I had to stifle it in order to not become a blubbering mess.

"Jolie, I need you to focus," Mercedes demanded, pulling my attention from my inner thoughts. "We must bring this battle to an end."

I couldn't help the confusion that warred through me. "End this battle?"

She nodded emphatically, her attention returning to the battlefield again. I followed her gaze and watched bursts of magic light up the dark sky, accompanied by war calls and the agonized screams of creatures dying, cries that raised the fine hairs on my body.

"Yes, you and I will do it together," she started, her attention on me. "I need your magic as well as my own."

She placed her hand on me and Rand grasped it, his expression hard. "Who are you and where did you come from?"

I pulled away from him. "You mean you don't know yet?" I assumed they must have already shared introductions. He shook his head.

"Mercedes is the prophetess," I said in a small voice.

Rand's eyes widened and Mercedes faced him with a small smile. "Hello, Rand."

He frowned and swallowed hard. "You know me?"

I grasped his hand and his gaze followed. His eyes suddenly widened. "My mother's ring?" he started.

I'd forgotten about the ring. But there was no time to explain. "There is so much to tell you, Rand. So much has happened. I barely know where to begin."

"Don't concern yourself with it now, Jolie," he said, shaking his head. "You need to recuperate."

"No," Mercedes interrupted. "She can recuperate later. We must end this battle now."

"H … How will …," I started.

Mercedes squeezed my hand and I noticed she'd already grasped Rand's. She stood up as Rand gathered me in his arms and moved right beside her.

Thunder suddenly deafened the night sky and lightning followed, casting an eeriness onto the battlefield. A thick curtain of rain began to fall, assaulting me with its coldness. I watched the dirt and blood wash away from Rand's face. He caught my gaze and offered me a warm smile.

"You must focus on me, Jolie," Mercedes said, demanding my attention. "I need you to focus your magic and direct it toward me. Rand, you must do the same."

Rand pulled his attention from me and nodded toward Mercedes. I gulped as I wondered if I even had any magic remaining. Guess I'd have to give it an old-fashioned try and see what happened.

"Focus on me, Jolie," Mercedes said, just before she faced the battlefield of Culloden. She closed her eyes while gripping my hand tightly. I imagined a tidal wave of magic growing to extreme heights and widths, power cresting and foaming at the top of the wave. When I couldn't hold the wave of magic back any longer, I imagined it roaring into Mercedes, filling her up.

She kept her eyes shut and tilted her face upwards. With her clenched teeth, it looked like she was in pain. Within seconds a beam of light broke through the clouds and highlighted her face as the rain poured down on her, cementing her hair to her cheeks. But she was impervious to the rain. And the rain was nothing compared to the beam of white light. It was as if the moon were radiating its milky rays to Mercedes alone. The pain in her features softened and she dropped her head back even further. The light penetrated her and after another few seconds, she began glowing—almost as if the moonlight had filled up a reservoir within until she was now overflowing.

Her feet left the ground and she levitated a few feet in the air, eyes still closed. I heard Rand gasp but my attention was riveted to Mercedes. I continued projecting, sending all my magic into her.

She dropped our hands and held hers skyward. Bringing her hands together, the light seemed to move out of her and into her hands until the glare was so intense I had to shield my eyes. Mercedes dropped her head and closed her eyes tightly again. She threw her arms wide and the glow left her, dispersing into a blinding light that ricocheted throughout the battlefield. Rand dropped me and I fell against the ground, but never felt any pain. Rand collapsed right next to me and I reached for him, needing his touch and reassurance. He grasped my hand and squeezed it, offering me a small smile before we both turned our attention to Mercedes again. I tried to stand but I was too weak. Instead I looked out over the battlefield, and noticed that all the warring creatures had fallen as well. It was difficult to separate the living from the dead.

There wasn't a sound and the rain had stopped.

The light emanating from Mercedes's hands went out and she collapsed next to me. I pulled myself toward her and grabbed her hand.

"Are you okay, Mercedes?" I whispered.

She nodded but she was trembling, her face pale. I gazed back out to the battlefield and watched as some of the soldiers started to get up and shook their heads quizzically. None of them reached for their weapons.

"They are getting up," I said, worry lacing my tone.

Mercedes shook her head. "The fighting is over."

"How?" I demanded.

She took a deep breath. "I have taken away their reason for fighting; I have instilled within them the Goddess's message that there will be no more fighting."

I didn't understand, but at the moment, it didn't matter. All that mattered was the fact that I was here … Rand was here … we were safe.

"Jolie, are you hurt?" Rand said, offering me a hand up. I took his proffered arm and he pulled me close to him. I was still too weak to stand and collapsed against him.

I shook my head, a new round of tears starting in my eyes. "I'm okay."

"I thought I had lost you," he whispered in my ear and I could feel his warm tears against my cheek.

I wrapped my arms around his neck and held him as tears began streaming down my face.

"You have been through too much, Jolie. We need to get you somewhere you can rest and heal." He faced Mercedes. "The battle?"

"Is over," she finished. "And now we begin to rebuild."

"Rebuild?" I repeated.

Mercedes nodded and scanned the battlefield again. I followed her gaze and saw all of the creatures of the Underworld caring for their dead. It would be a big job to reanimate the fallen.

"Bella?" I asked, wondering what had become of the witch.

"She lives," Mercedes announced flatly.

"Even though she is alive, is it still over?" I asked in a small voice.

Mercedes merely nodded, her breathing ragged.

Rand held me tightly and kissed the top of my head. "It's over."

I glanced at Mercedes again. "Was this what providence wanted? Have we fulfilled our missions, our fate?"

She nodded. "Yes, it is as providence dictated although your duties are not yet complete."

I shook my head as anger swelled within me. I'd imagined my duties were done, that the war was over and I could return to my life at Pelham Manor to sleep off the next few weeks. "I've gone to hell and back in the name of providence and the Goddess," I paused and glanced at Mercedes. "I'm done."

She faced me impatiently. "No, Jolie, your role is far from over."

I felt a new rush of tears stinging my eyes. "What else do I have to do?"

A cold breeze lifted her hair as her cat's eyes glowed in the moonlight. "We will rebuild our legion," she started with a voice nearly lost on the wind. "I will help you."

She paused and seemed to be taking note of the survivors. When she faced me again, there was warmth in her smile. "Jolie, your fate, your destiny, is to be queen of the Underworld."

"What!" I said at the same time Rand did. I felt like my stomach was going to drop right on the ground. Queen?

"You have proven yourself—your powers and your courage." She paused to catch her breath. "This is your fate, Jolie. You were meant to unite the Underworld creatures. And I will serve as your advisor."

I shook my head and closed my eyes, feeling a headache developing. My life was no longer my own. Queen of the Underworld. It was a hefty title and one I didn't want.

"I don't want to be queen," I started, glancing at Rand.

He said nothing and I couldn't read his face.

Mercedes shook her head. "It is your fate."

I squeezed my eyes shut. I couldn't fight against my fate … there was no way to sidestep it, to deny it. I studied Mercedes again, searching for any loophole, some way out of this.

She merely shook her head again and kept her lips tight.

It looked like the throne was calling and I'd have to answer.

Queen.

Son of a …

WITCHFUL THINKING

Book 3 of the Jolie Wilkins series

AVAILABLE NOW!

Flip to the next page to read the first chapter of Witchful Thinking!

ONE

Journal Entry

Queen.

I'm not even really sure what to make of the word.

And the worst part is that it's not a detached, unfamiliar, or unthreatening word. Nope, Queen *is an up-close-and-personal sort of thing, as in I'm going to be living and breathing it. Some would say being* Queen *is my destiny, I don't know about that but what I do know is that* Queen *is now my reality.*

I am Queen of the Underworld.

Jolie Wilkins, Queen of vampires, werewolves, and other creatures you wouldn't want to invite to dinner.

Somehow the title just doesn't fit me. It's like trying to wear a pair of shoes that are way too big for my size eight feet. I'm not a Queen, I never wanted to be a Queen, and I definitely don't have the makings of a Queen. I'm just me, a witch with some magical abilities—one of which is the power to reanimate the dead. But Queen? Not by a long shot.

One of the lessons I learned when I first became involved with the Underworld (less than two years ago) is that whatever the Underworld wants, it gets. It's like the mob—once you get in, ain't no gettin' out. And I'm in—up to my neck.

So how did I become Queen? Was there a royal celebration? Were Prince William and Harry in attendance? Was Kate Middleton pissed? No, no, and no. My entry into the royalty of the Underworld was more like trial by fire—I'd been in the middle of a war; Gwynn (the bitch) had just run me through with a blade in return for destroying her lover; I'd died and then I'd been on the receiving end of reanimation, myself.

The crowning glory of the whole battle came when Mercedes Berg, the supreme witch of all witches (also known as the prophetess), basically shell-shocked everyone with a magical burst of energy that lit up the entire sky. It was like God's television had short-circuited. Everyone just stopped in their tracks, as if their brains had gone dormant. No one had been able to function. As if waving their white flags of surrender, everyone laid their weapons on the ground and just stared at one another dumbstruck. And that was the end of that.

Well, for them. For me it was just the beginning.

After Mercedes put the kibosh on our little war (a war for independence against the tyranny of the witch Bella, who wanted to be Queen), she informed me that I was now the Queen of the Underworld. And it wasn't like I ever submitted my résumé for the position. It had come completely out of left field, and the craptastic part of the whole situation was that I couldn't say no. Mob, remember?

So now I'm Queen and I want nothing to do with the position.

About now, Diary, I imagine your head is spinning. Crap, my *head is spinning and I'm the one who lived through all of it. In a fit of desperation, I decided to write it all down—to document how absurd my life has become in an effort to make sense of it all.*

Actually, this is my first journal entry. I never really got into diaries because my life didn't warrant recording. It was a quiet, mundane existence fixed in routine, but I liked it well enough. I had a best friend, Christa, who never ceased to amuse me with her frivolous talk about sex, sex, and more sex. I had my cat named Plum and I owned my own business—a tarot-card-reading shop. My skills, though limited, included reading people's fortunes through cards as well as detecting auras to determine if someone was sick or healthy by glancing at the colors reverberating off them.

The day Rand Balfour walked into my life, he changed it forever. Rand is a warlock and the first to inform me of my witchiness. He taught me pretty much everything I know . . . not to mention, I'm also head over heels in love with him. But more about Rand later.

At this point the important things to know are: First, the Underworld is polarized in a battle of good (Rand's side, which includes me, a handful of witches, a few hundred vampires and werewolves, and the entire legion of fairies) versus bad (the evil witch Bella and her minions, including an equal number of vampires and werewolves, none of the fairies, but all of the demons).

They say religion is at the core of most wars. Well, that wasn't the case with this one. This war began over me—and I'm not saying that to sound vain or to make you think I have an inflated sense of self-importance. Trust me, I'm really not that great. But once word spread throughout the Underworld that I could reanimate the dead, all the creatures went into a tizzy because no one before me had ever been able to do that. Bella, in true Bella form, wanted me on her side because like most villains, Bella sought power—power over all *the Underworld species. I guess I was a sharp arrow to have in her quiver.*

As with any other war, what happened was heart wrenching—vamp fighting vamp and witch fighting witch. Of course, I didn't get to observe too much—just as I was impaled by Gwynn's blade, I was whisked back in time to Alnwick, England, in the year 1878. There I met the prophetess, Mercedes Berg. Well, as it turned out she'd been the party responsible for sending me back to 1878, in order to save me as well as herself. To put it bluntly, Mercedes needed a ride back to the future to avoid her own untimely death, and I played the part of bus.

As I mentioned earlier, Mercedes ended the war by raising her hands and causing that big ol' magical burst, looking like a conductor leading the orchestra of the skies. After Gwynn stabbed me, Mercedes brought me back to life and I learned that she was the only other person besides me who could reanimate the dead.

And now? It's only been about two hours since Mercedes stopped the battle. Now I find myself sitting in a cottage, alone, in a fairy village in the middle of the Cairngorms Forest in Scotland, waiting for I don't know what. After the war ended, we took care of the injured and the dead, while also taking Bella's remaining forces captive. Oh yeah, I forgot to mention our victory—Mercedes was on our side . . . thank God.

So here I am, camped out in this room, with not a whole lot to occupy myself, just waiting for word on what our next course of action will be.

Present Day
Fae Village, Cairngorms Forest, Scotland

At the sound of a knock on the wooden door, I lifted my gaze from the parchment in front of me where I'd scribbled my journal entry. I laid my pen on the oak desktop and stood up, catching a glance at my outfit as I did so, and I had to laugh.

One fact about the fae and fae communities in general was that magic ruled. When you were in a fae village, and if you happened to be female, fae magic dictated you be dressed in what looked like Renaissance garb. My dress had an empire waist and was so long that it skimmed the ground. The material was light and gauzy, off-white, and bedecked with pink ribbon piping around the waist, the bust, and the wrist-length sleeves. I didn't even have to look at my hair to know it was three times its usual length, now grazing my butt in a mass of golden sausage curls, kissed by pink cherry blossoms.

I'd gone into battle dressed in stretch pants and come out of it looking like Rapunzel.

I pulled open the door and found Rand standing before me. His chest was bare, revealing ripples of sinuous muscle. Rand's physique is nothing short of awe inspiring, but his muscles aren't the type you'd find in the gym. He's not into lifting five hundred pounds and grunting as loud as he can to make sure everyone knows he's lifting five hundred pounds. No, Rand's physique was sculpted from hard work and training with werewolves, master vampires, and fae kings.

I couldn't help but stare as my eyes trailed his beautiful upper body and rested on his blue-and-green-tartan kilt. While fae magic bedecked women in gowns, the same magic endowed men with kilts. It was like living in the book covers of every Highlander romance in existence.

Rand still wore the filth and misery of the war—blood and dirt staining a face that surpassed all others in its beauty. Well, maybe the master vampire Sinjin Sinclair (who just happened to be Rand's detested ally—long story) could compete with Rand's good looks, but at the moment I wasn't thinking about vampires. No, instead, I was getting drunk on the beauty of a warlock.

Rand is tall enough, maybe six-two or six-three, but he appears even taller by the proud way that he carries himself. He has chocolate-brown hair, cropped short. If you took that same chocolate, melted it, and added just a touch of cream, you'd have the color of his eyes. His complexion is what could only be called sun-kissed, without interruption by freckle or mole. And his face is pretty angular—a strong jaw, cleft chin, and high, sharp cheekbones. The beauty of his lips—full and plump under his strong nose—is on par with his gorgeous eyes. When he smiles, his dimples light up his entire face until you would swear you were beholding someone heaven-sent.

Neither of us said anything for a second or two. We just stood there, staring at each other as if we were from different planets and unable to communicate. And it made sense because although we definitely loved each other, the best way to describe our relationship was as an emotional roller coaster. As such, I still didn't know where we stood—whether we were together as in boyfriend–girlfriend or . . . not.

Jolie.

It was Rand's voice in my head—complete with his thick English accent—a form of communication he and I have shared ever since we first met at my shop in Los Angeles two years ago.

"Rand." I said his name out loud and suddenly his arms were around me, holding me tightly. I felt the heat of his skin against my cheek as he pulled me close. He smelled like spice and sweat, the scent of masculinity, the embodiment of Rand. I closed my eyes and inhaled deeply, wanting nothing more than to fill myself with his very essence.

"I lost you," he whispered with a strained voice. He was referring to my death, when Gwynn's blade had pierced my stomach. He pulled away from me, and his eyes were glassy. "I will never forget the pain of watching you die. It will stay with me forever."

I didn't want to think about pain. I'd known my fair share but I also couldn't deny him the ache in his eyes. I wanted nothing more than to soothe him, to promise we would never be apart again. "Mercedes brought me back," I began. I'd only really been dead for a second or two, so did it really even count?

He crushed me against him, almost as if he were trying to remind himself I was really flesh and blood, and not some figment of his imagination. He held me incredibly tightly, as if he could erase the past twenty-four hours by smothering me.

"I don't know whether to be indebted to Mercedes or furious with her," he said. I wasn't sure where my feelings leaned on the subject either. I had a damn good hunch that Mercedes knew beforehand that I was going to die—there didn't seem to be much of anything she didn't know. But at the same time, she was the one who brought me back to life, so how mad could I be?

"Let's put it behind us now," I whispered.

"You said Mercedes was the prophetess," Rand continued. "Are you sure?"

I nodded. If I was sure of anything, it was that Mercedes was the prophetess—the fabled and legendary witch to end all witches. The prophetess was rumored to be able to change history, something Mercedes had artfully demonstrated by pulling me back to 1878. Her magic was so potent, it was scary.

"Yes, I'm positive." The image of her manipulating the sky came to mind. "Didn't you see how she ended the battle?" I mean, hello, if that wasn't proof I didn't know what was.

He nodded but didn't say anything else, just continued to hold me, stroking my head like I was a child. Finally he spoke, and his voice was soft.

"And what is this about you being Queen?"

That was a tough subject, and I could read lots more into Rand's question than the mere fact that he asked it. Rand wasn't crazy about any form of monarchy, no offense to the Queen Mum. He'd rebelled against Bella's plans to become Queen of the Underworld, and even though he and I were allies and I was as different from Bella as day is from night, I couldn't imagine he'd be any more eager to see me ascend the throne. No, Rand believed in the ideals of democracy and justice. Even though he was as English as tea and crumpets, he could easily have been an American revolutionary from the eighteenth century based on his feelings toward equality, liberty, and freedom. And he did make a mean apple pie.

"I don't know," I answered, which was sort of the truth. I mean, I didn't know what Mercedes had in mind for me, and although Rand had been there to witness everything she had to say about me becoming Queen, there hadn't been much. In fact, as I recall, she said I'd become Queen and it was my destiny to unite the creatures of the Underworld, and that had been that.

"Mercedes made it sound like prophecy," Rand continued, eyeing me as if he thought I knew more than I was letting on.

"You heard everything I did," I answered simply. "I don't know what to make of it or what it means, but I imagine Mercedes will fill me in at some point."

"You have freedom of choice, Jolie. If you don't want to be Queen, you don't have to."

How ironic—this was the first time "freedom of choice" had ever been mentioned with regard to the Underworld. Freedom really wasn't something that came easily to Underworld creatures. Their society wasn't structured like ours—a lesson I'd learned the hard way.

"Mercedes assumes I have no choice in the matter." I sighed, not really wanting to shatter the beauty of the moment with thoughts of my new career path. "She said it was my destiny to unite the creatures. And if it is my true destiny, how can I avoid it?"

Rand was quiet for a second or two before he shook his head. "Let's not think about it right now," he said, pulling me closer. "We can figure out all of the details later." He kissed the top of my head. I closed my eyes as I held him, but it was a false sense of security. As if foreseeing my own future, I realized Rand would most likely oppose me if I chose to follow my destiny to become Queen. It wasn't a reality I wanted to face.

The sound of cheering and laughter broke my reverie. I was suddenly aware that our alone time was nearing its end.

"What's going on out there?" I asked, although I wasn't really all that interested. Instead my mind was teeming with all the discussions I needed to have with Rand—centering on a turn of events in 1878. So much had happened, and unfortunately what happened in 1878 couldn't stay in 1878.

"A celebration, Jolie. That's why I came to get you—to escort you to the festivities," Rand answered absentmindedly, as if the last thing he was interested in was celebrating. He and I were on the same page.

A celebration. I hadn't even considered it. The overall tone after the gruesome battle was one of mourning and charity as our soldiers cared for their fallen, separating our dead from the maimed and injured and bringing them to this fae village.

One of the benefits to having me on Rand's side was the fact that I could reanimate all of Rand's deceased soldiers. It was going to be a long and arduous job, but I had promised I would do it both to myself as well as to our legion—those soldiers who had stood beside us from the beginning and vowed their loyalty to Rand. And it was something I wanted to do—something I needed to do. As far as I was concerned, death was no longer permanent; it was merely an inconvenience to be overcome.

"How many are dead?" I asked in a hollow voice.

"No final count yet," Rand responded in the same barren tone. He secured a stray tendril of hair behind my ear and grazed my cheek with his fingers. "Everyone is asking after you—apparently word of your death spread, causing quite a bit of anxiety. I want to prove to everyone there isn't anything to be worried about." He paused, and a sweet smile lit his face. "I know you're exhausted, but it is important for both of us to make an appearance. Will you oblige me?"

I really had no choice but to oblige him. Rand was the captain of our legion and as such, he had to be there, congratulate his men, and play his role as their leader. And so would I. I needed to promise the family members of the fallen that I would bring back their dead. I'd have to hobnob with Mercedes and introduce her to everyone as the prophetess, the highest of all witches. Most suspected she was only a legend. Little did they know . . .

"Yes, of course," I answered with as sincere a smile as I could muster. The truth of it was that I was beyond exhausted, physically and emotionally. And times like this called for nothing more than an amaretto sour and an early night.

The war and reanimating our fallen legion weren't thoughts I wanted to address at the moment. Not when I was in the arms of the one man I loved with all my heart. And more so, there was so much I had to tell him.

Before my little excursion back in time, things with Rand had been strained. Although we loved each other, our relationship had never been an easy one. Rand had begun our affiliation as my benefactor/employer and consequently, he restrained his carnal feelings for me, fearing he'd be taking advantage of the situation. As that became less of a problem, we were faced with the issue of bonding.

Ah, bonding . . . what a bitch.

When witches love each other, they form a bond that is like a marriage on crack. Bonding lasts forever—there's no divorce. And witches live longer than humans, by a few hundred years at least, so bonding is definitely a long-term commitment. When witches bond, their powers increase tenfold, but so do their vulnerabilities. So ,if one bonded party dies, the mate also dies. And bonding isn't something you can actually choose—it's as if your body decides for you, usually right about the time you're getting hot and heavy. And I know this from personal experience. Talk about a buzz kill . . .

Prior to the war, when I was still in the present time, Rand and I had succumbed to the heat of the moment—and just when he'd been ready to seal the deal, he'd freaked out and proceeded to take a cold shower, literally. Later he explained that we'd nearly bonded, which in turn freaked me out. And scared as I must have appeared, Rand looked like he'd just gotten up close and personal with the headless horseman. Needless to say, all sexual bets were off and we were relegated to star-crossed lovers who couldn't get it on.

To say I'd been sexually frustrated for the last two years of my life was the understatement of the century.

Sexual frustration or not, this is where my story gets even more complicated. Part of the reason Rand was so freaked out about bonding with me was the fact that he'd bonded with a witch in his past and had nearly died because of it. It had taken Mathilda, the wisest and oldest of the fairies, to keep Rand sane and alive. Little by little, she nursed him back to health, using her magic to make him forget the details of the witch he'd bonded with until he could no longer recall her face, name, or anything else about her. He survived, but only by a thread, and the fact that he endured the "death" of his bond mate was testimony to Rand's incredible strength and stamina.

But there's more. On my tour de 1878, I met Rand during his initial steps in warlock training. To make a long story short, we both fell madly in love and bada bing bada boom, we had the best sex ever and yep, you guessed it, we bonded. Our happy little tryst didn't last long, though. Before I knew it, Mercedes insisted that I return to my own time, saying I had to save the world or some other such crap, and I reluctantly had to leave my Rand of 1878 behind.

If you're following my story, you probably just figured out the whole thing. If not, let me spell it out . . . *I* was the witch Rand bonded with, and my departure nearly killed him. It was a truth that had been hard for me to digest . . . one I had to share with Rand.

"What happened out there, Jolie?" Rand asked as he glanced down at me. "Where did Mercedes come from? And why were you wearing my mother's ring?"

It was the same question he'd asked me when I died on the battlefield. God, it felt weird to say that. I didn't imagine I'd ever get used to it.

I swallowed hard and glanced down at my hand, where I still wore his mother's ring. Suddenly I wanted to cry over the injustice of it all: Rand had once loved me and given himself to me and I to him. He'd also asked me to marry him and I'd said yes, although I knew all along that I would have to return to my own time. He'd given me his mother's ring and forced me to promise him that he and I would reunite in my own time. Even as I made him that promise, I'd wondered if I'd be able to keep it; if I'd be able to convince the Rand of today that we were meant to be together.

"Something amazing happened," I said simply and racked my brain, trying to figure out the best way to explain.

Sometimes the best route is the direct one. "I traveled back in time, Rand," I said slowly, hoping the words would sink in.

"And?" he prodded, as though my comment was completely understandable. That was one thing I could appreciate about Underworld creatures—nothing really surprised them. When you got hairy during a full moon or had a hankering for O negative, it only made sense that what might be considered unusual by some standards seemed little more than commonplace and ordinary.

"I traveled back to 1878. Mercedes is the one who orchestrated it."

He nodded but didn't seem to get the gist of what I was saying, so I figured I should start from the beginning.

"It was wintertime, Rand, in England. Even though it was summer when the battle here began—"

"About that," he interrupted in a scathing tone. "You knew I didn't want you anywhere near that battle, Jolie."

Yeah, that was true. But I was stubborn and I'd made up my mind to fight even though Rand had forbidden it. I was determined if nothing else. I'd also been smart about it, though, realizing I would need some form of false identity in order to deceive Rand into letting me participate in the battle. With the help of Mathilda, I had managed to drum up a spell that changed my outward appearance so Rand wouldn't recognize me. I fought alongside him, alongside our legion, and none of them was the wiser. That was before I nearly died. Once that happened, and I'd been transported back in time, all my careful spell preparations had been for naught because my false identity was stripped from me. Upon my return to my own time, with Mercedes in tow, I was again sans my disguise, and of course Rand had recognized me instantly.

"Rand, that's in the past," I reminded him, not up for being chided about something that really didn't matter now.

"If you had listened to me, none of this would have happened." His tone wasn't angry, more wistful than anything, as if he were imagining a completely different outcome, one in which he'd been spared from witnessing my death.

I shook my head and smiled up at him. "No harm, no foul."

"So stubborn." He chuckled. "Jolie." He tilted my chin up and gazed down at me lovingly. "It's been too long since the last time I kissed you."

Before I could even respond, his warm and sumptuous lips were on mine and I melted into him, feeling my body wilt against his. He chuckled and held me more firmly, running his hands through my hair as I felt his tongue enter my mouth. Suddenly, in my own mind, I was transported back to 1878 when Rand loved me freely and neither of us had to hold back. The thought depressed me so much I thought I might start crying. So I pulled away, thinking I should focus on the rest of my story. I had to get it out in the open, just to get it over and done with.

"I nearly froze to death when I arrived in 1878 but two maids helped me. One was named Elsie."

Elsie had been one of the attendants at Pelham Manor, the same manor Rand now inhabited and owned. But in 1878, it had belonged to Rand's best friend, William Pelham. Upon Pelham's death, William had bequeathed his property to Rand. Either way, the name Elsie wasn't ringing any bells in Rand's head. I could tell by the blank look in his eyes.

"It was Pelham Manor, Rand," I admitted finally. "Mercedes was responsible for bringing me back in time to Pelham Manor."

He blinked for a few seconds and then eyed me inquisitively. "Pelham died in 1878. I was in residence at the manor."

Hmm, about Pelham dying—that was another issue I had to address with Rand, but it wasn't at the top of my list. I'd sort of taken it upon myself to heal Pelham while I'd been his guest. As it was told, Pelham had died of cholera, but the ailing man I'd cured seemed to be dying of something else; his symptoms were different from those of a cholera patient. Well, I'd have to shelve that subject for another day. Now I had more serious stuff to get off my chest. Big stuff.

"Yes," I said firmly. "You were there."

"I was there?" he repeated, his eyes narrowing as he considered my words.

"You gave me your mother's ring."

He shook his head as if he was finding it difficult to believe. "I have no recollection of any of this," he said and pulled away from me, beginning to pace as he always did when agitated. "When I first met you in your store, there was nothing that seemed in any way familiar about you."

I nodded, but I had no clue what the laws were about time travel either. "I don't know what to tell you. Maybe I didn't seem familiar because you didn't know me yet at that point? Maybe technically you hadn't met me yet?"

"But if you traveled to 1878, we had already met—over one hundred years earlier."

I shook my head. Somehow I had to tell him that we'd bonded. But suddenly it was like a figurative light switch went off in my head. Rand and I were no longer bonded. Of that I was convinced, because when you're bonded with someone you're one with them—you can feel the same emotions they do, hear their thoughts. And I couldn't feel any of Rand's emotions. Nor could I hear his thoughts, and it didn't appear that he was cognizant of mine. In traveling back to my own time and Rand nearly dying, the bond between us had to have been destroyed . . . We were two separate beings. With this discovery I felt nothing but an isolating numbness.

I swallowed hard as I further considered it. There was a big chance that Rand might not take news of our bonding very well. Bonding had nearly killed him, and I didn't imagine that would be easy to swallow, especially since over the past one hundred years he'd carried with him the void of believing that his partner had died. So really, wouldn't it be better not to tell him, better not to dredge up something that was so incredibly painful to him? I mean, we weren't bonded anymore, so maybe it was better just to let that conversation die and focus on the future? Focus on a fresh start? Besides, Rand had made it pretty clear that he wasn't interested in bonding again, not after the first time around nearly killed him.

"Rand," I began.

"Rand an' Jolie, where be ye?" The voice boomed from outside and seemed to rattle the walls of my makeshift cottage room.

"Odran?" I asked Rand with a smile, referring to the fact that the baritone voice could belong to none other than the King of the fae.

Rand nodded with a sexy grin. "You and I have a party to attend. Are you ready?" He held out his arm and I took it with a nod, pushing thoughts of bonding conversations to the deep recesses of my mind.

H. P. Mallory is the author of the Jolie Wilkins series as well as the Dulcie O'Neil series.

She began her writing career as a self-published author and after reaching a tremendous amount of success, decided to become a traditionally published author and hasn't looked back since.

H. P. Mallory lives in Southern California with her husband and son, where she is at work on her next book.

If you are interested in receiving emails when she releases new books, please sign up for her email distribution list by visiting her website and clicking the "contact" tab: www.hpmallory.com

Be sure to join HP's online Facebook community where you will find pictures of the characters from both series and lots of other fun stuff including an online book club!

Facebook: https://www.facebook.com/hpmallory

Find H.P. Mallory Online:
www.hpmallory.com
http://twitter.com/hpmallory
https://www.facebook.com/hpmallory

19267208R00135

Made in the USA
Lexington, KY
12 December 2012